Crime Pays?

The First of a Trilogy

by

Tha Twinz

D1714236

Published by:
Prestige Communication Group, LLC
PO Box 1129
New York, NY 10027
Email: Info@Prestigecommunicationgroup.com

ISBN-13: 978-1484807767

Crime Pays Credits:
Written by: Tha Twinz
Edited by: Zach Tate
Cover Concept by: Baby Born, Damon & Marion Design
Cover Graphics by: Marion Design

Printed in the USA

ACKNOWLEDGEMENTS

First, I want to thank the Creator for giving me life, insight, and the love and support of so many people. To my mother Elizabeth, I am grateful to you for always having my back no matter what! Momma Joyce, you'll always be in my prayers. Grandma Catherine, I miss you so much. To my future: Borneisha, Carlton, and KoKo, continue to aim high.

To my brother and business partner, Sha Bee We had worked so hard for this moment and still the best is yet to come. Robin, thank you for your unselfish love and support. To my nephews: Rodney, Eric, KJ, Jason & Lil Terry – Nothing can impede your progress but you. To my nieces: Jasmaine, Macasia & Jeanette – Take the world by storm ladies.

Hassan & Julie Hines, we'll weather the storm together. A special warm acknowledgement goes to Tonia, Tee Tee, Boop & the Taylor family. What's up Mel? Stanly Davis, thank you for those small talks. Shelly, your happiness is contiguous. To my entire extended family, you know it's way too many to name, but I love you all.

An extra special thanks goes to Prestige Communication Group. Zach Tate, for the inspiration and for challenging me to always do better. Marion Design for the great cover. Sexy, your special touch made this book just right. Alicia, your contribution to this project will always be remembered! Miz, an extra special thank you for everything.

To Derrick Morgan, thanks for always being there for me. Dewright & Sharon Johnson, Sharon Whyte, Uncle Charles Mcgriff, Kathy and Ernest, Keisha Green, Lamont Bryant, Derrick Braxton, Joy Harris, Da'mon & Troy Reed, Darren Coleman, Cino Mike, Azarel, Adid, JoeLovett, Uncle Don Juan, PA, Liza, Carmen, Harvey, Rel, Andrea, Sean Gantt, Ruler, Sharlene, April, Ruthie, Kim, Frank Betts, and Sandra Mila, Thank you for your love and support over the years.

If I forgot anyone, put your name here (   ). I Love You!

Baby Born

When you've lost a great deal in life, you have to learn to appreciate the small things. So here's a big thank you to all of the important people, who without them this would not be possible. My mother first and foremost Elizabeth Bragg for being the unwavering support I need. To Robin Bragg and Sharon Whyte for a sister's love that every man can appreciate.

My other half Baby Born-Bee, your loyalty and integrity is incredible! Helping me turn a dream into reality. To Prestige Communication Group, thanks for being a part of the process.

To this group of individuals you have all had a special impact on my life that hasn't gone unnoticed: Zate Tate, Cino Mike, Mon-D, Justo Richards, Big Mazi, Roberto Pascal, Big Nuke, Money, Swell, J Washington, Uncle Redd, GT, Sav, Lil Chris, Black Prince, Serk, Va, Gallo, Stacy Larkin, PA, Keliese George, Sherrice Hunter, Nicole, Sharon and Princilla, Keyjuana Jones, Majorie Reid.

To the reader of the past, present and future, we thank you for your continued support and taking the journey with us.

Sha-Bee

Crime Pays?

The First of a Trilogy

Prologue - Spring 2006

Manny thought about the trail of bodies he left from Panama to New York. While confined in a double-bunked cell of a New York State Correctional Facility, he was preparing for yet another debate with his young cellmate.

He laid the hip-hop magazine on his muscular chest and said, "Them rappers is clowns!"

"What? You bugging, papi. They keeping it thorough!" the 21-year-old on the bottom bunk said.

Although Manny was thirty-five, he remembered how he was his bunkie's age once. He remembered how his life went from rags to riches from one robbery. The pain of what his wealth cost him pushed his frustration.

He looked down at the youngster and replied, "Hermano, rappers are legitimate business men. They are citizens quoting poetry. Any fool that ever got paid in the streets knows how great it is to be a citizen. Here it is these loco fools are legitimate citizens trying to be gangsters, while maleantes (gangsters) are trying to be legitimate citizens. But when these so-called gangster rappers get shot or locked up, they start telling. Where's the gangsta in that? Remember Lil Kim's trial? Those rats swear they're gangsters now."

"I don't know what you yapping 'bout. They getting paid, and that makes it all okay to Baby J. Crime pays, baby. When I get outta here,

I'ma get paid." The skinny, light-skinned youngster that was no taller than 5'7" started beating on his chest and singing, "I'ma hustler. I'ma I'ma hustler, homie. Nigga, ask about me."

Manny swung his feet off the bunk, letting them dangle. "Oyeme, Baby J. Escucha (Listen)! How many times I got to keep telling you that you playing with fire thinking that way? Crime don't pay, lil homie."

"Man, I ain't trying to hear dat. I'm going to get some paper! Baby J ain't comin' up empty for nobody."

"You think you so smart? You fail to realize the game only got two roads. That's death or prison. There ain't no 401K, pension, or retirement plans attached to that life."

Standing defensively, Baby J said, "All you old-timers always be talking dat bullshit. I don't see none of y'all doing shit different. Man, I'm from Harlem. All I know how to do is hustle. I ain't 'bout to change my game now."

Manny looked at his young bunkie while he paced back and forth. His posture reminded Manny of his wild brother. He sized up the situation, thinking of the right words to say. "Yeah, that may be true, but that doesn't mean you have to do what we did. Look at me, man. I'm sitting in this box rotting away. Learn from my mistakes. Baby J, be a citizen, man, Change your hustle up. Be legitimate."

Baby J pondered Manny's words before he asked, "Yo, what makes you the expert? You're in here with me."

"Mi pana, you really want to know?"

"Yeah, I really want to know."

"Well, I hope you ready to stay up all night." Manny lay on his bunk and stared at the ceiling like he did a thousand times before, then said, "Back in 2000…"

ONE

"**N**INE! EIGHT! SEVEN! SIX! FIVE..." shouted the massive crowd of close to a million people in Manhattan's Times Square.

Manny Black waited for the shiny ball to drop so he could finally pull off his big score. The electrical flaws of the new millennium would guarantee that his big plans would materialize. All news stations reported that all computers in the world were scheduled to crash for the year 2000, better known as Y2K. Manny's hand was in his coat pocket gripped around his gun, while his eyes were locked on his million-dollar mark. He skillfully eased through the crowd, impatiently waiting for all the lights in America to go out at the same time.

"FOUR...THREE...TWO...ONE...HAPPY NEW YEAR!" the crowd erupted, blowing party horns and singing *Celebration* by Kool & The Gang.

Shit! What the fuck happened? Why didn't the lights go out? Manny thought, while blinded by the shiny crystal ball. *Those lyin' muthafuckas! This shit is fucked up*, he complained before his blurry eyes went back to his mark and discovered that the man was gone. Things had gone from bad to worst. "Damn!" he yelled while racing across Times Square.

The Russian who transported diamonds from Avianne's Jewelers in the Diamond District had disappeared. This was Manny's big score. He was counting on bringing in the New Year right. His head bobbed over the crowd in an attempt to find his payday. After taking a half-hour to run from one corner of the crowded Times Square to the next in search of his mark, Manny walked through the crowd mad and upset at how his plan came apart.

A week earlier, Manny was coming from selling stolen jewelry, when his thirsty eyes spotted a young man dressed in oversized jeans and a hooded sweatshirt. Through the jewelry store window, Manny saw the young man receiving a black velvet bag. Like a gift from God, Manny watched as the young man slipped the bag into a knapsack, then strolled out of the store. Like a true thief, Manny trailed the courier from 28 West 47th Street to a Jewish man in Williamsburg, Brooklyn. For a whole week, he watched the man's movements and discovered that all his major moves were done at midnight instead of business hours. After a little more investigation, Manny found out the courier was a Soviet named Avi. On the night of New Year's Eve, Avi was leaving his hotel in Times Square for the purpose of transporting a large number of diamonds to Brooklyn. It was Manny's plan to pull the heist when the lights went out and then use the crowd to help him get away, but now those plans were over.

Knowing his heist was dead, Manny's nerves were rattled. He walked up 46th Street between 7th and 6th Avenues, reaching into his coat for a Newport cigarette. He found his pack and let one dangle from his mouth as he searched for his lighter. When he passed the USTAV Indian restaurant and a seafood restaurant next to it, he realized he didn't have his lighter.

"Fuckin' bullshit! First the lights don't go out, and now I can't find my muthafuckin' lighter? What's next?" he asked himself.

As the words left Manny's mouth, he saw a shadow in front him. A thin, middle-aged man was walking his way with his head bent to the grimy pavement. Manny looked at the man's full-length cashmere coat, fedora hat, the Burberry scarf wrapped around his neck, and his expensive briefcase, and then wondered if the man was a smoker.

Just as the two men were about to pass each other, Manny asked, "Excuse me, you got a light?"

The man stopped short. Manny realized he was looking in the eyes of a Latino. The stranger glanced around before answering, "Sure."

The man pulled out a solid gold lighter and extended his right arm. Manny leaned in to light his cigarette. Instantly, the diamonds that encircled the stranger's gold Rolex danced from the flame. Manny inhaled while his thirsty eyes tallied the worth of the watch.

Once the smoke drifted from the orange tip, Manny said, "Gracias."

"De nada," the man said before walking away.

Shit, that watch costs money. Tonight might not be a waste, Manny thought, while his heels turned with the quickness. He followed the man in the direction he came from. As soon as he passed the USTAV restaurant, the stranger made a sudden cut into the steamy alley that separated the two restaurants.

Quickly, Manny scanned the block to make sure no one was following them. He dashed down the alleyway with caution until he came across an open service entrance to the seafood restaurant. Manny crept through a mist of steam and passed a foreigner in the kitchen washing dishes. As his eyes suspiciously scanned the kitchen, he saw his new mark walking through saloon-type doors that led to a dark room. Manny pulled out his most trusted friend in the world. He took the safety off his 10mm and then quickly tiptoed behind the man.

Just as his mark stepped through the swinging double doors, Manny put his gun to the man's right ear. "Puta, give me the briefcase and the watch," Manny ordered, showing he meant business. Manny had him where he needed him. The element of surprise did half the work in a robbery.

"Wow," the victim said with a sigh under his breath.

Manny's eyes were adjusting to the darkness in the room. A single, low-watt light bulb hung from the ceiling. In a split second, Manny realized he and his mark weren't alone. His blurry eyes could make out a portable water cooler to his left. Alongside that were boxes stacked on top of each other. Ten feet away was a long table with someone sitting in front of it. Something was wrong.

Manny heard laughter from the darkness. Instantly, the light from a small black and white monitor came on. Manny swung his best friend in the direction of the sound, but it was too late. When the small screen came on, a huge, extra black man with piercing yellow eyes and a mouth full of gold teeth grinned at Manny. He was sitting behind the table laughing at the images on the small monitor. Manny inched closer with his mark and saw himself on the monitor creeping through the alley and entering the service entrance.

"Hands up, Maricón!" Manny senselessly demanded from the dark man.

The beast laughed deeper this time while sudden movements in the small storage room startled Manny. A tall Latino, with a long ponytail and dressed in all black, stepped out next to the beast. In his hands was a modified AR-15 machine gun.

"Puta, drop the pistol," Manny heard behind him. When he quickly glanced around, using his victim as a shield, a short brute of a man had two chrome revolvers pointed at him.

The gold teeth of the black beast shined when he chuckled. With a Latin accent he asked, "Pedro, chu come with company now, huh?"

Manny quickly spun back around, holding the gun tightly. His heart was about to pop out of his chest. He was about to die.

Without a hint of fear, the man in Manny's grasp said, "Pantera, perdóname. I don't know. This kid is good. I didn't feel him behind me."

"Puñeta muthafucka, drop the gun!" the short brute behind Manny yelled again. This time, he placed his cold steel at the back of Manny's head.

"Go to hell. If I die, I'm taking this man with me," Manny barked. Then to the amazement of all in the room, he said to his victim, "Damé the briefcase. We leaving together." There was a brief silence in the room. When no one moved or showed a hint of fear, Manny took a deep breath and said, "I'm leaving with the briefcase."

The man called Pantera laughed.

Behind him, a five-foot-seven, thick and honey golden complexion woman that looked to be in her late twenties stepped out of the darkness. The tweed, cream-colored pants suit and caramel leather riding boots complemented her round, brown eyes and short hairdo. She was plain, but flawless. In her hands was a silenced, infrared MP5 machine gun. With a sudden squeeze of the trigger, a volley of shots spat out and whizzed by Manny's ear. The dust from the bullets hitting the bricks sprinkled on Manny's shoulders.

Shit! I ain't got no wins. Instantly, Manny's gun dropped to the side of his leg, where the brute behind him quickly took it away. Manny looked at the woman in front of him and stared death in the eyes.

"You want me to kill him?" the woman asked, while the red beam twinkled between Manny's eyes. She looked at the black beast, waiting for his approval while the red dot bounced around Manny's face.

"Xia, don't kill him," the man in Manny's grasp responded. "This fucking guy got a lot of heart coming in here like that." He eased his way out of Manny's arms, then spun to face him. While looking into Manny eyes, he said to the group, "The kid definitely got some big cojones. But, I like that!"

"Cabrón! Put your hands up in the air!" the short brute yelled to Manny from behind.

Pedro walked to the other side of the table and took off his hat, scarf, and coat. He then came back around to the front of the table. He leaned up against it, then put two cigarettes in his mouth and lit them.

The black beast snapped his fingers. Submissively, Pedro leaned back, and Pantera whispered in his ear. When he lifted his ear from Pantera's lips, he turned to Manny, handed him a cigarette, and then asked, "Tell me something. What are you...Panamanian? What's your name?"

With no hesitation, Manny inhaled the cancer stick to calm his nerves. On the exhale, he said, "Si! My name is Manny. You all Cuban?" Manny asked while puffing away and looking into the red beam that stopped at his forehead.

Pedro nodded that Manny's guess was right. Since his girlfriend was Cuban, Manny knew these people's ways very well. As far as he was concerned, his life was over.

Pantera laughed, then called Pedro to his lips again. While Pedro was nodding, he said, "Si...si...I should have thought of that." He then faced Manny and said, "My boss really likes your style."

"Cabrón! Don't let me tell you again. Keep your hands up." the brute ordered, then turned to Pantera and said, "Boss, please let me kill him."

If this short bastard calls me a cabrón again, I'm gonna rush him. I don't give a fuck how many guns they got on me, Manny thought to himself.

10

Pedro looked at the brute and said, "Relax." He then focused his attention back on Manny. "You came in here ready to kill me for a briefcase full of papers that could only benefit the people that issues liquor licenses. You were ready to die for that." He waved his hand around the room, then said, "As you can see, if we wanted you dead, you would have been dead, but we like your hunger. You are hungry for something only a few of us can dine on. At the time of your death, you were still ready to kill. My boss truly appreciates that. If you are interested in making some real money instead of doing petty robberies, then come back in a few hours around ten o'clock. Pantera has some work for you. Let's see if you really have some heart... and really want to make some money."

The red glare disappeared when the woman lowered her gun. Manny dropped the filter from his cigarette to the floor and asked in total shock, "That's it? I can leave?"

Pedro responded, "Yeah, you can leave. Pick up your gun and take it with you."

Manny looked down at his weapon and then back at the brute holding the two revolvers. "Nah. What's this, some kind of a trick?"

Pedro answered, "No, really, it's okay. Take your gun with you. You're going to need it. If you're interested, we'll see you in a few hours."

The woman they called Xia looked at Manny's honey complexion, his tapered beard, and his short, curly Afro. She smirked like she was disappointed that she couldn't put a bullet through his head. Manny wasted no time picking up his gun and slowly backing out of the double doors wondering, *Damn, what the fuck I got myself into?*

When Manny reached outside, the cold air slightly calmed his nerves. He tried to make sense of what just happened in the back of the restaurant. He walked as fast as he could, while checking to see if he was being followed with each step that he took. What just happened was straight out of the movies, and no matter what they offered, Manny had no intentions of ever seeing the room full of killers again.

* * * * *

The morning after his unofficial meeting in the back of the restaurant, Manny was fully dressed and pacing in his Eastern Parkway apartment in the Crown Heights section of Brooklyn. He was wondering if he should take the Cubans up on their offer, or should he try to track down the Russian courier for the jewels. Manny needed money for his big plans to come alive. After coming to the conclusion that his pockets were on empty, Manny snatched his 10mm, headed for the door, and said, "Fuck it!"

An hour later, Manny walked back through the saloon doors of the restaurant, realizing that the occupants never left. The woman called Xia was the only one who had changed her clothes. The black beast Pantera's gold teeth shined when he saw Manny walk through the door.

Pedro stood, dusted off his suit, and then said sarcastically, "I didn't think we would see you again. You just cost me a grand to my boss by showing up, but that's good. Now we can see what you're made of."

Manny liked being his own boss. "I came to see what you're putting on the table. If I like what you have to offer, then maybe we can do business."

Pantera laughed. Pedro chuckled before saying, "I *really* like you now, kid. You remind me of someone I know." He opened his briefcase and removed a sheet of paper. "Now for business. You have a problem with cleaning? I need to know how you feel about spilling blood."

Since killing came easy for Manny, he replied, "If the price is right, then it's done."

Pedro looked into Manny's eyes. When Manny didn't flinch, he said, "Okay, big man. You talk tough; now for some action. If things go bad, you never been here before. If things get really bad, I'll make sure you get a proper funeral. In the meantime, you show me how hungry you are. You know anything about heroin and cocaine?"

Manny thought of his brother Rico, then asked, "How much you need?"

Everyone in the room exploded in laughter. Pantera's yellow eyes glared while Pedro handed Manny a page from the phone book. Manny glanced down and saw a name underlined in red. It read *Rodriguez* with a Brooklyn address next to it.

Pedro guided Manny by the arm out of the storage room and into the kitchen. When they stopped in front of a loud dishwashing machine, Pedro leaned into his ear and whispered, "We need to know that this man will no longer be with us in the morning."

Manny nodded.

"You have to be there exactly at noon. You'll see two tipos (guys) leaving the building. If they're carrying a briefcase, you make your move up to the apartment on the paper. Knock on the door and say, 'Miguelito, Juan had a car accident a block away. He sent me to tell you to bring all the papers before the cops come. He said to hurry.'" After a brief pause, Pedro added, "Everything you find in the apartment is yours. Consider it a token of our appreciation. You do this right and your whole life will change."

Manny saw dollar signs dancing around in his head. "It's done."

He left Pedro standing there while he made his exit. It was feeding time, and Manny only had two hours before his feast.

* * * * *

Five minutes before noon, Manny walked down Knickerbocker Avenue in the Bushwick section of Brooklyn. He was whistling to himself while carrying a big jar of Skippy's peanut butter in his gloved right hand. Each time he inhaled, the cold air filled his lungs. Manny made a left at Stockholm Street and walked up a slight hill towards Wilson Avenue. When he passed the address that Pedro had given him, a gray Chevy Impala was parked a few spaces from the entrance. Manny doubled back and sat on the stoop. His dusty black pea coat, sweatshirt, jeans, and boots gave him the look of a drug addict that was looking to purchase drugs.

At exactly twelve o'clock, two Latinos walked out of the building carrying a briefcase and jumped into the Impala. When the gray smoke from the car's exhaust trailed down Wilson Avenue, Manny's heart started pounding as he approached the building. His gloved hand unscrewed the Skippy's peanut butter lid and sent it scaling like a game top. For a moment, he wondered if Pantera was setting him up to get murdered.

But if they really wanted me dead, I would've been dead already. I came too far to turn back now. Whatever happens…happens, Manny reasoned as he climbed the stairs two at a time. When he got to the apartment door, he knocked twice.

"Who? Y ahora qué?" came from the other side of the dull gray apartment door.

While acting like he was out of breath, Manny bent under the peephole and said, "Juan just had a car accident a block away! He sent me to tell you to bring all the papers before the cops come. He said to hurry!"

Like Pedro said, the door flew open revealing a wide-eyed, chunky Latino, who asked in shock, "Juan?"

Without hesitation, Manny withdrew his 10mm. He stepped in and kicked the man in his stomach. The force of the blow knocked the wind out of the man, causing him to fly back onto the dirty floor. Manny quickly stepped in and closed the door behind him. Before the man had a chance to recover, Manny placed the Skippy jar above his face and put the gun to the silver foil at the top of the jar. Instantly, he squeezed off two muffled shots and a third one to the man's throat. Blood and peanut butter splattered onto the beige carpet of the floor. The unique scent of gunpowder and roasted nuts pulled Manny into focus.

He looked around, scanning the studio apartment to make sure no one else was there. What he saw instead was a table with a large Cuban flag behind it that had stacks of rumpled bills and two clear plastic

Ziploc bags of white powder. In haste, Manny searched the apartment trying to find something he could put the money and powder in. When he looked over by the bed, the space was empty. He skipped the small bathroom and ran into the kitchen.

Time was ticking. Manny looked around for garbage bags, but the kitchen was bare. A big aluminum stockpot filled with water was sitting on the littered stove. Manny poured out the water and used his shirt to dry it out. After putting the items from the table inside the pot, he covered it with a silver lid. On the way out the front door, Manny cautiously stepped over the dead body.

Wilson Avenue was empty when Manny exited the building carrying the aluminum stockpot. As he cut the corner onto Knickerbocker Avenue, he headed towards the J train, whistling in an effort to calm his nerves. His mission was done. The weight of the pot and the worth of the items inside were all Manny could think of. He patted himself on the back knowing that he still had what it took to pull a successful hit on his own.

* * * * *

Only in Brooklyn could a man walk down the street with a large silver pot in his hands and not be looked at twice. During his ride home, Manny was stopped by a few homeless people asking for food from the pot, but besides them, his task of making it home safely was easy.

Manny stepped inside of his tenement apartment with his gun in hand. He was paranoid that someone was there waiting for him. The job went so easily that he wondered if Pantera was sending someone to kill him to cover their tracks.

Once the search of his own apartment came up empty, he went to his hall closet. After removing the floorboard, he pulled out a triple beam scale that he stole from another heist. He then took the scale and stockpot into the kitchen, where he dumped the illegal contents out on his small glass table.

Damn! This is a lot of paper. I don't believe this shit. I done came up big. I'm sure they could've had someone else in their crew do the job. Why me? Manny thought, as he opened one of the plastic Ziploc bags, dipped his pinky into the pile of powder, and tasted it. "Oh shit!" he said, spitting into the kitchen sink. "This ain't coke. It's Manteca (heroin)," he joyously announced to himself.

Manny moved the cast iron beams and dropped the Ziploc bags onto the shiny, circular plates of the scale. After the scale bounced, both bags came up to 253 grams. Manny didn't know the street value of the drugs, but he knew that in New York, a big bag of heroin equaled enough money to lay back for awhile, and also a lot of time in a state prison. Still paranoid, Manny went into the bathroom with the drugs. He put the two bags into one big Ziploc bag and then placed it on top of the toilet tank in case the police kicked in his door. *Better to be safe than sorry*, he thought.

Once the drugs were secure, Manny rushed to count the money that would put food on his table for a long time. Avi, the jewelry courier, instantly earned a permanent pass to transport his diamonds. Forty-five minutes later, Manny counted up $84,000. The day of catching a big score had finally arrived. Manny couldn't believe it. Instead of celebrating, he became more paranoid. He put $24,000 to the side before stashing away the remainder of the cash.

Manny planned for this day for a very long time. Ever since he came to America, he knew exactly what he wanted to do when he got his big score. Now with the heroin, things would really run smoother, or so he thought.

Manny got on the phone and called his younger brother Rico, who was his confidant and the one he turned to when he was broke. Ten years ago, Manny sent for Rico to come to New York from Panama. Crazy-ass Rico reached America on a Monday and was running cocaine errands for drug dealers in Harlem by that Friday. With Rico's discipline and militant mind, Manny counted on his younger brother to take care of business. Their personalities were like night and day, but together, they could make moves without looking over their shoulders.

"What?" Rico answered after the phone rang four times.

"What's going on?" Manny replied in his Panamanian accent.

"I'm just chillin', fam," Rico said lively.

"Listen! I need to see you right now. Right now! It's very important."

From the urgency of his brother's tone, Rico asked, "How many I gotta kill, son?"

Manny sucked his teeth. In his smooth demeanor, he said, "Estúpido you on the phone. I need to see you right now."

"I'll be there, fam!" Rico said before he hung up.

Manny clicked the phone and then called his man Edeeks. The Andy Garcia look-a-like was a legitimate businessman who was like Manny's little brother. People often mistook Edeeks for being white, but his bloodline told another story. When Manny had to flee Panama, his mother contacted her Puerto Rican girlfriend in New York City. Thereafter, Manny went to live with the lady and her two sons, Louie and Edeeks. Louie was Manny's tutor in the art of robbing until he slipped up. One night in the Bronx, outside of Jimmy's Café, he bumped into one of the drug dealers he robbed and got murdered. After that, Edeeks contemplated dropping out of school, but Manny stepped up and convinced him to do the opposite. Since then, they've been family. Edeeks had a degree in law and accounting, and specialized in managing other people's money. Manny had a lot of plans for Edeeks, and now he was going to put them into action.

When Edeeks answered his cell phone, Manny said, "Yo, I got an important matter I need to see you about. I need you to come by right after work."

After listening to his brother, Edeeks replied, "Sure, I'll leave early." Then he hung up the phone.

With most of his business out of the way, Manny clutched his best friend and headed for the bathroom to put all the clothes he wore during the murder into a garbage bag. When the bag was full, he opened his bathroom window and dropped the bag down into the courtyard of garbage below. After shivering from the cold that came in, Manny cut on the hot water to his tub. He planned on following his ritual since Panama of soaking in a tub after he took someone's life.

* * * * *

Manny had just finished putting on his sweatpants and tank top, when he heard a knock at the door. He peeked through the peephole with his gun in hand and saw Edeeks standing in the hallway. Manny opened the door. He pulled Edeeks in quickly, then scanned his gray Brook Brothers suit. In his hand, Edeeks held a burgundy leather attaché case.

"Manny, what's so urgent that you had to see me tonight?" Edeeks asked, while walking inside and removing his trench coat. "I have a shitload of paperwork to take care of. I hope this is important."

Manny cleared his throat. "When I call you, you come. You really need to calm down, tiger." He left the room and then returned with the heroin and $10,000. He tossed the cash and Ziploc bag into Edeeks' lap.

"What do you expect me to do with this?" Edeeks asked with a puzzled look on his face. While extending the heroin back to Manny, he said, "My man, you know I don't touch none of that." He held the stack of cash and added, "But, I'll take this. What you want me to do with it?"

Manny was waving the bag of heroin in one hand with his weapon in the other. "The cash is for you. I know you don't handle dope, but I wanted to show you how I'm getting ready to make my big plans a reality. I told you a long time ago that..."

Manny's words were interrupted when he heard his front door open. He lifted his gun to the entrance until he saw Rico march in drinking a Welch's grape soda. Edeeks quickly did a magic trick of making all his cash disappear into his suit jacket. Rico stopped and looked at his two family members, wondering what was going on.

16

Although he was Panamanian, Rico could pass for the rapper 50 Cent. He walked into Manny's apartment dressed in all green army camouflages with black Timberland boots. Underneath his clothes, a bulletproof vest added a few pounds to his stocky frame. The way he marched into the living room, he looked like a commando soldier ready for war.

Rico nodded at Manny and then at Edeeks, before asking, "What's good, my peoples?" His eyes gazed at the bag of white powder in Manny's hand. "Hermano (brother), what you working wit'?" he asked, while pointing to the heroin.

Manny glanced down at his hand. "Before you came, I was just telling E that we're about to do some big things."

"What you talkin' 'bout?" Rico questioned.

Manny tossed the heroin to Rico and said, "That's a quarter-key of dope...my dope."

Rico spun and excitedly asked, "You bullshittin' me, right?"

Manny was hype and filled with power. "Nah, I ain't bullshittin' you."

Rico tasted the product to see if it was real. When his test was confirmed, he said, "Oh shit! We can *really* do it big now."

Manny asked Rico, "You still on 117th Street moving that coke?"

"Yeah. Three hundred grams every two weeks," Rico replied.

With his hands clasped together in a praying position, Manny's eyes zeroed in on his 21-year-old brother. "Hmmm," he said while thinking. "Brother, remember you thought I was bugging when we were over in Panama? I was running wild doing all that crazy shit for short money. Then after the invasion of Panama, I came over here and started making little moves to make ends meet. Remember when I sent for you with the money I was slaving at the airport for? And when you came here, I kept telling you I'm gonna make it big. You thought I had lost my mind, huh?" Manny stopped talking and turned his attention to Edeeks. "Yo, E, just like when I was living at your house. We only use to have rice and beans to eat on some nights, but didn't I always tell you that things would one day change?"

Rico didn't want to hear the victory speech. He wanted to get down to business. "So, what you got in mind?" He shook the heroin to emphasize his next point. "This right here is a lot of work. I can do some big things, for real. Just give me the word, hermano. Fuck that small shit I been doing! Everybody knows that heroin is king. It brings in the most paper. I can get with my man Rashid, and we can put together a mean team to move this shit." He pulled out a Walter PPK handgun and said, "From now on, cats is gonna feel us. When they mention money, murder, and mayhem, they'll think about us! 'Cause we ain't taking no prisoners!"

Manny added, "Exactly what I was thinking." He turned to Edeeks and continued, "What I need to know is that I can count on you, Gringo (white boy). You an expert in that counting shit, and got connections with all them white boys on Wall Street. You can manage our money, E. Make sure it grows. Make everything in Panama cool so we don't ever have to worry about money again."

Edeeks was momentarily lost in his thoughts, considering what Manny said.

Rico was too excited. He smiled as he nodded and said, "Money, murder and mayhem. Hmmm...3M. No, betta yet, M3." He nodded again, then looked at his brother and said, "No doubt, kid! No doubt! I'm feelin' your ambition. I'ma handle my business to make this shit pop off, fo' sure."

Edeeks stood up, then turned to face the two brothers. "It sounds like you two are determined to do this thing. I know if you two are putting y'all heads together, then it's going to be something big, but tell me something. Do either of you know what an 848 Kingpin Statue is? How about the RICO law?"

"What the fuck are you talking about?" Manny asked with a confused look.

Rico sat with a blank stare before asking, "They got a law named after me?"

Edeeks exhaled with a sigh. "I'm talking about what you two are about to get yourselves into. You realize running a continuing criminal enterprise can get you twenty years without any parole, right? Not to mention a possible two-million-dollar fine. And if killing is involved, you can get the death penalty. Money and guns don't mix."

Manny shot Edeeks a nonchalant look. Then he plopped down beside his brother. "Who said anything about running an enterprise? We trying to get paid. What's this enterprise stuff?"

Edeeks took his hands out of his pockets and started pacing in front of Manny and Rico. "By law, drug dealing, money laundering, and tax invasion just to name a few, are all considered enterprising. It doesn't make a difference if you a major player or just a small player on the team. If the government can prove you're making moves on the street, like buying and distributing drugs to sell or even receiving money off the product, you're lining yourself up for an 848 indictment." Edeeks stopped talking when his eyes shot up towards the ceiling like he was trying to remember something important. "And under the Racketeering Influence Corrupt Organization, RICO Act, shit is even crazier. The government will indict you on conspiracy for the smallest shit...like if someone says you did something or going to do something. Or for us just sitting here now talking about making moves even if we never make them. It's all conspiracy under the RICO law. Just like when you asked me to manage and invest the money you going to make from selling the product, that's considered a racketeering enterprise."

Rico turned to Manny and asked, "Yo, what the fuck is dude talkin' 'bout?"

Edeeks sat down on the arm of the recliner. "If I leave y'all two together, your best thinking is going to put you in the worst situation. Here's what's going to happen. Being that y'all dealing with heroin, if the product is above average, it's gonna sell faster than White Castle hamburgers on a good day. The money will roll in faster than y'all can count it. Then those stick-up and kidnap kids are coming for you."

Rico raised his gun and said, "Okay. That's when I come in."

Manny looked at his brother, nodded at him like he said something really smart, and then the two touched the tips of their guns like they were shaking hands.

Edeeks sighed again. "The second thing is all the drug traffic is going to generate attention from the local police and maybe the feds. It won't be a thing of *if* they will come, but *when* they're coming. And when they do, you have to make sure you're as secure as possible."

"So when the money starts coming in," Manny began, "your place is to hold the cash, invest it into some legit shit on Wall Street with the rest of your Gringo friends, and make sure everything is safe."

Edeeks realized he was wasting his breath. He didn't want to see the two brothers fall to the law, so he went against his best thinking. "Okay, I will keep a set of books of all the transactions somewhere safe. Through my so-called 'Gringo' friends, I'll find a safe bank to stash the money. But first, you have to make the money before your *big plans* can work."

Manny smiled with a burst of energy. "That's why I called you. We gonna do some big things together."

Edeeks said, "Just contact me when you're ready, and I will handle everything from there. I have a pretty good networking system. A few people owe me some favors. Just let me know when and where, okay? Now, if you will excuse me, I have a lot of paperwork that I have to catch up on."

After standing, Edeeks put his coat on and headed towards the door.

Manny laughed and shouted out, "E, one day you ain't gonna have to bust your ass working for those crackers. I'll be your boss."

"I hear that," Edeeks' faded voice shot back as he walked out the door.

Manny quickly raced to his bedroom, then returned with another $10,000. He proudly threw the stack of cash into Rico's lap. "That's to get you started. Let's finally get ours, bro."

A big smile cracked on Rico's face when he looked at the bundle of cash. "Manny, we gotta do this, hermano. We got to do it right. Make Papa proud for once after we rob America clean. M3 baby, Manny-Manteca, and money…all the things I need."

* * * * *

Manny's girlfriend knocked on his door a half-hour later. He had the lights dimmed with slow music playing and the bedroom was spotless. When he opened the door, he looked at her almond-shaped eyes, her full lips, and the C-cups that peaked through her button-up shirt, and he let the Eva Longoria look-a-like in. His woman was as scrumptious as ever.

"What's up, mami?" he said, using his best attempt at seduction.

Brushing off his greeting, her long legs walked through the door. She looked around the room before sarcastically asking, "You must've had a great day at the office, huh, papi?"

"Si, something like that." Manny's hand dug into his baggy sweat pants and pulled out a $4,000 stack of cash. He looked at his woman like he was the boss of all bosses. "Here, Carmen, this is for you."

With a look of surprise, she studied his facial expression, then asked, "What's this for?"

Manny pulled Carmen to him and kissed her. "Remember that big plan I was telling you about?"

Carmen nodded before answering, "But what does this got to do with…"

Manny cut her off in mid-sentence. He grabbed her by her small waist, pulled her closer, and stuck his tongue into her mouth. The deep, passionate kiss caused Carmen's pussy to moisten. Intense heat surged through her body as she felt Manny's big dick grind into her crotch. When his left hand squeezed a hand full of her ass, a soft moan escaped from her mouth.

"Mmmm, when I met you at the airport, papi, I knew you was gonna be trouble."

Manny unbuttoned her clothes, slipped his right hand inside her thong, and finger fucked her wet pussy. His thumb moved in a fast, circular motion on her throbbing clit.

"Oh God, papi! This feels so good."

Manny whispered all the freaky things he wanted to do to her while his fingers played inside of her. Carmen reached back, clawed at his neck, then her body went limp.

"I'm getting' ready ta cum…Mmmm, yes, right there. Keep movin' it right there. Oooo, baby, I'm cummin'." Her body trembled as she humped his thrusting fingers.

After Carmen climaxed, she pushed Manny back onto the couch. She pulled down his sweatpants and his boxers. Then she knelt down between his legs and seductively looked up into his eyes while grabbing his dick. Her head dropped, and she started working magic with her tongue. Manny loved the way she ran her long, wet tongue in a snake-like fashion across his dick, while playing with his balls. He reached down and ran his fingers through her hair while he enjoyed the sloppy noises she made.

When Manny came, Carmen fucked him up when she deep-throated him and then slurped his balls into her mouth. She gagged while trying to look into his eyes, but her tongue never stopped moving. Carmen drank every drop of her man with pleasure. When she was done, she walked seductively into the bedroom, calling Manny behind her. When he entered, Carmen was lying on his bed with her legs wide open.

Manny looked at the smile on her face, along with her hairy patch, and said, "Okay, mami, let me return the favor."

Manny crawled in between her legs, spread her pussy lips open, eased two fingers inside her, and opened it wide so he could have his second feast for the day. The slithering of his wet tongue drove Carmen crazy.

"Yes, papi, suck it a little harder...yes...yes." The more Manny sucked, licked, and dug into Carmen with his tongue, the harder she bucked. "Ay papi, ay papi, I'm cumming! Oh God."

After Carmen climaxed, Manny raised his head up, wiped away all of the sweat and juices from his face, then licked his hand. He flipped his lover over so he could enter her from behind. As he eased into her inch by inch, Carmen reached behind to prevent him from going too deep into her being. After he hit the bottom of her wet hole, filled with passion, he slammed into her. Their bodies moved like they were dancing to erotic Salsa music. Manny put his hip, back, and all his energy into driving his woman crazy.

"Yes, papi! This is yours! All yours! Ay dios mío. Ay dios mío. Ay dios mío," Carmen yelled while sweat dripped off of her body.

Manny took a deep breath and asked, "Ma, are you really wit' me?"

"What do you mean am I with you? Papi, you know there's nothing I won't do for you."

Manny smiled. "My whole life is about to change. I want to make some serious paper, and I might be on my way. I want to put a team together." Manny thought about running away from the Cubans, then said, "I might not be living here tomorrow. I was talking to Edeeks, and I need to know that no matter what happens to me that you gonna be there to do whatever I need you to do...to be my soldier."

Carmen smiled, looking more like Eva Longoria every day. She slid next to Manny on the bed and said, "Yes, papi, anything, I swear. I love you. I'm here till the end of time for my Manny." She reached for his limp dick and then started rubbing it. She put her lips to his ear and whispered, "I will die for you, papi."

Manny looked into her eyes. While his dick got harder, he replied, "I hope you ready to prove it."

TWO

T he following morning, Manny was awakened out of his sleep by the sound of rapid knocking on his door. The noise startled him, causing him to leap out of bed. Half asleep, he blurted out, "What the fuck?" while grabbing his gun off the nightstand next to his bed. His body hugged the paneled wall as he slowly tiptoed to the door. Hesitantly, he looked through the peephole. His plans of running away from the Cubans came crashing down. After a lot of resistance, Manny swung open the door.

With his gun in hand, he asked his visitor, "How you know where I live?"

His visitor's attire was nice. Underneath the black full-length sheared mink coat, Xia wore a black wool wrap-around dress. The material hugged every inch of her thick, curvaceous, plus-sized body. The stiletto boots did justice to her ensemble. Manny exhaled and took a few steps backward to clear the entrance. Xia accepted the unspoken invitation by stepping through the doorway. As she looked around his home, Manny could see that she lost her appetite. When her black leather ostrich-gloved hand came out the pocket of her mink coat, a small chrome Glock with an octagon nose was produced.

She ordered, "Get dressed."

With his eyes glued to the gun, he closed the door, lifted his own gun a little higher, and asked, "What? I served my purpose. Your fine ass is here to kill me now?"

She ignored Manny's question. "Let's go! Pantera wants to see you."

Xia's answer was disappointing. His charm wasn't working, and he realized she wasn't making a social call. He quickly turned and headed towards the bathroom. While washing his face, he thought, *The black beast must've had me followed home the first night. I hope this motherfucker don't kill me now that I finally got some money. I should have never taken the job.*

Manny was dressed in record time. As he walked into his living room, he thought, *I can kill this bitch right here. Leave her dead in the apartment and be gone.* When he entered the living room, Xia's back was to him. She was looking out the window at her car. Manny held the gun tightly with thoughts of murder. She suddenly turned around and his heart melted. Her round face was a reflection of beauty, and her deadly eyes made Manny's dick hard. He never felt love at first sight or met someone that changed his mind about killing them, until now.

Xia and Manny exited the apartment looking like a couple going to their jobs. When they emerged from the building, a new burgundy BMW X5 truck was sitting out front. Xia hit her remote and the lights blinked, while the alarm was disarmed. He looked around at the walnut leather seats and the wood grain around the dash, and came to the conclusion that his new Cuban friends may be the best company to be with.

The powerful engine moved the wheels of the BMW in the direction of the Brooklyn Bridge. Manny smiled to himself when he thought, *A classy car for a classy woman.* "Summer Rain" from Carl Thomas' CD played at a moderate level while they cruised in luxury. Neither Manny nor Xia spoke a word. For the first ten minutes, both were lost in their own little world. Manny glanced at Xia, admiring her tough and sexy demeanor. Her thick golden thighs showed through the long split of her dress. He smiled while wondering what made a big woman like Xia tick.

His thoughts were cut short when she looked at him and asked, "What you smiling at?"

"Nothing," Manny shot back with a bigger grin on his face.

"Oh really? Nothing, huh?" Xia asked sarcastically.

"Yeah," he replied, licking his lips like LL Cool J. He then turned to her and asked, "What type of name is Xia anyway? How you spell that?"

Xia kept her eyes on the lanes on the bridge and answered, "You spell it X-I-A, and it's the name my mother gave me. Don't ask me what it means because I don't know."

Manny felt like he was getting somewhere, so he continued. "Baby, how did a fine-ass woman like you end up so mean?"

Xia instantly looked into her rearview mirror when she heard the sound of the police siren wailing behind her. Her eyes bounced from the road to the mirror until two police cars jetted passed them. When the cars were out of sight, Xia turned to Manny.

"That gun on your hip is the one you used on the job last night?"

"Yeah, why?"

She sighed. "Genius! Take it out and hand it to me!" she ordered, while holding both hands on the steering wheel.

"What?" Manny asked, looking at her like she was crazy.

Xia responded calmly, "Unless you like the idea of going to prison for the rest of your life, you'll give it to me."

Her words slapped him with a hard dose of reality. He pulled the 10mm out of his waistband and then placed it in her lap. Xia pulled over at Houston Street under the Brooklyn Bridge. She reached her gloved hand under her seat and pulled out a hand towel. She placed the cannon in her lap and manipulated the gun. Manny sat quietly amazed as he watched Xia expertly dismantle his gun into pieces, then wipe each piece down with the towel. She wrapped up the handle and trigger part of the gun. Her eyes searched the grimy city streets until she found what she was looking for.

A sewage drain was at the corner from where she was parked. Xia got out of the X5, calmly threw the wrapped towel down the drain, got back in the car, and pulled off. Right before she drove onto the FDR highway, she retrieved another hand towel from underneath her seat. While driving, she wrapped the clip, slide, and barrel of the gun inside the towel. She handed it to Manny, then raced the engine of the small truck. As she was approaching a short tunnel, Xia glanced into her rearview mirror before rolling down the passenger's window. As soon as the darkness of the tunnel covered the car, she drove extra close to the cement barriers that separated the East River from the highway.

With a huge green dumpster quickly approaching, she barked, "Toss that...now!"

Quickly, Manny did as he was told. He looked behind him and saw the evidence he dumped fall into the dumpster where men were doing construction on the highway. He was impressed with how she handled everything.

"I see you've been around and know how to handle yourself, mama."

With a cocky attitude, Xia replied, "Yeah, it's a dangerous world. A real woman has to know how to take care of herself."

That was the most Manny had ever heard from her, so he tried to make a mile out of the inch she gave. "I really like that attitude, Ma, but tell me something. When does a real woman like you let the man step in and do the job?"

Xia stared at Manny and then back at the road. She sighed like she was painfully annoyed. "That depends." She then played with the CD player until Dru-Hill's "Tell Me What You Want" came on.

"Depends on what?" Manny asked with new interest.

Again, she posted her warning sign with her eyes. She gunned the engine when she drove off the 155th Street exit. Driving past the famous Rucker Park, she made a left on 8th Avenue. Manny relaxed while she came out of the 7th Avenue tunnel, made the sharp left, then headed over the Macombs Dam Bridge. Upon entering the Bronx, she drove onto the Bruckner Expressway.

As if she was continuing the conversation a second ago, Xia said, "It depends if the man is capable of handling his business and getting all jobs done."

"Oh yeah?" Manny asked, remembering what his question actually was. "How does a brother get an application for getting all the jobs done?"

Xia smiled without showing teeth. Manny couldn't believe it. He realized he was actually getting somewhere.

That is until the smile disappeared and she said, "You're already in over your head. Live long enough to do the small job. That's your application. Then we'll see if you can get to the interview in one piece. I would love to see that."

Before Manny could respond, they were pulling up in front of a social club at the Circle on Westchester Avenue in the Bronx.

When they stopped in front of the club, her door cracked. Xia checked her mirror to make sure she was presentable. When she hopped out, Manny quickly followed suit. He trailed Xia as she strode in the direction of the small storefront that had "Havana's Paradise" in blue, red, and white scripture printed across the front windowpane.

Manny walked in and scanned the dim room. A Cuban flag, like the one that was in his victim's house, was behind a long, worn, wooden bar to the right. Two guys who looked to be in their late thirties stood near one of the two pool tables in the center of the floor. "Usted Abusó" by Celia Cruz played from the old jukebox hidden in the corner. Another man by the bar reached over to hit a button when he saw Manny's escort.

Xia led Manny past a bathroom before entering a back room. The cluttered space was the size of a small bedroom. The fumes of a Cuban cigar hovered above Pantera's desk, as he watched TV laughing. Pedro sat in a fold-up chair to the left of him. Together, they acknowledged Manny and Xia walking through the door. Pantera continued to laugh, then looked at Manny.

In a hard Cuban accent, he said, "Tú eres funny, Peanut Butter? Ha ha, tú mucho funny, my man."

Manny was wondering what Pantera found so funny. His feet moved closer to the small TV screen. When he saw what Pantera was watching, his heart dropped to his shoes. The screen showed Manny killing the Latino in the drug spot.

How the fuck did they get that? Manny thought. He stood frozen with confusion while watching Pantera rewind to the part where Manny kicked the guy in the stomach, put the gun to the peanut butter jar, and shot him. Pantera watched the killing over and over while laughing. Manny was hit with the new reality that he was dealing with a sadistic man.

"Yo, I need that tape. I need that right now!" Manny barked, wishing he still had his gun.

Hearing Manny complaining, Pantera snapped his fingers. Pedro obediently leaned in, and Pantera whispered in his ear. Pedro then

26

looked up at Manny with a plastic smile on his face and said, "Big Manny Black, don't get all worked up. You did a fine job, but you forgot a piece of evidence, that's all. You family now. Don't sweat a thing. You do a favor for Pantera, and he gives you more money than you ever saw in your life. The heroin was good, no?"

Manny thought about the heroin and cash he gained from the heist and nodded.

"You see? We take care of you, you take care of us, and you worry about nothing. We called you here to tell you that we're proud of you, tipo. You have our full support in being the king of Nueva York, if you want. When we have another problem, we will call you. I'm sure you won't deny us. Then when you need more Manteca, you come see me, Tio (Uncle) Pedro."

Manny nodded and asked in anger, "What about the tape?"

Pantera barked, "Muévete!" telling Manny that he was dismissed.

Pedro hugged Manny, then whispered, "The tape is safe in the boss' hands. It is the only entertainment he likes. When he grows tired of seeing it, you have my word that I will give it back to you." He nodded at Xia, then said, "Take Manny wherever he has to go. When you come back, your papa has something for you to do."

Xia stood like a soldier at attention, then hurriedly escorted Manny out of the social club.

When they were outside under the overpass of the 6-Train, Manny asked, "What's the deal with Pantera holding on to that tape?"

Xia ignored his question while jumping into her truck. Manny hopped into the passenger side waiting for an explanation. Xia started the truck, put the stick in gear, and gunned the engine.

A few blocks away, they drove onto the Cross-Bronx Expressway and Xia said, "If Pantera has it, then it's in the best hands. You shouldn't trouble yourself about small things."

Manny looked at her like she was crazy. "That's easy for you to say. It's me he got some shit on."

"That's true. But before today, you never knew the tape even existed. If he didn't want you to know, you wouldn't have seen it. Consider yourself lucky to be alive. If it wasn't for him making sure your mess was cleaned up, your future would've been bleak."

"What are you, his pit bull or something?" Manny asked defensively.

"I'm whatever he needs me to be."

Manny reached over and touched her shoulder. "In bed, too?"

"People have received broken bones for less. Watch where you put your hands, and what comes out of your mouth."

Manny quickly snatched his hand back. He thought of the way his emotions were getting the best of him. He went back to his usual calm demeanor. "No disrespect, Ma."

Xia smirked. "None taken or you would be dead."

Silence gave Manny enough time to think things through. Pantera had him in the palm of his hand. He knew Xia had the ability to end his life and he could end hers, but there was no benefit to killing such a gorgeous woman.

Manny allowed his need to get closer to Pantera guide his tongue when he asked, "So, Mamacita, tell me something. What's up with a Bonita like you? You got a man? Maybe I can get that job interview now."

Xia didn't take her eyes off the road to the Tri-Borough Bridge. "What difference does it make?" she harshly asked.

Manny squirmed in his chair. He never met such a strong woman in all of his twenty-nine years. "I'm thinking maybe we could go out or something. You know, maybe work on you not being so mean. You too beautiful to be so mean."

"Brother, please!" Xia answered quickly, dismissing such ridiculous thoughts.

Manny looked at her in shock and licked his lips, but when he was ready to talk, none of the words came out. He exhaled, giving up on trying to get through to the woman next to him.

Xia commandeered the vehicle through the Brooklyn-Queens Expressway, then through the streets of Crown Heights until she pulled up in front of Manny's apartment building. As he was exiting the truck, Xia leaned over her steering wheel.

While looking out the windshield, she asked, "I followed you here, but do you actually live in this place?"

There was no need for her to insinuate anything further. Her message was clear. She thought Manny's apartment building to be beneath her standards. Manny looked at the stubborn woman while holding the passenger door open.

"Well, maybe you'll take me to your house one day, and then I'll see how the other half lives."

Xia looked Manny up and down and then straight ahead. Waiting for him to close her door, she blurted out, "Yeah, whatever."

Manny knew a tough woman when he saw one. Her attitude aided in his depressed mood. He slammed the car door and watched the deadliest woman he ever met drive away.

* * * * *

On the other side of the Big Apple, Rico was assembling his team so he could sell the heroin his brother gave him. Early that morning, he met with his partner Rashid on 117th Street and Manhattan Avenue. Rico and Rashid met at a satellite school where they were supposed to be getting their G.E.D's, but both decided selling weed in Harlem was better. After they smoked up most of their supply, they switched to selling tall bottles of raw cocaine. Through the years, Rashid helped Rico stay focused every time he thought a problem could be solved with killing somebody. Rico helped Rashid to understand that a hustler had to save for a rainy day, and that all his money didn't have to go into his wardrobe. Together, they hustled, partied, and handled all the casualties that tried to stop the little bit of cash they made.

Rashid's home on 117th Street was littered with tenement buildings and sprinkled with a few relics of decency. The drug traffic that rode down the major street of 116th caused him and Rico to run a smooth operation without too much trouble from the police. From the east to the west side of Harlem, 116th Street was legendary for selling heroin since the late 1950's. That one street made plenty of millionaires, sent many men away to prison to serve life terms, and caused a bloodbath of bodies back in the late 80's. Now that Rico had the one product that a lot of people loved, he had to convince his partner to run the operation.

Rico and Rashid were standing on the corner when Rashid asked, "Yo, you ready to open up? Our custies will be here in a minute."

Rico looked at his reflection in his partner's Cartier glasses and replied, "Yo, Rashid, I got good news and bad news. What you want first?"

Rashid nonchalantly brushed his suede jacket off. He glanced down as he licked his finger, then wiped his Timberland construction boots. He brushed off his corduroys, ran his hand over his cashmere sweater, and then looked in the reflection of a car window. Rico waited for him to finish the same ritual he did five times a day. Making sure no cold was in his eyes, Rashid ran his finger under his tinted glasses and rubbed his hand over his long, chocolate-complexioned face. He then made sure his Yankee cap was tilted just right.

When the adolescent stubble on his chin was laid down correctly, he said, "Give me the bad news."

Rico answered, "Whew, a'ight. That coke we selling is a rizzy rap."

"What the fuck is you talking 'bout, Rico? I got kids to feed, a bitch in need, and palms to grease. I need some paper, papi."

Rico was usually the one with the short fuse, so he chuckled. "Nigga, we about to get rich. That's the good news."

Rashid swung around his 6'2" frame. "Man, what is you yapping about with my paper?"

Rico put two hands up and said, "Yo, Rah, I got a quarter key of dope in the Path. A quarter key of dope, papi! That lil bit of coke we've been movin' is dead. We 'bout to play in the big boys' league."

Rashid pulled Rico's short frame across the street and away from where they conducted business. Leaning against the wall, he whispered, "Oh shit! Yo, Rico, where you get that from? Who you kill now, nigga?"

"Don't sweat that! Manny running things now. We just got to get a team together. I can't mess this shit up or my brother will body me." He looked around, then back up at Rashid. "Check it. Our crew is gonna be the M3 Boyz for Money, Murder, and Mayhem!"

Rashid laughed. "You fucking wit' me, right, son?"

"If I'm lying, I'm dying, and I'ma bust a fool before I fold. So what up?"

"Show me," Rashid demanded.

It was Rico's turn to pull the tall figure back across the street to his truck. He opened the door, pulled out the package, and then slammed the door. He ran past Rashid playfully, and they headed up to the apartment that Rashid shared with his baby's mother.

When they reached the back room where he and Rico usually hung out while their younger workers were outside, Rico opened the Ziploc bag.

Rashid gasped. "Oh shit, son! You ain't got to show me no more." He looked at Rico and asked, "It's already cut?"

Rico was stumped. He hadn't thought of that. As a matter of fact, he didn't know a damn thing about processing heroin. He stared at Rashid with his mouth open.

Rashid raised his voice. "This nigga don't even know if the shit is cut?" He slapped his forehead and playfully announced, "This dumb muthafucka!" Quickly, Rashid spun up off the couch and flew open the window behind him.

"What you doing, son?" Rico quizzed.

Rashid had his head out the window when he said, "We gotta find Fee-foe." Rashid hollered downstairs, "Yo, Betty, where Fee-foe at?"

From outside, an older feminine voice replied, "That no-good lowlife 'round here somewhere. Why?"

"I got two bottles for you if you get him right now," Rashid proposed.

"Sheeeeit, I'll span the globe for two bottles. Wait right there," the woman proudly said.

Rashid pulled the window down, then plopped next to Rico. He cut his wide-screen TV on and asked, "Nigga, what would you do without me? That quarter of a key is probably a half a key after we step on it."

Back in 1990, Rashid had watched his uncle Bill handle heroin. Rashid was just a child, but after his uncle received a life sentence in the federal prison, Rashid never forgot what his nosey eyes saw. He knew one day his street wisdom would come in handy.

He turned to Rico and asked, "How much we owe your brother for that? That's probably 'bout forty gees wholesale you holding right there."

Rico hid his surprise at how much money it was worth. He knew what he had was valuable, but not exactly how valuable. Trying to impress Rashid, he said, "We gonna flip it until we can cop a whole key. Then Manny will take care of us. That's the plan."

Rashid was fixing his lips to agree, when he heard someone outside yelling, "Aaaaaay yo!"

Rashid and Rico both jumped up and went to the window. When they looked outside, a dope-fiend that was old enough to be their father, and who used to be rich in his hayday, was standing outside fixing his worn clothes. Next to him, Betty was wearing shorts and a housecoat, standing in the freezing cold with an old scarf on her head.

The man saw the two partners and asked, "You got something for me to do?"

Betty protested. "Uh uh, not till I get paid first."

Rashid reached into his pocket, pulled out a fifty-dollar bill, crumbled it, and threw it at the woman.

When she saw the cash sailing down, she frowned. "No, Rah, I want what you promised me."

Rashid's face tightened. "You nasty bitch, stop playing wit' me. Work will be out in a minute." He then pointed to the man and said, "Fee-foe, come up. I got something for you."

Rashid closed his window and headed for the kitchen. He returned with a teaspoon and a piece of wax paper. He dipped the spoon into the bag, poured the beige powder into the wax paper, and then folded it. He signaled for Rico to leave the drugs and follow him. With spoon in hand, they met Fee-foe in the hallway and carried the man up to the top landing by the roof door.

Fee-foe inhaled a small pinch of the heroin and suddenly realized the drug needed to be stretched. From the potency of the drug, his whole life could change if he played his cards right. In the year 2000, heroin that could be stretched or cut more than twice was rare. From what Fee-foe felt, he knew the youngsters had something extremely rare. Immediately, Fee-foe transformed into his old hustler mode. He spoke as if he was still the boss of heroin back in the early 80's. He didn't know how much heroin the youngsters had, but he negotiated hard with Rashid and Rico to set up apartments, cut the dope for them, and if they wanted, he could bag it up in the small glassine bags for them, too. Rashid knew a dope-fiend came a dime a dozen, but one with wisdom and principles was hard to come by. They all shook hands. Rico made a few threats, and from there, everything was in motion.

For the next couple of days, Rico and Rashid were busy setting up their operation on 117th Street and Manhattan Avenue. With Fee-foe's help, they went to the local smoke shop and purchased all the paraphernalia they would need. They then visited a stationary store where they bought a few small stamps with "M3" written on it, along with a box of red ink pads. Later, they rented two apartments on 119th Street and Morningside Avenue. The first floor apartment was going to be used as a cutting mill to process the raw heroin, package it, and store it. The third floor apartment was for stashing the money. They hired four more young boys to assist the two who sold their cocaine, and the M3 Boyz started with a crew of eight men. Before they were done making up all the bags, Fee-foe spread the word to all the top dope-fiends in the area by handing out small samples. In comparison to the heroin in the 'hood, M3 was certified a ten.

Once everything was set with the spot, the workers and the customers were ready to line up. Rico decided to use his expertise. His main objective was to make as much paper as possible for his team. He wanted his dope to knock all the Harlem dope spots out the box. Over the objection of Rashid, he took the already potent material and made sure Fee-foe put the least amount of cut on it. Since the majority of the hustlers who sold heroin used cutting agents like quinine and lactose to stretch their product, Rico and Rashid used the drug morphine to boost the potency of their product. When they were done with the packaging, Rico and Rashid stared at 20,000 glassine bags of heroin that was going to be sold for ten dollars a bag. They looked at the product and were scared to death. Wealth was right around the corner, but they knew a lot of men would kill them quickly for what they had in their possession.

The first day the dope hit the streets, three people overdosed and had to be revived. Their heroin became known as the "super bomb". The six workers Rashid had pushed the product 24/7. It only took a matter of days for the word to spread about the potency of M3. As expected, the paper started rolling in. Rashid became a workaholic, and Rico made sure no one on the workforce got out of line. Not only were the streets watching, but the streets were talking, too.

* * * * *

Under his closet, Manny had the most money he ever had in his life. Yet, he was in a funk of depression. He never imagined that after getting his big score that he would feel sad. The incriminating tape Pantera had troubled his mind. He replayed how he could kill everyone in the Havana's Paradise Social Club, or at least use his robbery tactics of torture to get the tape. Then he thought of Pantera's team and how lovely Xia was.

In an effort to change his mood, he wanted Carmen to freak him off, but while they were having sex, his helplessness got the best of him.

"What's the problema, papi?" Carmen asked when Manny couldn't get hard.

Manny moved her hand from his limp dick. "I got shit on my mind."

Carmen looked at her man. Then filled with rejection, she dropped his limp dick and said, "Oh."

When she turned away, Manny expected her to probe to find out what was bothering him, but she was lost in her own thoughts.

Manny caught her looking up at the ceiling. "What's your problem? I can't get it up and you got an attitude?"

"No," she said curtly.

That drove Manny crazy. He needed the attention, and his woman wasn't paying him any mind. He nudged Carmen. "Qué te pasa?" he said, asking her what her problem was.

"Nothing, Manny. I got shit on my mind, too."

Manny sat up, demanding an explanation. "What type of problem?"

Carmen fixed her mouth to tell Manny, but changed her mind. When she saw that he wouldn't stop staring, she said, "I did something I wasn't suppose to do, trying to look out for you, but...but...just forget it, Manny. You got your own problems."

Manny became furious. He didn't like anyone keeping anything from him. "Stop playing with me, Carmen. What's the problem? I'm not gonna ask you twice."

Carmen sat up, pulled her knees up to her naked breasts, and then rested her chin on them. "You kept complaining about not having money, and the bills were backed up before you became Señor big spender."

"So? What happened?" Manny asked, waiting for the drama to come.

She sighed again, not wanting to upset her man. "I know if I don't tell you, it's the same as lying to you, so don't get upset. Okay?"

Manny lost his patience. "Coño (Shit)! Tell me already!"

"Okay, this girl...this black girl who works in baggage in Atlanta approached me way back about getting some cocaine for her. She mad cool, so I figured I could do her a little favor. I went up on Broadway and bought five grams and took it to her. I thought that was the end of that. Then, two days later, she came back with five hundred and asked me could I get her some more."

"You transport coke now?" Manny asked, sort of upset, yet proud that his woman was criminal minded.

Carmen exhaled, then sighed. "Papi, just listen. It was stupid, but I gave her an ounce. Then she came back with two thousand and asked me to get her some more."

"How long you been doing this shit behind my back?" Manny snapped.

"No! Don't say that," Carmen said, hoping not to upset him. "It all happened so fast. I didn't get paid. I was just doing it, but then, I liked the adventure of doing it. It made me feel like I was in charge. You know?"

Manny looked at her like she was insane, so she went back to her story.

"So, last week, when I had a stopover down there, she introduced me to her boyfriend. He's a gringo, but, papi, he cool. Anyway, his name is Matthew, and he lives down in Marietta, right outside of Atlanta. He's moving cocaine in a place called College Park. I was hanging with them, and he started telling me how he's trying to hook up with some solid people that can give him good coca from up here. So, I told him I'll look into it and get back to him, but I don't know what the hell to do."

Manny thought about how many different ways there was to make money as a flight attendant. "Out of all the times people ask you to do things for money, why you do this one now?"

Carmen looked away in shame. "Cause this was the first time my man was complaining about money, so I wanted to help you out. I don't like to see you sad. I told you I'm with you, Manny Black. I love you, and I will do *anything* for you."

Manny's dick got hard when he heard her declaration of loyalty. "So what you want me to do?"

"You gonna laugh at me or get upset again."

Manny laughed at the way she knew him so well. "No, tell me."

Carmen turned to face him with a half smile on her face. "I want to make us some money. *A lot of money.* Like fifty thousand. Then I want to give it all to you because I know you will take care of me. Then I want us to move in together, and if I can get mi mamá and papá from Cuba, everything will be okay." She bounced on the bed. "Come on, papi. Tell me what to do."

Manny was proud of Carmen, but she wasn't wife material. He loved the sex, and she was technically his woman. So, he wanted to take care of her. "I don't sell drugs. You want me to get Rico to take care of this?"

"I want you to tell me what to do, papi. Whatever you tell me to do, I will do."

Manny thought about it for a moment. When he thought of making more money, his dick got stiff as a diving board. "Okay! That sounds like a good avenue. Hold him off for now and don't go back to Broadway. I will take care of it. You can take care of your business down there."

Carmen was overjoyed. She kissed Manny, then said, "You the best, papi. You really gonna let me do it all?"

Manny nodded, while Carmen looked down at how hard he was. She put her hand on his stiffness.

"I make you money, papi. You see." Her head went towards his crotch, and she kissed the head of his dick. "Now let me make you cum."

Manny and Carmen made love, had sex, and then fucked to seal the deal.

THREE

F or two weeks, Rico and Rashid were busy selling heroin and counting money. Manny was in Brooklyn avoiding his new Cuban friends.

Early one morning, Rico walked in on Manny while he was sitting inside his small living room watching TV. After Manny cursed himself for not having a gun in the house, Rico handed his brother a black book bag.

"Hermano, you not gonna believe this, but that's a hundred thousand right there. A hundred thousand in close to three weeks, Manny. We gonna get rich! I ain't got much time. I gotta go take care of some more business."

Manny asked, "How you make so much so fast?"

Rico beamed with pride. "Homeboy, this ain't the stick-up game. This is the dope game."

Manny opened the bag and peeked in. "That was all of it? You finished? With what I got, we can take this and go to Panama right now."

Rico laughed. "We ain't all the way done yet! But, I told you my man Rashid is the truth."

"You and your man took some paper for yourself, right?"

Rico sat on the small table across from Manny's couch. "Nah, man! We ain't takin' no cut off that. The only people getting paid right now is the workers. We gonna build this to a key, then we take our cut."

Manny thought about his brother's words as he calculated all the money that could come. "So what am I suppose to do with all this paper now?"

Rico sighed. He knew how dangerous his brother was, and how serious Manny was when it came to money, but it was too obvious that he didn't know a damn thing about selling drugs. "Yo, fam, *you* the boss now. It's time you start actin' like it. Save all that going to Panama shit. We made a hundred gees in a few weeks, so *we got* to make a mill in a few months. Then we can fuck around and buy Panama."

Again Manny pondered on his little brother's words. "Si, I

understand."

"Oh yeah, I'm tellin' you now. At the rate that shit is going, we gonna need some help, so get on your job. You gotta get some more of that good shit. Them dopeheads love it!"

Manny realized exactly what he had to do. "Don't worry," Manny said more to himself than to Rico. "I got this. For real."

The two brothers embraced, and then Rico headed out the door. Manny was giving himself a pep talk. While he was getting dressed, he thought, *New York, New York, big city of dreams, Manny. You got to get all the money you can get. You the boss now. You better start acting like it. Rico was right. Little Rico telling me what to do. You got the plan. You got money now, but now it's time to get rich. Mucho fucking rich.*

Manny was dressed with the book bag in his hand. He was heading up to the Bronx to handle some unfinished business.

* * * * *

It was a little over three weeks since Manny was ordered out of Pantera's social club. On this day, he walked through the doors of Havana's Paradise to personally see the black beast.

Manny was dressed in a goose-down coat, sweatshirt, jeans, and boots. As soon as he walked through the door, the warm air unfroze his face. As he was unzipping his coat, he was ambushed. The tall Latino with the ponytail and the short brute that he dangerously met on the night he tried to rob Pedro appeared at his side. Without warning, they threw Manny up against the wall and started frisking him.

"Cabrón, put your hands on the wall," the short brute ordered.

Pedro stood by the pool table with his back to the action. The loud thud of Manny being manhandled caused him to spin around.

"Hey! Hey! It's alright." He ordered the two henchmen to release Manny. He then waved his hand in an inward motion and said to Manny, "Come with me, kid."

Manny followed Pedro into the backroom. The furniture in the room had been rearranged differently. Across the room, Manny saw the black beast sitting with his horse-sized cock in his hand and a devilish grin on his face. Before Manny turned his head away, he saw a naked, fiery, red-headed petite girl kneeling between Pantera's legs.

Instantly, Manny looked at Pedro and asked, "What the fuck is this?"

Pedro lit his cigarette, then said nonchalantly, "Don't worry about that kid. It doesn't concern us. Tell me, what brings you here?"

Manny watched both men simultaneously. His eyes strayed from Pedro to Pantera, then down to the girl between Pantera's legs. The movement of her sucking Pantera's dick had frozen him. Pantera's gold teeth shined through his crooked smile, as the girl worked her tongue and lips. While distracted by the sexual slurps, Manny said, "You told me to come see you when I needed more product. Well, I need more. I brought money with me."

Pedro looked into Manny's eyes. "Okay, but your money's no good here. The product is no problem. You just have to go get it yourself. I'll send Xia to pick you up in three days. Be ready to do what you do best."

Manny met his gaze, knowing what Pedro was hinting at. "Need something else done, huh?"

Pedro nodded, then simply reiterated, "Be ready in three days."

As the words left Pedro's mouth, Manny's eyes returned towards the desk where the black beast was grunting. "Drink, Puta, drink!"

Manny wanted to avoid Pantera's sexual sideshow. He quickly made his way back to the front of the social club. He spotted the brute sitting with the tall Latino at a table near the front door, puffing on cigars. As Manny was about to exit the establishment, the brute looked up and locked eyes with him. Manny met his gaze as he thought, *You little, short bastard. Don't worry. Your day is coming,* while walking out the door.

* * * * *

When Manny left Havana's Paradise, he walked up Westchester Avenue and caught a luxury cab. The Lincoln Navigator wasted no time burning up the miles on the Cross-Bronx Expressway. As the V8 machine headed to Harlem, Manny was in deep thought while slow music pumped through the speakers. He had accumulated close to two hundred thousand in cash and had more cash in the streets. The thought of how things came together so soon made him wonder what was going to go wrong. Silently, he said a small prayer.

"God, I know this is crazy, and I don't pray much, but please protect me and my brother so we can get this money. Amen."

Manny opened his eyes feeling like a hypocrite, but hoping there was a god to answer his prayers.

The Navigator pulled up to 117th and Manhattan Avenue. When Manny stepped out, he told the driver to wait for him.

A crowd of people was moving up and down the block buying drugs or trying to sell stolen merchandise. A long line of customers was lined up along the side of the building where Rico sold his drugs. Out in front, four young guys dressed in blue army fatigues were directing traffic. Directly across the street was a well-dressed, young man who stood over six feet tall. Manny watched the man observing the transactions while sipping out of a Styrofoam cup.

"Pardon me, homie! You know where Rico at?" Manny asked the man.

The puzzled youth reached his hand under his coat and asked, "A yo, who you, playboy? What you want wit' Rico?"

Manny saw how overeager the boy was to make a name for himself. "I'm his brother Manny."

Instantly, the young kid's face registered recognition. His gun hand went up, as a smile spread across his face. "Oh shit, Daddy-o. That's my bad. I don't know why I ain't make the connection when I first saw you. You look just like that muthafucka."

Manny nodded with a slight grin, thinking of the young kid's stupidity.

The kid took the nod as a sign to continue. He stuck his hand out. "A yo, I'm Rashid, Rico's partner." Rashid wiped his face in embarrassment, then licked his finger to wipe off his boots. When he was sure his shit was tight, he said, "And you my boss. My bad, son."

Manny smiled. "I heard a lot of good things about you. It's definitely a pleasure to meet you."

"No doubt, kid! I've been waitin' to meet you, too," Rashid said with enthusiasm.

Manny had other things on his mind. "Yo, where Rico at? He around?"

"He went to shoot some Cee-lo up at Butch Cassidy's spot over on a hundred and thirty-six between Seventh and Lenox. The joint is right across the street from the funeral parlor."

Manny gave Rashid another pound. "A'ight. I'ma try to catch up with him. Be cool." He jumped back in the SUV and directed the driver where to take him.

The Navigator cruised up 116th Street and made a left on 7th Avenue. Expensive cars of all kinds passed them while they traveled up the four lanes of the avenue. When they reached 136th Street, the Navigator made a right and worked its way toward Lenox Avenue. Halfway through the block filled with brownstones, Manny spotted his brother's old black Pathfinder parked outside the funeral parlor. Manny hit the driver off with some money, got out, and walked up the steps to a brownstone.

The black door looked like any other house on the block until Manny rang the doorbell. A peephole slid, exposing the light inside. Then a steel reinforced door swung open. A tall, dark-skinned man stood there scrutinizing Manny's unfamiliar face.

"What up? How can I help you?" the big man asked.

Manny looked up. "I'm here to see my brother Rico."

Fireworks went off in the doorman's eyes when he heard Rico's name. "A'ight, come in. But, you gotta get searched."

Manny stepped into a small vestibule where another door separated him from the action inside. After his pat frisk came up empty, Manny was allowed inside the dwelling of the brownstone. The inside of the large house had been converted into a nice earthtone lounging area with tables, chairs, and a makeshift bar. The space was semi crowded with young thugs sitting around drinking and talking. In the corner of the huge room, men draped with jewels moved like moths to a light down a flight of steps. Since Manny didn't see his brother, he slowly made his way towards the light, too. Carefully, he took the steep, wooden flight down into another gambling area, where all the big money boys came to shoot Cee-lo on top of a green felt craps table.

At the end of the table, Rico had his fist above his head as the plastic dice crackled against each other. When he released his grip, he yelled, "Crack ass, bitches!"

By the moan of the crowd, Manny could tell Rico wasn't doing well. As he made his way to Rico, he saw a tall, brown-skinned, bald-headed kid who looked like a rap superstar. He had a platinum Hebrew star on one chain and another diamond-studded, platinum, Jesus piece on another chain. On top of that, a platinum star and crescent chain was dripping with diamonds. On his wrist, Manny saw a rainbow of colors from the light that bounced off the big diamonds of his matching bracelet. Counting the diamond rings on each of the man's pinkies, Manny calculated that he had on at least $350,000 worth of jewelry. Instantly, Manny's second nature told him that he had to rob the man, until the book bag in hands reminded him that he was there for business.

Manny's eyes darted to another corner of the room. Past the bodies of the young thugs, two other guys were rolling dice and talking shit while the crowd looked on. The tall, slinky one of the two had pop-eyes. He resembled a black fish that sucked on the side of a tank. He held the money while his short, pudgy partner rolled the dice.

Manny eased up on Rico, and Rico smirked. His eyes quickly went back to the craps table when Manny asked, "What's up, brother? You're a hard fella to find."

Rico's eyes darted from his brother back to the table. "Yo, what up, fam? What ya doin' here?"

Manny looked at the dice shakers, then said, "Looking for your ass. I have to talk to you."

Looking down at the bag in Manny's hand, Rico asked, "Hermano, you got any paper on you?"

Manny didn't like what his brother was implying. No way was he going to support the foolishness of gambling. Then he reminded himself that it was Rico who made the cash that he was holding.

"Yeah, a little. Qué pasa?"

"Let me hold somethin'. Ten thousand so I can git back in the game. I want to crack..." He pointed with his chin towards the pop-eyed and pudgy dice shakers. "...these bird-ass niggas."

Without hesitation, Manny reached inside the bag and withdrew a $10,000 stack. All eyes were on Manny, who silently prayed that his little brother knew how to handle the dice.

In the course of the next forty minutes, the tables turned. Lady Luck became Rico's best friend. He moved his way to the head of the dice table, stopping the bank and talking trash. He was laying it on the crowd thick. Before releasing the crackling squares, he blew into his hands while speaking intimately to the dice. When he was done pleading, he released them and yelled, "Get 'em, girls."

All eyes watched the three green squares tumble out of Rico's sweaty palms. The first die hit the felt, bounced, and then landed on six. Right next to it, the second die to hit the table matched up with the first, and six dots showed when it rested. The last die spun around on an axis for what seemed like an eternity, and then finally stopped. When everyone in the room leaned over the table to see the number, it was another six, and Rico yelled over their roar, "That's trips, muthafuckas! Pay me my paper!"

Some celebrated over Rico's victory, while the majority moaned. Pop-eye and the pudgy man threw their money in with sad faces. The man with the jewelry stared at Manny, while Rico was scooping up over twenty thousand dollars.

Manny didn't like the envious eyes on him and his brother, so he whispered in Rico's ear, "Let's get out of here."

Rico turned and quickly counted out ten thousand. Filled with cockiness, he patted Manny's chest. "Here, put this back. I'm gonna break these birds a little more." He then reached into his front pants pocket. "Here's my truck keys. I'll meet up wit' you in a half hour at my crib."

Manny didn't want to leave his brother amongst a den of thieves, but he agreed. "Okay, hermano, but don't have me waiting too long."

Rico wasn't paying attention to his brother. He was too busy pleading with the dice. Manny looked around, then headed for the flight of stairs that would take him outside.

While Manny walked down the empty street, the brisk winter air caused him to shiver. The cloudy sky added darkness to the Harlem block of brownstones. Once Manny reached Rico's truck, the cold air made his bladder beg for mercy. Manny quickly used the driver's door for a block and pissed in the street. While shaking the last drips of piss from his dick, he caught the shadows of two figures moving through his peripheral vision. His instinct was to reach into his waist, but he was unarmed. He had given his last gun to Xia to get rid of. Manny quickly spun around towards the approaching figures, realizing he couldn't get in and drive away. In the semi-darkness, the pop-eyed thug from the gambling spot and his pudgy partner were pointing two 9mm Lugers at him. Manny looked around for a little edge, but he was caught slipping.

The cold stares of the two robbers told him everything he wanted to know. They were seasoned stick-up kids. He knew the look of a robber's hunger too well to make a mistake. The men got the drop on him. Manny felt like he was looking in a mirror.

"What's this all about?" he asked in a calm tone, hoping his pause would help him negotiate more time in his life.

"Yo... Yo, nigga," replied the tall, pop-eyed one. "Stop-stop playin' games. You...You...You know...You know what it is. Hand over the bag."

Manny's mind raced as he contemplated the stuttering man's words. He had made too much money to die now. He saw no other option but to give up the money and hope they would allow him to leave alive. If everything worked in his favor, he would hunt them down later.

"Okay, you got it," Manny said, slowly reaching for the bag.

"Shut the fuck up. Hurry up and hand over the paper!" the pudgy one of the two replied with no patience.

As the fat kid spoke, Manny's eyes focused on a shadow creeping up behind the two kids. He thought it was Rico until the streetlight above allowed him to see the sparkle of diamonds. Before anyone knew what was happening, twin .357 Desert Eagles were pressed up against the heads of the two stick-up kids.

The owner of the giant guns calmly said, "Drop da guns. Self only telling you once."

The two robbers immediately recognized the voice. Manny raised his hands thinking somebody was robbing the robbers like he had done in the past.

Instantly, the tall, pop-eyed kid asked in a whiny voice, "Yo...Yo... Sel...Self? How...How ya...How you gonna do this shit, man? Yo...you one of the biggest stick-up kids up...up...uptown. We was here...here first, man. Come on, kid. You know how...how the game go."

"Drop the guns, you stuttering muthafucka!" Self ordered, while cocking the hammers back.

Manny noticed for the first time that the man had a mouth full of platinum with diamonds.

The robbers suddenly wised up, realizing they were in a no-win situation. They followed Self's orders. With the quickness, Manny bent down and scooped up both Lugers, ready to pop Self. When he raised his weapons at all three men, the two robbers were standing stiff while

Self was doing a light drum tap with his guns on top of their heads. That's when Manny realized Self wasn't there to rob him.

The fat one muttered, "Yo, Self, man, you violating by interferin' wit--"

The force of Self's Desert Eagle caved in his front teeth before he could finish his sentence. The sound of the steel butt hitting bones caused the stuttering, pop-eyed robber to jet off without his partner.

Self looked down at the fat kid's body. He turned the gun around so the nozzle was in his hand. With each swing of the steel hitting the fat kid, he said, "You...lucky...ya got...that...and Self didn't kill your fat ass." His final blow sunk the butt of the gun into the man's fat nose, exploding blood everywhere. While the pudgy kid leaned over with both hands covering his bloody face, Self said, "Now beat it, and tell your partner to move outta the hood. This Self territory to rob!" Self watched with a smirk as the fat kid struggled to boogie in the direction of Harlem Hospital a half a block away.

Self turned to face Manny and was met with two Lugers pointing at him. Manny cocked back the hammers. He couldn't resist his second nature. He thought of an extra six figures when he said, "Move real slow. Hand me the guns, then take off all the jewels. Everything, bro."

Self looked at his two cannons that were facing the sidewalk. His platinum smile appeared while he stared at the ground. "Another stick-up kid getting stuck up, huh?"

"Just move slow. I ain't got the time. Pass the jewels!" Manny ordered.

Self's fingers moved closer to the triggers. He looked at Manny. "These come off when Self dead. Self saved you, and you want to kill Self? Well, you coming wit' Self. So, either you squeeze and we see who meet the devil, or you can hear how we can really get rich."

Manny started getting nervous. He waited too long to do something and knew it would be a senseless killing, but he was too far ahead. "If I don't get you now, you get me later. So, what you want to do?"

Self chuckled while tucking his guns into his waist. He covered the weapons with his coat. "Come on, Slick. By the weight of that bag, you holding anywhere between eighty to a hundred and twenty gees. But, Self don't want it. If Self wanted to get you, you would've been got. Self's far from them two clowns I chased up off you. Ask your brother 'bout Self."

Manny realized Self had to be in his late twenties. He uncocked the Lugers and lowered them a bit. "So, what's up then?"

Self pulled out the twisted brown stick of a marijuana-filled cigar. He lit it, and by the time the potent weed hit his lungs, he exhaled. "You, papi. You and Rico's what's up. The streets is talking 'bout that work y'all movin." He tapped himself on the chest, then said, "And that's where Self come in. Self see what y'all can't see. Some big thangs are about to happen. You gonna need a dude like Self to help keep the wolves in check."

Manny examined Self from head to toe before replying. "Who you bullshittin'? You gotta have on at least three-fifty worth of jewels. Why you wanna fuck with us?"

Self looked like he was in deep thought. "Self getting too old for the jooks game. Like I said, Slick, the heroin you got is a winner. Self ain't blind. Over the last few weeks, Rico and Rashid been cuttin', baggin', and hittin' off that six-man crew they got moving 'round the clock on a hundred and seventeenth. Them fiends been lining up in two and three cheese lines at a time for that dope. Rashid, Rico, and their lil' man must've made a hundred trips up to a hundred and nineteenth to re-up over the past two weeks. Then he go out to Brooklyn to drop off the big paper. It's Self's guess that it's your crib by Eastern Parkway. That M3 shit is the truth 'round here. Self figure they gonna see a few mill by the summer, and Self wanna be wit' da winning team." He glanced around before continuing. "Yo, I don't know if anybody seen us, or if those clowns ran to da poe-poe. Let's get up outta here so we can talk."

Manny was shocked how Self knew his brother's entire operation. With his hand on the truck's door, Manny hesitated before saying, "I know my little brother's gonna kill me, but I want to hear more. Get in."

Self didn't think twice. He jumped inside the Pathfinder, and they sped off heading towards Ennis Francis Houses.

Manny made the right on Lenox Avenue. When they passed two traffic lights, he asked Self, "Tell me somethin', fam. You always go around sacrificing yourself for people you don't know?"

Self pondered the question before answering, and then burst with enthusiasm. "Nah, Slick, Self here on business. Sometimes Self do thangs on impulse 'cause my heart tells me dat it's da right thang to do. Maybe this was one of them times."

Manny was starting to feel the energy from the flamboyant man sitting beside him. The more they spoke, the more comfortable he became with having Self in his presence. *I could definitely use somebody like him,* he thought as they parked on 124th and 7th Avenue at the front of the Ennis Francis Houses.

Manny parked, looked at Self's jewelry, then asked, "Yo, why you say Self instead of saying me or I? And what's up with them pieces? You confused on what religion you wit'?"

Self showed his platinum smile, then looked down at his jewelry. He lifted the Jesus piece, the Hebrew star of David, and the star and the crescent that were all dripping with diamonds. "Man is confused, but

Self understands. So, with all these symbols, I got all bases covered."
They both busted out in laughter, then Self said, "See when Self go in
Self mode, he all about Self. It's like a superhero when he put on his
cape. During the day, he got a job and shit. Then when he put on his
suit, he invincible. So when Self walk these streets, Self is the
superhero, saving my pockets from starving."

Manny liked Self more by the minute. His vibes told him that Self
was good people. He had an arrogance that people either hated or
loved, and there was no in-between.

While they were laughing and Self was telling Manny about the
weak links in Rico's organization, a light tap on the Pathfinder's
passenger side window cut their conversation short. When Self rolled
down the window, Rico recognized him and pulled his gun out.

Self raised his hand. "Whoa, cowboy. You should put that away
before you hurt somebody wit' that."

"Manny, you a'ight in there?" Rico asked, while moving his gun
closer to Self.

Manny leaned forward. "Estúpido, put the gun away."

With his hand still on his gun, Rico realized the two were actually
together voluntarily. "What tha fuck, bro? You bringing this nigga to
where I live?" he barked at Manny.

"Calm the fuck down," Manny shot back, trying to cool down the
situation before it got out of hand. "At least I didn't take him up to your
house. Plus, he already knows everything about you, and maybe where
I live, too. Get in!"

Rico quickly tucked his gun, then opened the back door. He slid in,
slammed the door, and said to his brother, "Yo, I know about Self for a
long time. Homes be taki—"

"Aye yo, Rico, it ain't like dat kid!" Self cut in. "Yeah, you know
Self for a long time, and Self clapped up a few of your mans. But Self
never fucked wit' you. Believe me, Slick, Self been 'round enough real
hustlers to recognize a good nigga when he see one. Some lines Self
just don't cross."

"Hmmm," Rico moaned from the back seat, slowly untucking his
gun and holding it behind Self's seat.

After talking for ten minutes, Rico's rage simmered down. Manny
and Self conveyed to him everything that took place outside the
gambling spot. Self then explained all the weaknesses in his M3 team
and what the future would bring if the robbers of the five boroughs
knew that Self was with them. Rico learned how he was exposed and
didn't like it. Like a true boss, Manny decided he was putting Self on
the team. In due time, Self would have to show what he was worth.
They all exchanged phone numbers, agreeing that it was time to make
some money.

* * * * *

Everything in the M3 organization was in order after Manny and Rico's meeting with Self. The following day, Manny was sitting at home when he heard a light tap at his door. When he looked into the peephole, his heart started racing. He didn't hesitate to open the door. In front of him stood a woman of class, holding a gun in her hand. Xia stepped in like it was a habit, while Manny's eyes scanned the cocoa leather pants with the matching full-length coat. Her pointy-toed, low heel, latte colored boots with cocoa buckles going around it matched her wool, turtleneck sweater. *Damn, this chica knows how to dress*, Manny thought. Instantly, he noticed that her hair was sharply cut where it covered one side of her face. Manny caught an instant hard-on.

"Pedro sent me to get you. You have a job to do," Xia ordered.

"What's that perfume you wearing, Bonita?"

For a milli-second, Manny saw her face turn into a smile. Then she quickly frowned at him before putting her gun away and turning the television on.

Manny saw he wasn't getting anywhere, so he sarcastically said, "Go ahead and make yourself at home. Mi casa es tu casa."

He walked into his bathroom and cut the steaming hot water on. When he stepped into the shower, he was determined to make the woman outside wait. Her beauty trapped him, and he couldn't figure out why he was so attracted to her. There was something about her extra weight that turned him on. Ten minutes later, Manny was coming out of his bedroom. Xia was sitting on his couch with her head back and her mouth wide open. Manny looked at the sleeping beauty and wondered if she was like Carmen. He cautiously sat next to her, taking close to five minutes so he wouldn't ruffle the leather couch and wake her. Once he was right next to her, he sat for five minutes, allowing her to fall into a deeper sleep. Softly, he ran his finger across her hand to see how deep she was sleeping.

When Xia's gun didn't return to his face, he tilted his head to her ear and whispered, "Xia...Xia baby, you tired, mama?"

She stopped snoring and moaned out, "Huh?"

Manny stopped himself from chuckling. "Xia, you were up all night? You were out with your man, mama?"

Her head lifted slightly. "No...beauty...parlor."

Manny wanted to see how far he could go. He let her rest some more, then whispered, "Who you looking good for, mamacita?"

"Pick up Manny tomorrow," Xia said before she let out a deep snore.

Manny was stuck. He was bugging off the news Xia spit out. She was looking good *for him*. Suddenly, her head slipped to his shoulder.

He let her rest for ten minutes more until he made a sudden movement. Instantly, Xia's round eyes popped open. Her gun was out faster than Manny had ever seen anyone draw before. She was up on her feet staring at Manny, who was busy watching TV like a woman wasn't there pointing a gun.

"Oh, I must've fallen asleep," Xia said, while wiping her mouth and putting her gun away.

Manny looked up at her. "You tired? You must've been taking care of business all night, huh?"

Xia put a piece of Orbit gum in her mouth before she looked away. "Yeah, Pantera had me running errands all night." She turned back to Manny and added, "That reminds me. Come on. Pedro is waiting."

Manny went to the bedroom where he placed the two Lugers into his waist. He then placed his sweater over the guns and walked out of the door with Xia, laughing to himself while adjusting his coat.

* * * * *

During the ride into Manhattan, Manny and Xia glanced at each other. They cruised to the sounds of Kiss FM, while Xia gunned the X5 like it was a racecar.

Manny got into his Casanova mode. Turning to her, he asked, "So when I get that job interview, mama?"

Xia fought back her blush. Biting her tongue, she replied, "You're playing a dangerous game. When are you going to realize when a woman is not interested in you?"

Manny smiled due to the hidden information. "When I'm sure she's not. You, Bonita, you like me, but you afraid." Xia's head snapped his way like he was exposing her. "You afraid of all that loneliness going away and a man loving you."

"What you know about love?" Xia countered, while cutting the corner and entering traffic on the Avenue of Americans.

Manny looked out of the windshield. "I know you can't fight it no matter what you try to do. Either you accept it and deny yourself, or you let it happen and handle it from there, chica. But, no matter who you kill or how tough you think you are, you and me, Xia, we ain't stronger than love."

Xia pulled up to the restaurant where she and Manny first met. She put the truck in park and stared at Manny. Her eyes searched his face for lies. When she found none, she opened her door, leading the way into the alley of the restaurant.

Manny and Xia walked into the small storage room where Pedro was sitting at a square kitchen table. He was eating smoked salmon with eggs and drinking a glass of orange juice. When he saw Manny, he asked how he was doing in Spanish. "Cómo estás, Manny?"

Manny shook his hand, looked at Xia, then said, "I'm good! And you?"

In between bites, Pedro nodded. "Everything's all right for now. Just as long as you keep making money and taking care of the unwanted business." He looked up at Manny with a smile on his face. "You making big money now, huh, big man? Things looking good in your world because of Pedro, si?"

Manny thought of the incriminating tape Pantera had. "Yeah, you can get me that tape and everything would be better. Much better."

Pedro reached inside of his blazer's pocket and removed a piece of paper with a name and address underlined in red. He ignored Manny's request. "Pantera don't care how you do it. Just make sure it's done by this afternoon. Esta bien? The guy you're looking for is tall. His hair is receding, and he has a mole the size of a raisin on his face. He usually keeps one other guy with him at all times. You will be happier after this one, okay?" Pedro reached under the table and grabbed a black gym bag. "Here, take this. Use it wisely."

Manny looked inside the old gym bag. A blue Con Edison uniform with a meter reading device sat at the bottom of it. At that instant, he thought about how much money he had at home. While clutching the bag, he knew he could walk away, fly to Panama with his cash, and live better than he ever lived in his life.

"Hey, you okay?" Pedro inquired.

Manny snapped out of his daydream. He wanted all the money he could get his hands on. He promised himself that he was never going to be poor again. He looked at Xia, then at Pedro. "Let Pantera know it will be taken care of."

Manny snatched the bag, then spun to leave the storeroom. He was determined and felt like the man that he was going to see had done something personal to him.

Xia was right behind him. When they hit the sidewalk, she hit her alarm, opening the door for Manny. When she sat, she saw Manny adjusting the seat so he could recline.

She started the engine and asked, "Where do you want me to take you?"

Manny turned to her. "You can drop me off at the train station on 59th Street near Columbus Circle."

"You sure?" Xia asked. "I can take you wherever you need to go."

Manny contemplated Xia's offer for a moment, then said, "No, I appreciate that, but 59th Street will be cool."

Xia shrugged. "Okay. No problem," she said, while pulling off.

They rode in silence with their own private thoughts. Manny was focusing on what he had to do, while Xia gunned the engine.

When they reached 57th Street, Manny turned to Xia. "By the way, your hair is nice, and the perfume smells real good. I'll be thinking about you all day today."

Xia smiled. "Thank you."

Manny lit up from her smile. "You see, I made you smile. That's where it starts first. You smile, we kiss, and then I make your body feel good all over."

The look of a killer returned on Xia's face, letting Manny know he was going too far. He didn't care. He may not make it back home that night, so he continued. "You can kill me, but loving me and driving me around will make you feel much better."

Xia smiled again. "Why don't you have your own car?"

Manny chuckled. "My two feet are good. If I had a car, then you couldn't drive me around, and I couldn't spend any time with you."

Xia smiled a little bit more. "You won't always have someone chauffeuring you around."

The car stopped at his destination. Before he jumped out the X5, Xia pulled out a card and scribbled something on the back of it. "This is my friend. His name is Big Dave. He can get you any vehicle you want. You should give him a call. The number on the back is mine in case you need something."

"Bien bien," Manny said, while exiting the X5. "Maybe I call the number on the back for the job interview?"

Xia rolled her eyes. "Good*bye,* Manny. Be careful."

Manny blew her a kiss. "Goodbye is forever. I see you later, Bonita."

FOUR

When Xia dropped Manny off, he raced down the escalators to the train station with his black gym bag. Before he got on the train heading uptown, he called Self's cell-phone, telling him to be at 135th Street and St. Nicholas by eleven o'clock.

At a quarter past ten, Manny exited the train station on 125th Street and Lenox Avenue. He walked one block over and one block down to Rico's apartment on 124th Street and 7th Avenue.

When he got inside, Manny wasted no time getting dressed for his mission. He put on the Con Edison uniform wondering what it would feel like to work for the energy company. He figured with the money he had, he could get a job and live a square's life. He quickly dismissed the thought, remembering how much he hated working in the baggage department at the airport. After checking and then re-checking himself in the mirror, Manny headed out to meet Self.

After standing for what he felt was too long, Manny said, "Damn! I hope Self hurry up and get his ass here. It's chilly than a muthafucka out here." Manny laughed at himself when he pulled up the collar to his wool pea coat so he could cover his neck. He sat on a wooden bench while waiting on the park side of the street at 135th Street and St. Nicholas Avenue.

A few moments later, a blueberry Ford Expedition with dark tint caught Manny's attention when it made an abrupt stop. The passenger's window rolled down and Self's voice boomed, "Aye yo!"

A smile appeared on Manny's face as he jumped in and Self sped off. Like always, Self was dressed nicely. He was dressed in an all-white, Sean John, velour sweat suit, with a red New York Yankee hat and red rugged boots. On his neck was his diamond-covered jewelry.

"What's good, Slick?" He looked down at Manny's pants. "What's da deal wit' that uniform? You got a job now?"

"Nah, fam, I got it to handle my business," Manny said between his chuckle. He turned Self's music down. "Listen, I want you to roll with me while I go handle somethin' this afternoon."

Self chuckled. "That ain't no problem. What we gotta do?"

Manny thought of the best way to test Self, so he said, "Some faggot-ass puta who violated. I gotta go see him. He keep paper and material, so I'm gonna pay him one last visit." Manny turned to see Self's reaction.

Self smirked, thinking of the drama he craved for. "Self is wit' that!"

Manny's plan was coming together. "Before we go take care of business, you got to go change. Put on something less flashy."

Like a fish taking the bait, Self responded, "Slick, you ain't say nuthin'. Self stay prepared." He eased his body towards Manny, and while looking at the road, he asked, "Tell Self something? You and your brother plan on getting all this paper and then feeding the rest of the team scraps, or y'all the type that share the joy? What you think is better, a worker get paid like a worker, or everybody on the team get theirs in due time?"

Manny was stuck. His plans hadn't gone that far. He wanted every drop of paper he could get his hands on. With the Giuliani administration, he had to get that money and bounce while he had the chance. He thought of Carmen, and with nothing else to say, Manny stuck to the truth.

"You said we could see a mill soon. So, when I get a certain amount, me and Rico riding off in the sunset and leaving it to you and Rashid. Rico want to take this M3 to the next level like a gang or some shit. Me, I want familia! And right now, Self, you the only other brother I got."

Self stopped at the light while studying Manny's face. He pulled the truck over on Convent Avenue. "Slick, I knew you was real. So, drive so we can handle our business."

Manny slid over to drive while Self jumped in the back seat. While Manny drove, Self started taking his clothes off. After removing his jewelry, it took all of five minutes before he changed into a black hoodie, black jeans, and a pair of black boots.

Although Manny told Self the truth about the man they were going to see, some things didn't need to be said.

* * * * *

Self's Expedition exited the Bruckner Expressway onto White Plains Road. Manny drove around looking for the address on Gleason Avenue. When he found it, Manny pulled up behind Elmo's gym. He pointed his finger. "That lil' white house across the street."

Self watched as Manny took off his pea coat. On the left side of his shirt, there was a medium-sized blue and white Con Edison patch. Manny reached inside his gym bag and removed one of the Lugers he took from the stick-up kids, along with the meter reading machine.

"Slick, how this thing going down?"

Manny looked into his fearless eyes. "I'm going in there, hit the puta, and I'm outta there. He's a tall guy with a raisin-sized mole on his face. I got a surprise for him."

Self watched Manny cock the Luger. The temptation of getting down and showing Manny where he really stood got the best of him. He blurted out, "Yo, slick, let Self show you how a real pro work." He hit a compartment inside his sound system and removed a sawed off, double barrel shotgun. He slid the small cannon in his waist and told Manny, "You wait right here."

Manny watched Self walk down the block to a fruit stand and remove two small potatoes from the large green bin. Self handed the Korean worker a bill and started bopping his way back.

When he reached Manny, he asked, "Slick, you ready to do this?"

Manny followed Self's lead and then stopped. "Potatoes? I ain't use them since I was a little kid."

Self smiled. "Good, let me show you how Self make mashed potatoes."

Manny slid on his gloves, thinking he had met someone more anxious about killing than his little brother. He exited the truck, and his nervous whistle seeped from his lips as he and Self crossed under the train tracks of White Plains Road.

While Manny walked up the narrow walkway, Self swiftly ducked down behind a bunch of tall hedges near the front door.

Manny knocked twice before a man's voice asked, "Who is it?"

"I'm from Con Edison," Manny replied. "And I'm here to read your meter." Manny looked down at Self, who was stuffing a potato over the nozzle of the shotgun.

The door opened, and a tall man with a raisin-sized mole on his face stood scrutinizing Manny's uniform. He read the name tag that read B. Johnson, and then motioned for him to enter. "Okay, follow me."

In one motion, Self darted out of the hedges and crept behind Manny. By the time the door slammed, it was too late. Manny already had the cold steel of the Luger pressed against the man's face.

The victim gasped, while Manny whispered, "If you want your life, you do what I say, comprende?" The man shook his head. Manny asked him who else was in the house. "Quien mas esta en la casa? Y no me mientas!"

In broken English, he mumbled, "Just me," through each deep breath he took.

"Enséñame adonde estás?" Manny ordered the man to show him what was inside. He used the man's body as a shield as they roamed through the semi-dark hallway and into the living room that had a huge Cuban flag hanging over a fireplace. Before nudging the man forward, Manny wondered why all the men Pantera wanted killed were Cuban.

What's it to you, Manny? Stay focused.

Manny moved his captor towards the dining area where they heard Salsa music playing. Self walked closely behind, prepared for the unexpected. Just as they were about to enter the dining room, Manny spotted a giant Latino in the kitchen. The man was sitting at a table counting money with his back turned. His head bopped to the loud Salsa music. Beside him was a black briefcase with large bags of white and beige powder. A big, ugly revolver lay on its side. The sight of the giant man caused Manny to stop dead in his tracks. He backed up while pulling his hostage with him.

When Self saw the surprised expression on Manny's face, he cautiously peaked in and observed the giant. Quickly, Self ducked back and looked at Manny, shrugging his shoulders. Then on impulse, Self went into action. He moved fast when he crept up behind the unsuspecting Latino.

When the man was about to hit a high note, Self moved in, placed the potatoes to the man's open mouth, then ordered, "Put everything in the briefcase. Now!"

Sweat poured from the black curls that lay across the giant's fearful face. He nodded quickly while dropping stacks of bills into the small case. After he closed the case, Self slid the case to the opposite side of the table and said, "Goodbye," when he pulled the trigger.

The muffled blast splattered blood and brain fragments in Manny's direction. *This kid is the truth,* Manny thought, watching how Self stepped to his business without hesitation. In that split second, the raisin-faced Latino pushed all his body weight back into Manny's chest.

Manny blurted out, "What the fuck!"

The Latino attempted to dash back through the living room, but his escape was cut short. Manny's Luger spit out two hot slugs that spun the man's body around, making him stumble to the ground headfirst.

Manny turned to where Self stood and said, "After you finish him off, I'll be right back."

Manny remembered the error he had made on the first job for Pantera. He looked all around the room and then headed back to the bedrooms. When he reached the dark dwelling, he found what he was looking for. A 13-inch colored television sat on a stand. He looked at the screen, and Self was standing over the man he plugged. He watched Self methodically kick the squirming man over, point the shotgun to the man's chin, and lean back before squeezing the trigger. Manny closed his eyes when he heard the silent thud. When he looked back at the screen, Self was smiling down at the bloody mess with the mashed potato covering what was left of his victim's face. Instantly, Manny pressed the eject button to the machine and slipped the videotape into his waistband. Manny was certain now that Self was for real.

Manny walked out of the room in a rush to leave. While he was heading for the door, Self yelled over the Salsa music, "Yo, hold up."

Manny stopped. Seeing Self with the shotgun and briefcase in his hand, he asked, "What's up?"

Self tucked the shotgun in his waist. "Turn around. Walk backwards out the house and see if we left anything that can lead this shit back to us."

Manny thought about the tape in his waist, but when he turned around, he saw something. The spent shellcasings from the Luger were close to the man he killed. While he was picking them up, Self put his ear close to the victim to make sure he was dead. Together, they eased to the front door.

Manny was getting ready to walk out, when Self said, "Hold up." Manny prided himself in being a professional, until Self said, "Always look out the window before you leave the crib. Witnesses can be out there. Poe-poe could be coming down the block, or somebody else could be coming in the crib. We don't want no surprises."

Manny knew he put the right man down on his team. When they looked out the window, an elderly white woman was walking her poodle in front of the house. They patiently waited until she was gone before leaving the house. Then they walked to the truck, taking their time and making sure they didn't pass anyone that could identify them.

The Expedition cautiously cruised the Bruckner Expressway at a moderate speed, heading back downtown. Beanie Sigel's new CD *The Truth* pumped through the speakers. Manny took his dirty Luger and a tee shirt out the gym bag. He started dismantling the pieces and wiping them clean.

"Slick, where we headed?" Self asked with pride.

"Drop me off at the train station on a hundred and twenty fifth and Saint Nick." He opened the briefcase, took out the heavy bags of powder, and put them inside his gym bag. He then looked at Self and said, "It looks like close to fifty thousand in there. That's yours, okay?"

Self took his eyes off the road. "Slick, you don't want any of that?"

Manny made sure he had everything he needed. "Nah, that's for you, bro. Enjoy it. Welcome to the family."

Self slid the case to the backseat. "You ain't got to tell Self twice."

He dropped Manny off at the train station like he requested. Manny paid his fare, then descended the gritty steps until he reached the platform. He looked around the platform to make sure the four separate tracks were empty. He then reached into his bag and placed the clip and handle part of the gun in the huge garbage can. With the other smaller parts, he dropped them under the platform, knowing years would go by before anyone found it.

With one part of his mission done, Manny was heading to Brooklyn, hoping he wouldn't have to use the other gun he had tucked under his waist. If he could help it, no one was going to catch him with drugs on him or the incriminating tape that was now in the bag.

* * * * *

Manny exited the train station in downtown Brooklyn on Jay Street and Borough Hall. He called Rico's cell phone and his brother answered.

"Talk about it."

"Hermano, I'm on my way home. Meet me there. I got something for you."

"A'ight, I got some paper for you. I'm almost done wit' dat thing, too."

"Just come to my house," Manny demanded before terminating the call.

When Manny reached home, he rushed to his stash spot and pulled out his triple beam scale. After busting open the bag of white powder, Manny tasted it, and it was cocaine. He then dipped his finger into the bag of beige powder. The bitter taste told his almost numb tongue that it was heroin. He weighed the heroin first, and it came up to 512 grams. The coke weighed in at an even kilo.

Shit, this got to be too good to be true. Why the fuck these Cubans being so generous? Manny asked himself as he stashed the coke, his scale, and the videotape in his closet floor.

By the time Manny was settled, Rico was coming through the door.

"A yo, what's up? Here goes some paper," Rico said, while passing Manny a plastic shopping bag. "That's sixty-two gees. We finished, bro. That shit is moving faster than I thought. We need more now!"

Manny had the heroin in his hands, then handed it to Rico. "Okay, hermano, you got double of what you got before. That should hold you for a minute."

Rico asked, "This the same shit, right?"

Manny shrugged his shoulders. "I don't know. Just do what you got to do with it," Manny said as he sat at the kitchen table. "Have a seat."

Rico wondered what was wrong with his brother.

"Yo, hermano, this cash is really rolling in fast. We really got to keep things together. 'Cause I never thought it was possible this fast."

Rico shook his head in disbelief. "Man, you should see how them customers are lining up." He looked at the floor. "I didn't know so many people use drugs in one day. Poe-Poe is all over us, but this shit is crazy. It seems like the more hot the police made it, the more custies we got. Son, this drug dealing shit is more work than a job."

Manny laughed. "Si, just remember we have a plan to follow. This game is crazy." He thought for a minute. "Self is real. He's family now."

"I trust that nigga as far as I can throw him," Rico replied.

Manny's tone got serious. "On our family, he's real. He showed me. That's all I have to say. You can thank him for that Manteca you got in your hand."

"Word?" Rico asked. He looked at his brother and said, "You don't take me to do shit with you no more. What's up wit' that?"

Manny smiled and gave his brother a tap on his chin. "If we're both in trouble, what good will that do mama and papa? Just do your part, and I'll do mine."

"A'ight, you know I'm gonna handle my business."

Rico took the heroin and left, heading back uptown to meet Rashid so they could put the new work on the block.

* * * * *

After Rico left, Manny followed his ritual of soaking in the tub. On that day, he killed his ninth person. Manny wasn't proud of his skills, but he learned at a young age that nobody was going to give him a damn thing for free. Anything he wanted he had to take on his own. He didn't have the family, education, or money to make it in America, so he did what the rest of the poor who wanted to get rich did. He hurt and fed off his own until he was fat enough to walk away. Just then, he wondered how Xia felt and what her story was. He was tempted to call her, but he had some business to take care of first.

When Manny was dressed, history repeated itself. He made two phone calls to Carmen and Edeeks, telling them that he needed to see them.

Carmen shared an apartment with her gay co-worker. Ever since Manny had an argument with the roommate, he never returned. He left a message on her voice mail, knowing once she landed in New York she would come straight over.

By 8:00 p.m., Carmen came through the door. Underneath her trench coat, Manny saw her stewardess uniform. "Hi, papi," she said in a cheerful voice as she kissed him on the lips. "I missed you, baby."

Manny smiled at how he knew his woman like a book. "What's up? I was waiting for you to get here. I got that thing for you."

Carmen had completely forgotten. "What's that?"

"The material you asked me for." He sat on the edge of his bed. "Now tell me again how you met this gringo."

Carmen sighed like she was explaining something to a child. "Remember I told you, papi, I met him through his girlfriend. She works at Atlanta's Hatfield Airport handling baggage. She and I started doing a little business. I was taking her grams of cocaine. They got rid of it as quick as she got it. Then she introduced me to her boyfriend Matthew. He has a few thugs around Atlanta buying the cocaine from him. He asked me about a coca connection up this way. I told him that I'd see what I could do."

Manny looked at Carmen, wondering when she got the nerve up to sell drugs. "Ma, you didn't think about the policía, your job, nothing? How you know this gringo is not the FBI or somebody?"

With a smile, Carmen kissed Manny. "I didn't care. Mi papi was crying broke, so I did what I had to do. For the amount of money that she gave me, I think they sell it for a hundred dollars a gram."

Manny thought about the one thousand grams he had in his house at that moment. He threw precaution out the window. "Find out how much. You got a phone number for him?"

Carmen reached inside her pocketbook for her cell phone. "I'm going to call him right now," she said, while scrolling through the numbers in her phone. "Hello, Matthew...this is Carmen...I'm good, and yourself? Listen, remember you was asking about that stuff? Okay, I think I found somebody for you, but he needs to know the price down there. Okay...fine...I'll see you."

Carmen hung up the phone and started clapping with delight when she turned to Manny. "Papi, here's the deal. They go for one hundred apiece. I was right! I told you I know how to do this. Matthew said he got too many people that want some and not enough help."

Manny rubbed the stubble on his chin. "That's good. Mami, when you flying back?"

"I have a flight at seven in the morning."

"Okay. I'm going to give you a thousand grams."

Carmen's eyes popped open. "A thousand grams? Where'd you get that? Damn, papi, you serious about this, huh? Now you making me scared."

Manny chuckled. "Loca, tell him to take forty and give you back sixty. You make sure nobody follows you, and you don't tell nobody, Carmen. Nobody!"

Filled with foolish pride, she kissed Manny. "Baby, your mami can do it. You see, I'm gonna make us rich. They don't search us flight attendants for national flights. I'm gonna make you proud, Manny."

He handed her the cocaine and showed her where to hide it. For the rest of the night, Manny told Carmen the do's and don'ts of what she was getting herself into. His mind told him to meet her down there, but she wanted to do it. So, Manny was going to make her wish come true.

After her pep talk, Carmen was horny. She sat Manny on the toilet seat and rode him until she came twice. The thrill of breaking the law was turning her on. By the time she was ready to have her third orgasm, a knock came to the door.

Manny rushed to look at his peephole, praying Xia wasn't standing in his hallway. He knew Carmen was no match for Xia on any level, but he still worried about a confrontation. When his eye looked through the small hole in his door, Edeeks was standing there in a suit. Manny smacked his head for forgetting he had called him over.

Edeeks stepped in, asking, "What happen now? You hit lotto or something?"

Manny put his finger to his lips for Edeeks to be quiet. At that instant, Carmen was coming out of the room. Her long hair was flowing, her caramel skin was shining, and Manny wanted to fuck her again. Unfortunately, she was on her way out the door, kissing Edeeks on the cheek and waving goodbye to the man of her dreams.

Edeeks stared at Carmen when she walked past. "What you gonna do with that girl? You should let me have her if you not gonna marry her."

Manny sat on the couch. "I will marry a woman who can take care of me in every way. One who I can take to Panama with pride. Somebody that got her own or more than me. Carmen's pussy is good, but she doesn't think too well, and she always needs something. My mother wouldn't like her to be my wife."

Edeeks said, "Anyway, why you call me over? I have things to do."

Manny shot him a glance that he needed to slow down. "I want you to set up everything. You said to let you know when I was ready. Now I got the money for the plans."

Edeeks crossed his legs and placed his hands together on his lap. "I'm glad you brought that up. I've been giving some serious thought to what kind of business we could establish to clean the money. Then, last week, this guy comes to me who I swear is in debt to my firm. The man owns a small scrap metal company on a hundred and thirty fifth in the Bronx where the bridge to Manhattan is. Anyway, he's trying to sell it so he can retire and move to Florida. Basically, we can purchase it at a bargain."

"Scrap metal? What the fuck you talking about scrap metal?"

Edeeks held up his hand, signaling Manny to wait. "It's important that whatever we do, we go in a direction different from other hustlers. Most of them are running to open up barbershops, laundromats, and little record labels to launder their money. But, the government and banks monitor those types of businesses a little more than others. Besides, people underestimate the money a scrap metal company can generate."

"Bueno. I get your point. But, what the hell we know about scrap metal?"

"Big bro, give me a little more credit than that. I did my homework." Edeeks got up from the couch, finally excited to talk about real business. "This is how things work. Once we purchase the company, we start buying scrap metal from demolition sites and peddlers off the street. You can have your people put the word out to the fiends to bring scrap metal to us. Afterwards, we sell it to recycle and larger scrap metal plants at a higher price. Those companies will resell the refined product to construction companies across the country. We're guaranteed to make a profit in the process of washing the incoming cash. So what if we don't make huge profits? You're in this to clean the dirty cash."

Manny was beaming with pride. Edeeks went to school and got something out of it. "Little bro, that sounds good. What you need to put things in motion?"

"Tomorrow I can meet with the guy from the scrap metal company. I'll make the arrangements to take the company off his hands. Afterwards, I'll start working on putting the paperwork together so we can form a Limited Liability Corporation. Once the LLC is formed, you and Rico will come in as equal shareholders in the company. However, you and Rico will remain silent shareholders for protection. We'll have to establish a business account. For all paperwork purposes, it will reflect that each shareholder deposited seven thousand in the account. That is the new limit under the recent law, and it will keep the IRS red flags down. Once the account is established, I'll secure a hundred-thousand-dollar loan from the bank by utilizing the company's assets, the twenty-one thousand in our account, and then use my good credit as collateral. Then we'll purchase the company. I also have this Jew named Ken Rosenstein. He owns several construction and recycling companies, but I hear he washes money on the side. I spoke to him, but he was beating around the bush. If we give him a hundred thou, at a fifteen percent fee, he could issue our company a check for eighty-five thousand dollars for ghost scrap metal he brought from us."

"Damn, hijo, I underestimated you. You're definitely on your job," Manny excitedly said, while heading to the closet. He returned ten minutes later carrying an old plastic bag. "Here, take this. It's one-thirty inside. Take twenty-one out of the thirty to set up the account. The nine thousand that's left use to cover the cost of the paperwork you have to take care of. You know what to do with the rest. It's for your boy Rosenstein."

Edeeks nodded, then uncrossed his legs. Sitting forward, he said, "Now that the money is rolling in, Manny, you have to take a trip back to Panama. I just read recently that the government down there has been rebuilding. So, now is the time to buy up whatever you can and make it work for you. I want you to go there, buy up some property, and then start sending money down there at least once a month. That way, when things start falling to pieces over here, you and Rico will have something over there to fall back on. Something this government doesn't know about and can't touch. Another thing, I think you should give some thought to maybe opening up some kind of social club for Rico's crew or something."

Manny thought of Havana's Paradise and said, "E! What I need with a social club?"

"Mi pana, you gotta stop thinking small. You said you want to do big things. Well, you have to start thinking like the big boys if you plan to play in their league. You and your people can have somewhere safe to get together. Y'all won't have to worry about being bugged or caught in a vulnerable position. When you have to meet with legitimate business people, you can entertain them at your own establishment. It's the beginning of solidifying you as a business man," Edeeks said, getting up off the couch. "Just think about it."

After Edeeks transferred all the money from the bag to his briefcase, he dug inside his wallet and retrieved a business card. "Here, take this. Robert Boyle is a good friend of mine. He's one of the best criminal defense lawyers in the country," Edeeks said. He saw Manny reading. "I spoke to him about being on retainer for you, and he's agreed. So, I'm going to need some money to take him. Remember, it's not a matter of *if* the police or the feds are going to come, but *when* they coming. You don't want to be like most of them other guys who wait until the last minute to get one. Half the time, they end up broke with incompetent mouthpieces."

Manny shot back to his bedroom and returned minutes later with another $10,000. "Here, this should hold the lawyer for awhile." Manny exhaled. "One minute, I have a lot of money, and the next minute, I spend it all just so I can keep it? Only in America."

Edeeks laughed while both of them tried to cram the money into his briefcase. When that failed, Manny escorted Edeeks to his Ford Explorer, making sure his investment left Brooklyn safely.

* * * * *

60

Two weeks after Manny committed the robbery, news reporters said Cubans were at war with the Colombians in New York. The report worried Manny, and he questioned if he was in the middle of a war.

Carmen arrived in Atlanta and everything was going well. Rico reported the same news. In Manny's idle time, he thought about the first time he saw Xia standing inside the back room of Pantera's restaurant. Even though he stared at death in her eyes, he found himself attracted to her pretty face and thick body. It made him smile thinking about their flirting during the ride up to Havana's Paradise. He liked the classy way she dressed and her tough, sassy disposition. Manny pulled out the card she gave him. While lying in bed smoking a cigarette, he was contemplating whether he should call her or not. His fingers twirled the card around until his desire got the best of him.

Manny picked up his phone and dialed.

"Hello?"

"Hey, Bonita. How you doing?"

"You have the wrong number," the woman on the other end said. Then the phone went dead.

Manny pressed the redial button. When he heard a woman's voice, he tried a more humble approach. "May I speak to Xia please?"

There was a pause on the other end. "Who's calling?"

Manny didn't know if he was talking to her sister, mother, or her, so he said, "Tell her Manny calling."

"Tell her Manny calling? That's how you call people's house?"

"Um...ah...this Xia?"

The woman on the other end sighed. "Why are you calling me, Manny?"

Manny was glad it was her. "You gave me the number, so I was wondering if you didn't have anything to do, if we could hang out."

"And do what?" Xia asked in an annoyed tone.

Manny was about to give up, but then he said, "Relax, querida. You come get me, and we'll just hang out."

Xia paused. "And *why* would I want to do that?"

Manny was about to play the last card he had. "So the next time you stay in the beauty parlor all night to look good for me, you will know I'm worth it."

Silence was on the other end. Xia was lost for words.

Manny asked, "So you coming to pick me up or what?"

"You still haven't got a car yet? You should've called the number on the front of the card before you flipped it over and called me."

"Okay, I'm going to do that. Will you let me take you out then, or you coming to get me now?"

There was another short pause before Xia answered. "Why me? Why you want to spend time with me?"

"Come on! I can't stop thinking about you. I want to smell your perfume, see your hair and those nice clothes you wear. Okay, just let me look at you, and then you can go back home."

Xia was quiet again before she asked, "Where you want to go?"

Manny thought of the best thing he could say. After his pregnant pause, he said, "In your arms forever."

Xia melted. "Damn."

Manny was finally getting somewhere. "Come on, chica. Don't be so strong all the time. Let me make you smile again. You and me today. I promise to be a good boy."

Xia finally relented. "You don't have to beg. Okay! I will come get you, but the earliest I can make it is about eleven. I'll call you when I'm close to your building so you can meet me outside."

Manny was filled with joy. "That's what I'm talking about. I'll see you soon."

He hung up the phone, skipped into his living room, and blasted the music so he could dance while he dressed. A woman had never made Manny feel that way before. For the first time in his life, he thought he had met his match.

FIVE

Manny came out of his building just as the X5 pulled up. From the driver's seat, Xia examined Manny's clothes while he walked to the passenger's side of her truck. Manny was dressed in a black leather jacket, a black and gray Coogi sweater, black jeans, and suede boots. When he closed the car door, he saw the distasteful expression on Xia's face.

"What's wrong with you?" he quizzed.

Xia frowned. With an attitude, she replied, "Where am I suppose to go with you dressed like that?"

Manny chuckled before he shot back, "Dressed like what?"

With a passive voice, she said, "Like a damn hoodlum."

Manny looked over at her red leather boots, one-piece, flowing corduroy skirt suit with buttons from her ankles to her red leather collar, and her red ostrich driving gloves. He knew he was no match for her. He put his hands up in a gester of surrendering.

"Okay, you win. Since we can't go where you want to take me, then I'll take you where I want to go."

Xia put the truck in drive. "So where are we going?"

"Relax, just chill. We going to get something to eat."

Xia drove down Eastern Parkway. "Okay, I like food. We can get with that."

Manny thought of a nice restaurant. "Okay, let's go to Harlem. There's a place named Londel's that I want to go to."

Xia gunned the engine, back in her racecar mode. They cut through the Brooklyn streets until they reached the highway. Neither of them spoke until Xia asked, "Manny do you think I'm one of those women that's going to sleep with you because you take me to eat?"

Manny sighed. "Bonita, why you so angry? Just enjoy the day. Sex is sex, and any man with a little game can always have sex. But, me? I see the big picture. Why you so uptight? I do think you need some sex to loosen you up, though."

Xia smiled and they both busted out laughing.

Then she asked, "So why me, Manny?"

"Why not you, Xia?" Manny asked, while looking out the window. "Mama, you beautiful. Everything about you is beautiful. Even your gun is beautiful. You the type of woman that makes life a little better, you know?"

Xia smirked and gunned the engine harder. "Make life better, huh? What makes life so good? In our business, there is a lot of bad."

Manny thought about her question. His mind told him not to speak, but his mouth didn't obey. "Let me tell you something. I lived in Panama, and things were rough over there, real rough. When America kidnapped General Noriega during the invasion of Panama, I had to go. Mi papá? He worked in a cement factory his whole life to take care of me and my two brothers. After the invasion, everything started closing. All the businesses went down. Teachers sold their bodies for money; government officials turned their asses on the poor; and children took over the streets looking for blood. Papá got laid off. I'm the oldest, and since papá wasn't feeding us, I left for America. I did things I didn't like to come here, but I'm here. I live well. Not like you, or how you want me to be, but I always think about how I came here with nothing but highwater pants and a shirt. Now? I do a little better. Soon? I do the best. Better than anybody in the Black family ever did. All I need is a good woman by my side, and I can have the world."

Xia was on the BQE in deep thought. She could understand how Manny was trying to make a better life for himself. He could never know what she knew, but she understood struggling and admired him more.

She mumbled, "I guess things can be worse."

Manny turned to her. "The load of life can get heavy, Bonita, but it makes us strong. When you find a good man, he can help carry the load and make life a lot easier."

She raced across the Tri-Borough Bridge when she asked, "A good man? What the hell is that? Somebody that tells you he loves you, then hurts your heart later and makes you hate all men?"

"Chula! You too angry. I wish I could find the man that did that to you. I would kill him dead right now." Xia smiled and Manny chose his words carefully. "A woman has to ask herself why she wants a man. Why she *needs* a man? Then when she finds one, she has to stay focused on that one thing. Everything else makes the love complicated. A good man, Bonita, is one who will look you in the face and tell you he is weak, help you make him strong, and let you choose if you can handle his weakness. Life is no fairytale. Man and woman do wrong, but it can't be wrong if you know what to expect. The problem is women think they can change a man without ever knowing who he is inside. When you know how your man thinks, Bonita, he doesn't surprise you. He doesn't hurt you, because you know his next move." Manny smiled, then said, "Like me. When I become your man, you'll learn what I like to eat, how I make love, and what I need to keep me happy. Just let me be the man for you that mi madre showed me how to be and my papa taught me to be."

Xia was on the 125th Street exit when she said, "Don't reach too high, Manny. You might fall and hurt yourself."

"You'll see, Bonita. You'll see."

Xia pulled up to the small restaurant on 8th Avenue. When she put the car in park, Manny was acting silly. He raced around to the driver's side and helped her get out the car. He opened the back door, pulled out her full-length, red leather coat, and placed it around her shoulders. He then held her hand up high like a queen being escorted into the establishment.

As soon as they were seated, a waiter who saw the X5 rushed to their table for their orders. When their soul-food meals came, they ate in the semi-lit dining area of the cozy supper club. Between bites, they talked while slow Jazz music played in the background.

When their meal was finished, Manny asked, "Did you enjoy the food here?"

"Yeah, it was good. I have to come here again," Xia said, while licking her lips.

Manny got up and paid the tab. "So, you see, a hoodlum does know some good places. Now let me show you something else. Come on, let's get out of here and take a walk."

Xia stood. "Where? In Harlem?"

"Nah! Just come on," he said, while pulling her out of the restaurant. When he reached the curb, he said, "Bonita, let me drive. I want to surprise you."

Xia smiled and put her hands on her hips. "Hell no! I just got that for the New Year. We on a date, but we're not that close. Just tell me where we're going, and I'll act surprised when we get there."

Xia followed Manny's directions until they reached Boston Road in the Bronx.

Manny said, "Pull over right here."

Xia pulled over, then asked, "Where we going?"

Manny pointed outside his window. "In there for a walk."

Xia put the car in park and checked for her gun in her coat. "In the Bronx Zoo? Who the hell goes walking in the Bronx Zoo in the cold?"

"It's okay. Come on," Manny said when he exited the vehicle.

"I can't believe this."

"Be easy, Ma. Trust me."

Manny guided Xia though the entrance. The zoo was empty. Only a handful of employees and spectators were walking around preparing for the late spring crowd. When they passed different animals, Xia stared and looked like she wanted to cry.

Manny saw her watery eyes. "What's the problem, Bonita?"

"They looked trapped, like this is a big prison for animals."

Manny laughed. "A coldblooded killer with a heart. Good, then this is visiting day. So, let's keep them company." They walked into the darkness of the reptile house, when Manny asked, "Xia, how you hook up with a man like Pantera?"

Xia's eyes canvassed the room of animals behind plates of glass. She pondered whether or not she would answer his question. Finally, she decided it couldn't hurt to tell him, so she took a deep breath.

"When Pantera first came over here from Cuba, he and his wife moved in the same tenement building that my mother and I lived in on Webster Avenue here in the Bronx. When my mother was thirty-nine, she was diagnosed with terminal brain cancer. I was only fifteen at the time and my mother's only child. Soon after, my mom passed away." Xia paused in reflection. She was reliving the experience again. Her eyes moistened and her voice trembled. She didn't tell that story often. "My mother's younger sister and her boyfriend moved in and received checks from the State to take care of me. Things were bad. My aunt was more concerned with spending the money on feeding her drug habit, while her boyfriend tried to feed his sexual appetite on me. I was only fifteen. I had nowhere to go and no one to turn to."

"Damn," Manny said, while shaking his head. He never imagined a woman like Xia having a rough past. "Where was your padre?" he asked tenderly.

"Pantera's the only father I know. Anyway, my aunt's boyfriend had forced himself on me and threatened to kill me if I ever told anyone about what he was doing. I was so devastated that I ran down the stairs crying my eyes out. Pantera just happened to be coming home at the time, and I damn near ran right into him. When he saw the tears running down my face, he stopped me and asked what was wrong. At first, I was ashamed to tell him what happened. He had always been kind to my mother and me. He even used to lend my mother money until she got her check. But, on that day when he hugged me to calm me down, I don't know. For some reason, I felt safe for once in my life. I just broke down and told him everything. From that day, Pantera made sure my aunt's man never touched another girl again. Thereafter, I went to live with him and his wife. He raised me like his own daughter. Not only did Pantera teach me how to defend myself, but when he really got himself established, he sent me to college."

Xia and Manny passed a huge glass enclosure with Boa constrictor snakes in it. The giant reptile shot out at the glass where Xia was standing. The sudden movement caused her to jump.

"Oh my god!" she yelled, with one hand on her gun and the other on her chest.

Manny was grateful the place was empty. He chuckled. "Don't tell me the big killer is scared of a snake?"

She put the gun back in her pocket. "Boy, you better stop playing with me. I don't like those things." Xia quietly moved away from the snakes.

Manny reached over and gently pulled her into his arms. Their eyes locked. Xia's eyes then looked at Manny's lips. He looked at her lips while his head leaned in. When he could smell her breath, he licked his lips. When Xia didn't beef about him holding her so close, he slid his tongue between her lips. Her tongue explored his mouth, while her breathing got heavier. Passion took over.

In the darkness of the reptile house with all the snakes looking on, Manny fumbled through Xia's coat until he reached her D-cup breast. When his hand squeezed her firm breast, she moaned out, "Damn, Manny, you getting me hot." His tongue raced down to her neck, as her hand reached down to the stiffness in his pants. When Manny began to unbutton her skirt, she said, "Not here. Oh...okay." Manny was about to pop one of her nipples out of her bra, when she said, "Damn. No!" She grabbed Manny's hand. "Come on. Let's go," she said, while leading him out of the Bronx Zoo.

The X5 raced across town until they reached the Major Deegan Expressway. Manny nibbled on Xia's ear and sucked her neck, while his fingers were under her skirt as she pressed down on the accelerator. When they reached Yonkers, Xia pulled into the Holiday Inn.

At the check-in counter, Manny and Xia's tongues locked between their request for the room. Once they were issued their card key, their passion led them to the elevator, where buttons, zippers, and belts came loose. They kissed each other like long lost lovers who were rekindling something they once had.

When they reached room 803, Xia wasted no time slipping off her boots. As she kicked the left one off, a black .380 automatic fell to the floor. She kicked the right one off, and a long Tanta dagger fell. Her and Manny looked down at the weapons and went back to their passion.

Xia's coat was still on with a few of the bottom buttons to her one-piece skirt undone. Manny saw her thick flesh peeking from underneath her skirt, and he couldn't help himself. He backed her up against the bed. The sudden pressure of the firm mattress against her legs caused her to fall back. Manny raised her skirt up to her waist, removed her panties, and pushed her thick legs back. When his head went between her legs, the musty stench of her crotch brought the animal out of him.

"Oh shit, Manny. Ssss...ah. Ohh damn!" Xia moaned out, while Manny's tongue made a wet figure eight on her swollen clit. While he ate her, she was half pulling, half popping the row of black buttons on her skirt. By the time the skirt was open and her curvaceous body was on full display, she felt the earth move under her feet. "Oh yes...yes...yes, Manny!" was all Xia said before her eyes rolled up in her head.

Manny took her orgasm as an invitation to take her over the top. He stripped his clothes off in two moves and pulled Xia up to face him. He then removed spare clips to her gun, her coat, skirt, and bra. When he dropped her coat to the floor, he heard the thud of her baby Glock. Again, he looked at the killer in front of him, wondering just how dangerous she was. He then looked at her naked body and turned her over. Slowly, he traced his tongue down her back until he reached the clean crack of her ass. Manny opened her ass cheeks, stuck his nose in-between them, and began sucking Xia's clit from behind. With each thrust of his tongue on her wet pussy, Xia started rocking while she was on all fours. Manny fucked her with his tongue, and again, Xia lost it.

"Ohhhhhhhh...my...god!" she screamed out. "Make love to me, please. Please, make love to me."

Manny climbed onto the bed and eased his big penis into her. Xia felt her vaginal lips being stretched little by little. She let out a low moan as Manny slowly pumped inside of her. He felt Xia squeezing her thick thighs against his body to regulate the tempo of their lovemaking. Xia was enormously wet from cumming, but her vagina was tight as a drum. With each thrust, her pussy accommodated Manny's girth. He had never felt anything quite like her before. It was like her body was made for his. Xia's open eyes penetrated his soul as they made love in the missionary position. The sexual feelings were so intense that her fingers intertwined with his while their passion soared. Her thighs trembled and her pussy contracted around his hard shaft. Sensing Xia was on the verge of cumming again, Manny pumped harder and deeper while grinding her walls.

"Ma, you got a sexy-ass body. Damn, this pussy is so so good!" Manny yelled out with each stroke of pleasure he delivered.

Xia blushed seductively. "Stop playing. Stop playing. Oh, cum for me, please."

Manny leaned forward while stroking the hot, wet folds of the big woman. He sucked her nipples like she birthed him, until her cries of passionate moans caused him to cum deep and hard into her.

"Oh, that was so good, but I'm not finished yet."

Xia's soft fingertips skillfully moved down his neck, across his shoulder blades, down his chest, and stopped at his nipples. Each spot Xia touched on his body, her hot mouth and wet tongue christened. Manny began feeling things within that he never knew existed.

Xia held his limp dick in her hand when she straddled him. With his soft tip, she positioned herself so it could stimulate her clit. She moved his tip in circles while it grew stiffer by the second. By the time she was rocking from the stimulation on her clit, Manny was sliding his newly stiffened shaft deep in her wet hole.

Xia bounced on her new lover, while Manny thrust in and out of her. The new couple made love for another hour until they passed out and fell asleep.

Click click! Manny heard the sound before his eyes opened.

"Xia, what the fuck is up? What you doing, Bonita?" he asked, while she stood over him holding her Glock with tears pouring from her eyes.

Xia waved the gun at his face, preparing to squeeze the trigger. "I don't know how you did it, but it's over now! Let's make this quick and get it over with. Goodbye."

"Wait…wait! Why you gonna kill me, Ma?" Manny pleaded.

Xia put her eyes to her shoulder in an effort to wipe her tears, while aiming at Manny. "You motherfuckers are all the same. You talk nice, you get what you want, and then turn into bastards after you crush our hearts. I don't know how you got me to sleep with you that easy. All you sweet-talking men are the same. Now that you got what you want, I'm going to crush your heart my way. Better you than me."

I got to keep this loca talkin', Manny thought with his hands up. "Chica, I like you, mama. I like you a lot. I'm not like those other guys. You're beautiful. You'll see. Just give me a chance. Why you want to kill me before you give me a chance?"

Silence invaded the room. Xia lowered her gun a little. "Y'all are all the same, Manny."

"Baby, I'm different. Come here. Let me show you." Manny held his arms out for her to hug him.

A smirk cracked across Xia's face. She lowered the pistol, then said, "I know. That's why you're not dead already. I don't normally mix business with pleasure."

"Xia, your pleasure is my business now. I'm not one of those guys out there. You can trust that you in good hands. I won't mess this up." Manny cautiously pulled her into his arms and held her.

Xia pulled back. "But, there are boundaries to this thing of ours," she said, while staring into his eyes.

"Boundaries? What kind of boundaries?"

"You have to promise not to ever ask me about my business, and I'll never ask you about yours," she replied in a serious tone. "If you hurt me, I'm going to kill you."

A few seconds passed while he was thinking. Manny broke the brief silence. "Okay, Bonita, it's a deal. I'll respect those boundaries."

Xia sunk into Manny's arms while he carefully moved the Glock from her palms. He didn't move his position until the early morning when they made love again, and Xia eventually drove him home.

* * * * *

After Manny reached his apartment, he ate a bowl of cereal and then called Self to pick him up.

By noon, Self pulled up in front of Manny's building. He called Manny on his cell phone to let him know that he was waiting. In a flash, Manny walked out of his apartment building, hopped inside Self's truck, and they drove off.

"What's the deal, Slick?" Self asked Manny.

Manny was distracted with thoughts of Xia and how his world changed. "I want to check on Rico. Everything's changing so fast that we have to be ready for anything."

Self understood what Manny was talking about. He was a boss, and today was the day he realized it.

The blueberry Ford Expedition reached Harlem within an hour. Self pulled up to where Rico and Rashid stood on the corner of 117th Street. As Manny and Self exited the vehicle, everyone greeted each other. The block was crowded with the usual lines of customers on the opposite side of the avenue waiting to buy drugs. Manny took a quick glance, calculating that each fiend was more money in his pocket. After that, the four men talked and looked on, smiling as their M3 heroin sold like hotcakes.

In a flash, their little party was cut short when they heard, "Squally-O! Squally-O! Aye yo, Squally!"

Hurriedly, the crowd of people waiting to buy started walking away in different directions. When the unmarked police car got right in front of Manny and his men, it came to a sudden stop.

"Hey, you...you!" a dirty blonde detective in jeans and a Yankees shirt barked at Self, who ran into the nearest building.

Manny, Rico, and Rashid didn't move fast enough. They were getting rounded up by the dirty blonde's filthy-looking partner. The officer's clothes looked like he was fixing cars in a garage. His receding hairline had bits and pieces of hair on it like he was in denial about his baldness.

The blonde cop watched Self flee and quickly gave up on chasing him. He turned to the other three. "What da fuck a youse boys standing out here for? All of youse get up against the car."

The three men were spread eagle and searched against the car.

"What's the fucking problem, officer?" a foolish Rashid asked, as the balding officer searched his pockets.

"Aye yo, what tha fuck!" Rico barked out when the dirty blonde detective squeezed his testicles.

"Shut the fuck up! Youse don't wanna be searched? Then youse shouldn't be out here loitering. And tell your friend I'll catch up with him later."

"Yea, whatever, man," Rico bitterly shot back as his anger started to boil.

The dirty blonde walked behind Rico and said, "This is a hazard of youse occupation. You want to sell dope? Find a better place to be instead of in the open, asshole." The officer began roughing Rico up. He threw everything in his pockets on the floor, pulled his pockets inside out, and then made him take off his shoes.

"Laope, suave! Suave!" Manny whispered to Rico to calm him down

After completing their search and coming up empty handed, the dirty blonde said with anger, "Now youse niggaz get da fuck off the avenue before we haul youse assholes in. Giuliani don't like youse niggaz up here loitering anyway!"

Manny, Rashid, and Rico walked down 118th Street towards Morningside Avenue as the police car pulled off. The way the officer roughed them up was eating at Rico. As they were walking, he wasted no time voicing his complaints.

"Aye yo, you see how that bitch-ass motherfucker squally was handling me? I'd like to catch his bitch ass at a Knicks game with his fam."

"This is the business, son. We got a job to do, and they got to do they shit. When we rich and living up in the burbs, we ain't got to worry 'bout them faggots unless they our neighbors," Rashid said with a chuckle, while fixing his clothes.

Rico was still steaming. "I'm done with that corner shit, hermano." He turned to Manny. "We finding someplace else to meet when you come up here."

Before Manny could answer, Self was easing their way. When he reached them, he was cautiously looking for the police. "Self trying to get rich. Ain't got time to lay no pigs down, and Self can't stand a search or a gun charge."

Manny already knew that Self must have been dirty with his Desert Eagles. He didn't want his team at risk. *Social club* flashed in Manny's thought. Edeeks words came to him when he said, "I'm going to take care of it." He then turned to Rico. "Hermano, keep that paper rolling. We have to do everything different. We gonna work this thing out."

All four men gave each other pounds, then Rico said, "Yeah, it'll be spring in a minute, so let's make sure all this pays off by the summer."

Everyone was in agreement. The M3 name was moving up from a drug operation to an organization.

* * * * *

Four days later, Manny woke up with Carmen in his arms. His fingers slowly moved through her long, silky hair as he leaned in and lightly kissed her forehead.

"Sleepyhead, wake up. It's time to go," he whispered in her ear.

Carmen's eyes opened. She hopped up, then walked out of the bedroom. Manny hated to disturb her peaceful sleep, but she had a flight to catch at 9:50. The clock mounted on the wall read 8:45.

Quietly, Carmen came back into the bedroom and started putting on her flight attendant uniform. Halfway through, she turned to Manny with a look of despair on her face. "Papi, last night something was wrong. Qué pasá? You fucking somebody else?"

From the start, Manny had always made it his business to be straight up with her. "Something like that."

The reality of his words made her heart drop. They confirmed what she felt the night before. Tears welled up in the pockets of her eyes and slowly fell down her pecan cheeks.

"Carmen, what's the problem, mami?" Manny asked with an attitude. "I told you from the beginning I didn't want to complicate things. I like what we have. Let's not fuck that up. No matter what, I'm always gonna check for you."

Carmen contemplated Manny's words. She ignored half of them, thinking she was going to change his mind. Then she reasoned she would rather have him in her life than not at all, and that in the long run, he would be all hers anyway. Her thoughts helped her to regain her composure.

"You know what, papi? I don't even care about no other bitch, because I ain't going to stop lovin' you. And I'm damn sure ain't goin' anywhere. You got a problem with that, Manny? No bitch is moving me out. Comprende?"

Her little emotional outburst made Manny smile. *Now that's my girl, rolling with the punches,* he thought. One thing Manny knew was women. He knew he had to smooth things over since Carmen was now one of his businesses partners.

"Mami, tell me something. If you could have *anything,* what would it be?"

"To have you as my husband," Carmen said without thinking about   it.

"Come on, ma. Be serious."

"What's so un-fucking serious about that, Manny?" Carmen barked.

Manny looked at her, then raised his voice. "I'm not marrying you. Stop the shit! Tell me now! What do you want more than anything?"

"Pendejo, I want you," Carmen said between sobs. When she pulled herself together, she quietly added, "To have my family in Cuba over here with me." Looking down at her watch and realizing that she was going to miss her flight, she stood and headed for the door. "Papi, I have to go to work."

Manny walked up on Carmen and hugged her from behind. He then slipped his hand down her flight attendant skirt and moved her thong to the side. When his finger found what he wanted, he started softly rubbing her clit. Carmen leaned her head back, sucked on Manny's neck, and closed her eyes.

"Oooo, papi, stop. I have to catch my flight."

"If you late, you catch another one," Manny said, running his fingers down her wet split and then back up to her erect clit. "Watch how you talk to me." His slippery fingers created more excitement. "This chocha belong to Manny. You do what Manny say, si?"

"Umm. Oooh, papi. Yes, papi. Anything for Manny," Carmen moaned, powerless over his touch.

With his hand busy at work inside of her skirt, Manny whispered, "Tell me about your family."

"Mmmm, what you wanna know? Ohh yeah, right there, papi."

Manny licked her earlobe, then pumped his fingers in and out of her. "Cómo se llaman?"

In Carmen's state of ecstasy, she mumbled, "My mother...mi padre. Ohh shit, Manny. Marisol and Luis Cerro! Ohh yeah, right there, papi. Ummm. Margarita is my little sister. Fuck me, Manny, before I go to work."

Manny bent her over, lifted her skirt, then pulled down and stepped on her panties. He stuck the head of his stiff dick inside of her, then quizzed, "What part of Cuba?"

"Ummm. Ahh, Marianao." Manny stroked faster. "Oh, papi, stop asking questions. Fuck me."

"Puta cállate!" Manny barked for her to shut up. "You do what *I* say!"

"Oh, I love you, Manny. Si, I feel it. I feel it. I feel it. Ohh, Dejesus, I'm cumming." When Manny felt her cumming, he started pounding into her until he came.

While she was still bent over and gasping for air, Carmen said, "Papi, look at what you started. Now I gotta take another shower."

Manny smiled. "Puta, go to work like that. When your panties drip, you think about your man. Don't wash until you come back to me. Now, go catch your plane before you miss it."

Carmen fixed her clothes. "You make me feel like a slut." She smiled, then said, "That's why I'm never leaving you."

As Carmen headed out the door, Manny said, "Carmen, make sure you see Matthew. He should be finished by now. Sixty grand, mami."

Carmen blew Manny a kiss before she walked out the door. "Adios, you big dick, black motherfucka."

Manny closed the door knowing his business and pleasure was in order.

* * * * *

An hour after Carmen left, Rico called and told Manny that he was on the highway headed to his house. Manny made breakfast, ate, and then started cleaning up his apartment while he waited on his brother.

Twenty minutes later, Manny heard the lock opening. Rico walked through the door of his apartment. In his hand was an extra large shopping bag. Rico greeted his big brother in Spanish.

"Como esta'?"

"Todo está bien." Manny let him know everything was good.

"Here, take this!" Rico said and handed his brother the bag. He took off his thick, calfskin leather coat and cotton knit hat that matched his sweater. "It's hot as a motherfucka out there, son. Don't wear no hot shit today." Rico remembered why he was there. "Yo, I'm gonna need some more work. Shit is almost running out. We only got a little left."

"How much is in here?" Manny asked, while holding the red and white bag up.

"Three hunned and thirty gees!" Rico said with pride.

Manny's eyes blew up with surprise. "Word! Get the fuck outta here. All that in here?" He nodded to himself. "Bien! I got this, hermano. I'm going to see my people tomorrow."

BANG-BANG-BANG! The loud banging startled both of them. Manny and Rico quickly reached for their guns.

"Yo, you brought somebody wit' you?" Manny whispered.

"Nah, that's why you gotta move out this dump," Rico said, slowly inching towards the door.

Rico looked into the peephole, then said, "Motherfucka, knock on the fucking door like you got some sense." He flew the locks open, and Edeeks was standing outside. Rico wanted to shoot him for scaring him. "Why the fuck you banging so hard? You got us thinking some crazy shit up in here."

Edeeks walked in. "Nice to see you, too." He walked closer to his part-time boss after Rico slammed the door. He opened his briefcase and produced a stack of papers. "I'm glad to find the both of you here. I need you two to sign a few papers."

With his gun still in his hands, Rico asked, "Damn! How much shit we gotta sign?"

Edeeks cut his eyes at Rico's foolishness. "Before I can do anything further, I need you two to sign these corporation forms so I can get things started. By the way, Manny, I'm in the process of making the transaction through the bank for the loan to acquire the other guy's company. Another thing, my guy Rosenstein is looking forward to doing long-term business with us."

Manny signed his name after Rico did. Then he said, "Good. I see you're on top of our business. I like that, fam. Let me know when things are completed."

Edeeks made an arrogant promise he couldn't keep. "Not to worry. This is a walk in the park. Things will go well."

For the next hour, Edeeks patiently explained the purpose of each form to Manny and Rico. After taking care of business, Rico headed for the door.

Just as he walked out, he turned to Manny. "Big bro, I was serious. You need to move outta this dump. You're making too much money to be still living here!" He nodded at Edeeks. "Talk some sense into his rabbit-ass mind."

"You so worried about where I live, when you need to find somewhere else to live yourself," Manny fired back.

"Yo, I'm *waaaay* ahead of you," Rico said, while closing the door.

"You know he's right," Edeeks said as he headed for the door.

Manny had too much shit to do. He looked at the bag, then back at Edeeks. "Yeah, everybody knows what's right for me now. Take care of business, E, and then give me advice later."

After Edeeks let himself out, Manny put all three locks on his door and headed to his hall closet. He had more floorboards to pull up so he could make space for all the cash he had coming.

SIX

C lose to three weeks had passed since Manny left Pedro and went on the mission for the black beast Pantera. During those three weeks, life had never been better for Manny. Carmen's business in Atlanta was doing well; he and Xia were making love in the best hotels New York had to offer; and Rico was bringing in the currency. Since the M3 brand was selling off the hook, Manny's team had practically finished the half a key he received from the job in the Bronx. Once again, Manny went up to Havana's Paradise to see the Cubans. He carried a bag containing two hundred and forty grand.

When he walked through the door of the social club, he immediately spotted Pantera's two goons sitting beside the bar. The dangerous men were talking while facing Manny's direction. Based on their sudden movements, Manny anticipated another search, but the pat frisk never happened. The tall, ponytail-wearing Latino and his short, brute partner acknowledged Manny's presence with a nod. The tall Latino reached his arm over the counter of the small bar and pressed a buzzer. Less than thirty seconds later, Pedro appeared.

As soon as he saw Manny, Pedro cracked a warm smile. "Qué háy, Manny?"

"Tranquilo."

"Come on, follow me," Pedro ordered.

He and Manny headed towards the small office. Pantera was sitting inside the dim room, puffing on a big Cuban cigar while sipping from a glass.

"Hola," Manny said to the black beast. Pantera returned his greeting with a slight nod. *Fuck you, you disrespectful bastard,* Manny thought, while standing in the middle of the room.

"My friend, Pantera wants you to know that he's impressed with the last cleaning job you did. But, tell me. How can we help you?" Pedro asked.

"Vine a verte, porque necesito comprar un kilo de manteca y dos kilos de perico." Manny indicated that he wanted to buy a kilo of heroin and two kilos of cocaine. "I brought the money with me."

Pantera started chuckling when he heard how much money Manny had.

Pedro beamed with pride when he looked at Manny. "You rich now, Pana! You doing big things. Never forget who got you there." He lit a cigarette, then on the exhale said, "So, one and two?" Manny watched as Pedro looked to the ceiling while calculating a price. When he was done computing, Pedro said, "Okay, give me one-twenty-six. That's ninety grand for the Manteca, and eighteen apiece for the coca. Someone will call you and give you the time and location."

"How long it's gonna take?" Manny asked, counting out the prearranged stacks of money.

"How long before you reach where you going?"

"About an hour."

Pedro nodded, then said, "Si, where's your car?"

Manny smirked. "I don't have one."

Pedro frowned with disappointment. "You a big man now, Manny. You walk with so much money and you don't have a car?" Pedro turned to Pantera. "I told you jefe he was different." He turned back to Manny. "Most guys your age buy cars before they have a place to rest their heads. Fix that!"

Manny nodded. When all the cash was on the table, he turned to Pedro. "There's one more thing." He tried to speak to Pantera exclusively. "Ah...want to know if you got any connection to get people from Cuba."

Pantera ignored him.

Pedro asked, "Who you been talking to, kid?"

"Nobody. I just need a friend's family brought over."

Pedro pondered the request. "You want credit, or you want to pay up front?"

Manny was grateful he was getting somewhere. "What's the damage?"

"For you? Twenty-five grand a head. Just give us the names and where they live. It's your job to get them from Miami."

Another one of Manny's plans was coming together. "Okay, I'm good with that."

When all the business was finished, Manny shook Pedro's hand and then made his way out of the social club.

* * * * *

Manny walked to the 6-Train. While waiting on the platform, he pulled out the card Xia gave him. The name *Big Dave* was printed on the front. He pulled out his cell phone and then dialed the number.

The phone rang twice before it was answered. "Hello."

Manny cleared his throat. "A lady friend of mine told me to give you a call."

"Who this? Manny?" the man asked.

"How you know I was calling?"

"That same lady friend of yours is a mutual friend of ours."

Manny wondered what type of relationship he and Xia had. With a hint of jealousy, he asked, "Okay. Just tell me what kind of vehicles you working with?"

"What you want? I can have you, your moms, and your whole crew in a ride by sunup. What you looking to cop?"

Money, Murder, and Mayhem flashed across Manny's mind. He smiled, thinking of Rico. "Four BMW M3's. All black. Tinted windows. Make them look the same."

The man laughed. "I feel you, my man. What kind of sneakers you want on them?"

Manny didn't know what he was talking about, but figured his crew would. "Put what's hot on all of them. Just make sure they're the same."

"Yo, I can do that. Not a problem."

"Okay, how much?" Manny asked, hoping Xia's connect was good.

"It depends on whether you want to lease or finance. I think it's better to lease. You got a company name? You can write them off and that'll keep the heat off y'all."

Manny thought of Edeeks. "Okay! We go that way then. Now how much?"

Manny heard buttons on a calculator pushing. Dave said, "Seventy-six kay. You'll be paid up for two years. Can you handle that? Another thing, I'll need to know if you want to pick them up or you want them delivered."

Manny chuckled out loud. "I didn't know you deliver. I tell you what. Get them ready. I'll call you tomorrow and tell you what to do."

"Whenever you ready, holmes. Just bring cash."

Manny hung up just in time to see his train pull into the station. When he exited the train station on 125th Street and Lexington Avenue, his cell phone rang.

A husky voice on the other end ordered, "La Marqueta on 116 at Park Avenue. Go to de first fishstand. Ask for three flounders."

Before Manny could question the caller, the phone disconnected.

Instantly, Manny walked into the middle of 125th Street with his hand in the air. He hailed a gypsy cab and told the driver to go one block over to Park Avenue, then to 116th Street. During the short ride, Manny thought about how much his situation had changed in a matter of months. Life was good and getting better with each passing day. He wished Edeeks' older brother, Louie, was still alive so he could share his good fortune with him.

The cab pulled up in front of the fishmarket under the Metro North train tracks. Manny stepped out. He walked inside and the strong odor of fish hit him. He followed the orders he received on the phone and stopped in front of the first fishstand he saw. The market was excessively bright and crowded with people doing their daily shopping. A large variety of fresh fish lied on crushed ice along the stand. A short, dark- skinned man wearing a blood-stained white smock worked behind the counter serving the line of customers.

"Hi. How can me help you?" the man asked when Manny reached the front of the line.

"Bien... need three flounders."

After looking at him through squinted eyes, the man asked, "You Manny, no?"

"Si."

The man reached under his counter, looked all around the market, then passed Manny a white plastic shopping bag. He nodded at Manny, then said, "Guaranteed fresh, amigo. Flounder for you, Panama."

Before he walked away, Manny peeked inside and saw the fresh fish wrapped up on top of three heavy packages. He smiled, then nodded back at the man behind the counter. He spun quickly for the exit out of the market. He headed across 116th Street in the direction of Lenox Avenue.

When Manny reached Lenox Avenue, he stopped off at Salaam's restaurant on 116th Street. The Black Muslim-owned establishment was a place of refinement, but Manny didn't care. He wanted to unload the drugs and head home. He ordered a Halal-bacon cheeseburger, fries, and a ginger ale. He then pulled out his cell phone to call his brother Rico.

"Talk about it," Rico said on the other line.

"Hermano, I'm at Salaam's on 116th. Come get what you need."

"Give me twenty minutes. One," Rico responded.

Close to a half-hour later, Rico's black Pathfinder pulled up to Salaam's restaurant. Instead of Rico exiting the vehicle, Rashid jumped out and walked inside carrying a medium brown paper bag.

"What's poppin', Daddy-O?" Rashid greeted Manny, as he sat at the small table.

"Everything good."

"Your brother had to address somethin' dat just came up, so he sent me to get that." Rashid slid the paper bag across the table. "And he gave me this paper for you."

Before Manny made a move, he scanned the semi-empty room to check if any eyes were on them. A few Muslims were talking and eating when he said, "Give me a minute."

Manny got up from the table and walked into the bathroom carrying two shopping bags. Inside, he took out the two kilos of coke and put them in the other shopping bag along with the thirty-four thousand. He then exited the bathroom and handed Rashid the shopping bag with the flounders.

"Fam, make sure you and Rico are on the block early tomorrow morning."

"Why, what up?" Rashid asked, ready for drama while he was wiping dirt from his boots.

Manny thought about their relationship. "Because I said so. Early in the morning. You and him on the corner of Morningside."

Rashid nodded at his boss with ultimate respect, then headed out the door with enough drugs to make the M3 crew a whole lot of money.

Manny grabbed the brown paper bag of cash, paid his bill for the food, and left in the opposite direction.

* * * * *

Once Manny arrived at home, he quickly undressed and took a hot bath to ease the built-up tension from his long day. Unlike his brother Rico, who loved the limelight at the neighborhood hot spots, Manny was more comfortable with just chilling at home with a good cooked meal, a gangster flick, and a hot woman curled up next to him. Sitting in the tub was the first step of his enjoyment.

Thirty minutes later, Manny came out of the bathroom feeling like a new man. The hot bath did wonders to his mind and body. He felt rejuvenated when he sat down at his kitchen table to count the money Rashid gave him. The money came up to $75,000.

Manny laughed to himself. *Damn, I'm making money now. I would love to see the faces of the people who laughed at me for being poor in Panama. I'm going to show them who is the mothafuckin' king of Panama and New York. Money, Murder, and Mayhem like Rico said. We come for the money, all of the money.*

Manny walked into the living room, then looked around the house Rico called a dump. He thought of the $400,000, realizing it was the most money he ever had in his life. He then nodded, knowing exactly how he wanted to live and how he was going to do it.

He slid the first part of *The Godfather* trilogy in the DVD player and watched it for the hundredth time while waiting on Carmen. Halfway through the movie, Manny's phone rang.

"Papi, I'm in Atlanta," Carmen said on the other line. Then she whispered, "I'm on the pay phone in case the phones are tapped. You see, I know how to do this, papi. I'll be there in a few hours. I have a gift for you. Get that big dick ready, 'cause I want you to do something for me." She kissed into the phone. "I see you soon."

Manny had plans for Carmen, but then Xia entered his mind. He knew for sure that he would be dead if he hurt her. He thought of how they made love and didn't get caught up in the relationship. She had issues with trust, and he had issues with his attraction to her. So, they agreed to take it slow. Xia didn't come to his house, and he had never been to hers. That agreement was made by both of them, and Manny liked the way it worked out. While he tried to get through the second half of *The Godfather,* his eyelids got heavy.

Two hours later, the sound of knocking woke Manny. He stumbled his way to the door with his gun in hand. When he opened the door, Carmen walked in and kissed his cheek.

In her sexy voice, she said, "Hi, papi." She tiptoed into the living room and took off her trench coat. The dark blue, flight attendant uniform she wore hugged every curve of her petite body. Manny watched her fat ass shake with an extra switch as she moved through his small apartment with her overnight bag.

"Qué pasa? What you up to, Carmen?" Manny asked, while standing in the middle of the floor.

Carmen sat the small overnight bag on his table, unzipped it, and then pulled out a stack of cash in a red rubberband. She snapped the rubberband and slammed the money on the floor. She then reached in and did the same with the remaining five stacks of cash.

While Carmen was losing her damn mind, Manny looked on. "What the fuck is wrong with you? Stop doing that."

Carmen held the last stack of cash in her hand. She seductively licked her lips, while popping another rubberband so the cash could fall over Manny's floor. In a sultry voice, she said, "No...no, Manny Black. Not tonight. Tonight, I picked this up from Matthew. He said the people loved the product. I did good for my man, papi. Esta Cubana es la mas sabrosa. I'm the hot bitch now, huh, Manny?"

Carmen frantically started unbuttoning her uniform. She pulled her skirt off, then ripped off her stocking and panties. She shook her head and said, "My pussy was so wet from having all that money, papi. I never *saw* so much money before." Carmen laid down on her back, spread her naked legs open. "Fuck me, papi! Fuck me on top of all the money. Fuck me hard while I look at all the dinero I made for mi papi chulo."

Manny's dick was rock hard. He looked down at Carmen begging him for sex, along with the cash that she made for him. He didn't hesitate to get down on his knees. He used the carpet for cushioning while he eased into her wetness.

Carmen kissed all over his face. "Yes, papi. Mmm, go deep, papi. Oh yeah, right there." Manny cupped her ass cheeks under him and rode Carmen like a roller coaster. The cash under her body created more excitement for him. He quickly flipped one of her legs back as he sank deeper. "Oh shit, Manny. Yes...I'm cumming!" Carmen cried out. Manny felt her whole body tense up, so he moved faster until he was meeting his woman in pleasure. Carmen kissed everywhere her mouth could reach on Manny, while he was growing limp inside of her. They both gasped for air as their heartbeats bounced against each other.

"Let me go and freshen up. I was so hot for you. That money got me so wet." Carmen wiggled her way from under Manny's weight.

While he was in the nude, Manny scooped up all the cash and placed it on the living room table. A smile spread across his face when he created a stack of money and put a rubberband on it. When he counted up ten thousand dollars, Manny put it to the side. With the quickness, he counted out the other fifty thousand. When he was placing the cash in a neat stack, he heard the door to the bathroom open. Then from the bedroom, Manny heard, "Ven aca', negro."

When Manny entered his bedroom, Carmen was laid across the bed on her stomach. Her fat ass was glistening with oil. With her legs spread wide open, she started humping the cool sheets like she was making love to the cotton. Her ass bounced each time she pushed her pussy into the soft mattress. "Oh, papi, I want you. All night, negro, I want you inside me," she whispered with an erotic moan.

Manny took his time climbing on top of her oily body. He placed the $10,000 stack of cash next to her face. "Here, Mami, this is for you."

While her pussy grind into the sheets, she looked at the cash and moaned out, "Thank you. Please...please...please...fill me up. Dame pinga."

Manny walked over to the small entertainment console and hit a button. "Lose Control" by Silk filled the room. He spread Carmen's legs further apart and started eating her pussy. His wicked tongue game was driving her up the wall.

"Papi, eat...this mothafuckin' pussy. Dejesus! Yes...yes. Just like that," Carmen shouted out, and he pushed his tongue harder into her hole.

Manny's tongue pumped, and it flickered faster as it went from her clit down into her wet lips, then back up to her clit. Carmen couldn't control herself any longer and came back to back.

Manny raised his head and licked the juices off his lips. He slid his swollen dick into her again. Suddenly, Carmen sat up, pushed Manny unto the bed and climbed on top of him. Her oily body slid down every inch of his dick. When he couldn't go any deeper, she moved her hips into a hard rhythm. Carmen then grabbed her titties and placed one nipple into her mouth and then the other. She rode her man while sucking on her own tits and moaning in pleasure. When she came again, Carmen reached over and spread the cash all over Manny's body. She then put one foot on each side of him, eased herself up, and while she held onto his neck, she fucked her man like tonight was the last night with him.

All the dirty talking Carmen did drove Manny crazy. That was the thing that turned him on with her. He loved the way she didn't have a problem telling him what she wanted or how she wanted it. Her hot-blooded nature kept him wanting her.

For two hours, they worked on pleasing each other. When the lovers were fully satisfied, they laid back to catch their breath.

Carmen rubbed Manny's chest. "Papi, I love you. I love you. I love you." She looked at the clock on the entertainment console. "I got to go home, then catch a flight. I'm going to be tired, but it was worth it."

She jumped up and took another shower. When she came back into the bedroom to get dressed, Manny pointed to the two keys of coke wrapped up in the brown paper bag. "Take that for your friend Matthew."

"Damn, Manny, that's a hundred and twenty thousand he has to give me?"

Manny smiled at how interested his woman was in breaking the law. "Tell him to give you back one-ten instead. That's how you do good business."

Carmen kissed him, double-checked her clothes, then said, "Okay, papi. You so smart. I see you later."

Manny walked her to the door, placed the locks on it, and then dragged himself back to bed.

* * * * *

Manny slept for twelve hours straight. He awoke to the sunlight hitting his face. He hopped up out of bed and rushed to the shower. While the hot water beat against his body, he made a mental note about the security of his cash being in that tenement apartment. Thoughts of a pit bull, a security system, or an armed security guard in front of his door came to mind. Manny knew he hadn't awakened yet.

After his shower, he stepped into his bedroom with a lot on his mind. He was going to spread the joy with his team that day. He went to his closet and pulled out a pair of Fortune Hunter's jeans, a Zo-Gear sweater, and a pair of boots. After getting dressed, he bagged up the cash he needed to take care of business and slipped his gun into his waist.

On the way out the door to his building, Manny dialed Big Dave's number. While walking on Eastern Parkway, the other line connected.

"Yo, Dave, it's Manny."

"What's good, holmes?" Dave asked.

"Listen, I need those delivered now. I got that loot for you."

"Where you want them?"

Manny thought about his run-in with the police on 117th Street. "Bring them to 123rd and Morningside Avenue…by the park."

"It's eight o'clock now. Right about twelve is good?"

Manny was hailing down a cab when he asked, "Damn, that quick?"

"Come on, holmes. This is what I do," Dave said.

Manny chuckled. "Good…good. I'll see you then."

By noon, Manny was standing on the block with his team. It was business as usual on 117th Street and Manhattan Avenue. Crowds of people paraded the small avenue, while the young hustlers worked pushing the M3 product. As Manny stood on the crowded block, his palms started sweating. Silently, he prayed the police wouldn't catch him with all that cash on him. He glanced at his watch, realizing it was time to make his move.

He called Rico, Rashid, and Self. "I need everybody to take a walk with me."

"Where we goin'?" Rico questioned as he stood canvassing the avenue like a general in battle. He was dressed in black fatigue pants, black boots, a black hockey shirt, and a black skullcap that compressed his 360 waves.

"Hermano, just come on!" Manny shot back and started walking.

Rashid and Self followed behind him as he headed up the desolate tree-lined street of Morningside Avenue.

Before Rico followed suit, he looked over at his six-man crew that was hard at work. He called out to his lieutenant, "Aye yo, Rich Dice. Let me holla at you."

"What up, homie?" the young hustler asked, while walking to his boss.

"Listen, me and Rashid gonna be gone for a hot minute. Hold shit down and keep your eyes open."

"Don't sweat that. I got it, dawg," the young hustler said in a confident tone. He watched while his boss marched off and caught up with his people.

When the top men of the M3 crew reached 122nd Street on Morningside Avenue, they saw four black BMW M3's with tints and twenty-inch rims. A silver Yukon was parked behind them.

"Ahhh. Those cars are proper!" Rashid marveled at the vehicles.

"Look like somebody moving in on our territory. Self gonna have to pay somebody a visit," Self said.

Rico looked at the cars, then at how calm his brother was. He then looked at the bag on Manny's back and started laughing. Everyone wanted to know what was funny. Manny looked at his brother and tried to keep himself from smiling.

Rico pointed to Manny and said, "Bro, you a funny nigga." He chuckled some more. "That's some old bullshit right there."

Manny looked away while Rashid and Self wondered what the two brothers knew.

As the crew stood admiring the caravan of cars, the back door to the Yukon truck opened. From where Self stood, his hawkeyes instantly spotted five figures sitting inside. Not knowing the occupants' intentions, he pulled out his gun. He ran to the driver's side, kicked the door closed, and barked, "What's this about?"

Rico didn't hesitate to pull his gun, and Rashid stood behind Rico empty-handed.

"Chill! Put that shit away!" Manny ordered.

Self looked at his boss, then half tucked the gun in his front pocket. Rico's cannon disappeared as fast as it appeared. By the time the occupants of the truck were safe, the driver's door slowly opened. A tall, brown-skinned man weighing close to three hundred pounds with a sharp blowout afro stepped out. He was wearing reptile boots, wool slacks, and a cashmere sweater.

He chuckled before he said to Self, "Hey, baby, don't kill nobody. Then Big Dave can't get paid!"

Self cracked a smile. "Big Dave, you can't be moving through Self town without telling Self where you at, baby." The two men embraced, and to no one's surprise, Self knew the man.

Big Dave looked at Rico and Rashid, and then at the bag in Manny's hand. "You must be Manny, right?" He extended his hand to shake Manny's.

"Yeah, that's me."

"I see you got Self rolling with you. I hope that means he won't rob me again?" Big Dave chuckled while looking at Self.

"That's a small thing to a giant, baby. Just don't grow no more or Self might come see you," Self said with a straight face.

"It's okay, mi Pana," Manny said, nodding and checking out the merchandise. "I'm really feeling these."

Big Dave smiled. "I only get the best, holmes."

Manny reached into the bag and removed a pouch. He then handed over the bag. "Yo, here's the paper. It's all there. You can count it if you want."

Dave looked over at Self and quickly threw the bag inside the truck. He pulled an envelope from the dash of the truck and turned to Manny. "Nah, that won't be necessary. You came highly recommended. Give Xia my regards." Dave handed Manny a manila envelope. "Holmes, you paid up for two years. All the papers are in the glove compartments, and I got your tags registered to P.O. boxes in case poe-poe tries to find your cribs. If you get *any* heat whatsoever, contact me at the address on the card. Everything's legit. Enjoy and tell a friend."

"Nah, these ain't for us." Rashid laid his face on top of one of the cars. He hugged the vehicle and said, "Tell me this is me, Manny. Tell me I'ma put shit on the map with this tonight."

Dave jumped back into his truck with his four deliverymen and drove away.

Turning back to his team, Manny began his speech. "Yo, we been doing some big things for a minute now by getting this paper out here..."

Self mumbled, "Self knew you was a good nigga from jump. I knew that shit."

Manny smirked. "We started small and grind our way up to making good money. This is only the beginning. As long as we stay strong as a team, we're gonna do big things. We just can't allow money or nothing else to come between M3. If we have to die, we die. Fuck it."

Manny paused for a brief moment. Rico stood in front of one of the cars smiling, when he said to his brother, "You a funny nigga. That's my word! You a funny ass dude, hermano."

Manny allowed his point to sink in. He made eye contact with each member of his team before he continued. "You know a lot of people gonna hate, but fuck 'em. If anybody forces our hand, then we'll punish them with no mercy." Manny handed everyone keys to the cars. "From now on, we *really* gonna be known as the M3 Boyz. Money, Murder and Mayhem...comprende?"

"Ahhhh shit, this is me. My first whip. A M3? Dawg, I'ma kill anybody that fuck wit' your paper," Rashid yelled, while hugging the car again.

"No doubt. No doubt, Slick, Self feelin' your energy. Self knew he made the right move by fuckin' wit y'all." Self turned and faced the cars. He was standing in the middle of the street. "M3 Boyz fo' sure. Self feelin' that money, murder, and mayhem thang." Self got serious for a second while looking down Morningside Avenue. He looked in the direction that Dave drove away in, then asked, "Yo, Manny, Dave got a lot of paper on him?"

Self started fumbling with the keys to the M3 when Manny asked, "Self, where you going?"

"Slick, be easy. Self gonna catch up to Big Dave. We could use that paper."

Manny started laughing. "Brother, stop. Let them go."

Self looked down the street filled with disappointment.

"Aye yo, good looking, Manny. These joints are hot to death, Daddy-O. Wait till the hoes see me coming through in this. They really going to be on a fella dick now," Rashid excitedly added.

Rico said, "I can't spend a car, big bro, but good looking."

"It's small thing," Manny said, as he turned to Rashid and Self. "Listen, Rashid, I want you to hold Rico down, and Self is gonna hold me down. When you finish that brick, I'm gonna have something for y'all." He turned to his brother. "Rico, keep the soldiers calm. We don't need no unnecessary problems. Close down when the kids are going and coming from school. Keep it quiet, hermano. Move in silence."

Rico was trading keys, trying to figure out which one fit the car he picked. When he found the right one, he grabbed the paperwork to it, then asked sarcastically, "This nigga gonna tell *me* how to work a spot?" He nodded at his brother. "Bro, you never had a car in America. Let's see if y'all can keep up with Rico. I'ma see what this bitch can do."

The men raced to get into their cars. After car keys were exchanged, the men of the M3 crew followed Rico. With their new cars, they drove through every major block in Harlem, announcing that the M3 Boyz had arrived.

* * * * *

Later that day, Manny was in deep thought while he tested his ultimate driving machine. After getting on the West Side Highway, he realized he had nowhere to go. He looked over at the pouch that rested on the passenger seat, and he wanted to celebrate. Instantly, Xia's image flashed in front of his eyes. He commandeered the car phone.

"Hey, Bonita?" Manny sweet-talked into his cell phone. "I didn't like the way you laughed about my clothes, so I wanted you to do something about it."

Xia chuckled. "Oh really? What do you have in mind?"

"Well, I wanna come pick you up. Then you can show me the type of clothes you want to see me in."

"Pick me up?" Xia asked with surprise. "Pick me up in what?"

"As soon as you give me your address."

"How do I know this isn't a ploy for you to finally see where I live?"

Manny laughed. "I woulda just followed you home, then surprised you."

"Oh yeah? What would you have told my man when you saw him?"

Manny was stuck. He thought she was all about him.

When he paused, she said, "I'm just playing, silly."

The blood left Manny's face and he took a deep breath. "Bonita, you cannot play like that."

"I just wanted to know why you didn't come pick me up sooner." Xia's tone got serious. "You know I'm not here for you to play games with."

Manny was close to the Henry Hudson Parkway when he asked, "You gonna give me your address, chica, or what?"

Xia paused then sighed before answering, "I know I'm gonna get in trouble for this, but it's my day off. So, come to Fordham Hill."

Manny ran what he knew of the city through his head and came up with a blank. "Fordham Hill? Where's that?"

"In the Bronx, stupid," Xia said with a warm chuckle. "Sedgwick and Fordham Road. It's the big beige buildings. Pull up to the security booth and tell him you're here to see Ms. Jackson. I'll be down when you get here."

"So that means I can't come up? I thought I had my job interview already."

"You had your interview, but who said you got the job? I'll be downstairs. If you get here before I come down, maybe I'll invite you up."

"Bonita, you don't know how far I'm coming from," Manny protested.

Xia said, "Exactly," and disconnected her line.

Manny gunned the engine of his new M3. He exited the Henry Hudson in Washington Height, where he looped around to the Cross-Bronx Expressway. When he saw the signs by the George Washington Bridge that led to the Major Deegan Expressway, he followed another loop from the skyline to the flats of the highway. He passed one exit and then exited at Fordham Road. He then climbed a sloping hill until he reached Sedgwick Avenue. Right across from Jimmy's Café was towering buildings in a complex.

Manny made the left and quieted the exhaust to the BMW when he stopped at a security booth. By the look of the small private complex, it was obvious to him that Xia had her own money to live in such a beautiful place. After dealing with security, Manny parked across from the armed booth. Instantly, and to his disappointment, Xia was walking his way in an earth tone skirt, white button-up shirt, a pair of ankle-length boots, and a brown leather purse in her hand that had her cannon safely tucked away.

Xia walked up to the car and asked, "When did you get this?"

Manny jumped out, playfully opened the passenger door, and hopped back in to enjoy her company in *his* car.

When he backed out of the apartment complex, Xia commented, "I wanted one of these, but Pantera wouldn't let me. He said I drive too fast and needed protection. So, I bought the X5 instead." She inhaled the new car aroma and scanned the interior. "This is really nice."

Manny beamed with pride. "So you like it? Now I can pick *you* up." He then leaned over and held Xia's face while his tongue slithered between her lips.

In a sultry voice, she said, "You starting something we can't finish in the car."

He looked into her eyes. "You almost killed me for loving you, so I should be able to have you where I want you."

Xia looked away. "I apologize about that, but it's complicated. We're good, but please don't get me all worked up in this car."

Manny pressed on the brakes in the middle of Sedgwick Avenue. "Good. Then maybe you can finally take me up to your house, and we can finish it there."

Xia ignored his come-on. She flipped the visor down to reapply her makeup and asked, "So, where we off to?"

Manny realized he wasn't going upstairs, so he put the car in drive. "To take your man shopping."

She turned in her seat. "So you're my man now?"

Manny pushed the pedal. "What's up, boss? I didn't get the job? What happened? I didn't make you feel good enough?"

Xia blushed uncontrollably. She looked like a little girl with a crush on her schoolmate. "I have no complaints whatsoever in that department."

"Okay, so I'm your man then. Today, you take your man to buy some new clothes."

She folded her palms on her thick lap. "I hope you brought enough cash. Let's start at the Galleria in White Plains."

"How I get there?"

Xia sucked her teeth. "Let me drive. We'll get there faster."

Manny mimicked Xia. "Hell no! I just got this. We on a date, but we're not *that* close. Just tell me where we're going, and I'll act surprised when we get there."

Xia was laughing hysterically from the way Manny's accent dramatized her words. "Just drive to Saw Mill and take it up to White Plains, and I'll show you where to go from there."

Manny put the car in overdrive, trying to impress Xia with his skills. He whipped his BMW up through the Bronx, then into Westchester County until he reached the huge parking garage of the Galleria Mall.

For the rest of the day, Xia led Manny through the stores to buy slacks, sweaters, ties, button-down shirts, hard-bottom shoes, and casual boots. After walking with a load of shopping bags, his pouch was ten thousand dollars shorter.

Manny suddenly asked, "Bonita, you ashamed of being with me?"

Xia smiled, then put her arm around his waist. "You would have never saw my body, saw where I live, or tasted my lips if that were the case."

"So why couldn't I go up to your house?"

"Because a *lady* doesn't allow a man into her bed until he becomes *her* man. I still don't know if you're serious yet."

They walked past a huge fountain in the mall, when Manny asked himself more than Xia, "Serious, huh?" Just as they were walking past the Charles Krypell jewelry store, Manny grabbed Xia's hand and pushed her into the store. He walked to a brightly-lit display case where engagement rings were shining. "Pick one!" Manny demanded, pointing down at the rings in the display case.

If eyes could kill, Manny would have been filled with holes. He saw Xia's seriousness, and for the first time, he accepted that she was deadlier than he was.

"You serious?" she questioned. "What type of games are we playing here?"

"Girl, just pick one! We see how serious I am when it's on your finger."

Xia pulled Manny in front of her, acting like she was being affectionate. "Manny, listen good. Don't play with my heart and your life this way. We can walk away from this store and act like this never happened. Think, Manny, and I'm going to think for you. You're getting ready to go somewhere where there's no turning back."

Manny sucked his teeth. "You'll see how serious I am. Pick one or don't ask me anymore about being serious."

Xia looked into his eyes for awhile. Everyone in the upscale jewelry store gazed at the black couple in awe.

Xia broke his gaze. "Oh yeah?" She looked down at the display case and pointed to a four-karat cushion-cut diamond setting in a platinum band. "I'm a great poker player. That one!"

Manny reached into his light pouch and pulled out five thousand dollars. He looked at the woman behind the counter. "If that's not enough, you tell me, and I'll be back."

The model-type cashier, who looked like she skipped too many meals, nodded for Manny to follow her out of earshot of Xia. Manny followed the woman's lead, while Xia beamed with joy.

The woman said, "Sir, the item you chose is retailed at twelve thousand dollars. But, for the way you demanded to please your woman, I will deduct two thousand off the price."

Manny nodded, and the salesperson put away the ring. She called Xia and measured her finger, and it was all set for Manny to pay the balance and pick up the ring.

On the way out the store Manny couldn't believe what he just did. The ring was the most expensive item he ever bought a woman. He was unsure if he even knew Xia well enough to be her husband. His life was on the line all in the name of love.

Silence separated the couple until they reached the parking garage. When they were about to get into the car, Xia said, "I don't know what kind of game you're running, but..."

"Be quiet!" Manny barked over the hood of his car. His voice was amplified from the low ceilings of the dark garage. "You said I wasn't serious. Now I show you I'm serious and you still have a problem? What's the matter, loca? You don't want me?"

Through clinched teeth, Xia said, "Stop yelling and open this car so we can discuss this like civilized people."

Manny followed her orders until they sat in the car. "Cuál es el problema?"

Xia exhaled while reaching for his hand. She sighed when she looked into his eyes. "This is not about you. It's about me." She reached into her purse, removed her Glock, and laid it on her lap. She then reached above her waist, pinched three inches of fat, and said, "It's about this and that gun." Xia looked down at the gun. "Manny, what do you want from your woman? I'm not one of those video chicks or some super model that comes with the hustling game. I'm not the type you can parade around your friends with pride or put in a bikini at the beach. I'm fat, Manny, and I don't need another man to have sex with me but give his love to a sexier woman." Her eyes started tearing. "You're seeing some money now, but in this life of ours, tomorrow's promised to no one. What do you want? A woman that gets a call in the middle of the night and has to change someone's life forever? What are we going to do? Have arguments like we are now and weapons are gonna get pulled? Are we going to raise our children to kill, too? Go to their graduations with guns? Will they have to bury one of us, or come on visits to a jail to see their mother or father?" She looked at Manny, then asked, "Have you thought this thing through?"

Manny had to admit she was right. He didn't think about any of that. All he knew was the woman across from him made him feel powerful, safe, and comfortable with who he was. The woman across from him made him feel like she was his home and a place he could go to escape the drama. No woman had ever made him feel that way before. He reached across to her.

"Xia, you fat! You think I didn't see that when I first met you? But, to me, you Bonita! Nothing else. Your face, your smile is Bonita. Your body is Bonita; the way you dress is Bonita; and your chocha? Oooo mucho Bonita!"

They both laughed.

"You worry about tomorrow so much that you forget about the good part of today. Today, Bonita, Manny want to be with you. Today, you home. Let's worry about tomorrow and our little bonitas when we get old." Manny reached across and kissed her passionately.

Xia looked at Manny with tears of joy dripping from her face. Her lips quivered. "Take me home, Manny. Come on."

Manny didn't hesitate to put the key in the ignition. He drove out of the parking garage and headed to the Bronx.

When the M3 was parked in front of Fordham Hill, Xia led Manny to her apartment door. The one-bedroom home was elegantly adorned with expensive furniture. Xia was a woman with good taste. She rushed to the Samsung stereo system, pressed a button, and Kelly Price's CD serenaded the first man that had ever entered her house.

Xia kicked off her shoes, then walked over to Manny. She slid her tongue between his lips while unbuttoning his pants. Right in the middle of the living room, she stripped him until all his clothes crumpled to the floor. She kissed him again before leading him down a wide hall.

When they reached Xia's bedroom, Manny was amazed. In the middle of the floor was the only customized bed he ever saw. The turquoise lacquer frame was the size of a small pool. The headboard reached the ceiling with rows of mirrors on it. The green wall-to-wall carpet and a custom-made green and white bedroom set took Manny's mind off sex. He was impressed. Then Xia took off her skirt, and his dick rose harder with each clothing item she removed. Manny couldn't figure out exactly what it was, but Xia's body type was the kind of woman he always wanted for his wife.

He walked up to her and pressed his rock hard penis against her ass as his arms wrapped around her large body. Manny started sucking on her earlobe and then her neck. His warm, wet tongue sent chills through Xia. Instantly, her pussy moistened. "Mmmm," she softly moaned, while pushing back and rotating her ass onto his dick.

Manny swung Xia around and passionately kissed her. He looked deeply into her eyes. "Bonita, I love you." He kissed her again.

Xia sat on the edge of the bed. Her hand reached out to his stiff dick. She grabbed it, squeezed it, and then put his massive flesh into her mouth. Manny looked down at the way she took her time trying to pleasure him. She was no comparison to Carmen, but with Carmen, he felt like he was doing something dirty. With Xia giving him head, it felt like a woman who loved her man and did it because of what *he* wanted.

"Yeah... Bonita, yeah," Manny cried out when her wet tongue kept flicking around the head and along the base of his cock. When she started licking and sucking it like it was a blow pop, he felt like he was on the verge of cumming. Quickly, Manny opened his eyes wide and took a deep breath so he could stop himself from shooting off.

After pulling out of her mouth, Manny traded places with Xia. He sat on the bed as she pushed him back while straddling his hips. As she held his stiffness, he watched her slowly lower herself onto his penis. When he was all the way inside her wet pussy, she started rotating and gyrating her wide hips. The up and down movement made Manny moan in pleasure. As he played with her breast, he pumped his hips eagerly and met each of her down strokes. As her tight vagina gripped his cock like a Lifestyle condom, Xia's moaned, "Yes, baby, yes. Come with me, babe, please."

Like a soldier following orders, Manny pumped faster into Xia's tightness until he couldn't hold out any longer. The semen spilled out of his penis and into Xia's warm womb.

While lying in bed, Xia looked Manny in the face. "If you're serious about putting a ring on my finger, you have to be honorable and get Pantera's approval."

Manny slapped his forehead. "Damn, this just gets harder."

SEVEN

A fter four weeks of Manny, Self, Rashid, and Rico putting all their manpower into the spot, Manny counted out $850,000. The block was generating a lot of money, and everything was unfolding just like he planned.

Carmen's outlet in Atlanta started to pick up. In five weeks, she made three trips transporting six kilos of cocaine to Matthew. She brought Manny back $360,000. Her money created a bulk of the cash in his house, and he was nervous. Manny gave her two more keys to take down, and he was willing to wait for that money to return. The cash was piled up on the closet floor and extended to the closet in his bedroom. Manny knew he was wrong for having all that cash in his apartment. He changed the locks and put gates on the windows, but the more secure his apartment became, the more insecure he felt.

Edeeks was busy setting up the scrap metal business. Over the weeks, he hustled between his job and running errands for Manny. At the end of the current week, he was done with all the installations of the M3 Auto & Social Club. The small storefront was located on 108th Street at Columbus Avenue. The busy, three-lane avenue was met with a lot of traffic, but at night, it belonged to the Latin flavor of New York City. Edeeks laid the place out with liquidated furniture, pool tables, video games, and pictures of every BMW ever made. He installed a reinforced steel door, a safe, a stash place for the single office in the back of the club, and a top-quality security system. On the day everything was done, he called Manny to announce the good news.

Edeeks' call was exactly what Manny needed. He picked up his phone and called for the top men of M3 to come to the social club.

Later at the meeting, everyone popped champagne and celebrated the opening of the club. They teased Manny about the button-up shirt, slacks and hard-bottom shoes he had on. After they had all their laughs, they agreed that only the members of the M3 family were allowed in. The purpose of the social club was for handling business and nothing more. They were allowed to park their cars outside of the club so it would fit the front that they were putting up, but no outsiders were allowed. When all the ground rules were established, Manny handed everyone a key to the club. He and Edeeks went to the back office and returned with a handful of the same Gucci bags.

"Hermano, this is for you," Manny said, handing Rico a bag containing $250,000.

When Rico looked at the cash in the bag, he had mixed feelings. A hint of greed came over him. He felt it was because of him that the cash was being made in the first place. His loyalty beat out his greed when he looked at his brother. "Bro, I'm fucking rich, but what about Panama?"

Manny nodded and cut his eyes at his brother, letting him know that was the wrong place and time to have that discussion.

Rashid looked at his man, then said, "Rico, from the day I met you, I knew you was going to get me paid." Manny handed him a bag with $150,000 for himself. Rashid pulled a stack of the dirty paper out his bag, busted the rubberband, and then threw it in the air. While the cash rained down on him, he said, *"Parrrtay* up in this bitch. I got the whip, house, money, and we just getting started." He turned to Rico and said, "Son, you know how hard I'm gonna shit now? I'm moving *today!* But before I'm done, Harlem gonna think Rich Porter came back from the dead out this bitch. Let them fuck wit' me."

The whole crew laughed during their small celebration. Manny handed over another Gucci bag with $100,000 in it. He winked at Self when he handed him the bag. Over the weeks, Self didn't have anything to do with the drug dealing of the M3 crew. He occupied his time by copping a new platinum Range Rover from Big Dave, changing up his jewelry, and sending hot slugs to all those who opposed M3.

With a feeling of self-glorification, Manny said, "That's the reward for hard labor. Y'all been doing all the work so enjoy it."

Self didn't even look in the bag or concern himself with how much everyone else was making. He casually dropped the bag at his feet. "Good lookin', Slick. You stay comin' through for Self."

"Aye yo, thanks again, big homie," Rashid gleefully said, while fixing his wardrobe so the Gucci bag wouldn't clash with his clothes.

"Listen, make sure you put some of that up for a rainy day. Remember, forever never lasts." Manny said, while glancing around at everyone in the room.

His crew nodded in unison, agreeing with his advice. For the next hour, they conversed about how good the block was doing and what they could do to make things better for the summer. After everybody gave their opinion, the meeting ended on a high note and the crew dispersed.

After Rico, Self, and Rashid left, Edeeks was the only one there. With a look of exhaustion, Edeeks spoke slower than usual. "Manny, I'm sorry I couldn't get this done a little sooner. My supervisor dropped a stack of paperwork on my desk Monday, and it tied everything up."

Manny studied Edeeks' face. He thought of the role Pedro played in Pantera's organization. "Fam, the first thing you can do is quit that job. I don't like to see those gringos working my man to death. We can use a man like you."

"What do you mean quit my job?" Edeek questioned. "I have a family to provide for."

With a cold stare, Manny shot back, "Fuck that bullshit! Why work for somebody else when you can work for yourself? With the money from the scrap metal spot and what I'll be giving you, you okay now. Trust me, pana, things are looking better now. We got the money to start expanding our businesses. So, stop playing games."

As Edeeks sat contemplating his words, Manny passed the last bag with $50,000 in it. "Here. This is a little sumthin' for you. I want to show you I'm serious and that I appreciate all you been doing for the family."

When Edeeks opened the bag and looked at the cash, a part of him knew right then there was no turning back. "Manny, thank you. I appreciate your generosity. Rest assured, I will continue to do whatever I can to keep things right, but no disrespect, fifty gees ain't enough for me to quit my job." Edeeks chose his words carefully. "Manny, you're giving all this money away like it's Christmas, but you haven't taken care of yourself, and you didn't mention anything about Panama. Have you lost focus?"

Manny thought about the benefit of having someone around him to keep it real. Over the weeks, the money, Carmen, and Xia had him distracted. He thought about himself. "Si, I thought of myself, but things are getting crazy. I need a new place to live, I want to get married, and then I want to send as much money as possible to Panama."

"Married? You mean you and Carmen got serious? What happened? Is she pregnant?"

"Not Carmen. Somebody else. A Bonita. She got her own money. That's why I chose her. She makes me feel safe, she got some meat on her bones, and she so so..."

Edeeks smirked at how a man was smart enough to give away a half a million dollars, but not wise enough to handle his personal affairs. Edeeks carried on. "Okay, Manny, okay. I hear you crying out for help. Give me fifty, and I can get you a down payment on a little house somewhere in Upstate New York. It's time you go somewhere safe to rest your head. You're getting money now, and it won't be long before some cowboy comes for you." Edeeks got professional. "Anyway, I'll use another thirty to put down on a nice condo in Westchester. I can furnish it, add the locks and all. You can stash your money there. Keeping all your money under one roof isn't a good idea. From now on, start spreading your capital. Should the authorities run in one house, you'll still have a backup of cash. Do you understand? Give me a minute to set up the accounts."

"What about those offshore places where you hide money?" Manny probed.

Edeeks laughed. "Hold on, big spender. Your money is too short for that. I can wire six figures through Rosenstein or get a safe deposit box. If you have a buck thirty now, I'll take that and set everything up."

Manny nodded and agreed with Edeeks' advice. "Yeah, that's a good idea. I'm gonna keep the condo to stash my money. Then the house is for Mrs. Black."

"Mrs. Black?" Edeeks questioned. "You're really serious about this woman, huh?"

"Si, longevity, mi pana."

Edeeks shrugged. "You're the boss man."

Manny chuckled. "Exactamente, and don't you ever forget it." Suddenly, the thought of having Edeeks working for him full time popped into his head. "E, I've know you for a very long time. I need you, mi pana. It's lonely at the top. Please, I beg you. Make sure this business thing works. I need you to work for yourself instead of making some gringo rich."

Edeeks smirked. "Don't worry; I'll take care of it. I'll set it up where you and Rico are paying taxes. Your checks will be enough to cover the condo expenses. As far as the tax situation goes, that's already taken care of. Being that the scrap metal company is formed as an LLC, you, Rico, and I are required by law to file taxes based on any earned income annually. I'll prepare the 1120 and 8832 forms when it's time. Then you and Rico can file them, but I'll jump on cutting those weekly checks immediately." He thought of their days of being broke. "Oh yeah, Manny, do me a favor. You take care of the small things, and I'll take care of the big things. So, for now, I'm going to hold on to my job."

"Okay, mi pana," Manny teased, chuckling out loud. "Just let me know when you take care of the house business." He went into the office and took $150,000 out of the safe. He pocketed $20,000 and brought the rest out for Edeeks to stuff in his Gucci bag.

Edeeks said, "So, boss, when do I get my M3?"

Manny laughed, knowing that Edeeks would never show how much money he had, so he said, "When I die, you can have mine."

The two men hugged like the brothers they were. They then locked up the club and went their separate ways.

By the time Manny got home, he went to his stash and counted out $144,000 to purchase a key of heroin and three more keys of coke. Things were finally coming together, but Manny was learning a lesson with the game. The more money you made, the more expenses would pile up.

* * * * *

In the following days, Edeeks was making the arrangements to purchase a house and condominium for Manny. He made sure everything was legitimate. Through his connections, he found a cozy, one-family, Colonial house in Ossining, New York. The house had a great view of the Hudson River and was only an hour away from the city. He arranged for the original owners to eventually accept cash and sign the house over to him as a gift.

While he was buying the house, Edeeks' connection referred him to a two-bedroom condominium in the Riverdale section of Westchester County. After dropping $30,000 as a down payment on the condo that was selling for $150,000, Edeeks went to work on Manny's other wishes.

When things were complete, Edeeks called Manny to tell him where his house was located. Manny drove up the New York State Thruway until he reached the town of Ossining, New York. He passed the huge walls of the world famous Sing-Sing prison and took the winding roads until he found his house on the silent block of Spring Street.

When he pulled up to the address, he saw Edeeks' Saab parked outside. The sight of the beige and white house filled Manny with pride. When Edeeks stepped out of the house, Manny was choked up. "All mine, huh, mi pana? All mine?" Manny asked. Edeeks hugged him and Manny said, "I told you. I told you. I told you. When we were eating rice and beans, man, I saw this. I saw this house, the cars, and the money. I don't care if I die today. I just had to know that I made it. I did it, E. *We* did it." Manny looked up to the sky and said, "Padre perdóname for my sins, but I thank you."

Edeeks motioned for Manny to follow him. "Come on inside before you get all emotional on me."

Manny shook his head. "I got to go down to White Plains. I got some things to do. Just give me the keys and hold all the paperwork."

Edeeks reached into his pocket and pulled out another set of keys. "This is for the house." He passed the other set over. "This is for your condo in Riverdale. You have to change the locks. The address is on the tag. It's right above a plaza, and all your neighbors are Jews, so no partying."

Manny thanked Edeeks, they hugged again, and they drove off together until Manny turned off at the exit for the Galleria Mall.

Once his business affairs were in order, Manny wanted to put other areas of his life in order. He stopped by the jewelry store to pick up the ring that would change his life. Once he entered the store, the saleswoman became excessively flirtatious with him.

"Are you sure you're doing the right thing?" she asked.

When he nodded that he was sure and paid for the item, the saleswoman scribbled her number on the back of the receipt.

"That's my cell phone number in case things don't work out."

Manny took her come-on as a compliment. Ever since Xia changed his wardrobe, he received more attention from professional women. He only hoped she could change his life for the better in every way.

* * * * *

On his way into the Bronx, Manny called Xia and asked her to meet him at Havana's Paradise. She told him that she was already there. He asked if Pantera was there, and when she told him that he was, the butterflies in Manny's stomach started tumbling.

When Manny arrived at the social club, it was a bit more crowded than usual. In the corner, the brute was sitting by the bar. He was tapping his feet to the rhythm of "Oye Como Va" by Tito Puente as the music blared out the jukebox. Manny observed how the short brute spoke a word or two to a stocky Cuban behind the bar. When Manny made eye contact with the brute, both men acknowledged the other with a slight nod.

"Nice car," the brute said to Manny, while putting his drink down and reaching over the counter to press the buzzer.

Manny nodded at his nemesis's compliment. Seconds later, Pedro appeared. He led Manny into the semi-dark office, where Pantera was sitting at his desk puffing on a fresh Cuban cigar and conversing with Xia. She was sitting in a small loveseat across from him. When Manny walked into the room, they stopped talking. Xia's pretty brown eyes brightened up and a smile spread across her face. Manny returned the warm smile when their eyes momentarily met. The strong cigar smoke made it difficult for Manny to breathe, so he was coughing when he asked Pantera, "Cómo estás?"

The black beast responded with a mild nod, while blowing a mouthful of smoke into Manny's face. Manny closed his eyes to stay calm. He then turned to Pedro.

"I came to get more Manteca and perico. The people love it. I can't keep enough of it. Another thing, I got the money for the Cuba situation."

Pedro opened his palms. "Okay, let's deal with the product first. What exactly do you need this time?"

"A kilo of Manteca and three kilos of perico."

"Umm," Pantera said, shaking his head when he heard Manny's request.

"Ah...I tell you what. You've been coming on a regular basis now, so you pay us upfront for one kilo of Manteca and three kilos of perico. I'm going to double the amount of product you get on consignment. You pay us later, esta bien? We know you good for it."

Manny thought about the proposition before he agreed to Pedro's terms. The idea of that much product made him nervous. He looked at Xia, then answered, "Bien, bien. Lo cojo!" telling them that he would take it. He unzipped his black knapsack and pulled stacks of money out. Pantera smirked at the pile of cash. Manny broke eye contact, then looked at Pedro when he asked, "Can I get that today?"

"Sure. No problem. You get a call when the package is ready. Now, who are the people you need brought over?" Pedro asked.

Manny looked at Xia again. She looked extremely interested in who he had coming from Cuba. He swallowed hard, broke her gaze, and then fumbled in the pocket of the slacks that Xia chose for him. He retrieved a piece of paper with three names and an address written on it. He handed it to Pedro. "How soon can I expect them?"

"Three weeks from today. They will arrive in Miami. You work on getting them to New York. I will have someone contact you the day before."

Manny nodded. "Gracias." He looked over at Xia then at Pantera. Manny humbled himself when he said to Pedro, "Pana, you been a great help to me. I'm grateful for the opportunity you gave me, but I need to speak directly to Pantera. It's very important."

Pedro put his hands up. "You don't speak to Pantera."

Manny wasn't taking no for an answer. "Si, I understand that, but it's about Xia."

Pantera's eyes turned evil. To everyone's amazement, Pantera said, "Xia? What? Qué esta pasando? Habla me," asking Manny for an explanation.

Manny's heart pumped faster as his mind raced to formulate the right words. Pedro was stunned that his boss spoke to anyone besides him and Xia.

"Pantera, I won't waste your time. Xia is like a daughter to you, and out of the respect I have for you..." Manny stopped talking to reach into his pocket. When he produced the ring, he said, "I am seeking your permission to take her hand in marriage."

Silence invaded the room. Tension was getting thick in the office. Xia was impressed that Manny had the balls to risk his life by offending Pantera. Pedro moved out of the line of fire. He locked eyes with Xia, looking for some form of sign that she knew nothing about this. Xia put on a poker face while Manny locked eyes with Pantera.

A wicked grin appeared on the face of the black beast. In a bewildering manner, he looked from Manny to Xia, then back to Manny. He pointed his finger to Xia. "You and him, Xia? Tell me why I'm hearing this now? And is it true what he said?"

Xia stood at attention. Without looking at Pantera, she said, "Yes! We have been seeing each other. Please forgive me for not telling you, but I know how protective you can be when it comes to me. I didn't want to worry you with the situation until it was serious."

"Are you in love with him? Tell me, do you wish to marry him?" Pantera questioned, smashing his cigar inside a crystal ashtray. "Are you having his baby?"

After a short pause, Xia browsed the room before resting her eyes on Manny. "Yes, I love him and want to be his wife."

Pantera watched her and understood the sudden difference in Xia. He had been use to seeing her by herself, and he couldn't recall the last time she even talked about any man. Lately, her cold, rigid ways had become more vibrant. As he studied her, he could see the love and joy in her eyes and before him stood the reason for her new happiness. Pantera smiled to the relief of everyone in the room. Then suddenly, his smiled turned upside down.

He pointed to Manny and barked, "Xia, kill him!"

Like a trained attack dog, Xia reached into her waist and removed her Glock. She pulled back the slide to her cannon and registered a bullet into the chamber. When her two hands aimed for Manny's head, she hesitated and then closed her teary eyes.

In the millisecond that she hesitated, Pantera barked, "Para!" telling her to stop. Xia dropped her hands with pure pleasure. She began to sob until Pantera ordered, "No crying!" Xia sniffled, then stood like an emotionless robot.

Manny was lost. He looked at Xia and thought, *This puta was about to kill me?* He couldn't take his eyes off of her. Pantera was irrelevant. He wondered how she could be ready to kill him if she loved him. Pantera started laughing uncontrollably. Right then, Manny realized that Pantera was a certified sicko. He laughed again, while pointing to Manny. "You see? She loves you, but she loves *me* more. *Never* forget that." He cracked a smile. "Okay...under uno condition I let you marry Xia. You have grandé Cuban wedding, and I give the beautiful bride away."

Xia exhaled a sigh of relief. "Thank you, Pantera. Thank you, papa."

Manny was still torn. He was staring at Xia amazed that she could kill him.

Pedro quietly sat off to the side trying to understand what just unfolded. He eventually broke the silence. "Congratulations! Looks like we are going to have a big wedding." He looked at Manny and warned, "Please understand that things will not be nice if Xia loses her temper. The consequences will be much different than any other woman you ever had."

Manny looked at the cold killer who would eventually be his wife and realized those were the truest words he ever heard. Quickly, Xia walked over to Manny. She looked down at the ring in the box and then up at her man. When she squeezed his hand with a look of an apology on her face, Manny's heart melted. He didn't want to offend anyone in the room, so he placed the ring on her finger.

"Pedro, I will be waiting on your call for the product." He then turned to Pantera and said, "Thank you. Please excuse us." Manny grabbed Xia's arm and calmly escorted her out of the office.

When the office door closed behind them, someone was coming out of the bathroom. Manny shoved Xia into the bathroom, slammed the door, and whispered, "You were going to kill me? That easily you were going to kill me because *he* told you to?"

Xia tried to calm him with her smile, but it didn't work. She humbled herself, then whispered, "Manny, I knew it was a test. If I were going to shoot you, I wouldn't have hesitated. I never hesitate. That can get *me* killed. Besides, I would have grazed you if he forced me to and acted like I missed. I love you, baby, but that's just how Pantera is. I'm his only daughter."

Her words weren't calming Manny. "You don't see anything wrong with this whole thing? You love me, but I don't come first."

Xia held Manny's face. She kissed his lips and said, "Baby, we promised to never get involved with each other's business. I love you, and that's all you need to know...all that matters. Me and you are in love. Please forgive me." She hugged him tight and the scent of her Carol's Daughter perfume invaded his nostrils.

Manny banged the back of his head against the white tiles in the restroom.

Xia looked up at him. "How you going surprise me like that? You asked me if everyone was here, but you didn't tell me why. I want to ask you who you have coming from Cuba, but I will stick to the bargain and stay out of your affairs like a good wife should."

Why the fuck she always know what to say and do? Manny thought as his heart melted. "You told me if I was serious, I had to see Pantera. So, I saw Pantera."

With her chin on his chest, Xia looked into Manny's eyes. "You really serious, huh?"

"You got that ring on your finger, right?" Manny said with an attitude.

102

Xia licked her lips, then grinded her big body against his hard-on. "So when you want to get married?"

Manny put his hand up. "Un momento." He got serious and continued. "The next time you pull that fucking gun out on me, you better kill me. Comprende?"

Xia looked into his eyes and smiled. "Okay, I promise to kill you next time. Now, when do you wanna make me Mrs. Black?"

"Soon. Do I have to ask Pantera permission to fuck you, too?"

Xia kept her cool when she jokingly said, "Damn, babe, you really pushing it."

Manny looked at the ceiling while Xia acted like they were dancing to slow music. In a beautiful voice, she started singing, "When we get married..."

"Stop playing," Manny whispered, while trying hard to keep his attitude. "When you want to get married?"

Xia sucked on his chin, then said, "Okay, let's set it for July 7th. That's three months away." Manny smirked, then Xia said, "Hey, dimples, July 7th will always be your special day."

Manny said, "Yeah, and maybe I'll calm down by then."

Xia rubbed her hand on the outside of Manny's pants, stimulating his erection. "Maybe I can work hard tonight to calm you down." She kissed her fiancé, and his attitude died while his erection came to life. The moment he started fumbling for her clothes, she backed away and looked down at the ring on her finger. "I'll see you at home tonight if you want me." She walked out of the bathroom leaving Manny aroused.

Manny ran out behind her. "I'm gonna call you later after I take care of business. I have something I want to show you, esta bien?"

Xia nodded, blew him a kiss, and then went back into the office with the black beast.

While Manny was walking out of the social club, he was sure he was in love and was worried. As far as he was concerned, he was a sucker, and only time would tell if he were right.

* * * * *

Manny's emotions were spinning out of control as he drove downtown. He was happy at the developments in his life, but confused over the way Xia had control over him. He still wanted the videotape that Pantera had, and he hoped in time that Xia could get it for him. His plotting was interrupted when his cell phone rang. Again, the caller instructed him to pick up the product at the fishmarket. Transporting in his personal car was a no-no, but Manny wasted no time in getting to 116th Street.

The aroma of fish hit him, and this time, it was stronger than the last. Manny ignored the scent and had no intentions of staying there long. He approached the first stand, made small talk, and received his package. On the way out the market, Manny was on his cell phone with Rico. Instead of going to his car, he walked down 115th Street and sat on a bench in front of Foster Projects. Ten minutes later, Rich Dice pulled up in an old station wagon. Without saying a word, Manny handed over one of the bags and walked away in the opposite direction of Rich Dice.

By the time Manny returned to his apartment in Brooklyn with the three keys of coke, Carmen's flight was landing within the hour. Manny liked that side of the business. He could send the drugs to Atlanta, never meet anyone involved, and still receive six figures from the deal. He didn't know how he was going to tell Carmen about Xia, but he figured he'd cross that bridge when he came to it.

At seven o'clock that evening, Carmen walked through Manny's apartment door dragging her overnight bag. Her disposition was as lively as ever. "Hi, papi," she cheerfully said, while throwing her arms around Manny and kissing him.

"What's good?" Manny asked, while observing that Carmen looked like she gained ten pounds.

"You what's good!" Carmen said, blushing. She started taking off her coat, kicked off her shoes, and strolled across the small living room to the couch. Manny smiled while watching her sashay across the room. Carmen quickly unbuttoned her blouse and skirt, then unfastened the girdle she wore underneath. Carefully, she removed stacks of money that were lined around her waist and hips. She put the cash together neatly on the coffee table. "That's one hundred thousand."

Manny smirked. "He's short. What happened?"

Carmen fixed her clothes. "I know...I know. He waiting to get paid, and I'll take care of everything."

When she refastened her clothes, Manny asked, "You sure you comfortable with transporting product and money back and forth?"

"Si, papi, I'm comfortable. I'm doing it for us. One day you gonna be my husband, so I have no problem. Qué? You got a problem?"

"I don't know, but I'm thinking about how you handling everything."

"What you mean?" Carmen shot back.

"Mira, have a seat." Carmen sat, then he said, "Me and you, we good in bed. We real good. Now things are different. We doing business now. You are a part of a bigger family now, and soon, you going to have to do things for me that you don't like doing...that you won't be so comfortable in doing. Right now, I don't want you in the open. Think like a boss now. Get somebody else to transport the product."

Carmen was disappointed. "Qué paso? You don't want me doing it anymore?"

"No, I'm not saying that. I only want you to handle the money part."

Carmen sat quiet for a moment. Suddenly, she asked, "What's bothering you, negro? What you gonna ask me to do that's so uncomfortable? I will do anything for you."

Manny thought about the wedding. "Oh yeah? Anything, huh?"

Carmen stood and licked her lips. "Si, *anything.*"

"Bien, you gonna have to prove it. Right now, you find somebody else to take the product down. You just get the money."

Carmen's eyes lit up. "Oh papi, I know who! My two girlfriends that work with me. If the money is right, they can do it."

"You trust them?"

Carmen waved her finger. "You teach me to not trust anybody. I think I can get them to do it, and that's what's important."

Manny thought about it. "I'll tell you what. I want you to feel them out first before we make any moves. Make some packages of flour, five pounds each. Tell them it's the coca, and you give them one thousand each. See how they do."

She started clapping, overjoyed that she was doing something deceptive. "Muy bien, papi. You so smart. I'll take care of it. I do everything. Okay, papi?"

Manny walked over to the coffee table and split the large stack of cash in half. He pushed $50,000 in Carmen's direction. "That's for you. Remember, you say you ready to do anything."

She looked down at the cash as tears of joy rolled down her cheeks. Instead of thanking Manny, she said, "Come to me. I have a flight in an hour, and I wanted to suck your dick all day, papi."

Carmen was a freak, and she knew it. She also knew that Manny loved every freaky bone in her body. Like a cat to milk, he bopped his way to her mouth, and Carmen took him to a place of comfort that only her lips and hot tongue could take him.

* * * * *

After Carmen left, Manny took a quick shower, got dressed in a blazer and slacks, then he hit the road. On his way uptown, he called Xia to tell her to meet him downstairs. He reached her residence in record time. Manny didn't want to drive, so they jumped in Xia's X5.

"Where we going, baby?" Xia asked.

"If I tell you, then it won't be a surprise," Manny said with pride. He pointed out the windshield. "Just drive, Bonita, and I tell you where to go."

Xia stomped on her gas pedal. "My words just keep coming back to haunt me, huh?"

Manny gave her directions to the New York State Thruway and then to the Taconic Parkway. Xia asked a hundred times where they were going, but Manny wouldn't budge. He pointed her through the town of Ossining until they reached Spring Street. When they stopped at the single-family brick house with cedar shingles and a two-car garage attached to it, Manny said, "For my wife. This is yours." He had wanted to say those words his whole life, but he didn't get the response he thought he would. To break her silence, he asked, "Bonita, what you think? You like it or what?"

An unsatisfied look appeared on her face. Xia scanned the house and said, "Let's go inside."

As they exited the X5, Manny was disappointed. He kept staring at her, wondering why she wasn't jumping up and down and screaming how grateful she was. For a second, he felt like there was no pleasing Xia, but he shook off his insecurities.

Manny opened the front door and took his fiancée on a grand tour of the home. He walked her up the creaky stairs where she looked at the cramped bedrooms and the grimy bathroom that only had space for a tub, a sink, and a toilet. He then walked with her on the bottom floor where the dining room was big enough to cram eight people in and the living room was smaller than her current bedroom. Manny wanted to go to the basement until she said, "That won't be necessary." Xia looked at the ceiling with a look of disgust before turning to her man. She kissed him, then said, "Thank you for everything you do. I appreciate this, but... " Xia looked around again and then shook her head. She turned back to Manny. "Babe, I don't want you to think that I don't appreciate what you've done. It's alright and all, but I think we should get something a little bigger with more rooms." Coolly, her eyes scanned the small empty living room once again. "How much did you pay for this house anyway?"

He didn't want to argue. In comparison to the house in Panama he grew up in, they were standing in a mansion. Manny walked away from her and looked out of the living room window.

"Edeeks paid the real estate agent a down payment."

"Edeeks? Who is he?"

"He's somebody very close to me. Like Pedro for Pantera."

Xia sighed, then walked over to him. She stood behind him and wrapped her arms around him. "Well, give me Edeeks' number, and I'll call him tomorrow. If you don't mind, I'm going to tell him to put the house back on the market." She turned Manny around. "If you tell me this is where we're living, then this is home. But, if you let me, I'll add two hundred thousand of my money so we can get a bigger house. With my way, I can cut them a clean check for the amount of the new

106

house, and we can move in immediately. No one will be snooping in our affairs, and you won't have to go around the world to get it done. My name is clean for up to a mill." She moved closer to Manny and sucked on his chin. "I want you to give me a lot of babies, Manny…a whole house full, and I always dreamed of having a big house with my husband. This is my dream, babe, and I know you can make all of my dreams come true."

What the fuck am I suppose to say to that? Manny reasoned. After swallowing his pride, he conceded. "Okay, we do it your way. Now let's get out of here."

Manny led her out of the house. When they were in front of the X5, he turned around at his house, trying to see what was wrong with it. He gave up, shrugged his shoulders, and reached for the passenger door.

Xia said, "Babe, can you drive please?"

Manny looked at his wife-to-be and wondered why she had to be so difficult. He immediately figured killing people probably did that to her. With no protest, he walked around to the driver's side. When he jumped in the truck and made all the adjustments to the seats, he asked, "Why couldn't you drive?"

Xia smiled. "I wanted to do something I've been waiting my whole life to do."

Manny put the truck in drive. He sped through the desolate Spring Street and headed for the highway. Once he was on the Taconic, he turned to Xia. "Where we going, and what is it that you want to do?"

Xia put on a devilish grin. While the traffic signs flew by them and the fast cars passed, she said, "This." She reached for Manny's zipper, pulled his limp dick from his pants, and placed her mouth on him while he raced through Westchester County.

EIGHT

The following day, Xia contacted Edeeks, and they met up to put Xia's dream in motion. Through enough haggling, Edeeks' money on the house was returned. Since that went well, Xia drove up to Ossining and found a real estate agent of her own. After seeing properties on a computer screen, she selected one she wanted to see in a small village called Cortland Manor.

The gracious four-bedroom, four-and-a-half bath house was the definition of luxury. When Xia walked into the house, it had a gourmet kitchen with granite countertops, a butler's pantry, a master suite with a private office, a pool with a spa, and a three-car garage.

She stepped out of the house, looked at the real estate agent, and said, "I'll take it."

She was going to surprise Manny. She drove into Ossining, where she met with contractors to remodel the house. Xia then used another hundred thousand dollars of her own money for a lavish shopping spree of furniture and other accessories for the home.

Manny was marrying an independent woman who had the ability to take care of the both of them. Although they both made their money from crime, it looked like crime was definitely paying.

* * * * *

Two days later, Manny was in Brooklyn packing up his personal belongings, when there was a knock at his door. He peeked through the peephole, and Carmen was standing in the hallway with a look of impatience.

Carmen came through the door with a troubled look on her face. Manny immediately knew something was wrong, "Qué pasa? Where's the money?" he asked.

Carmen's eyes nervously shifted as her hands dropped to her side. She fell to the floor in tears. "There is no money. Nada, nothing!"

Manny looked down at her. "What you mean nada? That's over one hundred and forty thousand dollars, Carmen."

The worried look on her face eased a little when she responded, "Papi, don't get mad, please. I went to the airport to meet the gringo Matthew like I do all the time. He wasn't there. So, I rented a car and drove to his house in Marietta. He wasn't there either." Carmen stood, wiped her eyes, then reached for a paper towel. She looked at the boxes in the house and asked, "Where you going?"

"I have to move these things out. I have something to do with the apartment." Manny waved his hand in front of her. "Él dinero! Qué pasó?"

Carmen moved her eyes from the boxes. "Oh, so I drove to his girl's house in Smyrna and he was there. He told me to tell you that somebody from College Park named Boss Hog got the money. He took the money and said Matthew gets nothing." Carmen walked up to Manny. "Negro, Matthew is bueno, but he's not tough, you know? That cabrón out there has our money."

Manny sat quiet for a moment and pondered the situation. He knew what he had to do. "What time your flight leaves tonight?"

"I got a few hours. Why?"

Without replying, Manny walked out of the living room into his bedroom. He grabbed his cell phone and returned to the living room. "Get your stuff. Come with me!"

"Where we going? What you going to do?" Carmen asked, while trying to fix herself.

Manny snatched her and said, "Puta! Just come on."

Three blocks down from Manny's apartment, they stopped at the parking garage on Underhill Avenue. Manny said, "Wait right here."

Manny walked into the darkness of the quiet hole. Five minutes later, his exhaust killed the silence.

When he pulled out on the sloped sidewalk, Carmen asked, "You got a car?" He waved her into the car. She looked at the leather interior and said, "Oh, Manny, I like this, papi."

Manny let the clutch loose on Underhill Avenue, heading for Flatbush Avenue so he could get to Harlem as soon as possible. He looked at Carmen, then said, "Chica, on the way you don't say nothing. Nothing." Carmen was obedient and would do anything Manny said.

On the way to the M3 lounge, Manny called Self and told him to meet him there. He then called Rico to tell him the same thing. Rico was his little brother, but he was also his partner. Over the months of them making money, instead of getting lazy over the cash they were seeing, he was more on point. Every dime was counted, and anyone that came up short felt his wrath. While Manny raced through the grimy streets of the Big Apple, his new plan came together.

By the time he and Carmen arrived at the social club, there were three M3's parked outside instead of two. Manny knew his whole crew was there, and felt a level of pride. When he stepped inside, Self was on his cell phone and Rashid was playing himself in pool. Rico was wrapped in a blanket on one of the leather couches while he ate Fruity

Pebbles cereal. Across from him was a large 60-inch television with BET on it, and across from that was a stainless steel Sub-Zero refrigerator.

"Hermano, what? You live here now?" Manny asked Rico. Carmen went to sit next to him, where she planted a kiss on Rico's cheek.

"What the fuck. *Somebody* got to stay close to the base." Rico looked around with milk dripping from his lips. "I just remodeled the spot some."

"What's up, Slick? You need Self for something."

Manny walked over to the pool table and pointed to Rico. "Fam, turn that TV off."

Rico pushed his bowl to the side and did as he was told. When everyone surrounded the pool table, Manny held the cue ball in his hand. "Carmen, I want to introduce you to our family. This is Self and Rashid. Rico you already know." He paused before finishing his thought. "I want you to know that Carmen is a part of M3. That's the only reason she is in here." Again, Manny took a brief pause to look at Rico, who was laughing hysterically. He ignored his brother, then looked in Self's direction. "Listen, I got a little situation down in Atlanta. Some pinga down there named Boss Hog is acting like a big man. He disrespects my people, and he owes us one hundred thousand and change. Self, I want you to pay him a visit."

"'Bout time you earn some of that dough. Let Self loose down on them backwoods muthafuckas," Rico blared out.

"ATL? Oh, Self gonna party," Self said, while brushing off his diamonds.

Rico stepped up and affectionately put his arm around Carmen's shoulder. "This bitch been getting paper for M3, and I ain't know, huh?" He kissed Carmen on the cheek, then said, "Big sis, why you ain't tell your little brother that somebody making you mad? I'ma go down there and let them feel the pain for you, baby."

Manny knew how off the hook his little brother was, so he said, "No, we need you here. Your small team grew to twenty on Manhattan Avenue. They have to eat, too."

"I got this shit up here in a smash," Rashid said, while licking his finger and then wiping a stain on his white, butter soft, leather jacket.

Manny saw what was about to happen with their egos. "Rico, you put all this together. Rashid, you keep it together. I need the balance of you two in New York. The summer is almost here, and we have to take care of our soldiers so they can drive in the summer sun. Self can handle it. If not, I go down there myself." Manny turned to Self. "You have somebody to take with you? I need you to leave now…tonight."

Self pondered, then snapped his fingers. "Yeah, Self can take nephew. He put in work, and he tryin' to get paper. Self will give Kev a call."

"He thorough like that? Don't have no bird-ass nigga repping M3, son," came from the underboss Rico.

"He's official," Self replied as he turned to Carmen. "Where Boss Hog at? What town? And how far you ready to go with this shit? How much he owe? You can hold water? If Self turn that whole town upside down, you gonna be able to take the weight for Self?"

Carmen squinted her eyes in confusion. She licked her lips and pointed at Self. "I thought you were Self? Why you keep asking about Self if you're Self?" She looked at Manny and Rico, who were both shaking their heads telling her not to ask. Carmen caught on. "Okay bien. Boss Hog is in College Park. I will stay in Smyrna with Matthew's girl. He is the man who takes care of Manny's business. He lives in Marietta. Me? You heard Self; I am Manny's *top* bitch! No puta can cause me to cross Manny. You Manny's family, then you my family, too. If the policia comes, I go to jail for Manny, do time for Manny, and die for Manny. I leave on the plane in a few hours. Where will you be for Manny?"

"Now *this* is a M3 bitch fo' sho!" Rico said, while laughing.

Carmen asked, "What does M3 mean?"

They all said in unison, "Money, Murder, and Mayhem."

Carmen nodded rapidly. "Si, that's me. All three in one."

Everyone laughed at Carmen as Manny beamed with pride.

Self rubbed his goatee while thinking and then said, "Boss Hog, huh? From out of College Park?"

Manny was confident of Self's abilities. "One-forty he owes. I want that back. Carmen can bring it back. You help yourself to anything you want down there. Stay awhile."

Self looked at his diamond watch, then said to Carmen, "It's ten in the morning now? Um…Self don't do planes, so Self a be in ATL by midnight or a little later. Self need a number to call when Self get there so Self can talk to that Matthew buster. After Self get the cash back, that's all Self gotta do."

Manny wrote on a piece of paper and handed it to Self. "Here's Carmen's number. Give her a call when you get there."

Self acknowledged Manny's request. "Slick, Self gonna make our presence felt in that town. Trust dat, homie."

Rico slammed his hand down on the pool table and asked, "Manny, please, I'm begging you. Let me go down there."

Rashid was feeling lonely. "Daddy-O, I know how to slang dem thangs. If Rico gonna stay, then let *me* go."

Self ended the debate. "Y'all amateurs never felt the wrath of Self. You only heard. Self keep it quiet uptown 'cause Self only shit a little where he sleep. As for ATL? Self don't live there. If Self need help, it means Boss Hog got the U.S. Army. Anything less, Self got it. So, stop the crying. Y'all the foundation of M3, so act like it."

The elder had spoken. Rico marched back over to his soggy Fruity Pebbles with an attitude. Rashid stood next to Manny waiting for orders.

With everything in place, Manny said, "Bien, that's what I'm talking about. I'm taking Carmen home so she can get ready for the trip. Anybody call me if there is a problem." While Manny and Carmen was walking out of the social club, Manny looked over at his brother. He saw Rico's adolescent attitude from him not having his way. He called over to him. "Aye, Rico, you the boss. Start acting like it." Rico's head bopped to a video rhythm, and Manny knew his point was well taken.

Before they exited the M3 lounge, Rashid stopped him. "Aye yo, Manny, hold up! Come back in."

Manny handed Carmen the keys. "Wait for me in the car." He stepped back in and said, "Okay, what's up?"

Rashid turned to Rico and asked, "Tell him?" Rico nodded, then went back to watching music videos. Rashid checked his wardrobe before saying to Manny, "Daddy-O, I wanted to holla at you 'cause I got this homie Stan down on the Lower East Side. He got a block dats makin' paper, but he ain't got no real work to meet the demand. Homie even got a lil' team rolling wit' em, but they ain't soldiers yet. They need somebody to take them to the next level. I already established dat it's my show if I come down there, but I don't move unless you say so. Rico? He doesn't give a fuck, but me and him ain't making no moves unless you say so. We can get really rich off this shit. The Lower built like they drink dope in the water or some shit. I want to know if it's okay for me to take four or five hundred bags of M3 to set up shop."

Manny was grinning inside from the respect his team had for him. He asked, "What did Rico say?"

Rashid exhaled with impatience. "He said ask you."

Manny looked over to his brother and said, "He's your boss. If it's alright with him, then it's alright with me."

Rashid jumped for joy. "No doubt! Money, Murder, and Mayhem. We gonna get paper, baby!"

Manny patted him on the back. "Homie, just keep your eyes open down there. Don't play games."

Rashid hugged Manny. "I'ma make you my father, that's my word. I love you, man."

Everybody cracked up. Manny waved him off, walked out of the social club, and had his mind on dropping Carmen off.

* * * * *

The day after the brief meeting at the M3 lounge, Rashid went down to the Lower East Side with Fee-foe and four of Rashid's pit bull dogs. Together, they repeated the same process like the Harlem operation. Fee-foe put the word out to all the dopefiends. He secured two apartments in a small complex on Baruch and East Houston Streets beside the F.D.R. Drive. After having the doors reinforced with steel rods and putting the pit bulls in each stash spot, Rashid wanted to meet with his homie Stan.

Rashid assembled a group of young Latinos and blacks. All ten of them stood in front of 4th Street on Avenue B late at night, Rashid had his polished M3 parked outside, and he made sure he wore his best jewelry.

Stan was half black and half Puerto Rican. He hailed from 140th Street between 7th and 8th Avenues. Rashid knew him from a girl that lived on his block. Once Stan saw how much paper was flowing uptown, he told Rashid about his crew down in The Lower.

Rashid stood on the corner with Stan in front of him. The light-skin male with neat cornrows, big eyes, chipped teeth, and a mean Newport cigarette habit was standing next to Rashid with pride. Rashid turned to the ten young males and started freestyling a speech, when he thought of Manny and said, "Stan brought me down here for us to get rich." He pointed to his car. "You see that? That's a M3. That's what this game is about…money, murder, and mayhem. If you ain't ready to bust your guns, bring the drama, and get rich, then leave right now." Rashid waited for movement, but nobody moved. "Good. Right now, y'all are a little ass crew. M3 is an army. I got a general over me, and he got a general over him. This ain't no broke-ass gang. We here to get paper. Right now, Stan right here is my lieutenant. We gonna make you into an army. Into soldiers! Ready to die and serve. Starting tomorrow, I want everybody back here in the morning with a gun on you. You gonna treat Stan like your general and follow his orders. I guarantee if y'all follow orders, we will have a bunch of M3's parked up by the summer. So y'all wit' me or what?"

The young team yelled in unison. They were just as hungry and thorough as the team in Harlem. Rashid opened shop the next day, and the word spread about the M3 heroin. From sunup to sundown, the young hustlers pushed the M3 brand in the infamous Alphabet City on 4th Street and Avenue B.

Within the first week, Rashid ran through a couple of ounces and had to call Manny for more dope. In a matter of weeks, he was sure the demand for the heroin would triple and the spot could start moving close to $40,000 worth of heroin sales a day.

At Rashid's request, Manny, Rico, and him drove down to 4th Street a week after he arrived. When the soldiers saw Manny and Rico, along with the three M3 lined up, they treated them like kings of the ghetto. That night, Rashid told them that there were five other generals with M3's and that he was buying the best soldiers BMW M3's by the summer. Once they heard that, and Rico telling them lies that they had thirty other M3 brothers uptown, the young men were tripping over themselves to take the Lower East Side over.

M3 was growing by the day. Rich Dice was given a promotion to run Manhattan Avenue. Rashid had Stan handling everything on 4th Street, and Rico and Rashid were out buying money counters and talking to Big Dave about purchasing used M3's.

* * * * *

While Manny and his crew were busy handling business, Xia spent her time getting the new house together, while planning for her and Manny's July 7th wedding. She had each room beautifully furnished with rich Italian handcarved furniture. Some of the room's floors were hardwood, and others had wall-to-wall carpeting. Entertainment consoles were in the four bedrooms and the family room. The basement was equipped with a stock bar and a mini theatre system. Xia's huge, detailed gourmet kitchen was done with custom cabinets and granite countertops with stainless steel appliances. When Xia finally finished putting her personal touch to the house, it looked like a celebrity's home on *MTV Cribs*.

With Carmen out of town, Manny spent most of his nights in Fordham Hill. Three weeks after he sent Self to Atlanta and a week after he made his appearance on 4th Street, Xia awoke in the middle of the night. She kissed Manny, then said, "Sleep. I'll be back in a few hours."

Two hours later, Xia was easing back into bed. The scent of her coming from the shower woke Manny up. Xia put his limpness into her mouth until he got stiff. She then got on top of him and rode him until they both climaxed.

Five hours later, Manny was up watching the news when the reporter said, "On this Mother's Day, two Cuban men were found dead in the Lower East Side. None of the men were relieved of their property. They each received two shots to their heads last night. It's believed the men were associated with..."

The TV went blank. Xia dropped the remote control on the bed, handed Manny his breakfast of pancakes and eggs, then said, "You shouldn't watch things like that. It will give you nightmares." She then quieted Manny by cutting his food and feeding him. She said, "I want to take you somewhere today. Do you trust me?" Manny couldn't tell her the truth, so he nodded with his mouth full. Xia said, "Okay then, you have to go blindfolded. You have to promise me. It's the first of my wedding presents to you."

Manny shrugged and that was that.

Later that morning, Xia put on a brown linen skirt that had big pockets on the front, a beige silk blouse, and a pair of brown leather clogs. She pulled out a pair of beige linen pants, a brown silk shirt for Manny, along with a pair of brown closed-toe sandals with a brown belt and silk boxers. She washed Manny from head to toe and then oiled him down with her favorite Carol's Daughter oil. When they were fully dressed, Manny kept his word, and she slipped a black blindfold over his eyes.

Xia led Manny down the elevator and helped him into her truck. She drove for less than an hour before the truck came to a stop. Manny knew he was somewhere out of the city because it was too quiet. He tried to cheat by rolling the window down, but then his door suddenly opened. Xia helped him out of the truck, walked with him a few spaces where he felt soft grass under his feet, and then she removed the blindfold, saying, "Voila!"

Manny was bugging. The first thing he saw was a wooden mailbox that had *The Black's* written above it. Huge trees and shrubs surrounded the house and the manicured front lawn. He looked up at the brown shingles, the beige stucco, and the white brick accents on the corners and over the front door.

She whispered, "Papi, this is home. For my husband. This is all yours." She kissed him. "Wait till you see inside. Come on." Xia handed him a miniature leather pouch with a set of keys and the button to a car alarm dangling on it.

Manny walked through the front door. He saw what Xia did, and he was amazed. His head was spinning because the house was exquisite. Everything from the floors to the high ceiling was immaculate. The crystal chandeliers, the huge dining table that seated twenty-two, and the huge kitchen made him want to cry. They walked upstairs, and she opened the double doors to their master suite. Manny saw a replica of her huge bed. It looked like two king-sized beds were put together, with a royal canopy above it and mirrors lodged into the mahogany canopy. When he walked into the small office in the bedroom, a plaque that had *Manuel Black-President* was sitting on the desk in front of a computer.

Xia then led him to the walk-in closet where a huge marble counter sat in the middle of the floor. On one side were suits, shoes, casual wear, and underwear. The opposite side had all of Xia's new clothes. Against a massive wall were rows and rows of shoes.

Xia put her hand under the marble counter and said, "Watch this." When she hit a button, the shoe wall clicked and a hidden door opened. Manny walked into another miniature closet and pulled a string for the lights to come on. When the darkness was gone, Xia had rifles, shotguns, handguns, bulletproof vests, and two sniper rifles hanging against the three walls. Loads of ammunition was under each weapon. "You see how your wife thinks of everything?" she asked him.

After playing with the Jacuzzi in the master bath that could hold four, he quickly scanned the other rooms that were designed for children and guests. Xia walked him out to the pool and the hot tub. Then she stopped at the three-car garage. She said to Manny, "Hit the button on your key chain." He hit two of the buttons, not knowing what each one was for. He heard an alarm disarming, and then an engine cut on. Xia laughed, pulled a garage opener out of her pocket, and then clicked the white button.

One of the garage doors opened, and Manny smacked his head. "Ay diós mío!" Tears came to his eyes when he saw a brand-new, all-black, 2000 Cadillac Escalade.

Xia said, "Wait." She handed him the button to that garage door and removed another one from her pocket. When she pressed the button, the garage opened to reveal an all-white Mercedes Benz E-class stationwagon with white interior. "It's hot, right, babe?"

"What? You hit the lotto or something?"

Xia pulled another button out of her pocket. "Wait, I'm not done." She pressed the button, and the third garage door opened to reveal a 2000 Plymouth Prowler in silver with a black convertible top and tinted windows. "These are Pantera's wedding gifts. He said we have some more coming after the wedding." She then turned to Manny, who had the biggest smile on his face. She kissed him and said, "All of this is yours with me included, Manny Black. You do what you have to do as a man, and I'll do what I have to do to keep your house in order. There is no divorce from me! Once I take on the Black name, I'll be keeping it for life." She spread her hands out to the house and all the material things, then said, "None of these things really matter. All that matters is our love, Manny. I hope it's to your liking and I am worth all the headaches I've been putting you through."

"Bonita, you the best, Ma," Manny said before kissing her.

Xia kissed him passionately like he was her last breath of fresh air. She then said, "I want to try out our Jacuzzi, our custom bed, and then make love in every room of the house. Then, by tonight, I want to swallow you while you're driving your new truck. When we come back from the drive, I want you to be the first man to make love to me in a car. I never had sex in a car before, so let's christen my Benz the right way."

Manny looked at his wife to be and hugged her. Then they both ran into the house to fulfill Xia's request.

* * * * *

On the day Self and Carmen arrived in Atlanta, Carmen went to Matthew's girlfriend's house. Self rented two hotel rooms at the Hilton Plaza. He drove his M3 down while his nephew Kev drove the artillery down in an old Honda Accord. In less than twenty-four hours after Carmen placed her complaint, Self was strapped in Atlanta, ready to handle his business.

The following morning, Self and Kev picked Carmen up, and they drove to Matthew's house in Marietta. Matthew answered the door dressed in a pair of faded blue jeans, a white tee shirt, and a pair of slippers. The smile on his face quickly disappeared when he saw Carmen with two black men standing on his porch.

"Carmen...I...didn't know...you...you were coming back down so soon," Matthew said nervously, while looking over her shoulders at the two thugs staring at him.

Carmen picked up on Matthew's nervousness and immediately eased his anxiety. She stepped in his house like a Mafia boss. "Matthew, I want you to meet my people." She pointed to Self and Kev. "This is Self and the cute one is Kev. They're here about the situation."

Matthew's eyes opened wide. "The situation? Oh...okay, right." He cracked a big smile, then exhaled in relief. "It's a pleasure to meet you guys."

Kev was Carmen's height with a caramel complexion. He favored the R&B superstar Usher. When Matthew greeted him, he nodded while scanning the house.

"What up?" Self asked, while focusing his attention on the tall, skinny, white boy with the long, black, shoulder-length hair. *Damn! Dis muthafucka look just like Steve Tyler from the band Aerosmith,* Self thought to himself as he flopped down on the sofa. After everyone was seated, Self leaned up to the edge of the sofa. While focusing on Matthew, he said, "Listen, Self need you to say everything that jumped off wit' you and this bird Boss Hog."

Matthew looked at Carmen and said, "I thought you said he was Self? He just said..."

Carmen nodded that he was indeed Self, and her eyes said not to ask why he referred to himself in the third person. While looking into Self's cold eyes, Matthew knew Self wasn't someone to play with.

After taking a deep breath, he exhaled. "Okay, dude, here's what went down. For some time now, I've been giving a little product to a guy over in College Park. You see, being white and all, it's been easy for me to move around without attracting any real heat. An additional bonus is that I grew up with one of the deputies from that county. I always take care of him by giving him a few lines of coke. Dude, he loves the stuff. He takes care of me by keeping me abreast with what's going on in the department. I pass the information on to my guy to keep him one step ahead. Anyway, dude, when I hooked up with Carmen and started getting that great 'caine, it seems like my guy's clientele quadrupled overnight. We went up to a hundred bucks a gram, and no one bitched and moaned about it. Dude, the product started selling faster than Carmen could bring it down." He looked at the ground, then said, "That's when so-called Boss Hog came into the picture. When Boss Hog heard about how good our coke was, he asked my guy if I could supply him. Dude, I didn't think it would be a problem. I gave Boss Hog a little bit just to test the waves. Then he came right back the next day with all the money and asked for more. Dude, I didn't have any more on hand, so I put him on standby 'til Carmen brought more. I gave him a shitload, and again, he came right back with all the money. So, I get to figuring, why not give everything I have to Boss Hog, you know? Thinking he'd be good for it. Thinking he would move it and bring the money right back like before. But instead, dude, when I went to see him to collect the money, he became very hostile, and the weapon in his hand was very persuasive, if you get my drift. So, dude, I left and got in touch with Carmen."

"Oh yeah?" Self asked with a smirk. "Why didn't you deal with Boss Hog to get the money back? You scared?"

"Fucking A-right, dude. Those nigg...I mean, those guys are gangsters. I didn't get into this to kill anyone. I just want to make some cash and then save my ass." He pointed to Carmen. "She gets the bigger split, so I called her. Dude, we have close to three hundred grand tied up with this thing. I just want to pay her back and keep my credibility. I guess that's where you come in, huh?"

Self nodded. "How much money you got now?"

Matthew looked around and replied, "About four thousand."

"Yeah, let Self get that."

Matthew left and returned with a rumpled stack of cash. He handed it to Self. "That's all you need?"

Self nodded. "Self got it from here."

Matthew sighed. "Dude, I don't know where he lives. I just know he has guys over in College Park selling *our* product for him. But I hear he likes to hang out a lot around Atlanta. He's some type of baller or something."

"A'ight, don't worry. Self gonna find this bird," Self said, while standing up to stretch his legs.

"How you going to do that?" Carmen asked. "You don't know anybody down here."

Kev butted in. "Just chill, Ma. Just let Self do Self."

Self and Kev left Matthew's house. They were leaving to put things into action the only way Self knew how. They were going to fit in, apply pressure, and then begin the M3 motto of getting the money, committing murder, and then leaving Atlanta with the mayhem they left behind.

NINE

Self and Kev returned to the Hilton. They had the door to the adjoining rooms open. Kev watched on as Self got dressed in a crisp pair of jeans with red teardrops dripping down the legs, a short-sleeve red and blue Rocawear button-down shirt with a pair of white and red Nike Air Force Ones. Self reached into his luggage and removed a black velvet bag. When he poured the contents out, a Bicentennial Rolex covered with diamonds and rubies fell out. Next, two platinum chains with diamond baguettes flowing through them, two diamond earrings the size of raisins, two canary yellow pinkie rings, and a bracelet drenched in diamonds.

Self put the jewelry on top of another necklace he already had on. When Self checked himself in the mirror, Kev asked, "So what you wanna do about this Boss Hog cat?"

Self brushed the lint off his shoulders. "Go shopping."

They left the hotel in the Honda Accord headed to Atlanta's Cumberland Mall. Self didn't want to attract heat on the M3, so he left it in the parking lot. The two looked like a pair of drug dealers out for a ride. Self was dressed in enough jewelry to buy a store in the mall, while Kev kept it simple. He wore a basic black Enyce velour sweat suit, a tee shirt, and a pair of black chukkas boots.

When they entered the mall, it was packed. Most of the younger people were just hanging out, while other shoppers moved about. As Self and Kev strolled along the lower level of the shopping center, they causally surveyed the action. Kids hung in small groups, parents of the younger children rushed through with impatience, and the eyes of the women followed Self's every move like he was a celebrity.

He and Kev walked around until Self stopped at Footlocker and Finish Line so Kev could buy the type of clothes the locals wore. They were there on official business, so Self didn't want Kev to be recognized as a New Yorker. As for him, he had to use his New York style to bring his plans together.

They walked out of the stores with ten bags of clothes and shoes. All eyes were on them, some from haters and others from admirers. A few young girls asked Self for his autograph, but he brushed them off. He was focused. His eyes scanned every level of the mall until he found exactly what he was looking for.

Standing with a group of three other women, a tall, thick, caramel-complexioned cutie with D-cup breasts she paid for and a fat ass that was peeking from under her clothes caught Self's attention. She was dressed in a red silk tank top and a white pleated tennis skirt. Her pedicured feet were squashed in a pair of sandals that had a six-inch heel. Her flawless red and black hair was in a short haircut that flared out at the back of her neck. She had a few diamonds in her jewelry, but when she saw the walking jewelry display on Self's body, she smiled to reveal her single gold fang. Her chinky eyes batted a few times while she covered her mouth with her long nails and whispered to her girlfriends about Self.

Kev and Self walked by the group of girls like they weren't there. When Self looked back and saw the chinky-eyed woman staring at him, he stopped short. He tapped Kev and said, "You get the other three while Self get the thick one. You know how to play, this is for a crib."

"No doubt! I got you." Kev replied, following behind Self.

When the girls saw Self and Kev walking back in their direction, the talking came to an abrupt stop. Their eyes immediately lit up and filled with greed when they saw all the diamond-encrusted, platinum jewelry Self had on.

Self walked up to the thick woman that smiled at him and stared at her. He looked at her from head to toe like he wanted to hurt her. Quickly, her smile disappeared. He turned his back to her friends and walked so close to her face that he could kiss her. Behind him, he heard Kev say, "Hey, y'all. What's happenin'?"

The women spoke to Kev, but all eyes were watching Self. Again, he scanned the stacked woman from head to toe while inching closer. Her eyes were on his diamonds, while she slowly backpeddled with every step he took forward.

"What up? You all right?" she asked Self when her ass backed into a store window and she was ten feet away from her girlfriends.

Self revealed his platinum and diamond-toothed smile. "No doubt, boo, now that I met you. Just tell me how I'ma stay alright with you by my side?" Self looked her up and down. "You look like you been waiting on a nigga like me yo' whole life?"

The woman smiled while looking at the diamonds in his ears. "You from New Yawk, right? I can tell by the way you talk."

Self nodded. "You wanna come up to the Big Apple wit' me, country girl? I wanna take you to meet my mama so I can show her my wife."

The woman blushed and her whole body went limp from flattery. "What's your name? Where you staying at?"

Self made sure she could see all the diamonds in his mouth when he smiled. "I can't tell you unless I know I ain't wasting my time." He picked up her hand, displaying his elevated pinkie ring. "I don't see no ring on this finger, so what up? You got a boy hollering at you?"

She blushed, then giggled again. "Naw, I ain't swinging wit' none a these broke-ass countrified niggas down here."

Self rubbed his hands together. "So you choosing this city boy right now or what?"

She laughed again. "You don't even know my name."

"I'ma call you something else anyway, 'cause you look like the prettiest Georgia peach I ever saw. So, come on, let me call you Peaches while I make you cum all night."

She blushed. "Well, what's your name then?"

"Well, you choosing me or what?" Self asked as he moved his lips an inch away from hers.

She looked over his shoulder at her girlfriends who were partly looking at Kev and partly motioning for her to get with Self. She asked, "How long you staying?"

"How long you want me to stay? 'Cause if I'm in your arms tonight, I might never leave, my Peaches."

"I like that, but my real name is Joy." She looked back at her girlfriends. "Okay den, if I choose you, I at least got to know a nigga's name."

Self thought about the name he used on women outside of New York. "Master! My mama gave me that name, but we got a lifetime for me to explain that to you." Self looked at his watch and made sure she got a good look at the jewels in it. "My time is paper, Peaches I came to Atlanta to get some serious paper, so you choosing me or what? You got some kids, 'cause I want you to have all of mine."

Her jaw dropped from shock, and she dropped her keys. Self quickly picked them up.

"Master, huh? That's crazy." She didn't want to seem easy, but she couldn't help herself. She exhaled, then said, "Okay, Master, you chosen. So what we do now? I ain't got no kids. They get in the way of my work. I'm a dancer over at Magic City. You got a problem wit' that? They call me Lusty, but you can call me Peaches, you hear?"

Self remembered the keys. "Peaches, if I got a problem wit' you stripping, I'll just have to pay you not to. If anything, we just gonna be husband and wife hustling together." He waited for the impact of his indirect wedding proposal to hit her. "What you driving, Peaches, and where we staying at?"

She smiled and covered her mouth because she was blushing so hard. She raised her head, then said, "I drive a Ford Explorer. I stay over in Allen Temple with my girlfriend April over there. We got a place, but she don't be tripping. So what you driving?"

Baby girl, if I can afford it, it's the same as owning it. So, I'm driving whatever."

Joy was sure her prince in shining armor was standing right in front of her. She looked at the diamond necklace around Self's neck and asked, "So, Master, you ain't answer my question. What we do now?"

From over her shoulder, Self saw a small locksmith stand. He pulled her to him, kissed her on her salty neck, then said, "I see you keep looking at how I'm blinging. You like my chain?" She nodded so hard her head almost came off. Self fumbled through the six chains, unlatched the diamond necklace that he smacked a kid in a dice game for, and put it around her neck. He lied when he said, "That's fifty gee's right there. That's for you as long as you mine. You mine, right?" She studied the chain in her manicured hand. "Fo' sho, Master."

Self pulled out a fat coil of bills. He unrolled two hundred-dollar bills, gave it to Joy, then said, "Pick up something I'ma like so when you get off work, I can see you in it." Self looked over at the locksmith. "Now come on and make a copy of your house keys so Master can get in. Me and my man coming over before you go to work. After I handle my business, I might stop by and see you work if I got time."

Self put his arm around her shoulders. They walked by Kev and her girlfriends like husband and wife. When they stopped at the locksmith, Self made her make a copy of her car keys, too. He then sweet-talked her out of her wallet, telling her that he wanted to see the pictures she kept in it. When he got to her driver's license, he complimented her on her picture, then asked her to write down the address where she lived. Before the night was over, Self would have a new place to lay his head.

* * * * *

Back in New York, Manny and Rico sat inside the M3 social club. With the new house, new cars, and $300,000 sitting with Edeeks waiting to be wired to Panama, Manny wanted to distance himself from the game. He called Rico over to discuss the future of their lives.

"Hermano, some things have to change now," Manny said.

Rico was playing his Playstation 2 on the large screen TV when he asked, "Yo, bro, what you talking 'bout? Everything good…too good. We got a spot uptown, a spot downtown, and with that paper for Panama, we a'ight. How much you got ready to send to Papa?"

"Three hundred plus the one from Self and the cash from The Lower should get us up to a half a mill. But, some things gotta change."

Rico was busy killing soldiers on the screen when he asked, "We getting close to a mill worth a paper and you want to change shit up now? Nigga, you bugging."

"Laope, listen. Look at me." Manny grabbed the game controller. When Rico looked at him, he said, "I'm getting married, I think."

Rico went back to playing his game. "'Bout time you and Carmen make that move. That bitch is proper. I woulda been put some babies up in her."

Manny knew Rico wouldn't be able to understand his decision. "Hermano, not to Carmen."

"What?" Rico asked, while stopping and getting killed on the screen.

"Si, la Morena. Her name is Xia. Bro, she bought me a big-ass house. She wants to have my children. She's a good woman. I want you to be my bestman."

Rico was staring at his brother, not believing that Manny was ready to settle down. "So what you going to do with Carmen? If you don't want her, then let me have her." Rico laughed.

Manny laughed along with him. "I don't want this new life to stop. I just want to go back to Panama with my wife. I want to see Papa's face when he sees all the money. As for Carmen? Chucha man, she making us a lot of money. I'm gonna take care of her when she comes back, but right now, I want some distance, so tell me what to do."

Rico cut the TV off and turned to his brother. "Bro, I don't want to live in Panama. I got a new condo, a new car, all the money I can spend, and I ain't even twenty-five yet. I'm in this game fo' life. What your ass need to be doing is taking me to see the connect so I can handle my business. You started all this shit. Now let me do me and get us this paper. You old, Manny. Retire and let your little hermano handle this shit."

Manny rubbed his chin in thought. He was suspicious why Rico was making it so easy. "Si, I'll set up the meeting. I want you plugged in with the Cubans, just in case something was to ever happen to me."

Rico shot his brother a scornful look. "Listen, I got no problem wit' none a dat shit you talking, but I ain't tryin' hear dat 'just in case something happen' bullshit. You need to stop talking dat stupid shit fo'real. You only burnin' bread on yourself."

Recognizing Rico's uneasiness with talk of something happening to him, Manny downplayed his statement. "Okay...okay. I'm going to work on putting the meeting together. As a matter of fact, hold on."

Manny pulled out his cell phone and called Pedro. He explained that he wanted to introduce them to Rico. Since he was marrying someone they considered their daughter, he was more laid back. The videotape was the furthest thing from his mind. When Pedro agreed that he could come down to the restaurant immediately, Manny was overjoyed.

He closed his phone and said, "Come on. We go now."

Rico stood, brushed off his camouflage army fatigue pants,

straightened the wrinkles in his tee shirt, and made sure his boots were untied. He followed Manny out of the social club. When they were closing the steel shutters to the club, the new Escalade was parked right outside. Rico looked at his M3, then looked around for Manny's car. When he didn't see it, he asked, "Hermano, where's your car?"

Manny pulled out his car keys and pressed the button to unlock the door. He then hit the other button to start the engine. When he saw that Rico was excited over the truck, he handed him the keys and said, "You drive."

"Get...get the fuck outta here. Say word? That bitch bought you this? Yo, bro, she ain't got no sisters?" Rico asked, while getting in the driver's seat of the Cadillac.

By six o'clock, Manny walked inside the service entrance of the midtown restaurant with Rico in tow. Manny was getting flashbacks on how that same place led to the beginning of his riches.

"What you think you doin'? You come wit' strangers now?" the short brute questioned Manny with disdain when they walked in. His partner with the long ponytail stood closely behind him with his right hand tucked under his button-down shirt.

Instantly, Rico's nostrils flared. "Yo, what da fuck is dis?" he asked, annoyed.

Realizing the situation could easily get ugly if he didn't do something, Manny held up his hands. "Suave! Suave!" He pointed to Rico, then said to the brute, "No, it's okay. He's familia. Pedro knows he's coming. Go check it out."

Reluctantly, the brute told his partner in Spanish to go check Manny's story out. The tall Latino marched off towards the back. He returned a moment later trailing behind Pedro. When Pedro saw Manny and the young man who resembled him standing up front, he ordered, "They're okay. Let them in!"

Quickly, the brute stepped aside and allowed the brothers to pass. When they approached Pedro, Manny introduced Rico to him. "Senor Pedro, this is my brother Rico. The one I was telling you about."

Pedro nodded, then turned to Rico. "Ah, you're the young man I've been hearing so much about."

Rico smiled. "Como está usted?" He then extended his hand to Pedro. "It's nice to meet you."

Pedro accepted Rico's hand by grasping it with both of his hands. "I'm doing fine. The pleasure is all mines. Now come. Let's go sit and have a talk." Pedro escorted Rico and Manny to the office.

When the three men were settled, Pedro looked around the small room before resting his eyes on Rico. "Your hermano has asked permission for you to meet me. Normally, I would never agree to such a request. In these crazy times we live in, it's just not a good practice."

Pedro extended his hand in Manny's direction. "However, your brother has provided a number of favors for us. Manny has proven himself to be a man of loyalty, honor, and integrity. Now that he's getting married I can understand his hesitance. He has been dependable. I trust for your sake that you cut from the same cloth." Pedro stood up and walked from behind the desk. He momentarily studied Rico's demeanor to get a better feel of the youngster. Rico remained emotionless with his eyes glued on Pedro's every movement. Manny, on the other hand, was lost in his own thoughts. "Okay, Rico, you the man now. We can do business. Take my number from your brother. You and only you, okay? Remember, we're not interested in meeting any new people. Comprende?"

Without blinking an eye, Rico replied. "Si. I understand."

"Bueno! You no take anyone with you to pick up the product...ever! Don't have anyone waiting in a car for you. Chamaquito, we are a quiet family. We have survived a long time by staying under the radar. It's important that we remain that way. Just follow the rules, and we'll do business together for a long time, my friend."

Rico showed he was raised right when he said, "It's a pleasure to meet you, señor."

Pedro escorted them out to the alley, then asked, "When will I be expecting you?"

Rico did a quick tally of the two keys of heroin he would need soon for he and Rashid. "Soon...very soon."

Pedro was pleased with his response. The three men hugged and then shook hands. While Manny was walking away, Pedro said, "Manny, don't forget what I tell you over the phone. Your package from Cuba is coming any day."

Manny waved to Pedro during their exit.

When they got back to the truck, Manny said, "Okay, hermano, you got the job. Make sure everything is straight with M3, Carmen, and Rashid. Call me when you need the money picked up, and put some people around you so you never get caught with nothing on you."

Rico exhaled, then blurted out, "This nigga gonna tell me how to run a drug spot."

Manny said, "Si, hermano. Remember, I'm the one with the brains."

Rico pulled off laughing, while thinking he finally had the power. What Manny forgot was that power corrupts.

* * * * *

"Baby girl, I'm on my way," Self said to Joy, while he and Kev were on their way out of the Hilton.

"Okay, how long you gonna be? I got something nice to show you." Joy, who was officially named Peaches, asked.

Self laughed to himself. "Give me a minute, Peaches. I'll be right there."

While Self was at the check-in counter of the hotel paying his room fee for a whole week, he pulled out a small container that had four purple diamond-shaped pills in it. In his hand were two small complementary bottles of Hennessey. He handed Kev a pill before swallowing his, and then he washed them down with the alcohol. After paying the hotel bill, he and Kev headed for the parking garage.

Self and Kev sat in the Honda Accord waiting for Self to adjust the two .40 caliber automatic handguns in his waist. For what he intended on doing, he needed to know that his guns were tucked when he walked into Peaches' house. He lit up his weed and placed six condoms in his pocket. He turned to Kev, then said, "Come on."

Kev followed the directions he received from the hotel until he reached the residential projects of Allen Temple. When they saw Peaches' Ford Explorer parked outside of a rundown house, they pulled the Honda Accord in right behind it. They double-checked the address. When they saw it was the same as the numbers on the paper, it was time to put the game plan in motion.

Self stepped out of the car to the amazement of a few heads that were hanging out. Kev popped the trunk and removed their luggage. Without locking the car, the two bopped up the cement walkway until they reached the front door. Self pulled out his key and opened up the door to the amazement of all the nosey onlookers. As far as they were concerned, Self and Kev had to be family to the two strippers who felt they were too good for them.

The door opened, and Peaches' jet-black girlfriend, with a gap in her teeth and a body that couldn't make too much money as a stripper, looked up in surprise. She was wearing a pair of low-cut shorts and a tee shirt that stopped at her belly button. She saw Kev, got up from the couch, then said, "Oh, hey Black," before kissing him on his cheek. She turned to Self, then said, "Master. Joy, oh I mean Peaches is all up in her room getting pretty for you. I ain't never seen that girl carry on like that for *nobody*." While flirting, she said, "I sure want to know what you told her."

Self raised his eyebrows and then turned to Kev, remembering the name he gave the naive girl, and said, "Black, I'll check you in a few hours."

Self made his way through the house until he saw a closed bedroom door. Without knocking, he pushed the door open, and Peaches was in the mirror fixing her hair. Her bedroom was decorated with pink carpet, black curtains, and a pink lacquer bedroom set. Pink satin sheets were on the queen-sized bed. She had a simple TV and radio, but her closet was bursting with all sorts of clothes. While standing in shock, she was wearing a pink, silk teddy with fur around the top and a pair of matching panties. Self smiled when he saw her and wanted to see how far his plan was going.

He walked up to Peaches, but Self didn't look at her fat ass or her D-cup breasts. He threw his luggage on the bed and ordered, "Take care of that."

Peaches quickly placed the bags into her closet.

Self then took the rest of the coil of bills Matthew gave him and dropped them on the dresser. He placed the condoms, his cell phone, and everything in his pockets, and dropped it next to the money. Instantly, he opened one of her dresser drawers, pulled out all the panties, and placed it on top of the dresser like he lived there his whole life. When he started taking his shirt off, he expected to hear some form of protest, but Peaches said, "Let me take care that." She slid her belongings into another drawer, did a quick tally of how much the coil of bills came up to, and then turned to help Self with the rest of his clothes. Meanwhile, he was lighting the blunt in her bedroom.

When she saw the two weapons tucked in his waist, she said, "Damn, baby, you moving like that?"

Self passed her the weed. "Master came to get all the paper in ATL. You think I'm taking my wife to meet my moms and she ain't gonna be rich?"

Peaches smiled at his announcement, then stared at the blunt when she said, "I don't really smoke."

Bitch, either you get high or you don't, Self thought. Never underestimating a street-smart stripper, he needed to know just how much he had her mind locked. "Yeah? Well, smoke that." He sat on the bed and kicked his sneakers off. He unbuckled his belt while Peaches inhaled the smoke. On her exhale, she was coughing up a lung, but Self ignored her while placing his two guns by the pillows. When he started taking his pants off, Peaches was hesitating about taking another pull. Self motioned for her to take another drag, and she puffed on the brown stick again. By the time Self was butt-ass naked, Peaches was blurry eyed and smiling at him, pleased with the size of his black dick.

Self put on a lambskin condom and then a latex one. He didn't like using condoms, but for what he was about to do, he couldn't afford to cum, so he was sure the two condoms would do the job. Romance and foreplay was for Self's woman in New York. With Peaches, he laid her down in the bed, removed her panties, and then climbed on top of her. Slowly, he slid the head of his dick into her loose mound. When she tried to kiss him, he said, "Master don't do that." He pumped his tip until she got wet, and waited for his Viagra to kick in.

For ten minutes, Self moved his dick in circular motions. Peaches held his sweaty back and was as passive as ever. "Eeeeeeeeeee" she groaned out when she came. Self was happy that his plan was working. He immediately slammed every inch of his stiffness deep into her. "Uh…oh shit, you gonna kill me!" she yelled for mercy.

Self pumped deeper in long strokes. He took his time pulling in and out of Peaches. When she knew he was on the down stroke, she started yelling before the dick hit her pelvis. Again, she started cumming, and again, Self changed the pace. He pushed her legs back, and she said, "Oh no…oh no… please," but it was too late. Self had her legs on his shoulders, and he was digging a new hole. He rotated his dick so her clit could feel all the pleasure, then he did ten shallow strokes for every ten deep strokes. "Oooooooh," she moaned out when she came again. Sweat was dripping from her body. Self ripped the teddy off her body while he fucked her. He watched her eyes go back in her head when she moaned out, "Ahhhhhh." Peaches was having multiple orgasms. Self pulled out and she hollered, "Good God! Please, Master, please. Just give me a minute. I can't handle all that."

"You mine, right? Yes or no?" Self barked while catching his breath.

"Yeah…hell yeah. I just can't…"

"Bitch, handle this!" Self said, while turning her around and putting her on all fours with her head damn near between her legs as he entered her from behind. He had her head down and ass up while he did a quick thrust into her. Peaches cried out for help, begging Self to cum. When he finally did, she was into her sixth orgasm.

Self grabbed his two guns and walked out of the bedroom. He was heading for the bathroom when he heard something in the room next door. When he peeked through the opened door, Kev had his pants around his ankles, and April was getting her face fucked. When she saw Self standing in the door butt-ass naked with a stiff dick, she stopped sucking on Kev, looked at Self, then began blowing Kev faster, imagining it was Self she was doing.

Self walked to the yellow, carpet-filled bathroom and was glad Kev came through with his part of the deal. When he took his piss and headed back to the bedroom, Peaches was snoring. Her legs were wide open, her arms were out on each side of her body, and drool was draining from her mouth. The other part of Self's plans was done. He took his time going through her cell phone, checking all incoming and outgoing calls. He then searched her room and closets. In the inside pocket of a coat, he found $6,000. He left it there, then searched some more. There was no sign of men's clothing or that Peaches had a man. That's when Self slipped on two more condoms.

"Oh...oh...oh, please no, Master." Peaches cried out with tears forming in her eyes when Self forced his way into her dry patch. "Let me suck it or something. My pussy is worn out, baby. Damn, you ain't had enough?" she asked Self, who was on his knees in the bed with a stiff dick in his hand.

"What type a game you running? You trying to get in my pockets or you want to be mine?" Self barked.

Her face turned passive when she said, "Baby, I ain't never had no dick like that. I ain't trying to let you go nowhere, but I'm sore. I need some ice in there or something." She looked at his stiffness, then said, "Let's do something else, but please just give my pussy a break." And that's what Self did. He snatched a jar of hair grease off her nightstand, slapped it on his stiff dick, and maneuvered himself down her dirt road.

"Ugggg!" Peaches cried out when Self had his entire dick deep in her tight ass. He started thrusting in and out of her, and she bawled out, "You ripping me in half! You ripping me in half."

When Self eased up a little, her cries turned into moans of pleasure. By the time Self was on his third pair of condoms, Peaches had fourteen orgasms. Her ass was throbbing, her pussy was swollen, and her jaw was sore from sucking him. As for Self, he had scratches on his back, rug burns on his knees, passion marks all over his chest, and a stripper that would do ANYTHING for him from that day on.

* * * * *

Manny was inspired by the decorations in his and Xia's new home. Since his package was arriving from Cuba, he had to get the last of his things out of his apartment in Brooklyn. Early in the morning, he removed $20,000 from his stash and then drove over to his condo in Riverdale. He walked through the door and a small kitchen was facing him. To his right was a living room with a terrace, a small dining area, and down a hall were the bed and bathrooms. Manny closed the front door and headed for the secured parking lot.

He jumped into his Escalade and headed for Central Avenue in Hartsdale, a few miles from Riverdale. The long strip had stores of all kinds. Manny drove in and out of different parking lots, buying everything the small condo needed. Once the back of the Escalade was filled to capacity, he stopped by an appliance store and filled up the front seat with appliances. With his furniture and TV being delivered within the hour, Manny rushed back to the condo where he had to make several trips to unload his truck.

Three hours later, Manny and two Puerto Rican deliverymen from the furniture store were setting up his house, calling the cable company, and offering their sisters to marry Manny after they each received one-hundred-dollar tips. As soon as the men walked out of the condo, Manny's phone chirped. He answered, "Qué pasa?"

Rico was on the other line. In a voice filled with panic, he said, "Aye yo, check it. Streets watching, so follow me. You follow me?"

Manny understood his brother telling him in code that he didn't like talking over the phone. Manny said, "So come see me."

"Nah, this nigga Rashid bugging the fuck out," Rico said with a chuckle.

Manny sighed, knowing things were running too easy for too long. "Explicame."

Rico said, "Yo, I went to see your man, but he sent me up to another fishy spot, right? And instead of me making sure I was safe, Rah got it. Now he blowing me out the box. The whole Lower going to see him. Bro, he brought me two in the time it took me to make one. Now you got to get this shit up outta here. Then he did some ole crazy shit with Fee and made another one in three days. How the fuck is that possible?"

Manny was annoyed. He listened while Rico told him that he went to see Pedro and was sent to the fishmarket for the dope, but instead of Rico using it for his spot on Manhattan Avenue, he gave it to Rashid. Since the dope was good, Rashid made $200,000 in the time Rico made one. Now he was sitting on $300,000 that Manny had to come get, but Rashid and Fee-foe did something to stretch the dope and they made another $100,000 in three days. He shook his head thinking about Rico. "So you couldn't wait until you saw me?"

Rico exhaled what Manny figured to be weed smoke. "That ain't what I called you 'bout. This nigga Rah on some little Manny shit. He took the one without my permission. Took the shit and went to see some cat in Queens. Now I got six white M3's running around in The Lower, and them little niggas multiplied to twenty-one strong. They talking 'bout getting two more by the weekend. Rah taking this M3 shit to another level."

"So this couldn't wait? I see you for the things. I come see you at M3," Manny said.

Rico raised his voice. "This nigga got me buggin'. Nah, that ain't what I call you for. Rah just called me from down low. He said two Spanish dudes in suits stepped to him talkin' 'bout they want to see us. I know that's cause he flossing too hard."

Manny thought of the police and then asked, "Who?"

"We don't know. They asked for Manny and Rico Black. These niggas definitely did they homework. Bro, what you think? You know I got no problem with doing me!"

Manny thought about Rico making the front page in the newspapers. He knew Rico could handle the day-to-day selling of drugs, but he didn't have the patience or the temperament in dealing with the politics of it. Like he did his whole life, Rico was calling his big brother when he was in over his head. Manny said, "No. Suave. Might be somebody wanting something. Make a meeting uptown and we see what's up."

Rico paused. "Why put both of us out there? Let me handle this."

Manny was losing his temper. For Rico to be on the phone this long something was bothering him. When Manny was trying to get out of the game, it was calling him back in. Now he had to put his foot down. "Hermano, listen! We all we have, familia. I don't want to say no more."

Realizing that his brother wasn't going to change his position, Rico said, "Bien. I feel you, but I'm handling things when we get there."

Manny knew better. "Bueno, I can live with that."

Rico paused before asking, "Man, I been on this jack too long, but how you think I should handle this nigga Rah?"

Rico's losing focus already. He made us two hundred thousand dollars, Manny thought. "Let him have fun. If he gets out of hand, we can handle it."

Manny said what Rico wanted to hear. "Cool, I'ma get up with Rah and set that up. I'll holla at you later. Make sure you go get that. One."

Manny hung up the phone thinking about the conversation he and Rico just had. He was so close to reaching his goal of getting rich and leaving the game. He was still amazed that he made so much money in so little time, all thanks to Pantera. He could run away to Panama and live like a king forever, or he could take his position as the leader of the M3 organization. Now that they had the best heroin in New York, Rashid's crew grew to twenty, and the news he got over the phone meant Manny was responsible for the lives of over forty men.

He sat in his new condo, looked around, and then said, "Fuck it."

TEN

On the night Self slept with Peaches, she was up in the mirror trying to save the perm she sweated out. Self had his back propped up while watching television. His eyes went from the television to the icepack between Peaches' legs. She was trying her best to walk straight while she was getting dressed for work, but every step she took was painful.

"Damn, baby, I swear 'fore God you tried to kill me. I'm be all crazy trying to slide down dem poles tonight. You coming to watch me and April at the club tonight?"

Self smiled, thinking how Kev must have handled his business with April. "You know I want to see how my baby works that thing. I'll be there to support my girl wit'out a doubt."

Peaches leaned forward and kissed him on his neck. She was extra careful that she didn't get him aroused again. After tiptoeing around Self, she was leaving for the club, when he said, "Aye, hold on." Self got up and walked to his luggage. He pulled out two .380 Walter PPK's. He turned to Peaches who had her eyes glued to the weapons. "Take these wit' you to work. When I show up, just bring them to me." Peaches was staring at the guns when Self asked, "You scared?"

She cracked a smile. "Is they loaded?" Self nodded and she said, "I ain't scurred. They git to actin' a fool when they git crunk up in there, so you let me know what else you want me to do, Master. I'm down for whatever when it come to my man." Self smacked her on her ass, and she squealed, "Oh, don't do that. I'm still sore."

After adjusting the diamond necklace Self gave her, Peaches and April left for the club.

Kev and Self searched the whole house to make sure no men would be there demanding anything from the women. When their search came up empty of any other hustler's relics, they got dressed in all-black clothes. Kev's style of dressing looked like he lived in Georgia his whole life, and Self had New York written all over him.

They jumped into the Honda Accord and stopped off at Ruby Tuesday's for a meal. When the time came for them to pay the bill, Self requested four hundred dollars in singles. He planned on giving a better performance in the club than any of the strippers.

When they reached Magic City, the long Friday night line snaked around outside of the club. The men wanted to know who the fool in the old Honda was, but when Self stepped out and brightened the entrance with his jewelry, all the men looked to the ground. Self was wearing jewels that were worth more than they would ever see in their lives. A few men gestured in his direction, and he and Kev walked past the line like they were V.I.P.'s.

Once they entered the dim club filled with naked women, mirrors, and a fully stocked bar, Self zeroed in on two bar stools that were open. He walked with Kev behind him and sat at a distance so he could see the sea of males getting lap dances and sailing crumpled bills at the naked women that were clinging to poles by the bar.

When the bartender walked up behind him, Self spun around on his seat, passed the woman a fifty-dollar bill, and said, "Ginger ale in a champagne glass. Keep it coming all night and I got another fifty for you."

The woman's grin appeared instantly and Self showed his platinum teeth as a reply.

The club was packed beyond capacity. Half of the men were lusting off the women, and the other half had their backs to the stage while they were talking about Self. Kev was busy talking country while giving job interviews to all the men who were so impressed with Self that they were sure Kev and Self could supply them with whatever drugs they wanted. Kev was bombarded with beeper, house phone, cell phones, and a few baby mama's numbers, without the fake hustlers questioning if he was a federal agent or not. Kev heard a few names of the major hustlers all over the Atlanta area. He was even warned about the Red-Dog drug task force.

Naked girls danced, and Self heard DJ Kool Ade yell over the sound system, "Big balla, she the one y'all came to see. That don't work for free. So, I present to you, Lusty."

All eyes went to the H-shaped stage and the gold poles when Peaches came out wearing high heels and a shiny bikini. From where Self stood, her oily ass looked twice its size. All the men in the spot went bananas when a Lil' Jon tune pumped through the system.

"No doubt, baby girl!" Self yelled, while he walked through the crowd to the stage. He walked up to the edge and threw coils of crumpled bills at Peaches. Instantly, a few of the local ballas didn't want to be shown up in their hometown. So, they started throwing coils of singles, too.

Self held the champagne glass to toast Peaches, and she stripped and did her floorwork while bouncing her sore pussy at Self s face. The more singles he pushed into the garterbelt on her leg, the more the local cats wanted to get her attention. Self motioned with his eyes that she should show them some attention and she did for a moment. The only person Peaches wanted to please was her man Master. Picking up on her actions, Self threw all the singles he had at her and walked back to the bar.

Peaches sped up her performance while having the best Saturday night of tips she ever had. By the time she was totally naked with a handful of green in her hands, the crowd of hardworking men didn't want her to leave, but she left anyway.

Self returned to the bar and found all eyes were no longer on him. The same fake hustlers that were trying to get Kev's attention were flocking around a damn near obese man. He was country all the way, carrying around a replica of a heavyweight boxing world championship belt. His jewelry was filled with ice, and he sat along the wall in the leather booths of the VIP section drinking Moet.

At the other end of the rectangular room, a skinny, dark-skinned man with a mouth full of gold teeth and a perm was checking his cell phone while strippers and men from the club tried to get his attention. He had bottles of Grey Goose and Hennessy at his table for his entourage of six.

Based on his observation, Self wondered if the fat man was Boss Hog. He nudged Kev to be on point, and Kev signaled that he was way ahead of Self. Just then, Peaches walked up wearing only a wet wife-beater shirt. Her round, black nipples peeked out of the tank top and her naked sculptured ass distracted all the customers so much that they didn't see the brown paper bag in her hand. She leaned over like she was whispering to Self as she placed the bag of guns in his lap. Self spun his chair around, then asked for champagne for the dancer and ginger ale for himself. While facing the bartender, he eased the guns out and used the bar to block the men in the club from seeing him put the weapons in his front pockets.

When everything was secure, Self whispered to Peaches, "Dance for me."

In front of the audience of onlookers, Peaches put her ass on Self and did a lap dance that was the envy of everyone in the club. When she spun around and started grinding against his dick, Self noticed the fat man looking his way.

He whispered into Peaches' ear, "Don't look now, but who's the fat kid over there?"

Peaches was a pro. She moved her body like a wave in the ocean, took a peek, and then whispered, "That's Boss Hog. He got dem boys over in College Park, Washington Road, and Commercial Ave moving that rock and 'cain for him. He got a baby mama over on Mechanicville that used to dance. He bought her an Audi a few days ago, I heard. He doing his thang. Come in here spending a lot a paper." Peaches continued grinding. Without Self asking, she looked over to the

Tha Twinz

permed, skinny man with the gold teeth, then said, "That's Peanut. He
stay by Cleveland Ave. He getting his rock from Boss Hog, but he
don't like him. Dem boys by the Bluff, Cascade Pines and Hollywood
Road move his stuff." Peaches was rubbing her sore pussy on Self's
stiffness and was caught up in the moment before she seductively
whimpered, "These bitches be yapping all day 'bout dem fools and
how much money they making." Peaches leaned over to Self's neck,
dug her nails into his shirt and whispered, "Eeeeeee, I'm cumming,
Master. What you doing to me?"

Self played it off like he was whispering in her ear while she came.
When she was done and opened her eyes, he said, "Take the Honda
home. The car keys is gonna be under the mat. I got some things to do.
Go take all these boys' paper. I'll see you later."

When Self tried to spin around on the bar, Peaches squeezed his
shirt and didn't let him move. She looked him in the eyes and said,
"You gonna be my baby daddy, you hear me? I'ma be a little late
tonight. I got to buy a shitload of KY jelly. I want some more tonight."

Self smiled for the crowd that was waiting to hand Peaches their
money. When Peaches wobbled away to give another lap dance, Self
ordered a bottle of Moet to be delivered to Boss Hog. When the
waitress delivered the bottle, she pointed to Self. He held his glass so
the canary yellow diamond on his pinkie that he "borrowed" from a
Harlem rapper shined. Boss Hog cracked a big grin and then lifted his
glass at Self.

Self leaned over to Kev. "Get the gatts out the car and meet me by
Peaches' truck. Leave the keys under the front mat."

Kev disappeared. Self paid his tab, left the fifty-dollar tip like he
promised, and stumbled out the club like he was drunk. He wanted to
know if any local robbers would try him and interrupt his plans, so the
drunken act was bait. The worst thing he could do was go rob
somebody and have to kill another would-be robber. That would be
unnecessary bodies with no cash at the end of the day.

* * * * *

Self stepped out into the cool night and no one followed. When he
looked out into the parking lot, Kev was hidden at the back of the Ford
Explorer. He waved Self over while scanning the other cars. To his
surprise, he saw a few other New York plates, but then he found what
he was looking for. A black SL500 Benz with vanity plates that read
"Boss" was parked a few spaces from the Ford. *This clown,* Self
thought when he read the plates. He jumped into the passenger side of
the Ford, and Kev jumped into the driver's side.

136

"Pull away from this clown," Self ordered. He didn't want to give away that he and Boss Hog were going to end up in the same place at the same time.

An hour and a half later, Boss Hog and his entourage were stumbling out of the club. Behind him was a group of fake hustlers begging to get put on. Kev and Self ducked a little lower in their seats. To the surprise of Self and Kev, Boss Hog sat in his Benz alone, and his entourage jumped into a Land Cruiser and a pick-up truck. When they all drove away, Self and Kev was in for another surprise. Boss Hog made a left at the light on Forsyth Street, while his crew made a right. Self couldn't believe his luck.

Boss Hog rode through Camp Creek Parkway and then over to Cleveland Avenue. While Self and Kev trailed four car paces behind him, they followed his taillights until he stopped behind an Audi TT at a home in Mechanicville Houses. When his car stopped, Self made Kev stop and back out of the projects. They slipped on their black gloves and black doo-rag headscarfs. Self took off all his jewelry, stuffed it into Peaches' glovebox, and locked it. He then climbed into the back of the truck and removed the tire iron. They got out of the car and jogged through the projects.

When they caught up with Boss Hog, he was struggling to turn the lights in his car off. It took him another five minutes to get out of the car. The alcohol had impaired his senses. When his 300-pound frame started wobbling towards his front door with the key in his hand, Self eased up behind him with the silence of a shadow. As soon as Boss Hog stepped into the house and slurred out, "Peggy, get up," Self used all his force to strike a blow with the tire iron behind his right ear.

Boss Hog's fat body poured to the floor while Self was trying to hold his collar to quiet the crash, but it was useless. Due to his weight and the force of gravity, the cotton shirt on Boss Hog's back ripped away. Kev immediately dashed in like a pro and tiptoed over Self struggling with Boss Hog. He closed the door quietly while making sure no one saw what he and Self just did. Confident that the coast was clear, he looked around the dark house and realized he was in the middle of the living room. He bent down and took the car keys out of Boss Hog's hand. He looked at Self and gestured that he knew what to do.

Kev walked into the kitchen and returned with a black skillet in his hand. Self inspected the skillet, then gave his approval. Self drew his guns and checked every room in the small house. When they made their way to one bedroom, a baby was sleeping in its crib. Kev closed the room door while Self covered him. They crept to another door that was slightly cracked. When Kev peaked in, he pulled his head back and put both of his hands together by his ear, indicating that someone was inside sleeping. Slowly, they eased the door open. Sleeping wild across the bed was a skinny woman with extra large breasts. Her head was wrapped with a scarf, and she was wearing a long nightgown.

Self walked around to one side of the bed, while Kev was on the other side. They only had a few seconds to do this right. While Kev held the skillet, Self tucked the guns in his waist. He then gestured to Kev, and they both counted to three. When Self reached three, he reached his hands to the sleeping woman's scarf. He snatched it off her head and then stuffed it into her mouth, waking her up. He then grabbed the nightgown by the collar and ripped it off, and then ripped off her panties. By the time she was awake and realized what she saw in the darkness, her body was raising up.

Bang! The skillet crunched against her nose and front two teeth. As soon as she was awake, she was quickly put back to sleep with blood leaking from her face.

Kev dropped the skillet and went to work ripping out phone, cable, and extension cords.

Self looked all around the room until he found what he was looking for. He snatched the item he needed along with a pillowcase and moved quickly to Boss Hog. When he reached the immaculate living room, Boss Hog was laying on his stomach the way Self left him. Between the blow that Self gave him and the alcohol Boss Hog drank, Self had a few moments to set up. He took off all of Boss Hog's jewels and clothes, then ripped the wires from the lamps and tied his swollen feet and hands.

Kev was coming into the living room with the naked skinny woman tied and gagged over his shoulders. He laid her down next to her man and then ran back into the kitchen. A few seconds later, he returned with a can of roach spray, a glass of water, and another extension cord.

Once Boss Hog and his woman were lying side by side naked, Self stood over him and smacked his face viciously. Seconds later, the impact of the violent blow against Boss Hog's face woke him right up. When his blurred vision cleared and his eyes adjusted to the darkness, he saw two men standing over him with calm looks on their faces. When he turned his head and saw his baby mama naked, his eyes bulged out of his head. Instantly, fear registered in his eyes, as his mind raced desperately trying to comprehend the predicament he was in.

"What tha fuck, man!" Boss Hog muffled out through the pillowcase that was in his mouth.

"Shut the fuck up, nigga!" Self whispered, while leaning in closer to Boss Hog. "Listen up, 'cause I'm only gonna say it once. If I don't get the answer I want, I'm gonna start burnin' your fat ass up in here." Quickly, Kev poured the water into the clothes iron Self took from the bedroom. He held the hot iron while the steam floated from it. Self looked into Boss Hog's eyes and caught when he recognized Self from the strip club. Self held the iron inches away from Boss Hog's face. "I'm a take the pillowcase out your mouth. You got one time to fuck it up."

With eyes the size of fifty-cent pieces, Boss Hog frantically asked, "What y'all want, man?"

"Where's the money at?" Self questioned.

Boss Hog licked his lips. "Aye, man... I ain't got no money, man. Take the cars out front and my jewelry, man. That's enough for you to get paid, man."

Self smirked, then handed the iron back to Kev and said, "Wake dat bitch up."

With a devilish grin, Kev flipped Boss Hog's girl over and held her face down. He placed the hot iron on her ass cheeks until he made the red impression on her pale skin. Instantly, her eyes popped open and she cried out a muffled yell. Kev used the roach spray to spray her eyes so she couldn't identify them later. The smell and sound of flesh sizzling consumed the room. Boss Hog's girl was shaking and weeping uncontrollably.

Self said, "Now I'm gonna ask you one more time. Where's the fuckin' money?"

Boss Hog didn't understand the severity of the situation until it was on his face. He looked Self in the face, then said, "Shit, man, I done told you I ain't got no paper, fool. Y'all might as well do what y'all gotta do."

Self stuck the pillowcase in his mouth, sat on his chest, and then sat the hot iron on Boss Hog's nipple. When Boss Hog's skin started sizzling, Self put all his weight on the iron. When he lifted the iron, Boss Hog was crying. He held the iron by Boss Hog's balls, and the man screamed out in fright.

Kev removed the pillowcase, and Boss Hog cried, "Okay, man...okay." Through tears and sobs, he whimpered, "Okay, man, I'll tell you where it's at. Just please don't hurt me no more, man. Please don't kill me." Self was moving the iron towards Boss Hog's balls, when he yelled, "Aye, man, it's behind the washing machine, man. Move the wall out and you got all the cash, man."

Kev rushed to the kitchen. He moved the washing machine, and low and behold, a small string was tied to a trap door made out of sheetrock. When Kev moved the door, the cash was piled up the wall in Ziploc bags between the wooded beams. He immediately grabbed a Hefty trash bag and loaded the cash into it.

When he returned to the living room, he said, "It looks short to me."

Self looked over to Boss Hog and then at his girl who was squirming in pain. Self had seen this a hundred times before. He ripped the scarf from her mouth and she cried out. Self leaned over, then whispered, "This muthafucka was gonna watch you get hurt over some paper. I'ma hurt you bad, real bad over him."

"Aye, Peggy, keep your mouth closed, hoe!" Boss Hog barked.

Self applied the iron to Boss Hog's cheek, then back to Peggy's leg. They both screamed out in pain while their skin bubbled up and oozed with puss.

"Motherfucka, you gonna let them kill me?" Peggy cried out.

"Shut your mouth!" Boss Hog cried out.

Self said, "Fuck it. Go get the baby."

"Noooooo!" Peggy tried to scream out when she heard someone headed to the bedroom.

Self put his lips to her ear. "This shit is short. Your man holding out on me. Now you can't see, but I'ma 'bout to put this hot-ass iron on your daughter's face. I'ma leave it there till she fucked up fo' life. Now let's make a deal. You ain't gonna see this fat bastard again. I'ma leave you some paper fo' yourself plus the cars. Tell me what he ain't, or I'm putting the iron down on your daughter."

Boss Hog heard the whispering and pleaded, "Peggy, don't say shit!"

Self let the steam mist touch Peggy's face. Then he said, "Pass me the baby..."

"No...no...no, fuck that!" she screamed. She turned her face in the direction of Boss Hog's moans and asked, "Victor, you gonna let them hurt me and your baby for some fuckin' drug money?"

"Bitch, don't tell them shit! They gonna kill us anyway!" Boss Hog cried out.

"Fuck it. Burn the baby!" Self barked to Kev.

"It's in the floor of the closet in the baby's room," Peggy burst out. "Plus his mama in Stone Mountain got that 'caine down in tha basement. It's across from the water heater. The safe in the corner. The combo is 5-24-37. She lives alone. The keys to her crib is on his key ring. Please don't hurt my baby. Y'all can kill him, fuck me, or even kill me, but please...please, don't hurt my baby."

Self turned to Kev, giving him the okay. He jetted out, heading for the baby's room.

Once Kev retrieved all the money from the room, they were going to have to take a trip. Kev returned, dropped the money in the garbage bag, then said to Peggy, "Whose name them cars in?"

"My mama and auntie," she quickly responded.

Kev pulled her hands free. He placed her baby in them and then turned to Self. "It ain't short no more. We gotta go get his mama."

"Ah shit, man. Don't do that. I got a white boy y'all can go get. I know where Peanut live. He ballin'. I know where his mama stay at and where all his folks at, dawg. Aye, come on, man. Listen, man, listen. I just got a new connect, man. He gave me a load of good shit, man. I can set his ass up sweet for y'all to get some mo'."

Self turned the iron off. He asked Peggy, "Where your car keys at?"

Through her whimpers, she said, "In the bedroom. Take whatever you want."

Self put his lips back to her ear. "Listen. I know you. I see you every day. You can't see me, but this is what you gonna do. I'ma take your man, and he ain't coming back. Your car gonna be up at Cumberland Mall. Go get it in the morning. Sell the Benz, and I'ma leave you a little something for yo'self. This is our little secret."

"Oh...okay...okay. Bet." Peggy liked the sound of her new arrangement.

"You trifling bitch! You over there bargaining, bitch?" Boss Hog screamed out when he heard Peggy agree to something with eagerness.

Quickly, Self stomped Boss Hog's face, then barked, "Get your fat ass up."

Kev rushed out to the Audi and opened the doors. Self felt the weight of the trash bag and knew they came off with more than they went for. He dipped his hands in the bag, pulled out a stack of bills, and threw them into Peggy's lap. In her blindness, she reached around until she found the stack. When she felt that the robber kept his word, she knew she wasn't going to die and would be a lot better off without Boss Hog. Peggy smiled knowing exactly what outfit she was going to buy so she could attract her next baby's daddy.

Self and Kev helped Boss Hog out of the house that he was never returning to. They used the darkness to hide their presence. Kev drove while Self and Boss Hog rode in the back. To Boss Hog's head was Self's .380 caliber weapon.

The three drove until Boss Hog directed them to Stone Mountain. When they reached the suburban home of Boss Hog's mother, Self used the keys to let himself in the house. Kev told his captive to open wide while he was sticking Self's other gun in Boss Hog's mouth.

By the time Self was down in the basement and opening the safe, he heard, "Victor, is that you? You bringing Mama some more money, baby?"

Self continued to empty the safe of the six bricks of powder that were inside. He peeked over his shoulder at a woman that couldn't have been more than ten years older than him.

When the woman got right behind him, she said, "Oh shit, you ain't Victor..."

Self quickly spun from the kneeling position with his back to her and put every bit of power into his blow. He heard the woman's jaw pop and her fall to the floor. He didn't know if she had company, so he took his time in the darkness and let himself out the house.

The following morning, a small section in the *Atlanta Journal Constitution* read: *Victor Andre a/k/a Boss Hog, an alleged Atlanta drug dealer, was found bound and dead in Mozley Park. He was badly mutilated and had one bullet hole in each eye. The police have no leads, but believe the homicide was drug related. When family members were questioned, they said they hadn't heard from the deceased in weeks.*

Kev and Self handled their business and then called Carmen. The cash they took from Boss Hog equaled $260,000. Self gave Carmen $200,000 and kept $60,000 to pay for the expenses of the venture he had in his head.

* * * * *

Self went to Matthew's girlfriend's house in the wee hours of the morning. He called Manny when he arrived. After the sixth ring, a groggy Manny answered his phone.

"Yo, Slick. Self handled what you sent Self to do. Self gave your girl two hunned as a token of Self's appreciation. A lot of gravy was left over with another six of them same thangs you sent down. Self gonna stay in the dirty with his little man to protect your interest. Tell Self to get back to the apple and Self ghost. If not, just call me dirty-dirty."

It took a minute for Manny to figure out what the hell Self was talking about. When he put it all together, he thought of Self's loyalty, then said, "Whatever you wanna do, Carmen will do. I need you back in July, bien?"

"One!" was all Self had to say before he ended the call.

Carmen loaded her carry on bag with the cash and caught a flight to work. A few hours later, the plane landed in Newark, New Jersey. From the airport, she called Manny and told him that she was on her way, thinking he was in Brooklyn. Quickly, Manny jumped up from the bed he shared with Xia so he could get to Brooklyn. He wanted to be there when Carmen got the surprise of her life.

When Carmen arrived in Brooklyn, she was entering the building when Manny pulled up. "Carmen esperaté," he yelled before she entered the building.

"Whose car is that?" Carmen asked when she saw the Escalade.

"Don't worry. I wanna show you something," Manny said.

When they reached Manny's floor, she handed him the bag of cash, then asked, "What you up to, papi?"

"Shhh!" Manny whispered, while covering her eyes with his hands.

"Okay, papi, you want to fuck me like that? Okay." Carmen giggled.

"Esperaté loca. I got a little surprise for you," Manny said calmly and then guided her inside the apartment and towards the kitchen area. When they walked into the kitchen, Manny stopped and asked, "You ready?"

"Yeah, papi, move your hands! Unless you like it better this way!"

Playfully, Manny shot back, "You sure you ready?"

"Yeah. Stop playing," Carmen shouted at him in annoyance.

Manny moved his hand, then stepped back a few feet. Carmen opened her eyes and couldn't believe what she was seeing. Standing directly in front of her was her mother, father, and little sister.

"Surprise!" Manny yelled.

"Mamá! Papá! Margarita, dio mío. How did you get here? Dios mío!" Carmen shouted in her state of excitement. Tears welled up in her eyes and fell down her cheeks.

After everyone finished hugging, crying, and kissing, Carmen's mother said, "Oh child, you friend Manny is such a saint. He pay for we to come from Cuba to Miami.. and he send people to git us from Miami. They bring us to Nueva York. We have everything. We live here now. Ask Manny."

"And he give us money to live. No rent," her father added.

Carmen turned back to look at Manny. He was standing close to the door smiling, when she said, "Muchas gracias, Negro." She was still crying when she ran into his arms. Carmen knew from that moment on there would never be a limit to what she would do for Manny Black.

Manny watched as Carmen was lost with her family. He couldn't stop thinking of the day he would be returning to his parents as a proud man. The money in his hands was going to guarantee that. When the time was right, Edeeks would be wiring the money down to a bank in Panama, and the other half was going to arrive in cash.

When Carmen looked up, she walked over to Manny, kissed him, and then held his jaw. "Nobody, Manny, nobody loves me like you. I will do anything for you."

Manny reached into the bag amd removed a $10,000 stack of cash. "Here. Take them shopping for their clothes. Make sure they have what they need. I already gave them pocket money."

She kissed Manny again. "Self is loco. He send more money than we expect, and he has six kilos of powder. Where he get that, papi?"

"The least you know the better. I have to go. Enjoy your family, and do what Self tells you to do. Later," Manny said after kissing her again.

Manny walked out of the apartment after Carmen and her whole family thanked him over and over. He jumped into his Escalade, picked up the phone, and called Edeeks so he could handle the money and get Carmen's father a job at the scrap metal shop.

* * * * *

Later that night, Rico and Manny were at the M3 lounge with their M3's parked outside.

"Rico, qué pasa?" Manny asked.

"It's on tonight, brother. I picked up some MP5's and a whole gang a shit. I'm gonna see what these chico's rapping about."

"What do they want? Who are they, hermano?"

Before Rico could answer his question, Manny heard the exhaust of a few cars pulling up right outside their door. He grabbed one of his brother's weapons and peeked out the door waiting for the drama to come. When he looked outside, Rashid was pointing his soldiers to stand across the street. Ten white M3's and one black one were lined up behind each other. A large group of black and Spanish men were all dressed in black hoodies, jeans, and black boots.

"What's this? Where all these M3's come from?" Manny asked.

Rico laughed. "Yo, these all your workers. I told you Rashid went shopping wit' all that money we making down there."

"Damn, bro. This is no good," Manny mumbled, while looking out at the group of men. He thought about the impression he was going to make at the meeting, then asked, "Hermano, why don't me, you, and Rashid go to the meeting?"

Rico's face screwed up as he angrily responded, "Man! We don't know these dudes. I ain't takin' no chances. We goin' ten cars deep!"

Rashid busted into the club and asked, "What the deal?"

"Manny's ass talking 'bout just us goin' to meet these cats," Rico said.

Rashid looked at Manny and his eyes quickly looked to the ground. He didn't forget who the boss was.

Manny looked at the two youngsters that were responsible for his riches. "Okay then, we go. Everybody."

Rico hopped up and said, "Money, Murder, and Mayhem, baby." He turned to Rashid, then asked, "I hope all your soldiers got heat on dem."

Rashid's smile appeared. "They stay ready, son, or they wouldn't be down with M3, baby."

The three strapped up, with Manny hesitating to go to the meeting. He wanted to take a step back from crime, but now he was the leader of a gun-toting crew. "Where this meeting at?" he asked, trying to put all odds in his favor.

"One fifty first on Riverside. Right by the park in the dark in case they come wit' some funny style shit," Rico announced.

Manny sighed. "Okay, let's go."

No one had seen Rico that happy in the whole time they were around him. When they stepped outside, Rico announced, "Holla at the general," to the youngsters. They held the presence of "Big Manny" in awe. They reached over each other to shake Manny's hand, and deep down, he liked their obedience. The praise the young men gave Manny told him that he was worthy of being praised, and that his influence over them would guarantee that he would never be broke again.

The M3 mob of thirteen cars and thirty-nine dangerous young men drove to Riverside Drive on 151st Street. To the amazement of everyone in the Harlem streets, the M3 Boyz were together. Something was about to go down.

* * * * *

At exactly 9:30 p.m., the M3 Boyz were scattered all over the park based on Rico's strategy. Suddenly, four black Lincoln stretch limos pulled up on the drug-infested block of 151st Street. When the back door of the limousines opened, two men dressed in black suits exited each car with their hands tucked inside of their suit jackets. When they believed the coast was clear, four other men stepped out of the limos, clearly showing Rico and his crew that those were the men they came to see.

One by one, with the cover of their two henchmen beside them, each man walked down the steep stairs connected to Riverside Drive. They were headed to the remote Riverbank State Park beside the Westside highway. Rico watched the disgruntled looking men and ordered members of his team to follow. Luckily, Rico positioned some of the M3 Boyz with Mac 11's and Calico machineguns in the park just in case things got ugly. Rico wasn't there to play any games with the men from The Lower. When the group of men reached the bottom of the stairs, ten members of the M3 Boyz suddenly surrounded them.

To Rico's surprise, the headmen stood as calm as ever, confident in the work their henchmen could do. From the distance, he could tell a bit of tension was building between his crew and the other men, so he and Manny started walking faster. Rashid, Stan, and their top soldiers from The Lower walked slowly in the direction of the group of men.

145

Instead of handling business in a calm manner, Rico pulled out his machine gun and cocked it when he was a few paces from the men. "We here! What up? What y'all want?" he said as his announcement.

A dark-skinned man with a tapered beard and a scar that ran from his right eye to his jawbone briefly studied Manny. He looked around at the mob of men and saw someone familiar. "Manny, my name is Miguel." He pointed to the other men the bodyguards were protecting. "These are my associates, Antonio, Felix, and Juan. We represent La Familia Mariel from Cuba. We needed to see you based on your business practices."

"What the fuck is this bullshit? Get to the point," an immature Rico barked.

"Esperate, hermano." Manny calmly ordered Rico to wait for the man. He didn't want to show any disunity in front of the strangers, but diplomacy had never been one of Rico's strong points.

The man with the scar nodded to Manny with respect. "I empathize with your hunger. Como se dice? Ah yes, I respect your hustle, but you must understand…there are rules. We are here to avoid bloodshed." He waved his hands to the M3 group. "Our conflict isn't over your heroin on Avenue B and 4th Street. That was fine. We can all eat, but now you're spreading your operation to Avenue A and Avenue D. Now *that* is not acceptable! The bigger you get, the more noticeable you become. Well, now we notice you."

While Miguel talked, Manny's mind raced to remember why La Familia Mariel sounded so familiar. Then it came to him. In 1980, Fidel Castro kicked all of the ruthless criminals out of Cuba. He sent them to the United States where they were placed into refugee camps in Miami, Florida. Eventually, many of them were granted political asylum and dispersed across the country and blended into other Latin communities. Since they were exiled from the port of Mariel in Cuba, they were known as the Marielitos. The U.S Government turned their backs on the ambitious men, and with nothing to eat, the men found a way for them and their families. As legend has it, many of the Marielitos would later come together to form an infamous underworld family known as La Familia Mariel. During the 80's, the Cuban family climbed to power by the use of violence and through the distribution of cocaine and heroin. Their operation was secured by networking with other ethnic groups, like the Colombians and Nigerians. Since then, they have been a powerful force to reckon with.

Manny's thoughts were interrupted when Rico sarcastically shot back, "Okay! You noticing us.. and? What dat 'pose to mean? We gotta stop what we doin'? You gotta be kiddin' me. Y'all ain't got no fuckin' monopoly on the city."

Miguel smiled with patience. "I would also like to know who's supplying you. Your product has a very close resemblance to product that we are missing."

"Dis nigga must be deaf! Chico, I don't give a fuck 'bout what you want. Y'all ain't got no fuckin' monopoly on the city," Rico blasted.

The other bosses couldn't believe what they heard. A young punk had the balls to speak to them like that. Out of anger, the Cuban they called Juan started twitching his mouth. In a gruff voice, he said, "Goddamnit! How dare you speak to us like that? You people are nobodies! I can have you and everyone out here dead before the end of the night! We try to be nice by coming here tonight, but that's done with. These are the rules from now on. You and your people can't operate on our turf! If any of you are found moving anything, there will be a price to pay. You got tha..."

Rico lifted his gun and aimed it at Juan's face. Instantly, the bodyguards of the Cubans pulled their guns out, and the M3 Boyz pulled their weapons out just as quickly and placed them at the back of the bodyguards' heads. When Rico saw that he wasn't dead already, he quickly squeezed the trigger. The hot slug shot out of his pistol and tore into Juan's warm flesh, shattering every bone in his face. He was dead before he hit the ground. Out of the thin air, Rashid's top gunners appeared, holding automatic machine guns in their hands. The Cubans quickly realized they were outnumbered. They stood their ground in fear, but and made no sudden moves.

Manny looked around, sizing up the situation. With the two guns in his hands, he said, "Listen, if you want a bloodbath, then let's get it over with. I promise you, none of you will make it out of here alive. If you don't want that, then I advise you to put away your pistols right now!"

While looking around nervously and then down at his dead comrade, the boss Antonio, who had a patch over his left eye, said, "This is not what we had in mind when we agreed to this sitdown. We are civilized people. We tried to resolve the problem we have, and this is how you negotiate?"

Rico knew the police weren't too far away and wanted to end the situation. He waited until his troops calmed down before he looked to the Cubans and said, "Okay, Chico, I hope I got everybody's attention. Nobody gonna shit on the M3 Boyz and live to talk about it...nobody! We already on the Lower Eastside, and we ain't goin' nowhere. Money, Murder, and Mayhem, muthafucka'! Now beat your feet and git up outta here."

The man with the patch over his eyes smiled at Rico, who reminded him of himself many moons ago. With a nod, he gave his useless bodyguards the order to leave. They picked up their dead comrade and quickly made their way back to the limos.

Manny knew what was coming, but knew it wasn't the time or place to reprimand his brother. Rico was drunk with power. Instead of them all standing around looking at each other, the M3 Boyz gave each other pounds and went their separate ways.

ELEVEN

Three days after Boss Hog caught a bad one, Self was lying in the bed watching television and waiting on Peaches. She was in love and never had a man who didn't make an issue from her stripping, or a man that made love to her the way Self did. She finally felt safe. When they made love, she felt like they were made for each other. She loved the way Self was a man's man, one who took care of home and wouldn't hesitate to put his foot in her ass if she got out of line. She was sure he was her soul mate. Ever since that first night of sex, Peaches was willing to do anything Self said, as long as he never left her house.

Peaches brought Self's breakfast of turkey bacon, cheese eggs, and grits. She placed the serving tray over Self's lap and tried to kiss him again for the twentieth time since she met him.

"Bitch, didn't Master tell you I don't kiss?" Self barked.

Peaches sucked air through her teeth, then seductively said, "That's right, Master. I'm yo' bitch." She licked his neck. "Baby, I love when you call me that."

It was hard for Self to keep from smiling. He knew a woman that was whipped when he saw one. As far as he was concerned, Peaches was naïve, but a good woman at heart. He thought about Kev lying up in the next room with April and figured it was time he put his other plan in motion. He held Peaches by the jaw with a firm grip and said, "What you willing to do for Master?"

Peaches smiled. "You taking me to meet your mama? Or you was running game, 'cause I been wanting to be somebody's wife for as long as I can 'member." Self nodded as she carried on. "Whatever you want me to do."

Self asked, "Yeah?"

Peaches slid her fine, caramel body off the sheets. "What you want me to do?"

"Bring me a hanger out the closet. Put it on the stove, and I'ma burn a M on the back of your ass." Peaches looked at Self, and her eyes started tearing. "See, you bullshittin'."

Immediately, Peaches stood and went to the closet. She pulled a wire hanger off the rack and headed to the kitchen. Self figured she was calling his bluff until she came back in the room and said, "I got the iron on the stove. I know that shit gonna hurt, and what about me going to work?"

Self channel surfed while ignoring her. He stood and threw the remote control on the bed. "Come on." He walked her out of the bedroom and down to the kitchen. When they stood in front of the stove, he ordered, "Take your clothes off." Peaches started crying while removing the bottom half of her sexy pajamas. She removed her thongs and then bent her fat ass over while the tears rolled down her cheeks. Self smiled, then cut the stove off. He looked at the red iron turning black, then thought that either Peaches was out of her goddamn mind or she was one of those women who loved a man with all she had. He opened his palm and smacked her ass hard. Peaches bawled out in pain, then Self said, "Get up."

She stood, turned around to face him, and asked, "What?"

Self looked her in the face. "You know how they say that 'death do us part' shit at a wedding?" Peaches motioned that she understood. "If you try to play Master, I'ma kill you. You feel me?"

"I know you ain't no joke. I would never clown on you," Peaches pleaded.

"Sit down," Self ordered. She sat at the round kitchen table. He wanted to unleash his plan, but there were a few more things he needed to secure. He said, "Today you gonna take me to meet your mama. You got credit, or you wasting that paper from twirking?"

"I got a few dollars saved up. I wanted to get a house, but if you need it, you can have it."

This shit gonna be easier than I thought, Self thought, thanking God for the love of a southern woman, He thought of the $60,000 he had at the Hilton and said, "This what you gonna do. We moving. You gotta get a crib up in a highrise where they got parking and security. Then you get some furniture. I need a driver's license wit' the new address on it. You switch some plates over and change your car. When bitches start to asking where you get all that from, you don't say shit. If you play me, I'ma have to pay your mama a visit."

Peaches kissed all over Self's neck and chest with gratitude. "I knew you was the one. I knew it. I saw it in your eyes at the mall. I love you, Master. Dang, I love you."

She grabbed his hand and took him to the bedroom. Peaches dropped to her knees and took Self into her mouth. She sucked on his dick like she knew it was the last dick she was ever going to give head to. Self looked down at the top of her head knowing he was going to change her life, and then end it if needed.

Later that day, Peaches dressed like a sophisticated lady and took Self with her to meet her mother. Self introduced himself, and Peaches introduced him as her fiancée. She explained to her mother what she wanted to do, and her mother called Peaches' uncle. He had connections with realtors who could get Peaches a condo in the upscale community of Buckhead if she could produce $20,000 for the closing fee. Her mother was putting the condo in her name, and Self didn't want anything to do with the transaction besides getting the keys to *his* new house.

For two weeks, Peaches and Self drove the M3 around Atlanta. She took him to all the places where he could buy groceries, clothes, and whatever personal effects he needed. He took her to pick out furniture for their condo that had a terrace, parking garage, spa, and a maid's service that did laundry. After everything was settled with the condo, Self put Georgia plates on the M3 and traded in Peaches' Ford Explorer for a silver Yukon Denali. Loyalty didn't come cheap, so he took her shopping for a new wardrobe and spent $5,000 for a cheap ring so she could believe they were really getting married.

Once his home was in order, Self moved Kev in with April. She saw the changes that happened with Peaches and foolishly thought her day was coming. All the firearms were moved into that house, and the drugs they stole from Boss Hog were safe with Matthew. It was Kev's job to act like Carmen's lieutenant, introduce himself to local dealers, and be seen all over Atlanta. Carmen and Kev got along well once he acknowledged that she was the boss. Thereafter, Self hatched his plan to Kev, explained that they had to get ready for Manny's wedding, but in the meantime, they had to lock ATL down. Once Kev agreed, Self leased him a white M3 and put a couple of Boss Hog's platinum chains around Kev's neck. He then secured a room and safe at Matthew's girl's house, and the black woman that worked with Carmen was overjoyed about the cash they were making.

While Self stayed in his new house most of the time, Matthew was moving the coke a mile a minute. Kev collected $400,000 in cash from the kilos of cocaine that Boss Hog had and packaged it for Carmen. She put two of her flight attendant girlfriends down with the operation, and they started transporting the kilos from New York to Atlanta for a thousand dollars off of each kilo they carried. On average, they made three trips a week transporting two kilos apiece. The operation was running smoothly. Self was staying low profile and was only going to get involved in case another Boss Hog surfaced, and Matthew was happier than he had ever been in his life.

* * * * *

A week after all the drama, Edeeks sat with Manny at the M3 social club. Manny was sitting with his head in both of his hands. He said, "E, Rico is out of control. The man came to talk…to work things out like a man, but Rico never gave him a chance. Now I'm looking over my shoulder and shit. This crew, this La Familia Mariel, I know they no joke, hermano. We wide open, and I don't know where to go find these guys. Shit is hot. They got the policia all uptown looking for us, and they didn't even find a body."

Edeeks knew things had to unfold this way in the game. He didn't want to leave his business partners stranded or watch them make mistakes. "Damn! Here it is you about to get married, and you trying to chill and raise a family. It's a bad time for war, but I've been thinking...there is only one way to take some of the heat off. We have to get more involved with the community and start doing some work in the neighborhoods."

"Gringo, you listening to me? I'm losing my mind over here, and you talking some community shit. What are you talking about, E?" Manny asked in a tone filled with irritation.

"Just listen to me for a moment. I'm thinking we can establish a not-for profit organization that gives back to the kids. We can set up a center in one of the local schools and start some afternoon programs for the kids. Do shit the way the old timers used to do it. Do dirt, but take care of the community while we at it. We can give out scholarships. Oh, and you know how every year the neighborhoods have block parties?"

Manny sunk his head in both of his hands. "Yeah."

Edeeks was overenthused. "Well, we can even fund the block parties for the blocks M3 is on. Do shit that corporate America do when they mess up."

Manny looked at Edeeks like he was crazy. "How much money you ready to send to Panama?"

"Two-fifty cash, two-fifty to be wired, and with the other thing from the south, about one-fifty spread out in the company."

Manny wanted to run away to Panama and not tell anyone, but then Xia and Rico labeling him a coward came to mind. In the social club was another $100,000. Rashid was bragging about taking the Lower Eastside over, and Rico started a new heroin spot on Lexington 116th Street. M3 was expanding when Manny wanted the ride to stop. He asked Edeeks, "You ever think the day was coming when we was tired of counting money?"

Edeeks smiled. "I *told you,* bro. How this whole thing gonna play out is important, but the Jew is happy. He wants to clean all the paper you can send him."

Manny nodded and calculated the cash he had in his condo, along with all his operations. Then he said, "Gringo, I'm almost a millionaire, can you believe it? I'm scared, E." He thought in silence for a minute. "Está bien, set it up. Do something for the kids. Whatever you need do it. Make the cash safe so the company is worth something and we can never lose that dinero."

"Sounds like a plan to me. Just give me a minute to check into a few things and I'll get back to you." Edeeks turned to walk out of the club and then stopped short. "By the way, I'm quitting my job in a few months. I want to open a lending institution. I'm being careful, but we partners, okay?"

Manny thought about making more money and became nauseous. He clutched his weapon, nodded at Edeeks, and filled himself with worry. "Bien, do what you gotta do."

The week after the meeting with Manny, Edeeks started doing his homework to put their plans into motion. He was able to secure a meeting with an old acquaintance who worked for the Reverend Al Sharpton at the National Action Network in Harlem. The same acquaintance owed Edeeks money and had a serious gambling habit. After explaining in detail what he and his associates were looking to establish, a favor was called and Edeeks was plugged into *"The Gang of Four"* who controlled the politics of Harlem.

Any major economical developing moves that involved rebuilding the community, which big corporations opened up in the neighborhood, were either orchestrated or approved by the most powerful and influential blacks in New York City. Congressman Charlie Rangel, former Mayor David Dinkins, former Borough President Percy Sutton, and Basil Paterson were dubbed The Gang of Four.

Based on Edeeks' impressive repertoire, The Gang of Four approved of the young accountant/entrepreneur's move in Harlem. Through their connections and under their tutelage, Edeeks planned to establish The Latin Avenue, a non-profit organization geared towards empowering kids ages 10-18. He wanted the center to hold photography workshops, sponsor basketball tournaments, give free bus rides, award scholarships, fund block parties, and donate backpacks equipped with school supplies at the beginning of the school year. The Latin Avenue was a concept that was on its way to being embraced by the community.

* * * * *

Days after meeting with the M3 Boyz, La Familia Mariel from Cuba met at their leader Miguel's home in Long Island. These men were professionals. They didn't move without getting the approval of all bosses. The situation with the M3 Boyz was over a few hundred thousand, and some of their men were dying over unrelated matters. So, they had to remain focused. They were not going to risk the millions they made in the drug trade over a bunch of young punks, but Juan's death had to be avenged.

Miguel was sitting at the head of his dining room table with the two other bosses. They had to vote on who was going to be the fourth boss in La Familia Mariel and how they were going to handle the ever-expanding organization known as the M3 Boyz.

The boss named Antonio argued, "In the old days, something like that would have never happened. If something is not done immediately, then control will forever be lost. Give them an inch and they take ten feet. Let's cut off the feet immediately!"

Miguel could clearly see that most of his partners had fear pouring from them. The same type of fear they created upon masses to establish themselves decades ago. Now that fear was being used against them, and it was working.

The best thing to do is plan and then hit back, Miguel thought to himself. The more he thought about his plan, the better the plan came together. Miguel had one advantage that none of the men in the room had; his niece was an Assistant District Attorney in New York. He looked to his comrades and said, "Gentlemen, please excuse me."

Miguel left the living room and went into his bedroom to call his niece, Maria Flores. After several rings, the other line connected. "Maria, this is your uncle Miguel. Listen, I have a little situation with some punks that call themselves the M3 Boyz. They're responsible for the death of one of my closest friends, Juan Santos. He was killed earlier tonight around nine-thirty inside the Riverbank State Park up in Harlem, but you won't find a body. Two brothers by the name of Manuel and Ricardo Black run the crew. The younger brother Rico pulled the trigger. They're running a heroin operation in Harlem on 117th Street and Manhattan Avenue. They're also running one down on the Lower East Side on Avenue B and 4th Street. Their product is stamped M3. I need you to find out what you can so you can work on getting rid of them."

After a slight pause, the voice that was missing a Cuban accent said, "Tío, with all due respect, with all the power you have at your disposal, why do you need my help? I'm only an ADA."

Miguel exploded. "Maria, don't ever forget that if it wasn't for me, and *me alone*, you wouldn't have that job! I made it possible for you to go to college! My money! Not your parents! I'm not concerned with how you're going to do it, only that it is done! I'll be in touch soon." With that, he disconnected the line.

With his phone call out of the way, Miguel walked back into the living room, cleared his throat, and said, "Okay, I was speaking to an associate of mine. What it's going to boil down to is to find the weakness of the M3 Boyz and use it against them. Right now, I think we all can at least agree on one thing, and that is they are very strong and well organized. But *not* stronger than us."

Everyone in the room was in agreement.

The boss named Felix said, "You know how I feel about having outsiders dealing with *our* problems. Many of you have your methods, and I have mine. Let me be the first to tell you that I do not waste money on security. Those fools who were supposed to be securing us at the M3 meeting are now being cremated. I had enough! As we speak, I have my men working on dismantling the M3 crew."

"You acted alone without consulting the group?" Miguel asked, ready to reprimand him for doing what he just finished doing on the phone.

Felix, the youngest of the crew, turned to the bosses. "Juan was mi hermano. La Familia Mariel. You can handle this the old way, but not me. They shed blood, so now I make theirs run in the streets where they sell their Manteca. If that's not good enough, I say we send for our wolves from Miami and then set them loose. It's important that we send a message to these chamaquitos. Juan was like a brother to all of us. We cannot allow his death to go unanswered. I don't know about you, but I can't live with that!"

After hearing what Felix had to say, Antonio adjusted the patch over his eye before responding. "I understand how you feel, but we have to be smart about this. We come too far to be reckless now. These are not like the old days when you can just leave a trail of dead bodies laying in the streets. It will eventually come back and destroy your house. It's important we handle these M3 Boyz from both ends. We can't stand an all-out war in the streets with a bunch of young gung-ho cowboys. Let's not forget, our hands are already filled trying to find the other faceless enemy who has declared war on our family."

A smile spread across Miguel's face as he piggybacked off of what Antonio had said. He hoped to convince Felix that things would be okay. "Felix, I agree. We should pull our resources together. Once the head is dead, the body falls. Then we can crush, kill, and destroy the rest of the M3 Boyz to take back what is rightfully ours." Miguel's gaze fell on Felix. "Amigo, I'm asking you right now, give me a little time to work some magic. I'll get the results that we want."

Felix looked around at everyone in the room and then focused his icy eyes on both Miguel and Antonio. "Okay," he began, "we will try things how you have suggested. If they don't work out, then we do it my way. Comprende?"

Both men nodded and shook hands. Felix stood, letting the older members know that the meeting was over. All the bosses of La Familia Mariel quickly exited Miguel's house focusing on bringing death to the M3 Boyz.

* * * * *

Tha Twinz

After the bosses of La Familia Mariel met, Rashid's lieutenant Stan was exiting a tenement apartment on 140th Street between 7th and 8th Avenues. One half of his cornrows were undone while the dark mami he had sexed all night kissed him at the door. After locking lips with the young girl, Stan walked down the hall and headed for the steps. After reaching the lower landing, he lit a cigarette. When he looked up, a dark man wearing a two-piece suit looked as if he was waiting for Stan. Stan walked down the next flight of stairs with his hand clutched around his .357 revolver. When he reached the next landing, a twin to the first man stood with gloves on his hands. The huge window that led to the courtyard of the building was wide open. The man stood with a tee shirt under a blue suit. When Stan was a few feet in front of him, he smiled. Instantly, Stan felt that he was sandwiched. He reached for his weapon, but the two men had the drop on him.

The first man punched Stan in the center of his chest. All the nicotine in his lungs tried to escape and folded him with coughing. Stan's .357 fell to the floor instantly. The other man looked out the huge fourth floor window, then grabbed Stan by the back of his neck and threw him out. Stan floated for a quick second and then the hard concrete sped up to his face. He didn't yell, scream, or make a sound until he hit the ground.

Pleased with the damage they created, the two Cubans took the steps as quickly as they could. When they reached the courtyard, Stan was groaning with pain. The first man Stan saw in the hallway walked from the courtyard, while the other dragged him by his collar across the slimy concrete. The smell of two-day-old garbage woke Stan. He saw that he was being dumped into a cargo van, and then everything went black.

A few hours later, Stan awoke to his nakedness. He felt something extra tight around his wrist. When his vision cleared, his hands were bound in rope and were being pulled over a rusty beam in an abandoned apartment. He tried to yell, but nothing was coming out. Everything moved in slow motion. The drug he was given allowed him to see what was going on, but he couldn't do anything about it.

Just when he saw the two Cuban men smiling, he saw the gleam of shiny objects in both of their hands. With one man on each side of him, he watched as their hands moved in rapid movements to his body and came out bloody. That's when it hit him, he was being stabbed, and he could feel the pain. As the minutes shot by, the pain started to wake him out of his haze, and that's when he felt it. The Cuban moved his hand in a sawing motion between Stan's legs. When the man held Stan's penis and testicles in front of his face, he blacked out and went where it was safe. The last thing Stan remembered was choking on something being shoved into his mouth.

The next day, a dope-fiend discovered Stan in an abandoned building on Avenue A. Instead of calling the police like most citizens would have done, the fiend went to a M3 soldier trying to get a bag for the information. When the Puerto Rican fiend took Fee-Foe up to the apartment, a newly sober Fee-foe found Stan tied up and stabbed more than two hundred times with his manhood hanging from his mouth. The fiend received his bag, and Fee-foe picked up the phone to call Rashid. Since Rashid wasn't built to see his number-two man dead, Fee-foe called the police and Rashid called Rico.

Four hours later, all M3 spots were closed while Rico, Rashid, and their solders had a meeting at the social club. When word hit the street about Stan, a few of the M3 soldiers quit on the spot, and Rashid was going to teach them that there was no quitting on him. In the meantime, Rico was on his cell phone setting up another meeting with someone he felt was going to help solve their problems.

Even though the M3 Boyz were moving two to three kilos of heroin a week between all three spots, Rico wasn't completely satisfied. He only wanted what all other men wanted when they received power. He wanted more money and more power, and he was willing to start stepping on toes in order to get it. When his phone folded up, he pulled a chunk of cash out of the safe and then told all thirty-three men in the room, "Come on. Let's go."

The whole M3 clan followed behind Rico's new black Lincoln Navigator until they reached 155th Street and Amsterdam Avenue. He turned, then drove inside the Trinity cemetery. When all the men exited their cars, it looked like a group of young people gathering to pay their last respects to a body that was being lowered into the ground. Although it took him a second to think about it, the cemetery was the perfect spot to hold the meeting. Rico exited his truck carrying a black knapsack. An hour later, the sound of a car horn filled him with anxiety. When he looked up, he was happy to know the man that he was waiting on was able to accommodate him so soon.

Across the street from the cemetery, a tall white boy with a shaggy beard and long dirty blonde hair was dressed in a pair of jeans, a tee shirt, and blazer. He was exiting an all-black pick-up truck. From the distance, he waved at Rico, removed two large duffel bags from the cab, and walked in the direction of the M3 crew.

"Hey, baby, good looking. Everything there?" Rico asked the man, while handing him the bag.

The shaggy-haired redneck looked around. It was obvious to everybody that he wasn't comfortable in that neck of the woods. "Shit yeah," is all he said after handing over the two duffel bags.

After Rico peeked inside the duffel bag to check out the merchandise, the white boy left just as quickly, carrying the knapsack full of cash.

Turning halfway around so he could face his whole team, Rico looked at everyone. "Yo, I brought y'all together 'cause the name of our clique is Money, Murder, and Mayhem. Y'all heard about Stan, right? Well, we been getting the money, but we been fallin' short on the murder and mayhem part. So, I got something for y'all." Rico bent down and opened both duffel bags. When his hands came out, he started distributing black plastic bags filled with MP5 machine guns. When most of his team had a weapon in their hands, he said, "It's time for a takeover. We takin' The Lower over! I want all of y'all to start putting pressure on all the dopespots. Find out who runnin' them. If niggas don't want to move out the way, then we rollin' over them. Tomorrow is a new day for the M3 Boyz. We gonna bury our man Stan in style. Then we gonna take it to the next level and get a bigger piece of the pie, naah mean?"

The M3 members stood in awe. Like kids with new toys, they examined their lethal weapons. Each man quickly looked around the Harlem streets to see if they were being watched. While some tucked the guns, others removed them from the black plastic. Rico handed out boxes of bullets.

When each driver for every M3 that was parked in the cemetery was armed, Rashid said, "A'ight, we meet up later." He turned to his men from The Lower and said, "All my people open the spots up. If you see anybody that *act* like they want it, lay they ass down! When y'all working, every time you make a gee, give it to the lieutenant. I need every dollar; war is expensive. Now get up outta here and I'll catch you later."

The men tripped over each other as they rushed to leave the cemetery. Some wanted to leave so they could test their new weapons, while others wanted to put the weapons away instead of standing around in broad daylight.

Rashid and Rico were the only two standing in the cemetery. Each was in their own thoughts while they watched dirt get thrown on a casket of someone they didn't know. The idea of Rico wanting to do a takeover and take people spots didn't sit well with Rashid. He knew such a move would bring a bunch of unnecessary beef for the M3 Boyz. *It was bad enough we got drama with the Cubans*, Rashid thought as he turned to Rico and questioned, "Daddy-O, what Manny got to say about all this?"

Rico's forehead wrinkled as he angrily shot back, "Fuck Manny! I run this! All he do is count paper. He marrying some bitch when he should be marrying the game." Instantly feeling Rashid's indecisiveness, Rico pulled back the slide to his machine gun and barked, "Nigga, you with me or what?"

"Whoa! What tha fuck ya doin', Daddy-O?" exclaimed Rashid, keeping his eyes glued to the MP5 in Rico's hand. "Come on, homie. We go too far back for this. You know I'm wit' ya," murmured Rashid, knowing Rico just made a detrimental move.

Rico was powerstruck. He put the gun in a duffel bag, then said, "I been meaning to tell you how you been wildin'. You getting crazy like we running two different spots. I run M3, Rah! Don't forget that shit. Don't forget who moved us to the dope game and got you paid, Rah. You my man, but don't let this paper have you thinking twisted."

Rashid couldn't believe the words he heard. He always heard about teams having internal beefs after they got rich, but now he understood. Rico deserved to die for cocking a gun on him, so he said, "Daddy-O, you my man. I got your back. Don't sweat nothing. I'm your top soldier." Rashid thought about how he was the one who got the dope cut, set up the spots, and made all the soldiers for M3, when he said, "Yo, kid, let me go make you some money, boss. I'll catch you later."

Rico was staring at the workers close up the grave. Without looking at Rashid, he said, "Yeah, later. Just tell Fee-foe it's time for him to come back uptown. I heard he quit using that shit, driving around in a Benz and shit. You shoulda told me that."

Rashid knew what he had to do. He said, "No doubt, kid. I'ma go take care of that right now." Then he left Rico in the same cemetery he may eventually have to bury him in.

* * * * *

Manny laid in the Jacuzzi tub with bubbles while he watched the six o'clock news on the TV that was mounted on the wall above him. He really wasn't paying attention to the news; he was more interested in sorting his life out. He wanted out of the game, but felt obligated to finish what he started. He could sense his brother getting power hungry. Whenever Manny questioned Rico, he always gave a sarcastic remark. At first, he didn't care. He wanted to concentrate on the scrap metal business, the public relations Edeeks was working on, and keeping his hands clean. Then when he thought about the cash that was coming in and how one mistake could make the whole thing fall apart, he realized he had to keep a closer leash on Rico. Manny slapped the water in the tub and made up his mind right there that he was going back in the streets to settle things with the Cubans. He thought he could ask Pedro for help, or maybe Pedro knew the men from La Familia Mariel, but he didn't want to seem weak.

"Manny Black? What you doing handsome?" Xia's seductive voice interrupted Manny's thoughts.

He looked at her leaning against the door frame. "Thinking."

Xia had become a homebody. She didn't go out much since she bought the house, and whenever Manny was around her, she smothered him with love. All she wanted to do was plan for her wedding, workout so her body could look toned for her wedding dress, and have sex. For Manny, the sex became more of a routine than the passion filled with love that they had in the beginning.

She walked around to face Manny wearing her sheer nightgown with nothing underneath. She disrobed and took her time getting into the hot tub. When she floated her way towards her man, she playfully blocked his vision from the television, and Manny became annoyed. She kissed his neck, then his nipples, and said, "I'm ovulating today." Her soapy hands jerked Manny's dick under the water. Seductively, she said, "Get hard for Bonita. Give me some so I can have your baby."

Manny got hard instantly. Xia got in his head; she knew just the right words to stimulate her man. When Manny's dick was stiff in her hand, she straddled him and slid his stiffness into her warm hole, then slowly rode him while bobbing up and down. Every time she came down on his dick, water left the tub. Her big body splashed the suds around, but Xia didn't care. She wanted a family and as many children as she could afford, and to her estimate, that was at least ten.

Five minutes later, Manny whispered, "Ai Bonita, I'm cumming."

Xia rode him faster and then sunk all of her body weight down on him so that his cum could go deep into her womb. When his dick stopped jerking inside of her, she kissed him and said, "Thank you. When you get out of the tub, can I have some more please?"

Manny closed his eyes while his fiancée eased her way out of the water. When she was out of his sight, he quickly rinsed off with the intentions of getting out of the house before Xia fed and fucked him to death.

Manny quickly dressed and left the house while chewing on one of Xia's homemade biscuits. He jumped in his M3 dressed like he was going to do a robbery. Suddenly, there was a knock at his window. He held his heart and barked, "Coño! You scared the shit outta me."

Xia smirked. "Remember, I need to know who's going to be in the wedding. Tell them to call me so I can tell them when their tuxes can be altered."

Manny nodded, kissed Xia, and put his car in drive. When the garage opened, he shot out of Upstate New York and headed down Interstate 87 until he reached his social club on Columbus Avenue.

Rico was inside the office of the M3 lounge packaging coke, when Manny walked through the door. After lowering his new machine gun,

Rico sarcastically asked, "What you doin' here? Ain't no money here fo' you to count."

Manny looked at his little brother and realized that his hunch was right. He stared at his brother, and like Rico did his whole life, he broke Manny's reprimanding gaze. Manny walked on the other side of the desk. "Hermano, I'm the boss. That's why I'm here. You got a problem with that?"

"The boss, huh?" Rico said, mocking Manny.

Manny knew a showdown when he saw one. He intended on showing his brother who was stronger. "Si, el jefe numero uno! What the fuck is your problem? I come up in here and you got an attitude like I fucked you last night or something. You forgot I put you in charge, hermano? You getting too rich to follow orders now? Let me know. I'll do the work if it's getting too hard for you."

"Yeah, whatever, man," Rico said, while packaging the coke.

It was Manny's turn to do the mocking. He removed his accent from his voice and replied, "Yeah, whatever, bro. Like when you was broke moving that little coke a few months ago. I was the one killing putas to get that dope. I helped you step your game up. Don't forget who introduced you to mucho dinero."

Manny's words stung Rico hard. He never knew how Manny was getting the dope, and now that he just slipped and told him that he killed people to get them rich, it changed everything. Rico sighed in surrender. He put his head down and said, "Bro, you right! My bad. It's just that this shit got me bugging. The cash rollin' so fast, them Cubans killed Stan from The Lower, and the pressure to keep shit right got me buggin' out a little lately. Love is love."

"They killed Stan? When? Why didn't you tell me?" Manny asked in surprise.

Rico raised his voice. "First, you want out da game. Then, you want in. Then, you want to get married, and then, you back to being the boss? *You* got me bugging, bro. My words is getting motherfuckas kilt. They stuck his dick in his mouth, bro. Stabbed him like a hundred times. I'm tryin' to stack this paper, but I can't enjoy it, hermano. I'm looking over my shoulder, and I got like three hunned gees in my crib. That shit got me so parro I don't even want to go to my crib. I been sleeping here with mad work in dis bitch. Yo, hermano, man, this hustle game ain't easy."

Manny knew he was right. Rico was still the immature boy who would get reckless when the pressure was coming down. Now he had to show him why he was the boss. He said, "Suave, suave. You got to keep it together, hermano. Remember, we on the same team. I'm with you, not against you. When nobody is here, your blood got your back, hermano. Never forget that!"

Rico cracked a smile in relief. "Fo' sure, familia." He continued to pack the shopping bag until it was filled with six keys. He packed the remaining six kilos inside another shopping bag. When he was done, he asked, "So now what?"

"Nothing. We have to keep our eyes open for the Cubans. They know us. You should have killed the man if it was going to make us more money or improve business. Instead, you kill a man that is going to cost us money and make business slow. I tell you, hermano, you have to think before you speak, and think three times before you act. Emotions are for women, bro. A man has to think with his head all the time, not his heart or ego, man."

"Shit, man, I ain't doing shit right," Rico complained.

"No. Everything's good because of you, but now we have to fix this, and I don't know where to look for these Cubanos. I will do some homework. Right now, I came to catch up with Carmen. If things get crazy, we maybe go to Atlanta until it cools down."

Rico looked down at his watch. It read 8:15. "Yeah, that's who I'm waiting on now. I hope she hurry up and get her ass here soon. I wanna take care of business so I can bounce. A fella finally got some ass lined up tonight."

Manny chuckled. "Playboy, where she from? She got a sister?"

"Man, stop playin'. Who you tryin' to bullshit? You know you already got your hands filled wit' Carmen and your wifey. They got your ass all pussy-whipped and shit," Rico said jokingly.

Manny looked at the ridiculous expression on his brother's face and burst out laughing. Quickly, Rico joined in. When the laughter died down, Manny said, "Hermano, it's about time we take a trip back to Panama. You know it's been too long, but now that our money is right, we have to go home for Mamá and Papá. We can set up some businesses over there. This shit is not going to last forever. Now is the time to go and follow the plan."

Rico thought about what Manny said. He had to admit that his brother did make a lot of sense. "No doubt! I'm feelin' you, but when you plan on goin'?"

Manny's July 7th wedding date flashed in his head. "Me, you, and Xia can leave right after the wedding reception. That's where I want to go for my honeymoon. Take Xia to see Mamá. I know Mamá will not come to America, so we have to go see her and Papá."

Rico started having second thoughts. The control freak in him made him feel like the whole M3 organization would fall apart if he was gone for a day. "I got a lot to do, bro. You know them Cubans can't catch me slipping. You go 'head, and tell the fam I said what up."

Manny leaned on the desk and looked into his little brother's eyes. "Listen, hermano. Right now, I really want to go to Panama and never come back, but I know you won't stay."

"You damn right."

"Si, that's why you can't forget why we make the money. We make the money to go home when things get bad. Everybody that sells drugs goes down or dies, so you coming home to see Papá. It might be the last time we ever see them."

Rico nodded in agreement. "Yeah, I guess we could use a vacation. But, you know Papá. You gonna have mad explaining to do when he see all this paper."

Manny thought of his poor father and his dislike for blood money, and agreed that he would have to hatch a plan for his father to accept the cash.

Rico asked, "How long you plan on staying? You know I can't be gone too long. I still gotta stay on top of getting this money."

"Suave. Two weeks tops."

Suddenly, the buzzer for the front door rang twice. Both Manny and Rico looked over to the television. Rico changed the channel, and they saw Carmen standing on the other side of the steel-plated door wearing a summer suit with a mini-skirt. Rico quickly reached under the desk and buzzed her inside.

Carmen walked in smiling. She dropped two shopping bags by the desk like she did a great deed. Without missing a beat, she strolled over to Manny. "Hey, papi." She bent over and kissed him on the lips. "Negro, I missed you so much," she said, while balancing herself on her new designer heels. She then turned around with another smile and said, "Hi, Rico."

Rico looked at his watch again. "I thought your ass was gonna be here at eight o'clock? I gotta get up outta here."

Carmen apologetically said, "Rico, I've been running a little behind. I'm sorry. I should have called."

Each one of them was putting on a show for Manny, showing him that his dream of doing it big had really come true.

Rico said, "Yeah, yeah, whatever. How much cash you got wit' you?"

Carmen smiled at her man. "Self gave me two-eighty. He said he'll have the rest by the time I get back down."

Rico asked, "Yo, you took paper outta that for you and your girlfriends, right?"

"Si, they ready for the trip in the morning, too," Carmen replied.

"How's Self doing down there?" Manny asked with a chuckle.

Carmen beamed when she said, "Kev is really good. He knows what he's doing. I only see Self when it's time to get the money. Your woman is taking care of everything, papi."

Rico stood and interjected. "A'ight, a'ight, that's all good. Right now, I got twelve bricks for you to take them." He took the money off the desk and packed it inside of a black knapsack between his feet. When he was finished, his cell phone rang. He snatched the small Star Trek-looking gadget from off his waistband, then answered. "Talk about it!" A second later, he smiled and said, "Oh. Hey, boo, what's up, hooker?"

Manny rolled his eyes at Carmen over the way his little brother always felt like he had to impress him. Carmen smiled at her man, then said, "Papi, let me tell you, business esta muy bueno. Matthew bought his girlfriend one of them new 300 Lexus. Oh, it is hot. Last night, we drove all around hot-lanta in that bad boy. Can I have one?"

Manny laughed. "Oh yeah? How you plan to do that if you scared to drive?"

Carmen playfully punched him in the arm. "Papi, that's not funny. Stop laughing at me. Okay, you think I'm playing. I'm going to take some driving lessons."

Manny switched the conversation. "You like everything in ATL? How much you save for yourself now? How's your family?"

Carmen sat on Manny's lap and cupped her hand over his ear. "Ssss, I need some pinga, papi. The more we do business, the less we fuck. Come on. Let's go in the bathroom."

Manny smacked her on the ass. "Espérate, business first. Tell me!"

Carmen sighed. "Okay, everything good. Family is good. Mi madre ask for you all the time. She wants me to marry you. Papá likes the job you gave him." She kissed Manny with all of her tongue in his mouth, then said, "I have close to two hundred thousand, papi. Thanks to you, but I know that once you have that, I have it. You know Self; he on top of business. The more coca we bring is the more they want. Kev is doing real good, papi. You should give him a raise. He knows everybody. All the Negritoes think he da boss." Carmen eyes widened. "Oh yeah, papi, I hear you in somebody wedding. Who getting married, us?"

As Rico was ending his phone call, he overheard Carmen questioning Manny about his upcoming wedding. Manny glanced at him with his eyes pleading for help. Rico rushed to get his things together so he could leave. He looked at his brother and said, "This is your bullshit. You clean it up!"

Quickly, Manny's mind raced as he thought about how he would handle the situation. *Yo, just keep it real*, he thought. "Come here. Let me talk to you."

Carmen shifted in his lap.

Rico stopped both of them in their tracks. He saw what was about to go down, and he felt that Carmen should have been Manny's wife. So, he knew Manny's blood might fly. He said, "Yo, there go the package. Put the cash away. I'm outta here. I'll catch y'all later."

Manny was on his own. He made a mental note to remind Self to keep his mouth shut or to keep a closer watch over Kev.

Rico did the dash and slammed the door shut. Carmen and Manny were on the couch, when she asked, "It must be true. Is it true what I heard? Who getting married?"

Manny exhaled, then said, "Si, it's true. I'm getting married to the woman I told you about."

Carmen's eyes locked onto Manny's. She thought it was some kind of sick joke. When he didn't budge, her eyes filled with tears. Manny's words ripped her heart into pieces. Her lips started trembling when she asked, "Maricón, how can you do something like this to me? Ay dios mío. I don't believe you. You gonna marry some other bitch? You know I wanted to marry you, Negro!"

Manny's face held no emotion. "Oyeme, I told you before we not fucking up a good thing. The wedding is nothing personal. It's about business. I'm always going to check for you and make sure you alright...no matter what. You have to trust me."

A stream of tears rolled down Carmen's pecan face. She sat up straight. "I don't believe you. Cabrón! This is bullshit! I can't stand you, Manny!"

Without thinking twice, Manny smacked Carmen. "Watch yourself!" he barked. Carmen held her face in silence. She looked at Manny filled with rage. In his disappointment, he ran his hand up between her inner thighs until he felt her crotch. Before Carmen could protest, he snatched her panties and pulled them down.

"Fucking me won't solve a thing come mierda. Go home and fuck your wife!" Carmen scowled.

"You told me that you would do anything for me, right?" Manny questioned, while fumbling to lift her skirt up.

Carmen turned her head to the side while he pulled his dick out. When he tried to penetrate her with force, she said, "You hurting me!"

"Good, puta, maybe you'll learn some respect," Manny said, while pumping inside of her wetness.

"Oh, papi! Yes!" Carmen yelled, while her legs opened and her hands clawed at Manny's back. The more he pumped into her, the tighter her eyes closed and the more she tried to push him deeper into her tightness. "*Anything,* Negrito." Carmen moaned out. "I would do anything for you. Umm, why you doing me like this?"

"Cállate, bitch. Shut the fuck up!" Manny moaned, while he sunk himself deeper.

"Fuck you, maricón!" Carmen passionately yelled before kissing him. Manny pushed her legs back and she moaned out, "Ay...pinga! Fuck me, Manny! Fuck me, papi!"

"You my soldier, right? You with me? Tell me." Manny was grinding her deep.

"Yes! Yes! Oh...yes!" Carmen cried. "I'm cumming, papi. Oh, papi...papi...papi." She moved fast, creating sweat as her cum dripped out of her.

Quickly, Manny pulled out and stood over her. While his stiff dick was in her face, he said, "Okay, ahora es mejor for you to be my soldier. You do what I tell you to do," he said, while gasping for air. You stay by my side. I want you there at the wedding. I want you to represent for us. You always been my women first and my soldier second. Now be my soldier."

Carmen had both of her hands between her legs, when she asked, "How you gonna ask me to do something like that? I love you, Manny."

Manny lied and pleaded. "Just work with me. I'm telling you, it's business. I made you rich, and I have more for you to make. Nothing will change. Everything you need I will give you. I give you your madre and padre, right? Do it because you love me, mami."

In the mist of Carmen's confusion, her head started nodding to her own surprise. Then, her mouth betrayed her. "Okay, Negrito. Just don't forget who's numero uno."

Manny started taking the rest of Carmen's clothes off. He knew her weakness, and he wanted to seal the deal.

TWELVE

High atop the headquarters of the New York City Police Department in Manhattan, a group of men and one woman sat in a large windowless boardroom. The elderly Manhattan district attorney, Robert Morgenthau, addressed a special anti-crime task force.

The white-haired district attorney stood and announced, "Men, I have assembled you here because one of my bright ADA's has brought a menacing force to my attention." He turned to the only woman in the room and said, "Men, I present to you Maria Flores."

The Cuban gangster Miguel's niece Maria Flores stood. "Men, I have been granted your undivided attention because we have a new gang ruling the streets of Manhattan. They call themselves the M3 Boyz. These geniuses even have the BMW cars to help us identify them. I've had some men from the old Pressure Point task force do some research. The leaders are Manny and Rico Black. The brothers are of Panamanian descent. Rico has a rap sheet, assault one, but it was later dismissed. The victim ended up dead a year later, but nothing points directly to Rico. Gentlemen, these men have killed a man in Riverbank State Park, unleashing terror in our streets on the lower Eastside and in Harlem."

A huge muscular, baldheaded black man with an unlit cigar raised his hand, but didn't wait for permission to speak. "Excuse me, miss. Tell me what exactly do you want my men to do, and how long do you intend to hold us up? We have other cases to close."

Robert Morgenthau cleared his throat. "Detective Clarke, you will assist my staff for as long as it takes. I personally selected you because I want this over before it starts. Your unconventional methods are welcome here, just don't get indicted in the process. I am giving you men six months to complete this investigation and disband M3 as quickly as possible. No leaks to the press on what you are up to either." He turned to Maria and said, "Mrs. Flores, the floor is yours."

Maria Flores ran down the procedures that she wanted the task force to follow in collecting evidence. Detective Clarke wanted to head over to Manhattan Central Booking to see how many snitches from The Lower would come forward or be his confidential informant. He explained how he could trace the arrest of a junkie who was from The

Lower, offer the felon a get-out-of-jail card, and that junkie would supply all the initial information he needed. Maria liked the plan, and they agreed to meet in a week to see how much progress was done. She promised the task force and her boss that she had a reliable informant, as well, and guaranteed more information before the next meeting.

At the end of the meeting, Maria Flores looked like a promising star to the men in the room. She thanked them, kissed her boss's ass for awhile before he left, then grabbed her folders. While she was walking down the dim hallway towards the elevator banks, she pulled out her cell phone.

"Hola?" the voice on the other end answered after the fifth ring.

"Tío, the first phase is complete, but I will need your help immediately."

"Very good, very good. I see that education is finally paying off," Miguel said.

Maria cringed at the reminder of who she was obligated to, but the promotion she would receive after she put away Manny and Rico Black was worth the abuse. She said, "Si tió, but I need you to help me connect the dots. Get me addresses, how far these guys are distributing, and get me conspiracy and racketeering evidence, plus the homicides."

"It sounds like you want me to do your job," Miguel replied sarcastically.

Maria sighed. "Okay tió, I understand, but I am doing this for you."

"Smart girl. Very smart girl. Okay, I'll call you in a few days with more information. I will put somebody on them now."

Maria Flores ended her call, knowing her uncle would come through for her. Miguel hung up the phone, knowing that the two brothers would either die or get arrested.

* * * * *

"Okay, sign there. Yeah, okay, now sign here. Rico, you sign there," Edeeks stated while the three men were in Manny's Riverdale condo.

Edeeks needed the Black brothers to sign the necessary papers so their business would be in order by the time they came back from Panama. Rico was impatient while Manny sat at the kitchen table wearing slacks and a blazer. He was more pleased with handling the legitimate business, while Rico wasn't interested in anything dealing with paperwork. Rico lived for right now, while Manny was concerned with having a successful future.

"How much longer we got to wait for this bullshit?" Rico asked impatiently.

"How much longer you want to make sure you keep the money you and your brother make?" Edeeks asked.

"Here we go wit' this bullshit." Rico exhaled.

Manny looked at Edeeks, singling for him to let it go, but Edeeks wasn't having it. It had been too long that he pacified Rico for the sake of Manny.

Edeeks got up close to Rico and said, "Let me explain something to you. I told you from day one that you guys combined would make a lot of money. It's the American way to start from the bottom by killing, robbing, and then earning cash off the back of the poor to get rich. What separates those who keep money and those who spend money is proper planning. That's where I come in."

Rico looked Edeeks in the eye, hoping to finally be treated as an equal instead of Manny's little brother. "And pushing a muthafuckin' wig back is where I come in, so get the fuck outta my face."

Edeeks stepped in closer, creating a cornered thug. If Rico reached, moved too fast, or flinched the wrong way, he was going to learn a lesson in violence that the Bronx streets taught Edeeks.

Rico could smell the garlic on Edeeks' breath when he said, "I'm in your face 'cause I'm all you got. Your ass go to the hospital, Edeeks get you out. You go to jail, which you never have a problem working your way into, Edeeks will be there with the lawyer and bail money. If your ass got to be buried and shipped back to your mama, it's me that got to take care of that. So, do me a favor. Leave the thinking to me, sign what I need you to sign, and if I need somebody killed and won't do it myself, then and only then do I want to hear what the fuck you got to say."

"You let him talk to me like that?" Rico looked across the table, asking Manny to save him.

Manny squeezed his bottom lip with his fingers and blew out a whistle. "Enough. Too many years of you two doing the same bullshit. Rico respect Edeeks like you do me. He's family. Edeeks, Rico is a man now. Treat him like one. I got to get home and call Self up for the wedding. So, are we finished yet?"

Edeeks blew off some steam when he exhaled. "You guys have to realize that there are only two roads in this game…a quick death on the streets or a slow death in prison. You hit the ghetto lotto already, and if I didn't love you, I wouldn't care. "'Cause if you two die, all the money you killed for goes to me. As your brother, I advise you to pack up and leave the game right now. Manny, you getting married. I know I'm wasting my breath with Rico because you got that young fire in your blood, but, fellas, listen. You have a half a million dollars in cash ready to be wired to the Bank of Panama. You have an additional two hundred thousand in cash you taking with you. Plus, by my calculations, you have at least three hundred grand a piece in cash floating. You have the cars, the women, and the house, Manny. What else do you need? We have the scrap metal making a profit when we were hoping it would take a loss. It's all clean, and they can't get you on RICO because the initial investment was under ten thousand each and it was all clean. Guys, what the fuck else do you need me to tell you? The politics I'm setting up, this lending company? Man we can get millions and walk away right now, today."

Manny wanted to jump at Edeeks' offer, but he couldn't leave his brother in the middle of a war. He turned to Rico. "Hermano, what's up? We can walk away right now."

Rico stood and looked at Edeeks. "Money, Murder, and Mayhem. That's what got us paid. M3 for life. Y'all muthafucka's scared? Go buy a dog. Are we done yet?"

Edeeks surrendered, while Manny shrugged his shoulders at him and said that Rico would always be Rico.

Manny looked at his watch. "Hey, we got a wedding to plan, and I got to call Self. So, come on."

The three men stood. Edeeks convinced himself that everything would be okay, but he knew better. Manny hurried to close his place up, and he escorted Edeeks out before him and his brother headed for the parking lot.

* * * * *

Self was sitting on the living room couch with his feet in a basin of hot water watching a bootleg version of *Little Nicky* on his big screen. Below him was Peaches' mother giving him a pedicure. Since he was introduced to her family, Peaches' mother treated the man that changed her daughter's life like her own son. Self never had a mother in the true sense of the word. After leaving foster homes, group homes, and then kiddy jails called the DFY homes, he graduated to prison where he did five years with no family backing him. His girl in New York was stressing him over his absence, and the more time he spent with Peaches, he realized she was wife material.

Peaches was in the kitchen cooking barbecued chicken cutlets, red rice, blackeyed peas, turnip greens, cornbread, peach cobbler, and fresh-squeezed lemonade. To Self, she represented what every hustler would ever want. She was independent, made her own money, and worshipped the ground he walked on. Although she was tired from being out stripping all night, Self woke up to getting head almost every morning, breakfast in bed when he wanted it, and a warm meal every night. His clothes were always clean and washed like the house was. Peaches never argued or second-guessed his wishes. She just trusted in her man and did what he needed her to do. To top it off, she washed him, bought him clothes, and gave him enough sex that he didn't even think about leaving the house. Whatever he wanted, Peaches was one step ahead of him doing it before he had to ask. Self had to ask himself if he was getting pussy whipped, or if what he felt was love for the first time in his life. With Peaches and her mother, Self finally had a family, and it was working his mind overtime, questioning if he was getting soft or not.

Ten minutes into the movie, Self's phone rang. Peaches stopped what she was doing in the kitchen to bring him the phone that was just a few feet from him. When he flipped it open, it was Carmen telling him that Manny wanted him to call New York. Self ended the call and started dialing his boss's number.

"Yeah, I think you starting to like it too much down there. I don't have anybody up here to keep me company anymore," Manny said, while chuckling into the phone.

"Playboy, everythang good." Self looked down at his mother-in-law and knew he wouldn't be questioned, but then thought, *Fuck it,* when he said, "You know how Self do. All that paper Self dropping can keep you company. Self got a gang more for you, too. Just being the family man, you know. Maybe Self in love or something."

Manny laughed. "Well, I'm happy with everything you did. Keep one hundred for yourself. That's my gift to you. Maybe I can meet her. I'm calling because I'm getting married next week. Kev didn't keep his mouth shut to Carmen, but I handled it. I need the three of you up for the occasion, and for everybody to get measured."

"You want Carmen there, too?" Self asked in disbelief.

"Si, it's all worked out."

"Damn, playa, Self knew he was rollin' wit' the right one."

"It's complicated. I need you here, so come up as soon as you can. Bring the girl with you. It will be fun."

"Self don't know 'bout all that. But Self a be there. One." He disconnected the call.

He stood from the couch and stepped out of the water and onto the hardwood floor. "Boy, where you going trailing that water all over the floor?" Ms. Culpepper asked.

Self then said, "I'll be right back, Ma. I gotta take care of some business."

He called Peaches from the kitchen and walked into the spare room. Everything in his heart told him not to do what he was about to do, but Self didn't care about the cash.

"Yes, baby?" Peaches softly asked when she walked into their bedroom.

Self pulled a duffel bag from under the bed and moved the AR-15 rifle that Matthew picked up for him off the top of the bag. He pulled out ten giant stacks of cash from the bag and placed them on the satin sheets to his bed. He sighed, then said, "This is what you gonna do. You going to a locksmith and buy a few of them flat fireproof boxes. Take nine of these stacks and stuff it in the boxes. Then go to a furniture store and buy a bedroom set. Get the dresser drawers and all that. Find a storage spot in Florida, right over the border. You gonna get a U-haul truck, load the furniture in it, and then put the furniture wit' the dough in it in storage. Take Ma wit' you."

Peaches indicated that she understood his every word. "You want me to go now or after I cook your dinner? I can make it to Florida by tomorrow if you want me to."

Self couldn't believe a woman like Peaches existed. He knew then that he was making the right move, because she was ready to handle his business immediately. He thought of his good fortune, then said, "Nah, that's cool. Do it tomorrow. Wit' the other stack, buy what you need. Then we goin' shopping when you get back. You gotta get some shit for my man's wedding next week. I'm takin' you and Ma to New York to meet my family."

A big smile appeared on Peaches' face. She closed the room door, then hustled over to Self. She sat on the edge of the bed, pulled his sweat pants down, and said, "Oh, Master, thank you for taking me to New York." Peaches then put Self's dick in her mouth and sucked him, deep-throated him, licked him, and slobbed all over his tip. She ignored the fact that her man just gave her six figures to put up. She was more overjoyed that she was truly accepted and was going to New York. Ten minutes later, Self was cumming. Peaches took her mouth off his dick and let the cum drip all over her face before she sucked him again. Peaches understood that every man wanted a nasty freak in bed and a respectable woman in public. If it was up to her, she was going to be everything Self ever wanted in a woman.

Early the following morning, Joy Culpepper and her mother Eva were at a furniture store with a U-haul truck. Peaches picked the first bedroom set she saw and paid $2,500 in cash for it. Her mother held onto the remainder of the cash and wouldn't let go of the bag with wheels no matter where they went. The lockboxes were in the back of the truck, and when the men were loading the furniture, Eva locked herself in the back with a flashlight. She insisted on packaging the cash while her daughter drove. The plan was set that by the time Peaches pulled over to the first rest stop, Eva would be done packing away the cash. She would hand Peaches all the combinations to the boxes, and they would drop off the furniture at the storage container.

Several hours later, Peaches and her mother were heading back into the city of Atlanta. With her mother at the wheel, they made it back in no time. They called Self to meet them at the mall. When he arrived, he picked out two gowns for the wedding, three outfits for each woman and the shoes to match. He traded in the diamond necklace he gave Peaches on their first meeting, and picked up diamond stud earrings, a stainless steel watch with diamonds, and a string of pearls to match her and her mother's blue gowns.

While they were in the upscale jeweler, Self told Peaches to remove her gold-toothed fang. With no hesitation, she struggled with the cap until it came loose.

When she smiled for her mother, Eva said, "About damn time. Now all I got to do is git him to get all that mess outta his mouth."

Self wasn't removing his mouth full of platinum for nobody. He wanted Peaches to take hers out because she was no longer his girl. She had graduated to being his woman.

When they left the mall, Self stopped at Dimple's Hair Boutique in downtown Atlanta. He took Eva and Peaches into the late-night salon and picked out a short-cut hairstyle for both of them. Eva thought the whole thing was fun, but Peaches didn't like the style he picked. She didn't protest, but by the time her hair was professionally cut low and curled in waves around her head, she would never be looked at as a stripper again. Self remade her into a lady, and on that day, she was ready to be taken to New York.

* * * * *

Manny and Xia's wedding was three days away when Rico met Xia for the first time. He followed Manny to Cortland Manor, and Xia gave him a grand tour of the house. Rico thought the house was a mini-mansion and was highly impressed. When they reached the walk-in closet of the master bedroom, she clicked the button to reveal the hidden room with all of her weapons.

"Oh shit. This shit is off the chiz-zain!" Rico exclaimed to Xia while his mouth was open in shock.

She ran her hand over the display of weapons. "Yep, I can use them all. I'm a sharpshooter by training; know hand-to-hand combat, defensive driving, and I make a mean banana cake."

Rico laughed while Manny found out the hard way that everything his wife-to-be said was true. When the tour was over, Rico was out by the pool when he said to Manny, "Yo, bro, you marrying the right bitch! That's my word. You ballin', son. She ain't no joke, though." Rico looked out at the half acre of land, then said, "Yo, I gotta go. I gotta get me a crib like this in Panama so when I get old I can chill down there. But right now? I got to get the whole M3 ready for your wedding, son. Give me everybody's number. I wasn't ever sweatin' it before, but now, hermano? After meeting her? Yo, it's on. That's my word; it's on."

Rico left his brother standing at the back of his own house after receiving the phone numbers he needed. On the way out, he went to see Xia, looked at her thick body up and down, and then came to the conclusion that his brother had scored. He then took down her instructions as to what she wanted all the groomsmen to wear at the wedding. Rico took down the list and told her to expect at least forty men there to represent for Manny.

* * * * *

Self and his entourage arrived in New York. He didn't want to fly, but agreed to meet Kev and Carmen in New York when he arrived. He put Peaches and her mother up in his Staten Island hideaway house that he rented. He gave them enough cash to go anywhere in New York for the day and directions to get where they needed to go in his new Range Rover. Eva was so impressed with his immaculate three-bedroom apartment and his Range Rover that she thought Self was a millionaire and started acting like she wanted to sleep with him.

While the women left to go see New York City, Self drove his M3 up to his Bronx Co-op in Parkchester, where his other woman was at home. When he walked through the door, the older nurse that worked nights looked at Self like he was nobody special. She didn't tell him that she missed him, how much she appreciated him, or how happy she was to see him. She didn't ask if he had been locked up, shot, or if he was having a bad day. Instead, she complained about how *her* needs weren't being met while he was gone, how she was all alone, independent, and didn't need no man telling her how to live her life. Then she caught an attitude and refused to talk to him.

Self looked at the woman that he shared a bed with for two years and came to the conclusion that she just simply looked tired. Her appearance didn't matter to her because she wanted her hair to be something low maintenance and practical. Her clothes didn't make a statement about who she was, and her overall appearance showed that she was not willing to make the extra effort for her man. Self thought about putting a bullet in her head, but he quickly cancelled the thought. Instead, he walked into the spare bedroom, opened the closet, and emptied his safe of the $70,000. He then packed his six handguns, his two machine guns, and a sawed off shotgun with the cash in the bag. He put on his bulletproof vest and then picked up his three diamond watches, his old pinkie rings, and a pair of black pearl earrings.

When Self had the bag in hand and heading for the door, his girl asked, "Where you going?"

Self was a man. He never gave an explanation about his whereabouts. He put his finger to his lips and said, "Shhh. Just wait for me right there. I'll be back to hear you beef some more. Don't go nowhere." Self walked out the door with no intentions of ever returning.

After dropping his bag of artillery off in his locker at the gym in the Bronx, Self headed down the Harlem streets that he had been away from. During his drive, things in New York didn't seem right. It felt like a large gloomy cloud was following him. In the Big Apple, he had to stay on point, wear his bulletproof vest, and if he got pulled over by the police, the punishment would be more severe. At that moment, Self was telling himself that he wanted to move to Atlanta, open a business, and just chill. Then his phone rang.

Rico was on the other line. "Yo, son, I need you and Kev down at the Lower Eastside immediately. We got to rep for Manny's wedding. Right now, son, ya heard?"

"Self a be there in a minute. Let Self get Kev, and we'll see you."

Rico said, "One," and hung up the phone. He immediately closed all the Uptown spots, and a caravan of M3's shot down to the Lower Eastside.

When he reached downtown, Rashid had the spot closed. Fourteen M3's with three men in each car waited on Avenue B. Rashid was leaning back in his car listening to his slow jams when Rico pulled up next to him. Rashid rolled down his window while Rico rolled his passenger window down. Rashid didn't forget how Rico had threatened him. He looked indifferent when he said, "Yo, what up?" while his head was rocking to Luther Vandross.

"Y'all ready? You seen Self?" Rico asked. Just then, the exhaust of Self's M3 was pulling up behind Rico. Rico looked in his rearview mirror and said, "A'ight, we set. The whole clique is here."

Before Rico put his car in first gear, Rashid said, "Nah, we got to wait for Fee-foe."

Rico took the suggestion like a slap in the face. He asked annoyed, "Fee-foe? What da fuck we waitin' on that dope-fiend nigga for?"

Rashid rocked to the music, ignoring Rico's temper tantrum. He stuck his head out the window, then said, "Yeah, that same dope-fiend that put us on, mixed the dope you ain't know how to cut, and that same dope-fiend who still cutting our dope. He's M3 more than most of these cats, so we waiting for Fee-foe. By the way, he don't get high no more. You ain't like the Benz, so I made him trade that shit in. So, we waiting for him to come back from Queens." Rashid went back to rocking to his music.

Rico reversed his car from being double parked and slid in behind Rashid. Ten minutes later, a charcoal gray M3 drove between the sea of white and the three black M3's. Fee-foe was smiling with a Panama hat on his head. He pulled up next to Rashid, apologized for his lateness, and then fell in formation.

The M3 Boyz turned all heads on every avenue while they drove through the gritty streets of Manhattan. Just like their lives, no one knew where they were going. All cars followed the first black car, and Rico was behind the wheel amazed that his army had grown so large. He drove through the blocks of his competition, then passed the local police precinct, eventually stopping at a midtown parking lot where they took over every available space.

Pedestrians, storeowners, and police officers wanted to know what the mob of youngsters walking up Fifth Avenue were up to. The entire M3 team looked menacing and caused terror in the hearts of the city dwellers. The only people that seemed non-threatening were Self and Fee-foe. They looked like the older parents to the gang of misfits.

Self had on a few of his jewels, with a polo shirt, a pair of jeans, and lace-up shoes. Fee-foe had on a white shirt, burgundy slacks, and a white Panama hat with a burgundy band going around the top. In his hand was an expensive cane, a gold rope chain laid on his chest hairs, and a gold Movado watch was on his wrist. To any stranger, he looked like a player from the past.

When the mob turned into the entrance of the Bergdorf Goodman department store, Rico was lost, so Fee-foe stepped forward. He eased the suspicions of the security personnel when he said, "Gentlemen, all of us are attending a wedding. We need clothes for this wedding, so what floor?"

The black security guards exhaled in relief that the small mob wasn't there to rob the store. They gave Fee-foe the number to the floor he was looking for and gave every member of M3 a pound except Self, who didn't show love to strangers.

The male and female staff tried their best to accommodate the M3 crowd, but the situation was unmanageable. Each member was trying to outdo each other in clothes, stacks of cash were piling up at the checkout counter, and Rashid was fixing his wardrobe by buying clothes that had nothing to do with the wedding.

After Rico consulted Manny on the phone, six gray tuxedos, one gray gown, forty suits, and thirty-three other outfits were purchased from the store. The management called the surrounding shoe stores up the block to accommodate the fifty pairs of shoes that were needed. Onlookers were convinced some rapper and his entourage were buying out the store. Photographers were trying to take pictures of Self, but Fee-foe jumped in the way of the camera. He wanted the attention and wanted to save the cameramen a few broken bones.

* * * * *

"Central two, what's your twenty? What do you have up there?" Detective Clarke asked the leader of a six-man team.

Officer Burke was parked at 117th Street off of 8th Avenue. "Zero, sarge. No activity here. A few dopeheads milling around, but no cars, no trace of our suspects, or any drug activity. Over," the officer responded in his walkie-talkie.

"Hold on, Burke," Detective Clarke said.

He was sitting in front of the M3 spot and didn't understand what was going on. It was obvious by the mob of disappointed customers hanging around that there was indeed a drug spot there. The informant that he hired to give him the directions on where to find the M3 stamp was right. He even entered the building himself to see what was inside, but no one was there. Instead, people asked him if he was working or had something to sell. He sat in the back of his Ford Excursion with three other men from his twelve-man team with an old arrest photo of Rico. Today, they wanted to get pictures of all the cars, run whose names they were registered to, and then begin dismantling the M3 crew, but there was no crew to take pictures of.

"Did you copy, sarge?" Detective Burke asked.

Detective Clarke said into his radio, "Either these guys are onto us in some way and closed because they heard we were coming, and I find that to be impossible, or this ADA broad gave us a bum wire. Observe and see if anyone shows up. If nothing happens, come back to HQ. Over and out." He stomped his foot into the floor of the truck, then said to the other men in the truck, "This broad is running circles around Morgenthau's head. I knew he was making a hasty decision, but who can tell that old battleaxe anything? He's probably drunk from the scent of sniffing up her ass. Hey, let's get outta here and see what other Intel we can find on our other cases."

The engine to the Excursion started, and the two trucks from the task force drove off. Detective Clarke really didn't want the case in the first place, so as far as he was concerned, the M3 crew didn't make things personal, yet.

* * * * *

Later that night, Rico manipulated his way to lock down the top floor of the Pussycat Lounge on Greenwich Street. The strippers called in reinforcements for the bachelor party of Manny Black. Cases of liquor were dropped on the tables, while the team got to know each other. They took turns sticking crumpled bills into the garter belts of naked women and bragging about who they killed for the M3 name.

Manny had one drink the night before his wedding. The glass of champagne was raised to honor his troops. He realized quickly that he had to play the role of a politician to each of the men who were willing to kill for him. All night different young boys were greeting him, telling him their deeds of loyalty. Self slipped out without anyone noticing. He wanted to get back to Peaches and Eva. When the partying started getting out of hand with Fee-foe telling the strippers stories of how he used be on top of the world and was the greatest player in his heyday, Manny and Rico stepped outside.

"You getting married, big bro! Get the fuck outta here!" Rico yelled while they were outside of the lounge.

Manny felt vulnerable and uneasy. He looked around for Cubans that he felt were determined to end his life before his wedding day. He led his drunken brother to the trunk of his car. He opened Rico's trunk, removed the tux and gown he needed, and then opened the trunk to the Plymouth Prowler he and his wife-to-be shared. Once the transaction was done, Manny led Rico back into the safety of the M3 Boyz. He didn't know how his men were getting home, and he didn't care.

While Manny was going through the Lincoln Tunnel, he picked up his cell phone and dialed a number. When the voice on the other line answered, he said, "I'm on my way." The caller acknowledged his announcement, then hung up the phone. Instantly, his line rang again. "Hello," he said.

"Are you sure you want to do this?" Xia asked on the other line.

"Why, you don't?"

"No...1 mean, yes, so bad. I just...I just need you to be certain. If you really don't, then we don't have to."

Manny laughed. "Bonita, you running away on me?"

"No, I just hope you know how serious this is? There's no space for disappointment, Manny. Once tomorrow is over, there will be no other women or fooling around. I'm not saying you are, and I'm going to try to stay secure, but...but, I will really mean 'till death do us part, baby."

Manny exited the tunnel and turned off until he reached Jersey City. "Bonita, I'll see you, okay? Just don't leave me standing at the altar alone."

"Manny?"

"Si?"

"I really, really love you. I'm the happiest woman in the world right now. Make sure I stay that way."

"See you, Bonita," Manny said before disconnecting the line. He made two turns, then headed to the West New York exit in New Jersey until he found Spring Street. He took the quiet, tree-lined, residential street until he stopped at a security booth.

The older white man in the booth leaned over to the Prowler and asked, "Who you here to see, mister?"

"Cerro residents," Manny said.

The man's face lit when he said, "Oh yes, the new people in condo forty-seven. I have the copy of your keys here for you, bub. Hold on."

The man reached into a top desk drawer and handed Manny a set of keys. "These are for you, Mr. Cerro. Enjoy your night."

Manny pulled out a twenty-dollar bill and handed it to the happy man. He then drove through the secured gate in a semi-circle of duplex condos. When he reached his designated parking space, he pulled up to the house. He looked up at the terrace for the top condo that he had the keys in his hands to, and the silhouette of the person he was going to see was standing in the shadows.

I hope you know what you doing, Manny thought as he climbed the stone flight of stairs until he came to the solid oak door with gold numbers on it. When he turned the key and opened the door, a row of candles led down a long hallway. Manny closed the door and walked down the hall until he stopped at an opened door at his right.

Candlelight flickered inside the darkness. A shadow was moving against the wall, and the cool breeze was coming through the window. In the middle of the huge canopy bed with sheer curtains, his woman was lying on her back. She had on a sheer teddy nightgown with lace at the top. On her elevated feet, she wore translucent stilettos. Since her feet were up and her knees were by her perfect breast, the shadow of the spiked heels looked like ice picks aiming at Manny. When he stepped into the room, his dick stiffened with the quickness. The woman had both of her hands playing in her wetness.

"Papi chulo ven aca. Please come fuck me now," Carmen moaned out.

Manny laid the tux and gown on the chair in the room and sunk to his knees. He opened Carmen's legs and placed his head between them.

When his tongue danced on her clit, she said, "Yes, papi, drink it up. Esta Cubana es la mas sabrosa. That's right. I'm the best. You love this chocha." Manny made two figure eights with his tongue, then made it move back and forth like a wave. Then he stuck all of his tongue out and licked her clit with all the pressure. "Oh fuck! Yes…yes, I'm cumming, papi. Oh, Negro, fuck me please!" Carmen screamed out with her moans.

Manny stood and Carmen was all over him. She fumbled for his pants, stripped off all his clothes. When he was fully naked, he pushed her on her back.

"I tell you it's me and you, right? Be my puta now," Manny whispered out.

He took off Carmen's shoes and sucked each one of her toes until she cried out for more. He then put both her big toes in his mouth, and she said, "Oh Jesus!" and started sticking two of her fingers deep inside of her wetness.

Manny's tongue worked its way up Carmen's body without him missing any part of her skin. When he reached her waist, he grabbed her two legs and flipped her over on her stomach. He pushed her until she was on her knees and then stuck his head between her ass cheeks while his tongue and lips pulled on her clit. When Carmen couldn't take it anymore, Manny poked his fat tongue in and out of her deep hole with quick thrusts.

"Coño, papi, you the best. I love you. I love you," Carmen barked out.

Manny then climbed on top of her and entered her from behind.

"Puta, you love it? You love this pinga. Take it all. Take it all," he whispered in her ear, while moving extra slow in and out of her.

Carmen was losing her mind and her body started trembling from the lovemaking. When Manny picked up his pace and started smacking her on her ass, Carmen moaned out, "Maricón, you can never leave me!"

Manny ignored her pleas, turned her on her side, and pushed her knees up to her chest. When Carmen grabbed both of her knees, Manny entered her straight up. To Carmen, it felt like he was way up in her stomach. Manny thrust hard and strong, then he stopped. Carmen opened her eyes and then quickly closed them when she felt Manny penetrating her asshole.

"Oh, papi, please...please, papi, tranquilo." When he started pumping into her snug fit, Carmen couldn't take it anymore. "Negrito, fuck me. Cum, papi, please."

Manny dug deep into Carmen, then prolonged his orgasm until she begged some more. That's when he exploded all he had for her.

That would be the last time Manny planned on sleeping with her.

THIRTEEN

On the day of Manny and Xia's wedding, an assortment of exotic cars were lined up from 142nd to 145th Street on Convent Avenue where the famous Convent Avenue Baptist Church was located. The huge elegant church had been selected by Xia and paid for by Pantera to house Xia and Manny's grand matrimony. Inside the house of worship, Brazilian rosewood adorned the walls, floors, pews, and overlooking balconies. The lights from the crystal chandeliers that covered the undulating bamboo ceiling illuminated throughout the church. The center aisle was lined with white flowers and covered with a series of white and lavender roses.

Pantera, along with Manny's people, piled inside the church to represent for their family. They were dressed to impress. On one side of the pews, the M3 Boyz sat dapper in silver tuxedos and white patent leather shoes. On the other side, Pantera's team was dressed in black tuxedos and hard bottoms. The scene was straight from a gangster film. Each crew socialized exclusively with their own while waiting for the ceremony to begin.

Manny, Rico, Self, Rashid, Fee-foe, and Carmen were in the back of the church waiting for Xia to arrive. Manny was dressed in an all-white tuxedo with tails, a white tie, and white patent leather shoes. He avoided eye contact with Carmen, who was stressed out from him asking her to stand in with the groomsmen. For some reason, Manny's mind was focusing on the handmade invitations Xia sent out, the silk, satin, and lace wedding gown she paid twenty-five thousand dollars for, and the six-tiered cake that he knew he wouldn't like. Manny had never been under that type of pressure before in his life.

Outside on the church balcony that overlooked the altar, the pianist played and started singing "For You I Will" by Kenny Latimore. That was Manny's cue, telling him that Xia was there. Instantly, he and his crew rushed out to meet Pedro at the altar.

As the song played, the bridesmaids that Pantera brought in and the groomsmen stood on each side of the aisle. When they were all situated, Xia appeared at the back of the church. Her exposed shoulder blades and voluptuous cleavage sent waves of envy through the pews. Once the traditional "Here Comes the Bride" tune belted out of the organ, Xia took her long walk with Pantera down the aisle.

Xia smiled when she lifted the train of her embroidered gown so she could walk up the four steps that led to the altar. She seemed to stop short at the sight of Carmen standing with the men, wearing a man's tuxedo top with the long gown flowing under the tails. The scene was something magical and the envy of all women.

Manny found himself captivated by how beautiful Xia looked in her wedding gown. They stood at the altar and held hands when they faced the pastor. When Xia's pretty eyes looked over to Manny, they penetrated his soul. In the short time that they knew each other, they established a bond stronger than couples who've been together for years.

"We are gathered here today to join these two beautiful people in holy matrimony," Pastor Katherine Dukes announced. Thereafter, she went through the entire spill about the importance of marriage and how marriage is a great institution for the black family.

Manny and Xia looked at each other, not thinking of anything but the other. When they were asked if they had their own vows, Xia said, "I love you, don't mess it up, and never forget till death do us part." Some people in the pews laughed, while others knew the seriousness of Xia's words.

Manny said, "I love you. I want to spend my life with you." He then looked at the pastor and said, "Make this woman my wife."

Pastor Dukes said, "You two may now exchange rings." Rico handed his brother the rings, and then Manny and Xia simultaneously placed the rings on their fingers. The pastor said, "By the powers invested in me, I now pronounce you husband and wife." She then turned to Manny and said, "You may kiss your wife."

Manny quickly took Xia into his arms and passionately kissed her. The guest jubilantly applauded, while Carmen stood behind Rashid crying. The husband and wife strolled down the aisle holding hands while everyone congratulated them. As they exited the church, they were showered with rice while the photographer was capturing the moment.

Manny and Xia raced into an all-white Bentley, while the two black Bentleys behind them were reserved for Pantera, Pedro, and their henchmen. Behind them were the caravans of the M3 Boyz. The scene of close to fifty cars running red lights and tying up the Harlem traffic made the residents of Harlem feel like ex-president Bill Clinton was coming through.

* * * * *

The caravan of exotic cars drove over to Riverside Drive and didn't stop until it reached Grant's Tomb. The large crowd for both parties exited their cars and posed for pictures until the sun made its decent. From there, they drove down to Club Lotus, where the owners were presenting a buffet to feed 150 guests Latin food.

By the time the food was done, all the tables were moved to the side and the dance floor welcomed the bride and groom. As "Here and Now" by Luther Vandross played over the immaculate sound system, Xia and Manny slow danced while the crowd looked on. The second the song was over, DJ Clue ordered everyone on the dance floor and played records from old to new.

In the middle of the dance floor, Rashid and a fine Latina were bumping-n-grinding enjoying each other. Eva and Peaches were leading Self, the Cubans, and members of the M3 crew through the motions of the Electric Slide. Self was smiling, and it was the first time in his life he danced in public.

On the other side of the room, Carmen, Kev, and Fee-foe were off at a corner table pouring bottle after bottle of Cristal and Hennessy in an effort to get totally drunk.

While everyone partied, Manny's eyes scanned the room, checking out the guests enjoying themselves. Ever so often, he caught Carmen glancing over at him and Xia. The way she looked at him and Xia made him feel uncomfortable. He wondered if he had made a mistake by inviting her to the wedding in the first place. His thoughts were broken when the music suddenly stopped and he heard a tapping sound on the microphone. When he looked over in the direction of the DJ booth, Pedro stood with the mic in one hand and a glass of champagne in the other.

Pedro lightly tapped the champagne glass against the mic again to get everyone's attention. "Excuse me! Can I please have everyone's attention for a moment?" When Pedro had everyone's undivided attention, he continued. "I'm grateful all of you came out to celebrate this special occasion. On behalf of the Pantera' family, we would like to extend gifts to the newlyweds." The brute and his tall partner stepped forward and handed Manny and Xia a set of keys. Pedro smiled, then said, "These are the keys to your new fifty-two-foot motor yacht in Boca Raton, Florida. May you two get as much mileage out of your marriage as you will that boat, and maybe make some babies while you're traveling the seven seas. Salute. Now let's get back to celebrating and enjoying the evening."

The crowd applauded. Rico was jealous that he didn't give an expensive gift. His mood instantly changed from drunken happiness to drunken rage.

Just then, someone was banging a fork against a champagne glass until it broke. Everyone looked in the direction of the shattering sound. Rashid was wobbling from side to side with the broken glass in his hand. His bowtie was hanging off to the side as he yelled, "I want to give a toast!"

"Nigga, you drunk. Lay yo ass down," Rico demanded from the table across from Rashid's.

Rashid looked at Rico, then up at Manny. The crowd was silent except for a few soldiers from The Lower cheering their boss on. Rashid held the broken glass up and slurred, "To my boss...the general...Manny, I love you, man! That's my word!" Rashid looked at the Cubans scattered all over the club, then said to them, "He changed my whole life, son. Daddy-o was like a father I never had. I was fuuucked up before he dropped the bomb on me. That's my word."

Rico said, "Sit down, man. You embarrassing us."

Rashid lifted his glass in Rico's direction. "You see, Manny? I ain't like some people. They ain't got no loyalty. They get rich and start bugging… forget who was doing for them when they ain't had shit. Not me, Daddy-O. I recognize. I know you the truth, son. You gave me shit nobody gave me." Rashid wobbled on his chair and then stood on the table. "Every muthafuckin' body raise y'all glasses." When all his troops and the Cubans followed his order, Rashid held up the broken glass and said, "To the last muthafuckin' Don, my boss and yours, Manny Black. We'll die for you, son."

The audience sipped their glasses and then gave a standing ovation.

Rico fumed with envy. He didn't like the way Rashid acted like he didn't have to answer to him. His lack of controlling Rashid was getting to him.

By the time the soldiers helped Rashid off the table, the DJ played the music again. While the crowd started dancing, everyone wanted to talk to the bride and groom. Edeeks walked over with two envelopes in his hands. He leaned closer to Manny and his bride, then yelled over the music, "This is your tickets to Panama. You already know you're leaving tonight. I gave Rico a package with two-fifty in hundreds. The rest is ready on the wire to Panama by the time you land. Ken Rosenstein took care of everything and told me to tell you it was his wedding gift to clean all the money up." He handed Manny the other envelope and said, "This is my gift to you two. Business has been good, and with the invitation to the mayor's ball, we are really ready to do some big things." He leaned to Xia and said, "By the way, I have your Benz outside like you asked me to." He handed over the keys to her car. "You two have fun and don't miss your flight. You'll have a ride waiting for you when you get there, so don't worry about a thing."

Manny and Xia thanked Edeeks, along with what seemed like a hundred people thereafter. While they were speaking, the guests pulled them apart. Before they knew it, they were on opposite sides of the room watching each other kiss and shake hands with people they didn't know.

From where Manny stood, he observed Pedro walking across the crowded room to where Xia was standing. Pedro then leaned over and whispered in Xia's ear. He guided her to the far end of the room and into the back of the club. Self walked over and interrupted Manny's thoughts with the details of their Atlanta operation. While Self talked, Manny waited patiently for his bride to come back to the dance floor. Fifteen minutes later, Xia came from the back dressed in an all-black, silk pants suit. She had an expression of urgency on her face, and in her hand was a cardboard box with a red ribbon tied around it.

Manny excused himself from Self before he marched in Xia's direction. He never took his eyes off her. When he reached her, she lied and said, "There you go. I've been looking all over for you." She kissed her husband on the lips. "Meet me back at the house. I have to take care of something. Tell Rico to meet us at the airport."

"Where you going? It's our wedding night," Manny asked.

Xia paused, shook her head indicating that he could never know, and then said, "I promise I won't be long. Meet me at home so we can make it to the airport on time." She then kissed him, rubbed his crotch, and said, "I'll make it up to you," before she mingled her way out of the reception hall door.

Just as Manny was about to stop his bride, he felt a strong tap on his shoulder. He turned instantly, and Pedro said, "Come with me," leading him in the direction of the mystery room in the back of the club.

Manny stood inside the small office that was cluttered with money counting machines and boxes of fine liquor. Pedro reached in a desk and removed a flat cardboard box with a blue ribbon tied around it. Manny remembered his wife having the same box and figured it was yet another wedding gift, until Pedro pulled out a sheet of paper with a red circle around a name and address.

"Oh, hell no," Manny said, while opening the box. Inside was a brand-new, all-black, Astra A-80, nine-millimeter gun. Beside it was a silencer. "Maricón, this is my wedding night, man! I got a plane to catch for my honeymoon in a few hours," Manny protested.

Pedro looked down at his watch. "You still have time. Best to get it done before you leave for Panama." He handed Manny a bag, then said, "Change your clothes and get a car. The guy you looking for will be wearing a tuxedo with a red bowtie. He wears a patch over his eye."

Manny thought about telling Pedro something foul for making such a request on his wedding day, but knew he got an order he couldn't refuse. He immediately began taking off the white tux while Pedro walked out of the office. When he reached in the bag, it held articles of clothing from his closet at home. He didn't even want to know how Pedro got in his closet; he had bigger problems to consider. After he was dressed in black fatigues, a pair of boots, and a black, long-sleeve tee shirt, Manny walked out the dressing room with the box tucked under his arm.

When he reached the reception hall, Eva and Fee-foe were on the dance floor showing all the youngsters the dances from back in the day. Manny called Rico over, knowing he had a mission to fulfill.

He said, "Hermano, I need your car."

"Why, what up?" Rico asked.

Manny waved his hand for Rico to hurry. "Business. I got to put in some work before we leave. Keep everybody busy, and make sure everything is packed. Xia and me will see you at the airport. If anything happens, I want you to still go see mamá and papá, okay?"

Rico handed over his keys and said, "Yo, you sure 'bout this? You want me to come? It's your wedding night, Manny. Let me go."

Manny sighed. "No, I gotta go. Just meet Xia and me at the airport. Our flight leaves at eleven."

Rico hugged his brother, and Manny jetted for the exit of the Lotus Club.

* * * * *

"Boy, you got my daughter calling you Master, but everywhere we go these boys calling you Self. What is your name, boy?" Eva asked Self while she was refilling her glass with rum and coke.

The one glass of champagne Self drank had him a bit off point. He looked down at the woman he would embrace as his mother and said, "I, Self, Lord, and Master."

Eva's whole face wrinkled like a prune. "What the hell? All dem is your names? So what you want me to call you, Self, Master, Lord, or what?"

Self hugged the woman. "Son. You can call me son, Ma."

Eva shot the glass back when "To Be Real" by Cheryl Lynn came on. She grabbed Self's hand and said, "Well come on, son," while she escorted him to the dance floor.

Across the room, Carmen had her eyes glued to Manny as he crossed the dance floor to leave the club. She tried to remain strong through all the ceremonies, but after her fifth drink, her whole world felt reckless. She broke down and started crying like someone died.

"Damn, ma. What's wrong? Why you cryin'?" Kev asked when he saw her body shaking from her cries.

"Hijo de Puta maricón, cabrón. I don't believe this shit!" Carmen blasted.

Kev moved closer to her. "Who? What happened?"

186

"That bastard Manny!" Carmen shouted and cried while the music drowned her out.

Kev put his arm around her shoulder, trying to comfort her when he said in a drunk slur, "Who you talking 'bout, the boss?"

Carmen slowly nestled into his arms. "I don't believe this motherfucker. He had me come to his wedding and the reception? I must be an idiot. My whole world is crashing down because of that bastard. I bought a car that I can't drive. I crashed on the way here, and now, I'm too fucking drunk to get home, all because of that bastard." She caught the spit that was drooling from her wet lips, then slurred out, "The boss, huh? Me! I was with that motherfucker when he didn't have shit! Before that bitch even came into the picture."

"Oh word, ma? Fo'real?" Kev asked, looking at the emotional wreck in front of him. "So why you come?"

"Some come mierda, M3 soldier bullshit," Carmen sarcastically replied, slurring each word. "Me mama loyal."

Kev looked around to make sure none of the dangerous men in the room heard her disrespect. She was his boss, but he knew how things ran downhill when he said, "Whoa, ma. You kinda drunk. You need to go home. We got a flight to ATL tomorrow."

With droopy eyes, Carmen looked into Kev's eyes and said, "Si, you damn right I'm drunk. And you know what, handsome? I'm horny, too!" Carmen pointed to the exit. "And my dick just walked right out that door." She looked down at Kev's crotch and asked, "You got a dick? Huh? Come on, take me home. I can't drive. I'm your boss. I tell you to do something, and you do it."

Kev didn't hesitate to do what his boss told him to do. He steadied himself, checked to make sure Self was nowhere in sight, and put one of his arms around her when they walked out of the door.

Rico walked right by Carmen and Kev when they were leaving. He didn't pay attention to them because he had bigger things to tend to. With his girl trailing behind him, he headed to the dark corner at Rashid's table. When he reached the darkness, Rashid had his back against the wall, with his head bent to his lap. Rico looked over the table, and the fine Latina that Rashid bought with him was sucking his dick. Her head was bobbing up and down while she jerked and sucked on Rashid.

When he caught that someone was standing over him, Rashid looked up at Rico, smiled, and then said, "What up, boss?"

Rico looked back at his girl wondering why she wasn't willing to handle her business the same way. "Yo, son, what you doin'? You in public. You buggin'."

Rashid was too drunk to give a damn. He looked down at the chick that was blowing him and said, "Bitch high off X. What the fuck you want me to do, Daddy-O? She want to give some head, so I'ma take some head."

Rico blew out frustration and then said, "Yo, I need your car. Manny jacked mine, and I got to get up outta here."

Rashid looked down at the woman sucking him, then emptied his champagne glass before he asked, "You got all these soldiers in here wit' cars you copped them and you want my whip?"

Rico sent his girl to the front door. He spun towards Rashid and lost his patience when he said, "Nigga, you drunk. You can't drive. When yo ass get up in the mornin', make sure my shit ain't fucked up by the time I get back. Stack that paper till I get back. I'm putting you in charge while I'm gone, and that's my word you better not fuck my shit up."

Rashid looked at Rico and asked, "Yo shit? What the fuck *you* do? All you do is count paper!" He lifted the girl's head off his dick, then mushed her away from the table. He reached in his pocket, pulled his .380 Beretta out, and placed it on the table before he said, "Nigga, I put you on to the dope game. I put you on the coke game. Me and Fee-foe out here putting in work. You got Stan kilt wit' all your bullshit wit' them Cubans. But guess what? I ain't Cuban, muthafucka, and Manny my boss. Yo shit? Nigga, you must be outta yo rabbit-ass mind."

Rico thought about the snubbed nosed .38 strapped to his ankle. He looked down at Rashid, thinking how easy it was to lay him down right in the club. Instantly, he thought of the plane he had to catch and how Rashid was the only one that could keep the money in order while he was gone. Rico nodded, then said, "A'ight, muthafucka. You drunk, so I'ma let that bullshit slide. Just have my paper right when I get back in two weeks," and he walked away.

His head searched the whole club until he saw his lieutenant from 117th Street, Rich Dice. He asked Rich to hand over the keys to his white M3 and told him to catch a ride with someone else. From there, Rico headed to the door thinking how Rashid had to go as soon as he got back.

* * * * *

Manny drove Rico's car wondering what his wife was doing on their wedding day. He sped to the Major Deegan Expressway until he exited at Jerome Avenue in the Bronx. He drove under the elevated train tracks of the 4-Train on the downtown side of the street. While both of his hands were on the leather steering wheel, the sheet of paper Pedro gave him was between his fingers. Manny looked at the number on the address and realized he was close. As soon as he picked his eyes up off the paper and onto the road ahead, Manny's head turned, looking behind him. A white Mercedes Benz wagon with white interior and a woman driving shot right by him. *That's Xia*, Manny thought when he searched his rearview mirror for something familiar. He thought of chasing her down, but the crowded street with cars wouldn't let him out of the flow of traffic if he begged them to.

Manny got back in focus as he passed the address on the sheet of paper. He looked to his right, and rows of limousines were parked out front of a limousine company. The garage door was wide open, so Manny moved quickly trying not to attract any attention of whoever was inside.

He circled the block once and then parked. Manny was a block away from the limousine company as he stared at the six hollow limousines out front. He checked his clothes, then screwed on the silencer to the 9mm. Manny walked into the night with caution and bopped his way down the dark block until he reached the garage. His adrenaline was pumping and his thoughts raced to his honeymoon, making it to Panama, and promising himself that he was leaving that garage alive no matter what.

Like any customer wandering off the street, Manny walked into the limousine company like he belonged there. Inside the darkness of the garage, six other limos were parked, and a small light shined in the back where a tall glass window to an office was located. Since Manny didn't see anyone, he pulled the gun out his waist and thought, *No turning back now*.

With the silenced gun in his hand, Manny went in search of his intended target. When he reached the belly of the garage, he smelled the pungent odor of cordite. Someone was shooting in the place. Manny's heart beat a bit faster as he walked towards a hill that dropped into a smaller garage.

A man with a heavy Latin accent was talking in the lower garage. He said, "I doe no. Dat hijo de puta sneak in wit' a pistola. Befo' me or Antonio see anything dat puta shoot Antonio. I duck, then shot back, but da mohón get away."

Manny crept closer to the voice. When he walked down the hill, he looked to his right and a desk was twenty feet away. In front of the desk were three Latino men crouching down over a man's motionless body. Fresh blood spilled from the back of the dead man's head and onto the cold, oil-stained concrete. In broken English and Spanish, the man with the heavy accent, wearing a greasy jumpsuit, frantically explained to the other two men in suits what happened to the man on the floor. The men in the suits senselessly struggled to stop the blood from spurting out of the wound. The hopeless look of their faces confirmed that their effort was useless; it was already too late for their comrade.

When the men in the suits gave up their attempts to save their comrade, they stood while the mechanic continued to struggle with the body.

Manny looked at the two men and jumped back. He recognized them as the bodyguards of the Cubans he and his crew met in the park. He ducked lower behind a parked limo without taking his eyes off the men. While the mechanic was below them, the taller man in the suit pulled out a handgun and screwed on his own silencer. He said to the other man, "I turned my head for one second and this cocksucker let's Antonio get shot? You weren't in here so that's explainable, but first Juan, then Antonio? Oh no, that's not explainable." The man pointed his hand to the ground, placed his cold weapon behind the mechanic's head, and then pulled the trigger twice.

Again, Manny jumped back when he saw the two shells exit the man's face, and then the man dropped onto the dead body. The mechanic pitched forward and his face froze onto the dead man's chest. When Manny caught a clear view of the lifeless figure laying on the ground, the dead man was dressed in a tuxedo with a patch over his eye. Instantly, Manny recognized that not only was he the man that Manny was sent to hit, but also one of the bosses of La Familia Mariel who was at Riverside Park.

What the fuck is this? What kind of beef could Pantera have with La Familia Mariel? Why Pedro send me and somebody else on the same hit? Manny's mind raced while he was inching his way out of his crouching position.

When he spun around, a black cat crossed his path and screamed out at his sudden movements. "Who's there?" one of the men in the suits asked.

Manny thought about finishing off the men inside the garage, but that was not what he was sent to do. He stood to exit the garage, and his sudden movement caused one of the Latinos to look his way.

The man in the suit saw a shadowy figure walking fast and hugging the darkness by the wall. In a rage, he yelled out, "Maricón," and fired four shots at the quick shadow.

The other man in the shadow was running towards Manny with a gun in his hand, and Manny went into action. While running backwards, Manny squeezed off three quick rounds before he used a limo for cover. Fear gripped his throat, and when the men saw the sparks spitting out of Manny's weapon, they filled the limo he was hiding behind with holes.

Manny was trapped. The only way out was through the garage door and leaving would make him an easy target. With his plane to catch and his mother on his mind, Manny ducked behind the rear bumper of the limo and fired three more shots.

One of the clumsy men ran right into the silent slugs that tore into his chest cavity. The second man kept Manny stuck behind the rear tire of the limo by firing by the bumper and under the car by the tire. Manny couldn't move. If he raised his head, it was coming off. Time seemed to stand still, and all he could feel was his heart beating out of his chest.

Again, the killer shot a round of bullets at Manny. Suddenly, he had an idea. Manny reached for the car door to see if it was open. *Chucha!* he thought when the door gave way. Slowly, Manny opened the car door and slithered his way through the small gap he created. When he reached the silence in the car, he looked through the tinted windows and saw nothing. The man that was shooting disappeared. Manny didn't know what to do, so he nervously waited.

In what seemed like an hour later, but was really four minutes, the man walked from the office with a silenced Mac 11 in his hand. Manny cursed himself because he could have gotten away, but instead, he was in the back of a limo trapped. Instantly, a hail of slugs slammed non-stop into the concrete pillar above the limo and on the ground under the car. When the shooter ducked behind a giant tool locker and didn't hear Manny shooting back, he stuck his head out to investigate. Manny watched the man's eyes searching for his lifeless corpse. When the man's search came up empty, he thought Manny got away or was dead. He started walking his way towards the exit of the garage with confidence.

Manny sat and watched as the man walked closer to him. When he was right outside of the car and his chest took up the space of the window, Manny lay down on the back seat and aimed his gun, releasing all the bullets he had left into the back window.

One by one, the hot slugs caused the man to do a dance before his body dropped to the oily pavement. Manny couldn't believe his luck. Without waiting to see if the coast was clear, he grabbed a stack of napkins from the dispenser in the limo and wiped down every item he touched in the car, including the door handle outside. When he was satisfied with his clean up job, Manny raced for the exit, hoping he wouldn't have to face more Cubans with his empty gun.

Manny jumped in the car and thought of his wife. Instantly, he began dismantling the weapon in his hands. When he pulled off, he drove over Mount Eden Avenue until he reached Claremont Park. When he pulled over by the row of lovers that parked by the darkness of the park, he dropped the dismantled pieces down a sewer and in a public garbage can.

During his ride home, Manny tried desperately to make sense out of what took place. When he finally arrived at home, he walked through the door confused and feeling jittery from the drama in the

Bronx. He checked his watch and only had an hour before his plane left. He sped through the double doors to his master bedroom. When he got inside, he heard a loud retching sound coming from his bathroom.

"Uh…Uh." The retching sound of someone throwing up their guts came from the other side of the bathroom door. Without any hesitation, Manny opened up the bathroom door and was stunned by what he saw. Xia was on her knees with her head bent over in the toilet, vomiting and dressed only in her white panties. Droplets of blood were slowly trickling down a two-inch gash across her left shoulder blade. She was so consumed in throwing her guts up that she never heard Manny come in.

"Bonita, que…" Manny tried to ask what happened, but Xia swung a karate chop that hit him in his balls. By the time his knees hit the floor, she had a handful of his hair in her hand, ready to smash his head into the hard porcelain toilet.

"Oh shit!" Xia said when she realized it was her husband she was holding. "You startled me," she said after letting him go, then hugging him for dear life. "We have to get to the airport."

Manny's hands were clutched on his balls when he said through clinched teeth, "What the fuck is wrong with you?"

"My stomach hasn't been acting right," Xia replied, quickly getting up off the floor.

She grabbed a bottle of mouthwash off the sink and was rinsing her mouth out when Manny caught his breath. "Cabróna! I'm not talking about that. Your back…what happened to your back?"

"Oh, it's nothing. I'm alright. I just had…a little accident."

Manny took his time getting to his feet and to the first aid kit behind the mirror on the wall. "An accident, huh? You was in the Bronx, right? I saw you, so don't lie to me."

He began to clean her superficial flesh wound as she said, "Baby, you promised. I never want to lie to you, but you promised."

Manny dabbed at the wound. "I promised? I promised what? I want to know what the fuck happened to my wife. Now!"

Xia sighed. "Baby, you promised that we would never interfere in each other's business. I had to take care of some business." She lifted her head, then kissed him before she said, "I'm okay. Now stop making something bigger than what it is. Let's get the rest of our things together. We have a flight to catch in an hour."

Manny allowed Xia to think that she had finagled her way out of telling him what had happened to her. Together, they jumped in the shower and scrubbed the traces of gunpowder that was on each of their bodies without realizing what the other was doing.

When the shower was over, and while Manny hurried to pack their last suitcase, he thought, *If it is the last thing I do, I will get the truth out of her.*

By the time Manny and Xia finally got to Kennedy Airport, Rico was already there patiently waiting. He looked at the faces of the newlyweds and asked, "Yo, what up? Why y'all lookin' like dat?"

Meeting his younger brother's gaze, Manny said, "Tranquilo, hermano." He looked at his wife, then said to Rico, "It's nothing." He quickly changed the subject when he asked, "You have the package?"

Rico said, "Yo, it's good. I did my part." He pointed to the bathroom a few feet from them, then held up a brown paper bag and said, "Now you can go do your part. We out in a minute, so hurry up."

Manny smiled while feeling a sense of relief. For once that night, something had gone right. He snatched the bag out of Rico's hand and headed to the bathroom. He rushed into the first stall, opened his pants, and then dropped them to his knees. Quickly, he unstrapped the nylon moneybelt around his waist and stuffed stacks of one-hundred-dollar bills inside of it. When all four pouches were filled, he piled the extra tight girdle around his midsection until he made 500 one-hundred-dollar bills disappear. He then filled his pants pockets, the spandex he was wearing, and all the pockets on his suit jacket with the bills. After Manny was dressed, he checked and rechecked himself in the mirror to make sure he looked slim.

He stepped out of the bathroom to hear that their plane was boarding. He pushed another stack of hundreds into Xia's pocket before they went through the metal detectors. Manny wanted to make sure they had enough cash when they arrived to put his plans in action in case the wire transfer that Rosenstein sent to the bank went wrong.

When he, Rico, and his new bride were safely tucked in First Class, Manny ordered a Seagram's Gin, laid back in his chair, and smiled knowing he was returning to his birthplace a rich man.

* * * * *

"Yes, papi! This is yours! All yours! Ay dios mío. Ay dios mío. Ay dios mío," Carmen yelled, while sweat dripped off of her body. "Oh yes! Mmm yeees! That's it. Fuck the shit out of me, Manny. Bang this pussy harder, motherfucker! Ah yes, Manny, this dick is good."

"My name is Kev...Kev...what's my name?" Kev asked while his balls slapped against Carmen's ass from the deep strokes he was giving her from behind.

"Si, Kev. Yes, Kev, dame esa pinga rica! This pussy is yours. Fuck me good, negrito," Carmen cried out while Kev steadily pumped away, digging into her guts.

The Hennessy and Cristal he drank had him so intoxicated that he couldn't cum if he wanted to.

Ten minutes later, Kev was on his back while Carmen rode him. She talked dirty to him, made him feel like he was her man, and then he came. All of his juices filled Carmen's hole and swam around with the cum Manny had left in her earlier that morning. Carmen accepted his cum and clawed at his chest while she came with him. When he flopped down, Kev's dick was shrinking inside of her.

She said, "Oh, Kev, you good, papi. You mucho grande, papi." She kissed him. Their liquor-stained tongues intertwined, then Carmen asked, "You like this pussy, papi? You want to make it yours?"

Kev kissed her deeply while he thought that she had the best pussy he ever had. The way she talked during sex made him feel powerful, and he wanted as much of Carmen as he could get.

He said, "Yeah, I want you, but I don't mix business with pleasure."

Carmen sucked on his chest and then licked his nipples before she said, "That was your bonus. I wanted to fuck you the first day I see you. Now you fuck me. That's your business now, papi. I give you all the money you need. You sell the cocaine and make your money. You let me take care of you in Atlanta. Just fuck me. We keep it our secret, okay?" Carmen looked into his eyes and slithered down to his waist. She held his dick in her hand, then said, "Now let me show you that I am all business." Carmen put his dick in her mouth, and the liquor flowing through her system made her lose all sense of control. She knew it was Kev in her bed, and by the size of his dick, she knew for sure it wasn't the man she loved. But, Carmen closed her eyes and sucked on Kev, convincing herself that it was Manny she was going to fuck until she was sober.

* * * * *

"PLEASE BUCKLE YOUR SEAT BELTS AT THIS TIME. WE WILL BE LANDING AT TOCUMEN INTERNATIONAL AIRPORT WITHIN MINUTES. ENJOY YOUR STAY IN PANAMA AND THANK YOU FOR FLYING WITH COPA AIRLINES," the captain of the plane announced.

After the pilot dropped the plane on the hot asphalt, Manny and Rico looked out of the plane's windows like little kids seeing Panama for the first time. The darkness hid most of the spectacular sights, but it didn't stop them from looking.

Xia got a kick out of the way the brothers were acting. After her and Manny joined the Mile High Club, his whole attitude changed. It seemed like the brothers became calmer after they left the thug images they had in America.

It was 2:00 a.m. in Panama when they arrived at Tocumen Airport. Since the only people in the airport were the people on their flight,

Manny, Xia, and Rico got their luggage and went through customs in record time. When they stepped outside, a sleepy blonde in a chauffeur's uniform held a white piece of paper that had M3 on it. They thought of Edeeks' sense of humor and busted out laughing when they saw the woman.

"Senior Manny?" the hardworking woman asked when Manny stepped in front of her.

"Si, me llamo Manny Black. This is mi familia," Manny said.

"Bien, this way please. Let me help you with your luggage," the woman asked, but was too frail to handle the bag.

Manny and Xia decided to carry their own bags, but Rico didn't hesitate to hand the woman his bags and drape his arm around her shoulders.

A black Lincoln limousine was parked to the side when they reached the semi-empty parking lot. The blonde popped the trunk, the Black family dropped their luggage inside, and Rico insisted on sitting up front with the driver.

The limo took off and passed the paved palm tree-lined streets heading towards the city of Colon. The night air was cool, a few people were outside their small homes, and poverty knocked on the limousine's window when the car passed the slums. As they drove through Panama City, Manny and Rico saw how much the place had changed. After the U.S. invasion of Panama, a day that neither Rico nor Manny would forget, everything changed for the worst. Crime picked up, drug use ran rapid, and economic opportunities fell short. The propaganda the U.S. spread was that American soldiers went into Panama to get the General Manual Antonio Noriega, but every Panamanian knew the real reason they were there was for free Panamanian labor and control of the Panama canal.

While houses whizzed by his eyes, Rico's mind was on Rashid. He thought, *Damn! I hope this nigga don't fuck anything up. I don't need no surprises when I get back.* His eyes and mind shifted to the driver of the limo when he thought, *I know she like my New York style. I'll fold her skinny ass right up, too. Her broke ass probably want to be my baby mama once she see these hunneds I'm a pull out when we get home.*

Manny's thoughts were racing through his head as they traveled along the hillside of his country. He hoped his mother would like Xia, and he hoped his father wouldn't be too hardheaded about taking the money he had strapped to his body. Manny had big plans for his family, and the only one in the way of those plans was his father. The fact that he was going to surprise them in the middle of the night was also enough reason for Manny to worry.

Rico liked what Panama had to offer, and he was only there for less than an hour. When he saw the old school he went to, the church his mother attended, and the street of his first girlfriend, he looked through the divider in the limo and said to Manny, "It's good to be home, hermano."

Manny opened his hands, then said, "We can stay right now. We don't have to ever go back. Just say the word, Rico, and we start a new life today."

Rico looked to see if Manny was serious or not. He knew his brother wanted to get out the life of crime, but the allure of the game was too deep in Rico's veins. He said, "Yo, I ain't say all that. I'm only saying it's gonna be good to see the family and country again. Don't get it twisted. I ain't staying here." Manny and Xia looked at each other, then busted out laughing at Rico. When he saw their response, he said, "Yeah, y'all some funny muthafuckas, but I ain't staying."

The driver pulled up in front of their parent's ranch-styled house and Manny was embarrassed. Tears came to his eyes when he looked at the house he grew up in. The two-acre front and backyard that he remembered being filled with banana, mango, and coconut trees was unkempt. The trees were bare with no fruit. The three-bedroom house that his father worked hard to build was falling apart. A section of the Spanish-styled roof had a tarpaulin covering it, the windows were gritty with dirt, and trash was in the front yard that, as a child, Manny received beatings when he didn't clean it.

Rico was distracted with getting the limousine driver's address and phone number while he was getting the luggage. When he slammed the trunk down and looked at the house, he barked, "What the fuck? Yo, what happened to our crib?"

Xia didn't know what was going on. She loved her husband and didn't care if they had to sleep in a shack, but by the response of the two men, she knew something was definitely wrong.

Manny knew what he had to do so he wouldn't wake his parents. He stepped over a small iron gate and walked around to the side of the house. He tapped his wedding band lightly against a window. A figure came to the window. After Manny convinced the person of his identity, the figure left the window.

Less than a minute later, Manny and Rico's seventeen-year-old brother, Puncho, came rushing out of the house. "Manuel, Ricardo? Oh my god, it's really you." Little Puncho started dancing in the street and waking the neighbors.

Rico pulled his old playmate to him, then said, "Shhh Cállate!" When Puncho calmed down, Rico said, "Qué pasó aqui?" asking what happened to the house.

Puncho looked at the intensity of Rico's eyes and calmly said, "Nothing wrong. I'm just so happy to see my brothers. Now things will be better."

"Where's mamá and papá?" Manny whispered.

Puncho looked around like they were keeping a secret from him, then whispered back, "Inside."

Manny whispered, "Okay, come on."

Puncho stopped his brothers and the beautiful woman. "Why are we whispering, hermano?"

Rico smacked him on the head and yelled, "It's three o'clock in the fucking morning, little man."

They all laughed and headed inside the house. When Manny walked through the door of the crumbling house, he immediately made a mental note of why his plan needed to work. The whole house was in a desperate need of a makeover. Instantly, his mother appeared in a housecoat with her eyes open wide in shock. When she saw her oldest son, she crossed her chest, said something about Jesus, then turned around towards her bedroom and yelled, "Jason! Jason! Los muchachos éstan aqui," telling her husband that the boys were there.

Mrs. Black rushed into Manny's arms like her life depended on it. She then pulled Rico closer to her, and they hugged her tight with tears in their eyes.

"Oh niño. My baby, I miss you so much," Mrs. Black said as she hugged Rico, who was smiling from ear to ear.

Instantly, all chatter stopped when they heard the slamming of the bedroom door. Everyone looked to see where the noise was coming from. Their father stood at the door with a mean look on his face. The dark man with beady eyes, a baldhead, and a small gut stood in the doorway wearing khaki pants only. In his hand was an old hunting rifle. He stared at Manny in his expensive suit, then at Rico, and then looked at Xia. The room was dead silent. Nobody knew what to expect except Manny.

Mr. Black started nodding his head, then took a step towards Xia. He got close to her face and articulately asked, "Senorita, who are you and why are you in my home?"

Xia didn't look for help from her husband. She had sent many men like Mr. Black back to God. She looked him in his face and said, "My name is Xia Victoria Black, the wife of Mr. Manuel Black. I am in your home because all wives should know their husband's family, even if they won't like them."

Mr. Black raised his eyebrows at his wife, then looked back at Xia. "Fine. My wife and I are pleased to meet you. Our home is yours to do as you wish."

Mrs. Black exhaled in relief, and Rico took it as a sign that his father was in a decent mood. So, he ran over to the man, hugged him, then said articulately, "Papa, I am happy to see you. We are here together for once. All of us together."

Mr. Black hugged Rico again, but he didn't take his eyes off of Manny. He looked at his older son that resembled him the most, then cut his eyes until he found Puncho. "Puncho, set up your grandmother's room for your sister Xia. Rico can sleep in his old bed." He grabbed his wife's hand, then said to Xia, "Please excuse us. We will see you all in a few hours."

No one said anything, and Mrs. Black didn't hesitate to move when her husband made the suggestion that they were going back to sleep. She was old school, back when a woman knew that a man had to rule his house.

Puncho ran to prepare the room that his father's mother lived and died in. Manny carried his entire luggage into the room and realized he was standing in the space that had the hole in the corner of the roof. He looked at his grandmother's antique three-piece mahogany furniture and remembered when he was forbidden from entering that room. While he unpacked, Puncho made up the king-sized bed with the quickness and then tried to leave the room. Manny grabbed his frail arm, reached in his pocket, and handed Puncho a hundred-dollar bill.

"Wow! Is it real, hermano?" Puncho asked. "I can buy food for us for the week with this. Papa will be proud of me."

Manny frowned. "What you mean buy food? Papa buys the food in this house."

Puncho looked down at his feet. "Oh...okay, but you can't tell him. When the money you send runs out, I help out at the factory and buy the food. Papa doesn't work. He just sits in the garden all day."

Manny was shaken. He couldn't believe what he heard. He was sending a few hundred here and there, but after he started getting money, he was so focused on going to Panama with a lot of money that he didn't consider how his family was going to make it without his contribution. He thought his father was working, but now he knew differently. Manny and his father had issues, but in the morning, he planned on changing everything.

FOURTEEN

F ive hours after Manny and Rico landed in Panama, they were up eating what their mother could put together for breakfast. Xia was still sleeping, and Manny liked it that way. For what he was about to do, he would either be considered the man of the house, or they would be sleeping in a hotel before the day was over.

Manny called Puncho to him in the hallway of the house, then stopped Rico from going back to sleep on a full stomach. He handed Rico a bag, then walked his two brothers out into the backyard. Their father was sitting in a rocking chair while smoking a cigar as Daniel Santos played through his old boombox.

Manny grabbed the cigar out of his father's hand and had a seat on an old tree stump facing him. Mr. Black looked at his oldest like Manny lost his mind. Rico slid in next to his father, while Puncho sat on an old beer crate at his father's feet. While father and son had a staredown, Manny puffed on the cigar as Puncho waited for the sparks to fly.

"You too tough to respect your father, Manuel Black?" Mr. Black questioned.

Manny took a puff on the cigar, then calmly said, "Papa, the time has come that you see me as a man."

Mr. Black ordered, "Puncho, Ricardo, leave. We have something to settle."

Puncho was ready to run, when Manny barked, "Puncho, stay." Puncho looked at his father confused and then back at his brother. Manny said to Puncho, "Hermano, this will be the first and last time you disobey your father."

Mr. Black surrendered, then said to Manny, "Okay, papá, you the father now. Say what you have to say and then get out of my house."

Manny nodded at Rico, who stood, went into the house, and returned with the bag that Manny handed him. He placed the bag next to his father and returned to his seat.

When Mr. Black looked down at the bag, Manny said, "That's two hundred and fifty thousand dollars in cash. I have a half a million dollars in the bank here in Panama. This morning, Mamá had to scrounge up food from empty cupboards to feed us. Papá, you raised us to be men. Let us be men and take care of you and mamá."

Mr. Black looked at both of his sons. In a voice filled with anger, he asked, "Where did you get this money from?"

"The money is ours," Manny quickly responded, trying to downplay any suspicions.

"Esto es mucho dinero. What did you boys do to get it?" Mr. Black asked suspiciously.

"We're doing some things over in the States," Manny replied.

"What kind of investment give you so much money? Shouldn't it be in a cheque or banco or something?" Mr. Black asked with a bit of sarcasm.

"That's one of the reasons we're here. Rico and me are interested in investing money in Panama for a family business. We have businesses in Nueva York, and we wish to do business with you in Panama."

"Did you bring blood money into this house? With that amount of cash, it cannot be legitimate. I thought you two were working at the airport?" Mr. Black turned to Manny and said, "This is the reason you leave Panama!" He pointed to Manny. "You were running around with those maleante boys, robbing and hurting good people. You kill Señor Delecruz for money and brought shame to this family. Now you involve your brother in that life? Hijo, if we do business with blood money, anything that starts in blood ends in blood."

Rico's patience wore thin. When he couldn't stand it anymore, Rico thought of the way his father demanded that his sons use articulation and said, "Look, Papá. The money is here now. It's a fresh start. It's good money. Look at *your* house, Papa. It has a hole in the roof. That is not how you raised us to be. Do you want to scrape all your life? You want you and Mama to die in this beatdown flat without seeing the better side of life? What about Puncho? Doesn't he deserve more?" Rico was getting furious so he stood. "You slaved in that cement plant for what? You have nada! Where are the benefits? Pops, you always told Manny and me to be men. So now we're being men by taking care of our familia. You gonna deny us that? America stopped the money from coming into Panama when they took Noriega and the drugs. Now we gonna take the money out of America and bring it to Panama."

Rico's words cut his father deep. It forced Mr. Black to examine the injustice he received. He shut his eyes and concentrated. For twenty-eight years, he worked hard trying to keep a roof over his family's head. Prior to the invasion of Panama in 1989, he worked as an executive at one of the biggest cement plants in Panama. After the war, his company was left badly damaged by the United States continuously bombing it. He thought of how the company he worked for was repairing the building and laid him off because his salary was needed to fix the place. He admitted that things had gotten bad. He didn't like filing for bankruptcy. He didn't like the way Manny turned to crime and then left for the States because his father was an embarrassment. He was really upset when Rico followed in his older brother's footsteps. Since then, his family had been getting by with the financial assistance his sons sent back home. Now that he was sitting before his two sons, he was reminded of how much he had fallen from grace. Mr. Black opened his eyes. He stared at his most loyal son Rico and felt a sense of pride mixed with fear. He then looked at Puncho wondering what type of future he would provide for him.

He looked to Manny, who was always reserved and calculated, before saying, "What do you expect of me?"

A smile quickly spread across Manny's face. He took a deep breath with a sense of relief. He said, "Papá, here's what Rico and me have in mind. We want to move you to a hotel in Panama City so we can rebuild our house and land. Later this morning, we will go see the contractors and get them to start the work immediately. The hotel will give you and Mamá a chance to have someone take care of you for once. Papá, use that money to pay for everything. From now on, we are going to send a hundred thousand a month to you. I want you to open up a food market with fair prices so the poor can eat. Let Puncho and Mamá run it. Me, you, and Rico will buy up the rundown property in Colon. We can fix the houses and rent them out at fair prices. With the rest of the money, you can keep it in the bank. It's all clean."

Mr. Black was stunned. He sat looking at his son's great ideas, along with the money to finance them, and felt sad. In front of him were two men who could have done anything with their lives, but if Manny was behind anything, he was sure blood had been shed for all of their riches.

Mr. Black sighed. "I was not always an old man who worked in a factory and became poor. The man that I was before I met your mother is unimportant. You are my sons, and I have lived my days. There comes a time when the parents must listen to the children. I just ask this of you. Remember, sons, that what starts in blood will end in blood. Do what you will with this house because it was built for you to share. I just hope Puncho will not be corrupted by greed, because before I die, I may have to bury the two of you." Mr. Black stood and looked like a broken man. "Tell your mother where she will be living. Do not make her worry. I will not allow you to kill her, too."

The sons of the Black family watched their old father walk away heading for his bedroom. Manny didn't care how the old man felt. Rico was glad their plan was going to be in action, and Puncho was amazed that his tough brothers from New York could tell their father what to do.

* * * * *

Back in New York, Miguel spent everyday on the phone with either his niece or the other Cuban bosses. They were losing a grip on New York, and Miguel wanted to prove that he was worthy of being the boss of the organization. With the death of Juan and then Antonio, two seats on the council were open. Only he and Felix were left with too many underbosses to consider as replacements. There was no way Felix could ever find out about Miguel snitching to the district attorney's office, but he wanted M3 taken care of.

While smoking one of his favorite Cuban cigars in his private study, Miguel listened to "De Mi Alma Latina" by Placido Domingo. He was wondering how long it would take for his niece to get rid of the M3 Boyz. The longer they stayed in business, the more they boldly expanded their Lower East Side operation into the Marielitos turf. He was too old and powerful to shoot weapons in the street, but the young gang didn't have any problems with killing or dying, and that was a bigger problem. Miguel didn't know how to fight an enemy that looked forward to dying.

In his frustration, Miguel realized he needed to step up his counter-attack or risk being humiliated. He picked up the phone and dialed his niece's Maria's house.

"Hello," the professional voice answered.

"Maria, this is Uncle Miguel. Listen. I want to see you at my house immediately!"

"Uncle Miguel, right now is not a good time. My family and I were just about to sit down to eat dinner. I can come by sometime tomorrow."

Miguel growled in frustration. Through clinched teeth, he said, "You little ungrateful come mierda! Who in the hell do you think you're talking to, your husband? Let me remind you that I'm the one that put you through law school! Not your husband, snot-nose kids, or your puta madre! So don't ever tell me when you are going to see me. When I tell you I want to see you, I want to see you now," and he slammed the phone down.

A half an hour later, Maria was standing before her fuming uncle. Miguel sat down and looked at her with venom in his eyes when he asked, "What's the problem? Why is it taking so long for these punks to be taken off the street? Where is the information on the Black brothers' investigator? Did you know that cocksucker is on his honeymoon in Panama with his wife and his brother that killed Juan?"

"No, I didn't. We keep coming up blank. We are having a hard time finding people to come forward and give us information. I have a task force in order directly from the DA, but we do not have the finances that you do to get information. These things take time on the state level. Tío, I really don't understand why you don't handle things yourself. Your people are only going to kill each other anyway. I will pick up the bodies and send away who I can when the smoke clears," Maria shot back in irritation.

Miguel started pacing. "You are too smart for your own good. I am aware that you do not have the resources that I have, you idiot. Why do you think I am helping you to help me? Do you want me to do your job and indict them, too?" Miguel didn't give her a chance to respond. "I put a tail on him since the beginning. His operation is spreading to Atlanta. I may handle that operation on my own. Crumble them where they least expect it. But in New York, the M3 Boyz are multiplying like roaches, and I want it to stop! I need your help here! When Manny and Rico Black come back to New York, I want a task force arresting them at the airport. Can you guarantee that?"

"Is anyone from your organization willing to testify? I can arrest them on Juan's murder if you produce the body."

Miguel looked at her like she was a fool and said, "Don't be silly or play games with me. Use the education I paid for."

Maria had enough. She stood and said, "Well then, you should have sent me to magician school because it's obvious you want me to pull a rabbit out of my ass." She spun for the door. While she was walking away, she yelled, "Tío, do what you have to do. I will resume the investigation, but I can't do magic," and she walked out the door.

On the way to her car, Maria thought about the case that they were building against the Black brothers and their ruthless M3 gang. Her uncle told her how Rico Black killed Juan Santos at the meeting and how his M3 soldiers were taking over the Lower Eastside. The problem at hand was if none of the Marielitos were willing to testify, what could she really do? The Cuban family had always been strong. Maria wondered why the Marielitos didn't use their own people to get rid of the infamous crew, but she promised herself that she would do whatever it took to please her uncle.

Back in the house, Miguel was on the phone. When the person was on the other line, he said, "Felix, it's time we take your leash off and let the beast take a walk. Si, everybody. Send the family from Miami to stop by Atlanta, too. Viva Marielitos!"

Miguel hung up the phone knowing a bloodbath was about to wash the streets of Manhattan, and then maybe Maria would take him more seriously.

* * * * *

The following day, Maria was back in lower Manhattan at the District Attorney's office. She and the city's Special Narcotic's

Prosecutor, Bridget Brennan, were in the midst of putting together a profile chart of the M3 Boyz. Thus far, they only had the allege heads Manny and Rico Black. The known informants seemed too scared to say anything about the M3 Boyz, and that in itself worried them. It was as if Manny and Rico were myths that her uncle made up. The ADA's were coming up empty, but agreed to continue their investigation until they caught some of the lower members in compromising positions. They hoped the soldiers from the M3 Boyz would turn over state evidence on their bosses the way most other drug crews did.

After her meeting with the special prosecutor, Maria Flores was back in the boardroom trying to get information from the anti-crime task force.

"So, Detective Clarke, what do we know about this organization so far?" Maria asked.

The black, baldheaded detective had both of his feet up on a table in front of his seat, when he said, "Not a damn thing worth mentioning."

Maria sighed, knowing it was going to be difficult dealing with disgruntled police officers. She wore a suit and wasn't a part of their fraternity of courage. She didn't lose sleep from the long hours of trailing a suspect, arresting him, and then watching the DA's office cut him some slack on a technicality. On the nights she was at home happy, making love, or eating with her family, Detective Clarke was having a cigar for dinner and losing his woman to the same criminals he was out trying to catch.

"What exactly do you mean?" Maria asked.

Detective Clarke dropped his Survivor boots to the floor. "I mean, my team and I have been sent on a wild goose chase. When we tried to collect Intel on these guys, nobody heard of them. Yes, there are drugs being sold at the locations on the complaints, but no one was there to sell them. I don't know if you have a leak or if our chains are being jerked, but we can't get a handle on these guys. None of the fiends even heard of Rico or Manny Black. The only names we recovered were one Stan and another named Fee-foe. Fee-foe drives an M3, and we have a hit on both spots, but these guys have spots all over. Stan took a dirt nap so that information was useless." He stood and then said, "These guys are selling drugs like half of New York. Either we build a nest where these guys are, and they don't seem to be that much of a threat that the boys in blue can't handle, or you can let us go close the rest of our cases."

Maria started shaking her head before he was done. "That's out of the question. I suggest you build that nest. Get me video on these guys. I don't care what happens. Just videotape until we have something solid. Stake the known drug areas out, do whatever you have to do, but I don't want these guys on to us until it's too late. Your orders are to videotape, investigate, and then penetrate the M3 organization. Nothing more! I want no petty arrest. Just audio and video."

"This is bullshit!" Detective Clarke exhaled.

Maria put her hands on her hips, and in a firm tone, she said, "These are your orders. If you prefer, I will get my boss to tell you."

Detective Clarke started chewing on his cigar, when he looked down at his team and said, "Come on."

When the door to the boardroom closed, Maria exhaled and leaned against the nearest desk. She was exhausted and knew for sure it was going to be a task to bring down Manny and Rico Black.

* * * * *

Since Kev was sexing his boss, he returned to Atlanta feeling like a new man. Finally, he was a hustler with the backing of a woman who wanted to have sex with him every chance she got. He controlled Carmen to the point where she would do anything he said in bed. He knew he would never marry her, but as long as she was supplying the coke, drinking his cum, and letting him keep most of the cash off his deals, everything was cool. For the time Rico was out of the country, Kev and Carmen set up a system where Carmen went back to Broadway and bought a few keys of coke. It was Kev's job to spread the coke all over Georgia, give Self the money he expected, and then save the cash off the other coke for him and Carmen. She set up a small town house in Sandy Springs as their love nest.

The first day back in ATL, Kev was flashing money in Magic City and calling the phone numbers of all the local dealers that wanted to re-up from him. Later that night, he met up with Peanut that the late Boss Hog was supplying. They hit it off immediately after Kev ran his mouth about how Boss Hog wanted to send Kev and his uncle over to Peanut's family's house. After more talking, Kev took a ride in Peanut's '64 Chevy to Stone Mountain where a Jamaican woman wanted a key and half of coke. She had Macon, Georgia, locked and needed a new supplier. When the woman handed over the cash before she received the coke, Peanut and Kev were partners in crime.

Two days later, Peanut arranged for a deal to sell four keys of coke to a man named Carlos from Savannah, Georgia. In the past, Peanut did business with Carlos, so Peanut and Kev was pleased to do business with him, but Kev wanted to meet him first. Later that afternoon, a black Chevy Avalanche with chrome rims, tinted windows, flood lamps on the roof, and a black fiberglass top covering the cab pulled up. A short, young, Latin kid with curly hair stepped out of the truck. "What up, blood?" The man smiled his gold teeth at Peanut.

"Carlos, what's up, my man?" Peanut embraced the man. He then turned to Kev and said, "This my partner right now. His name Black. What's crunking?"

Carlos looked all around to see if he was being watched. He then looked Kev up and down and asked, "You the Feds, man?" Kev looked at the man like he was crazy and turned to leave, when Carlos said, "My bad, man. I just been getting some heat, man, and I don't need no direct sale charge, you know. I don't know you and all."

"Man, this my boy!" Peanut said, vouching for Kev.

Kev was annoyed. "What up? What you wanna do?"

Carlos looked around again. "I need four keys, man. I'ma do some drops in Savannah. Then I'm heading over to Nashville. Those country singing fuckers can't get enough of that white lady. I got a hundred and sixty grand for you if you guarantee it."

Kev did the quick calculation of the cash. At that rate, he could tell Self and Manny that he was getting out the game while the going was good. He looked the nervous man over, then said, "Cool, we can do business. I'll meet you later tonight."

Carlos looked around nervously again and said, "Yeah, man. How's eight o'clock at Kennesaw Mountain Park?"

Kev smacked his hand, then said, "Yeah, meet you there. Eight sharp or I'm gone. Step out the truck when you get there and wait."

The men shook hands again and then jumped back in their vehicles to leave.

At eight o'clock sharp, Kev and Peanut drove the M3 to do the deal. They circled the park, and from a distance, they saw Carlos and another man leaned against the pick-up truck smoking. Kev looked around again, and for some strange reason, something didn't feel right.

Before he got out the car, Kev used his New York Street smarts and sat back in the car. He turned to Peanut. "Listen, youngin', this da deal. Something ain't right. When my mind tell me it ain't right, then it ain't right, so this is what I'm gonna do. I'm gonna leave the work here with you." Kev quickly took the four kilos out the gym bag and placed them under the driver's seat. He removed his Czech-9 sub machine gun from his waist and dropped it in Peanut's lap. "I'm gonna have my cell phone and da gym bag wit' me when I go in da park. If shit is good and he got the cash, then we do how we did with the Jamaican chick and drop off the work later. If you don't hear from me in da next ten minutes, drive this muthafucka back to my crib. Tell April I said to stash da work for me and to get in touch wit' my uncle." Kev opened the door to the car. "You know what to do."

He exited the car with the empty bag, then popped the trunk to the M3. Two minutes later, he closed the trunk quietly and took the hundred-foot walk to Carlos and the stranger.

Kev walked towards the park. When he approached Carlos and the mystery man, he asked, "What up? Who this? I told *you,* I was going to meet *you.*"

Carlos was rubbing his palms on his pants. "Playa-playa, err' things is good, amigo. This is my peoples, Big Red. He's here for my *security.* You know one-sixty ain't no bag of shells, man."

Kev shrugged his shoulders, then asked, "You got the loot?"

Carlos looked around nervously. "Amigo, you got the product, huh?"

The actions of the two men were spooking Kev. He said, "Be easy, partna. What's da big rush?"

"Boss, I gots places to be, so are we gonna do business or what?" the man named Big Red shot back in his fake southern accent while looking around the park.

At that moment, Kev caught a strange vibe about Big Red. His intuition told him to leave. Without delay, Kev turned to Big Red and said, "As a matter of fact, I don't feel comfortable fuckin' wit' you. Yo, I'm out of here, Carlos! I don't want to play ball tonight."

Kev started walking away, when Carlos started yelling, "Yo, Black! Why you actin' like that, playa-playa? You know I need that product, playa. Don't do me like that!"

Kev looked at Carlos and saw the desperation in his face. He also noticed how Big Red looked around like he was waiting on somebody. Kev said to Carlos, "Nah, I ain't fuckin' wit' this cat! I'll get up wit' you later on in the week. Be easy. We'll work somethin' out."

Big Red walked over while Kev and Carlos were talking and asked Carlos, "Cee, what's goin' on?"

"He don't want to do business wit' ya," replied Carlos.

Big Red looked around nervously, then pulled out a Glock and said, "Freeze, cocksucker! Police!"

Out of the darkness, local agents ran from every corner of the park with guns drawn surrounding Kev. "Get down! Get on the fucking ground, asshole. Now!" the agents yelled, as they closed in on him. Immediately, Kev dropped to the ground. While on the ground, he observed an agent escorting Carlos away.

Kev didn't know that Detective Thomas Stevens, a.k.a. Big Red, was from the Fulton County Sheriff Department. He and his task force of ten undercover officers from the Georgia State Bureau of Investigation (GSBI) were already at the Kennesaw Mountain National Park waiting for the deal to go down. Detective Stevens had planned the sting after receiving information from Carlos Martinez about a new supplier who was selling pounds of cocaine.

Carlos wasn't always a snitch for the GSBI. Most of his life he had been a hustler until the day he slipped up and made several sales to an undercover officer. When they finally picked him up and got him down to their headquarters, they made him an offer he didn't want to refuse. It was either he rot in the pen for the next twenty years, or get on their team and play ball. Like the weakling he was, he chose the latter and sung like Michael Jackson. When Carlos ran out of setting up hustlers from the Atlanta area, he promised to set up Kev and Peanut.

"If you move, I'll blow your damn head off," Detective Thomas barked, pointing his gun down at Kev's head.

When Kev heard the exhaust to his M3 driving away, he looked up at Agent Thomas, then at Carlos and he started laughing. "What's so fuckin' funny, asshole? If I were you, I would be crying like a baby right now. You are definitely going away for a long time!" Detective Thomas barked.

Kev continued to laugh. "Y'all are a bunch of funny muthafuckas. I wish I had a camera wit' me right now to film this funny shit!"

"Pass me the bag!" Thomas ordered his other officer. He pulled Kev by his handcuffs and led him to the front of a black GMC truck. He pointed to the windshield of the vehicle and said, "You don't need a camera, boy. Smile, you been punk'd in real life." Kev started dancing and laughing in front of the camera, and Detective Thomas felt something was terribly wrong. Usually when he had a perp under arrest, the suspect would try to make a deal in place of going to prison. Instead, Kev was standing with a big smile on his face. Instantly, he hurried to check the gym bag. When his hands came out of the bag, it held a pair of sneakers, a set of workout clothes, and a pair of gloves. "Where the fuck is the drugs, asshole?" Thomas barked.

"What da hell you talkin' 'bout?" Kev answered. He looked into the camera and said, "I came to play night ball. I don't sell drugs. Why y'all think all black men sell drugs, man?"

Realizing that the suspect had outsmarted them, Thomas decided to take Kev down in an effort to find something he could charge him with, or at least find out if he was wanted in any other counties of America.

* * * * *

In Panama, the Black family sat discussing their future. Mr. Black sat his wife down so her gangster sons could explain to her how they were going to change her life. When the two brothers were done and told her how much money was already in Panama, Mrs. Black surprised her husband and everyone else in the room. She clapped her hands together and started crying. She said, "Finally, we can live like normal again. In the beginning, your father took pride in spoiling me and gave me what no one else could." She looked to the ground, then said, "Those days have been gone for a very long time." Her head rose to her sons. "How soon can we leave?"

The men of the Black family were stunned. Manny looked up, and Xia was smiling with his mother. From the pleasant look on their faces, he knew that they had hit it off. The thought of his mother approving of his bride meant a lot to him. Usually, she was a hard person to win over. Then something hit him. He looked at his mother's face, the complexion of her skin, her wide hips, and thick body, and realized what he saw in Xia. Standing side by side, Xia could have passed as Mrs. Black's daughter.

Manny smiled and said to his mother, "Thank you, Mamá. We will take care of everything in the morning."

Everyone in the room was in for another surprise when Mrs. Black looked up at Xia and asked, "Xia how long have you been pregnant?"

All eyes shifted to Xia, then to Mrs. Black to see if the old lady was going crazy.

"Mamá, what are you talking about? Xia isn't pregnant," Manny said in Xia's defense.

Mrs. Black shook her head. "I have three strong Black boys. Niño, don't you think I know when a woman is pregnant with a Black boy in her womb?"

"Tell her, Xia," Manny said with confidence to his wife.

The tears fell from Xia's eyes when she nodded. She looked at Mrs. Black, smiled, then looked at Manny and said, "It's true. I took the pregnancy test on the night of our wedding, but I didn't want to tell you until I saw the doctor." She kissed Manny. "I'm pregnant, baby. We did it! I'm sorry from keeping it from you, but I wanted to be sure before I got your hopes up high."

"Hermano, congratulations!" Puncho said.

Mr. Black got up and kissed his daughter-in-law on both cheeks when he said, "Congratulations." He smacked his head, then pointed at Manny and said, "Your mother did the same thing to me. You can no longer be a Maleante. You have a family to think about now instead of being a gangster."

"Damn! Y'all didn't waste no time, huh? You betta be having a nephew for me," Rico said playfully, while hugging Manny and Xia.

Manny didn't know what to do. One minute, he was sitting there happy, and the next minute, he was worried. The answer to his problems was to stay in Panama.

"Okay, okay, let's eat!" Mr. Black announced.

After they all ate a feast, the blonde in the limo came to pick Rico up, and Manny and his mother took a walk. All his life Manny did things with her at the back of his mind. When they returned to their front yard, she said, "M'ijo, I love you boys, but you have always been my favorite. My firstborn." She held Manny's face and said, "Ricardo has been wild since he was inside of me. I just ask that you understand the gravity of having a lot of money. Please, son, be careful, and don't send any coffins home to me. Promise me."

Manny made the promise to his mother, then walked into the house. He showered before heading to bed where Xia was getting ready to dose off. Before she fell asleep, he whispered in her ear, "Bonita, let's do something," while rubbing his dick up against her ass.

Xia quickly moved her ass off of his penis. "Nooo. How are we going to do something like that with your mother and father in the next room?"

Manny felt like a kid again. "Don't worry. They won't hear us." He kissed the back of her neck, being careful not to brush up against the wound on her back. He then gently moved Xia so he could slide inside of her from behind. When he noticed how warm and wet she was, he said, "Damn, Bonita, you wanted some, too, huh? This feels good."

Xia was pushing her ass to meet Manny's deep thrust, when she moaned out, "Boy, you're crazy. I don't believe I'm doing this in your parents' house."

Manny steadily pumped into Xia. With his free arm, he reached around and started rubbing her stiff clit. Gently, he bit down and sucked on her neck as she threw her head back into him. "Ahhh...mmmm," Xia softly moaned out in her moment of pleasure. The feeling of Manny's dick digging deep inside of her, combined with him rubbing her clit, made her pussy throb and tingle.

Hearing Xia's soft cries made Manny buck a little harder. Their bumping and grinding made the old bed squeak like it was on the verge of collapsing.

Manny lost control and put Xia on her knees while he was penetrating her from the back. They both ignored the cries from the old bed. The moment he felt his body tingling, Xia moaned out that she was cumming. Manny bucked harder trying to make new space in her pussy, when he heard, "BOOM" from the bed boards breaking. Him and Xia dropped with the mattress to the old wooden floor.

They blew up the spot and were frozen in silence. They didn't know what to expect, until they heard his parents laughing from the other room. In embarrassment, the entire Black family laughed together before they went to sleep.

Early the next morning, the room door to where Manny and his wife slept slowly crept open. The intruder quickly stepped inside. When he looked down at the broken bed and the mattress on the floor, he saw a naked specimen of beauty lying on the bed. Instantly, he caught an erection, and his penis was bulging through his sweatpants. At that moment, he realized entering his brother's room was inappropriate, but it was too late. In his effort to step back, the wooden floor squeaked. Xia jumped out of her sleep, causing the covers to drop and completely exposing herself. Out of habit, she reached for her gun that was not there. In that instance, she realized who was there. In a whisper, she asked, "Rico, what are you doing in here?"

In that brief moment, Rico stared at her breast, naked stomach, and the lining of her crotch. Xia stared at the erection bulging out of his sweatpants when Rico licked his lips and whispered, "Came to get Manny. I didn't want to wake you up." Again, they both gave each other a once over. Xia pulled the covers over herself, turned over to go back to sleep, and then elbowed her husband. When Manny opened his eyes, Rico said, "Come on."

Manny slowly got out of bed. As he walked out the small bedroom, he glanced at the clock mounted on the wall. It was far too early for New York standards. "Hermano, what the fuck is the problem?"

"We have to meet Señor Rosá," Rico said.

Annoyed, Manny cleared the cold from his eyes and asked, "Who the fuck is Señor Rosá?"

Rico said, "The contractor. He's over in Rainbow City. You know how these old men is. This is late for these cats."

For the second time Manny could remember, Rico was being responsible. Manny walked into the bedroom and grabbed a new shirt, the pants he wore down there, and his suit jacket. When he slid the suit jacket on, he tapped his inside pocket and felt an envelope. He reached in and pulled out the gift from Edeeks. When he opened the envelope, a check for $50,000 was inside. Manny shook his head, still not believing how fast his life had changed. He leaned over, kissed Xia, and then laid the check next to her.

When the Black brothers stepped out of their parents' house on 9th Street, the blonde limousine driver was outside waiting for them. She ran into Rico's arms, kissed him, and then caressed him in a way that told Manny that they hadn't stopped having sex since Rico touched Panama.

It was a quick drive from Colon to Rainbow City. When Rico took the lead in speaking with Mr. Anthony Rose, Manny sat back. He examined the tall, dark, skinny man as he touched keys on the computer that eventually showed the brothers what their parents' house was going to look like when he was done. He showed them how he was going to take the weathered, three-bedroom, concrete and brick house, and convert it into a gated, six-bedroom, six and half bath home with all the futuristic features, including a kidney-shaped pool. He then gave the brothers the name of a Mr. Carlos Edeghill. He was a house decorator from New York that lived in Panama City. When Mr. Rose told Rico and Manny that he could do the whole house and work with Mr. Edeghill to furnish it in modern decor for $200,000, Manny jumped in and offered him $300,000 if he had it done by September. Like any true Panamanian would, Mr. Rose agreed to the terms, and the Black brothers agreed to send half the money by the end of the day.

By the time Rico and Manny returned to their parents' house, everyone was up. Mr. Black greeted Manny with a smile for the first time in many years. Xia was up helping with breakfast. The family sat down and ate in peace, and then Manny told his wife that they had to go. He wanted to enjoy his honeymoon, check the bank, and make arrangements for the hotel suites for his family.

The climate in Panama was much different from the weather in New York. Due to the excessive heat, Manny and Xia dressed in much lighter material. Xia's cream, linen skirt outfit and her black, wrap-around, open-toe sandals complemented Manny's white linen slacks, shirt, and matching loafers.

The blonde limousine driver took Manny to rent a convertible Ford Mustang. During his drive around Panama, Manny wanted to give Xia a grand tour of his beautiful country. They went to the bank first to see if the wire that Edeeks sent was there, and it was. Manny made the check out for Mr. Rose, transferred the account to him and his parents' name. From there, he cashed the check Edeeks gave him and put $40,000 in his brother Puncho's name. With the rest of the cash, he was going to secure the hotel rooms and then take his wife on a tour.

After business was done, Manny started his tour. He went to the famous statue of the black Christ in Portobelo, Colon, then to the monumental Cerr Anco Park overlooking the Panama Canal. Manny asked Xia how she felt about driving their yacht out there and staying for good, and she told him that she would go wherever he was and enjoy it as long they were together. Happy with her response, Manny showed her the rest of his country.

Xia quickly fell in love with the many different cultural and historical sites they visited. She loved the beautiful insides of the presidential palace in Old Panama City. They then drove to Juan Diaz in the capital of Panama and had a late dinner at the renowned Chimborzo seafood restaurant. While Manny and Xia were busy sightseeing around Panama, Rico was having sex with the blonde in the back of the limousine.

FIFTEEN

Kev was sitting inside the interrogation room of the Georgia State Bureau of Investigation headquarters in downtown Atlanta handcuffed to a table. The dingy beige walls felt like they were closing in on him as his mind drifted. He thought about the situation he was in. Kev knew they couldn't give him time for not having drugs, but he figured he could be charged for conspiracy. What worried him was Self. He figured his uncle had to know by now what happened to him, and if Self knew, then Carmen would know. What he counted on was Carmen sending someone to help him get out and Self being in the dark about the extra coke they were bringing down. Since it was Self's job to collect the money off every kilo, somewhere the math would be wrong unless Carmen covered for him. The footsteps of Detective Thomas and the state's prosecutor walking into the room cut Kev's thoughts short.

The two law officials sat down directly in front of Kev. After studying his face, the tall, pale-faced prosecutor said, "Kevin Brown, my name is David Mayers. I'm the prosecutor assigned to this case. I don't have time to bullshit around with you, so listen up. We have information that you've conspired to distribute narcotics in the state of Georgia. With the help of Carlos's testimony, that can get you a life sentence down here. It is in your best interest to fully cooperate with us, and you might make it out of here a free man. If you feel the need to play hardball with us, then we can play that way, too. So, tell us who you are working for, how much cocaine is being brought to the Atlanta area, and how are the drugs being transported down here? We can dismiss your attempted possession, unlawful acts, and conspiracy charge, and relocate you. I'm telling you up front that I am on your side, but this offer is only for the next hour. Once I walk out that door unsatisfied, all deals are off the table for good. So, what are you going to do? You better start thinking about yourself and your future while you have the chance."

Kev looked at the determined prosecutor and laughed. "Y'all really think everybody is a snitch and will go for all of that bullshit, huh? Well, let me tell you somethin'. I don't know what ya'll talkin' 'bout! Y'all ain't got shit on me. I know it, and y'all know it. So, let's stop playin' games. Just get me my muthafuckin' phone call. I went to play basketball with Carlos. I don't know shit 'bout selling drugs.

Check your snitch! If he'll snitch, then he'll lie. So, eat a dick, 'cause it's illegal to question me without my lawyer being here!"

Mayers couldn't believe what Kev told him. He jumped across the table and grabbed him by the throat. As the struggle ensured, agents walking by heard the commotion and ran into the room to help Thomas subdue Mayers.

"Ah ha, wait until my lawyer see all dis on camera!" Kev yelled, while laughing.

Detective Thomas walked the prosecutor out the door and left Kev in the interrogation room. An hour later, a white man with salt and pepper hair walked into the room with a short black woman that was a bombshell.

"Kevin Brown?" the intimidating man asked.

"Yeah. Who you two?"

"Matthew sent me. I'm Martin Smuckner, your lawyer." He pointed to the short, gorgeous black woman. "This is my Atlanta counsel, Phandra Parks. I'm originally from New York. I do law back and forth in ATL, and she is the best attorney down here." He looked impatient and then asked, "You ready to go?"

Things didn't work that way back in New York, so Kev asked, "What you talking 'bout, man?"

The man adjusted his glasses. "You're a real riot. The way you danced in front of the camera. Anyway, Peanut contacted Phandra and told her to get in touch with April, who called somebody name Carmen, who knows somebody that knows somebody like me. So, now, I'm ready to get you out of here. They posted a hundred-thousand-dollar bail, and I gave them ten grand for you. I don't want to talk anymore in here, but..." He handed Kev his card. "...you can come down to my office when you're ready. If I'm not in town, Phandra will handle it. We'll embarrass the state if they try to take this to trial."

Detective Thomas walked through the door angry at the world. He uncuffed Kev and said, "We will be seeing you, Kevin Brown, or Black, or whatever your name is. You fools can never hide for too long."

"Good day, officer," Kev said with a chuckle, as he and his lawyers walked out of the interrogation room.

The gorgeous lawyer said her farewells when they reached outside. Kev and his other lawyer walked to the parking garage. The cool air hit Kev when he rolled the window of Martin Smuckner's Volkswagen down. The lawyer made two left turns in downtown Atlanta, then stopped at a corner where there was an ATM machine. Across from the ATM was Kev's M3. A woman was in the passenger seat on the phone, but Kev didn't recognize his car because the front end was smashed in.

"What up?" Kev asked his lawyer when the car stopped.

"Carmen. Carmen is waiting for you in the car. With the amount of concern that was in her voice, I'm sure you rather spend the night with her than come home with me," the lawyer joked.

With no hesitation, Kev shook Mr. Smuckner's hand and exited his car with the quickness. He ran across the street to the driver's side of his car. Carmen was sitting in the passenger seat with a solemn look on her face.

When he sat in the car, she said, "Oh, papi, you have me so worried. That's it. No more business. We have enough money. I don't want nothing to happen to you, papi chulo."

Kev kissed her long and hard while remembering what it felt like to be handcuffed. He started the engine, then said, "Be easy, ma. Don't get all crazy on me. They ain't have nothing on me. Everything going to be business as usual." He put the car in gear and heard a slight drag against his front wheel. "What Peanut did to my car?"

Carmen exhaled. "Peanut is okay. He is loyal. I have all of the coca. He called the lawyer, and her friend April called me. I tried to drive the car here, but I can't move the stickshift right, so I kept it in first and ended up crashing into a pole. None of that matters. I'll buy you a new car. You are safe now."

When Kev heard April's name, he panicked. "What April say?"

"Everything cool, papi. She call to tell me what happened. Now I want to make sure you never go to jail, papi. Who gonna fuck me when you in jail? Let me take care of you."

Kev smiled at how enthused his woman was about taking care of him. He had big plans for Peanut and planned on making him the man in the state of Georgia while he pulled strings behind the scenes like Self and Manny did.

While Kev was driving downtown, Carmen made him pull into Smoky Bones for barbecue to go. By the time they pulled up to the townhouse in East Lake, they couldn't keep their hands off of each other. When they reached inside the spacious house, Carmen pulled him into the bathroom, stripped off his clothes, took off hers, and then stepped into the shower. While Kev stood against the wall, Carmen washed him, sucked him off, let him penetrate her from the back, and then begged him to fuck her in the ass. When Kev eventually came, she washed him off again and then walked him into the only room that had furniture in it.

"Papi, mi corazon belongs to you," Carmen said when she laid him on the bed.

Slowly, she licked him from head to toe and let Kev fuck her the way she liked Manny to. This time, Manny was no longer in the picture. It was all about Kev. While her legs were over his shoulders and he was cumming deep inside of her, Carmen made up her mind that she was going to support Kev if he wanted to quit the game or not.

If she could help it, no matter what Kev decided to do, he was going to be the father of the baby in her womb, and together, they were going to move Manny out of the picture for good.

* * * * *

The following day, things were bubbling on 117th Street at the M3 spot. Dopefiends were lined up, copping and going. Detective Clarke and his six-man team videotaped the activities from the corners of Manhattan Avenue and on the opposite corner on 8th Avenue that sandwiched the spot.

While the traffic flowed into the building, Rich Dice and two of his soldiers were across the street examining his platinum and diamond M3 medallion that he just bought. The medallion was the size of a CD that sat on his stomach and was overlaid with diamonds everywhere one could fit. While his men talked of getting their own medallions, Rich Dice had two other soldiers on each side of the street and two more in front of the spot.

"This is bullshit," Detective Clarke said in the back of the truck. His men were videotaping Rich Dice display the trinket that was worth more than his annual salary. "We're over here babysitting these nickel and dimers when we have bigger fish to fry." He picked up his radio, then said, "Burke, you have me up here doing what?"

"You're the boss. I'm just following the cunt's orders. Video and nothing else," Burke answered with a laugh.

Detective Clarke dropped his radio on the seat in frustration.

While Rich Dice was kicking it with his soldiers, an old Lincoln Town Car gypsy cab was easing down the block. The car stopped short in front of Rich Dice. When he and his soldiers looked down to see who was in the car, the soldier to the left made his way to a car tire.

"Em-three?" the Latino in the passenger side asked.

Rich Dice looked at the men suspiciously, then barked, "Yeah, park down the block if you want to cop."

The dusty man stepped out of the car with a Mac-11 sub machine gun in his hand. Before Rich Dice realized what was going on, he was quickly going to learn the hazards of his occupation.

The man yelled, "Viva Marielito," pointed the short nozzle at Rich Dice's chest, and let the bullets fly into the spaces of his new medallion.

"Oh shit!" Detective Clarke yelled, while looking through the binoculars, and was about to disobey his orders by yanking on the door handle.

Empty gold shells rained down on the black asphalt when the Latino sprayed Rich Dice and the soldier next to him. Instantly, Rich Dice's other soldier came back from the car tire, cocked the MP5, and let the machine gun do what Rico paid for. The five-shot burst penetrated the Latino, slumping him down in the street.

Instantly, the back doors to the Town Car opened. Two other Cuban men wearing bulletproof vests appeared with AK-47's in their hands. Before their doors were closed and their weapons were raised, two soldiers from inside the spot and one from the corner of 8th Avenue started shooting off the MP5's in their young hands. One Cuban aimed towards the customers and soldiers on one side of the street, while the other was picking off M3 soldiers from the other side of the street.

Rich Dice's loyal soldiers gunned down the man closest to the spot, but while the young kid was aiming from a distance, he caught someone moving in the corner of his eye.

"Drop the gun!" Officer Burke ordered the street soldier, not realizing that war meant soldiers would die.

The young M3 soldier raised his weapon and sprayed sporadically, while Burke's head split from the shells that entered it. Before he could pick off the other officers, they were standing over him unloading their Glocks into his tender flesh.

On the other side of the block, Detective Clarke barked, "Drop the weapon!" at the Cuban after shooting at the man and missing from fear.

"Cabrón, mamate una pinga!" The military-trained Cuban yelled for Clarke to suck a dick before he fired the small rockets from the AK at Detective Clarke, causing him to hug the ground for dear life.

Over his head, Detective Clarke heard rapid gunfire. When he finally looked up, the Cuban disappeared into the building where M3 sold their drugs. More gunfire was going off inside the building. Then Clarke saw his men hugging the walls, cuffing the dead bodies, and he heard the sirens of backup arriving.

The whole block from 116th to 117th Street was closed off within a half-hour. Rich Dice was rushed to the hospital in critical condition. Four other M3 soldiers were killed with two Cubans. The driver of the Town Car smashed the truck of the newly dead officer, Burke, and got away. Another officer was shot in the arm, and the Cuban that ran into the building couldn't be found.

Detective Clarke was in deep trouble and would be the premier article in tomorrow's *New York Post.*

* * * * *

Down in the Lower Eastside, Rashid and Fee-foe were in an apartment three blocks away from Avenue B. They were making sure the last of their heroin was being cut and bagged properly.

When all was clear and the product was bagged up and sent to the spots, Fee-foe said to Rashid, "Man, I got this fine young fox waiting on me in the car. She one a them bitches from downtown thinking I'm gonna be her trick. Man, I got some shit for her young ass."

Rashid smiled with gratitude to be around Fee-foe. He liked the way the old hustler kicked his dope habit and picked up the new habit of making cash. Fee-foe taught him style, grace, and to have finesse in the way he did business. Rashid said goodbye to Fee-foe while he left with the drugs to supply Avenue B.

Fee-foe strapped four hundred bundles of M3 dope into a knapsack and jumped into his M3. He knew he was wrong for having the girl know his business and for driving around dirty, but he was thinking with his dick that day. When he pulled up to the spot, he parked a few car spaces from the entrance to the building. He walked with his pimp cane, bopping into the spot while the young soldiers greeted their other boss. Without getting a tally of how much cash was in the spot like he was suppose to be doing, Fee-foe dropped the bag and headed out of the building.

At the end of the block, a black Ford Taurus was pulling out of its parking space when Fee-foe bopped out of the building. The car came to a slow creep while Fee-foe walked into the street. By the time Fee-foe sat in his car and kissed his young girl, the car stopped right next to him. When Fee-foe looked to his left to see who was stopping him from getting out of the parking space, the back window of the Taurus slid down and he was staring at the barrel of a 12-gauge shotgun.

BOOM! The blast of the barrel peeled off Fee-foe's face and sent pieces of his brain splattering on his dashboard. Before the redbone with the tight Versace jeans, diamonds in her ear, and new hairdo could scream, all she heard was, "Viva Marielito." Then the shotgun was fired at the back of her head, sending her face into the glove compartment.

By the time the Lower Eastside was awakened from the blast and the M3 soldiers ran outside to investigate, the Cuban hitmen were driving off in the direction of the other M3 spots.

* * * * *

"Damn, girl. Ooo, damn!" Kev was moaning while getting oral sex.

His girl got off her knees and then straddled him. When her wetness slid down his stiffness and she started to move her pussy in circles around the tip of his dick, she asked, "What's my name?"

"April!" Kev hollered out while his eyes were rolling into his head.

She started pumping fast and sending his dick deep inside of her when she asked again, "What's my name?"

"April!"

"Whose dick is this, nigga? Nobody else getting this, right?" April barked while she rode him like a pony.

"Your dick! No, it's all yours!"

"Yeah, motherfucker. Think about that the next time you get locked up and I got to call that bitch! Who it belong to?"

"April. That bitch ain't shit. This your dick."

"My dick! Sssss, ooh, I know you love this pussy," April boasted as she squatted on the tip of her toes and bounced her pussy, causing Kev to dig deep into her.

"I'm cumming!" he declared, while squeezing the bed sheets

"That's right, nigga. Come for mommy while she handles this dick," April said as she rode Kev faster while he was cumming. While he was gasping for air, April said, "I know you giving that dick to somebody else, motherfucker. But, I ain't even gonna trip. I'm just gonna drain your ass so you ain't got nothing left when you see her."

Kev shook his head going to the shower, when he said, "You bugging. You know this all yours, boo."

Once word hit the streets of Bank Head Court, the Bluff, Cascade Pines, MLK Drive, and Magic City about the way Kev played the police out and was back home before the night was out, he was labeled the man for real. Everyone recognized the man named Black with the white M3 as the biggest cocaine supplier in Georgia, even if it wasn't true. Between April, Peanut, and Kev's big mouths, the whole world knew he was moving weight and was too smart for the cops to get caught. Kev's cell phone was ringing off the hook with orders for pounds of cocaine, and met with everyone he could to see who he was going to get the benefit of taking the four keys from him at an inflated price.

By the time he drove away from April's house with a bag of cash and was heading to East Lake, a burgundy Dodge Caravan with Florida plates was trailing him. The two young Cubans and the older driver that wore a bandana on his head came in from Miami on the night Kev got arrested by Big Red. After spending a little cash and asking a few questions, they received the name and whereabouts of the kid from New York with the M3 that had all the cocaine. Their source from New York told them that it was two men and a Cubana they had to eliminate.

While Kev was bopping away to a New York mixtape, the men in the supercharged Caravan kept up with his every turn. When he pulled up to the parking space that was directly below Carmen's door, he sat in the car making sure his appearance was good for the other woman he was going to fuck that morning.

Carmen heard Kev's exhaust when his car pulled up under her window. She hurriedly sprayed perfume on her naked body, then draped a silk nightgown over her shoulders. She wanted to surprise her man by greeting him naked at the door. That way, she could drop the news on him that she got pregnant the first night they made love and was having his baby.

Carmen quickly descended the steps down to the front door. When she opened the door and exposed her naked body with her hands on her hips, Kev was getting out the car with a lustful smile on his face. Suddenly, the Caravan eased up quietly to the parking space next to him. Carmen quickly covered herself so her neighbors wouldn't think she was a freak, even though she was.

When the van stopped next to Kev, the front passenger stuck his head out the window and said to Kev, "Yo, Black." Kev looked over at the man while he was locking his car. The young man smiled and asked, "You that kid from New York that's down with that clique M3, right? Y'all blowing up all over, kid."

Kev smiled at the young kid that heard of him. "What up? Who you?"

The young kid's smile quickly turned into a grimace when he pulled out a silenced M92 handgun. The side door slid open and a twin of the kid in front had the same nine-millimeter with a silencer in his hand. They both aimed their weapons at Kev and said, "Marielitos hijo de puta!" and they each shot Kev in his chest cavity four times.

"Coño," Carmen said in shock, putting her hand to her mouth.

"Get that bitch!" she heard one of the men bark as she ran from her door while leaving it open.

Immediately, the two men ran up her steps with the intentions of ending the life of the Cubana they were sent for.

* * * * *

Manny and Xia came back from playing dominoes at the Broad Park in El Chorrillo, Panama. When Manny went inside the house, Rico had a look of distress on his face that Manny knew all too well. *Something is wrong,* he reasoned.

Manny looked at Rico and said, "Outside, hermano."

The two brothers walked out into the backyard where they played as children. Rico walked in front of his brother, then quickly turned around before saying, "Yo, shit is fucked up at home. I know this shit is Rah's fault."

"Qué pasó, hermano?" Manny asked.

"Yo, I called my girl at home, and she told me that M3 was on the front page in all the papers."

Manny knew it was just a matter of time. *Edeeks was right. The Feds came in and swept everybody up.* He asked, "How many arrested?"

Rico had tears in his eyes. "Arrested? Man, these niggaz was busting at the poe-poe. I called Rah after I hollered at my chick, and he told me them Cuban cats tried to body Rich Dice at my spot. Then Drama and Murder started giving them Cubans the business. Then the next thing, squally who was laying for you and me jumped out and all them niggaz, the Cuban cats and everybody, started busting shots. Everybody dead, even the poe-poe. Then Fee-foe got bodied the same time while he was in The Lower. Then Bone from the Westside got bodied in the middle of the street, right in front his spot. Then this nigga Rah telling me he need more dope on top of all this shit. Plus, Carmen called my cell and my chick took the call. When I hollered back, she was talking some old crazy shit about Kev. She was crying like a muthafucka."

Manny rushed to the phone. He made the long distance call to Carmen's cell phone, but there was no answer. He then called Self, who didn't even know something went down. Self called Matthew on the three-way, and Carmen was there.

Her voice was filled with fright when she yelled into the phone, "Negrito, you have to save me. Marielitos, I saw them. Tres muchachos, they killed Kev right in front of my face! Then they shoot the pistola at me, and I jump out the window and run. I come to Matthew house, and he scared Manny. They want to kill me." Carmen knew one of the possible fathers to her child was dead, so she lied when she said, "They was calling your name in the house, Manny. When I run, they tell me they going to kill me because I love you, papi." She started sobbing. "If I have to die for you, I will, papi, but kill them please. Kill them first!" Carmen's voice turned into a whisper when she said, "Papi, I'm pregnant. Please tell me we will be alive to raise our child."

Manny's heart was beating out of his chest. All the news had his mind tripping. He thought fast and said, "Don't worry, Carmen. I got you. Go home to Jersey now. I'll call you. I'm coming home." With Self still on the three-way, Manny said, "Self, you got to come through and clean this up. Go home, man, and leave that thing down there alone."

"Listen, Slick, Self got to take care of family. This *is* Self home now. Tell Carmen to get them pies to me, business as usual. Self got to find them Cubans that did Self family dirty. Ain't no way Self sending a body back to the Big Apple wit'out sending a few more to Castro. Self gonna take care of your paper, and then Self gonna have some fun. Self got this."

"Bien. I been on the phone too long. I'll call you. Carmen, do what Self say, then go to Jersey." Manny hung up the phone and then turned to Rico who was pacing in the middle of the floor. "Hermano, escucha.

I need you to listen to me." When Rico gave Manny his undivided attention, Manny said, "We can leave the game right now. We can walk away! Right now! Right here! We safe here, and we can be the lucky ones who leave the game, mi pana. We got close to a million in cash. With the business in Nueva York, we can do the right thing. A million dollars is mucho dinero in Panama, Rico. We followed the plan and did it."

Rico looked at his brother and lost all respect for him. What he was suggesting is that they run when he wanted to fight back. He looked at Manny and said, "That was your plan! I ain't no coward, Manny. I'm a gangster! M3 till I die. So either you gonna stay here and plant bananas while you collecting rent from a bunch a broke muthafuckas, or you gonna jump on the plane wit' me so we can handle our business and make another mill after we kill these Cuban fuckers."

Rico turned his back on his brother and walked out the room. He was rushing to pack his bags. Rico had a plane to catch.

Manny thought about his life, the two babies on the way, and his obligation to Carmen and his team. Everything in his body told him to let Rico go and stay, but he couldn't do it. He promised his mother he would take care of his brother, so that's what he was going to do.

After getting off the phone, Manny went into the living room where his family was packing up to move. "We're cutting our vacation short, and you guys have to move to Panama City tomorrow. Something important came up back in the States."

Xia looked at Manny and knew something must have hit the fan in order for him to be cutting their vacation short.

Mrs. Black clapped her hands and said, "Okay, you heard Manuel. Drop everything and we will make sure the poor gets the belongings."

Manny pulled Rico and Xia inside the bedroom where he was staying. He said, "Look, we have to make a change in plans." He looked at Rico, then said, "You said the police was looking for us. So, we can't go into Kennedy. Me and Xia will go to Liberty Airport in Newark, and you fly into Philadelphia. We take a private car or the train back to the city. That way, we can figure out what to do. Call Xia until you hear from me, then we will meet."

"Damn, good lookin'. I wasn't even thinking about that shit," Rico said.

Manny looked in his brother's eyes. "That's what I do for you, hermano. I think and you handle the rest. When we get home, that's what you have to do. But, I'm telling you two now, when everything is finished there, I am coming back here with my boat for good. Comprende?"

Everyone agreed to Manny's plan. From that point forward, Xia started flexing her muscles. She handled all the business over the phone to make sure Mr. Rose would start construction the following day and that the hotel had a two-bedroom suite ready for the Black family. Manny gave his family all the cash he had, told them where the rest of the money was, and then left to the airport with his crew.

* * * * *

The two remaining bosses of La Familia Marielitos were sitting in Miguel's study. Felix laughed while sipping on cognac, then said, "It is almost over, my brother. We lost a few good men, but many more are in Cuba waiting to come over. The situation in Atlanta is handled, too. I have given the young ones instructions to take over where M3 left off and flood the land with cocaine. Viva Marielito!"

Miguel chuckled. "Yes. We have to slay the head so the body falls. I'm sure Rico and Manny Black will be back from Panama to save the day. Then we can crush them. A few of their soldiers are making problems for our business, but I'm sure the new bosses we elect will be willing to earn their stay."

Felix leaned forward. "It is just us two. No more politics or secrets, okay?" Miguel shook his head in agreement. Felix said, "Okay, then. I will tell you in confidence. I think we should paint the streets red with the blood of M3. In the eighties, we became stronger from the blood we spilled. Now everyone thinks Marielito is old and soft. If we massacre all foes, then we can open the gates to prosperity. If things become hazardous, we return to Cuba and live like kings."

Miguel wasn't interested in Felix's plan, but he knew his only equal loved blood like a vampire. He laughed and asked, "What do you have in mind?"

Felix leaned back in the antique chair, crossed his legs, then said, "We don't fuss over the vote. I give you a name of an underboss and you agree, and the same for you. Then the East Coast council returns to four after we receive approval from Cuba. The familia is solid again."

Miguel wondered what the angle was, so he wanted to choose a name that was certain to keep him at the top position. He wanted to vote in his protégé, so he quickly said, "Mauro from Newark, New Jersey."

Felix sucked his teeth. "Mauro killed a lot of Africans over Manteca in Jersey without our approval. How do we know he will take the position and respect our honor?"

Miguel answered the question with a question. "So who do you have in mind?"

Felix smirked. "Roberto Sazón."

Tha Twinz

He watched Miguel's eyes balloon in fear. Then he spit his drink back in his glass before saying, "El maricón es un animal! He loves to see people die, and those eyes!"

Felix had him right where he wanted him. "Si, he has been denied a seat on the council and the fortune that comes with it, but this is the type of boss I need to make the family strong again."

Miguel rubbed his chin when he thought of the two new possible bosses. He shrugged his shoulders, then figured he could always eliminate Felix and Roberto with one swipe. "Si, it is done. We will meet with them. We will let them earn their way in by destroying the M3 organization. Give them their orders immediately."

Felix was overjoyed about spilling blood when he stood. He shook Miguel's hand and said, "Viva Marielito."

When Felix walked out of the door, Miguel picked up the phone. He wanted to share some information with his niece.

* * * * *

Inside the headquarters of the Major Crime Squad located on the 14th floor in One Police Plaza, Captain John Baylor and the city's Special Narcotics Prosecutor, Bridget Brennan, were sitting with her protégé Maria Flores and Detective Clarke.

"This anti-crime unit was a mistake from the start. Now we have a media frenzy because you once again didn't follow police protocol," John Baylor barked.

"I lost a good man on this case and one is wounded. Now you're telling me I can't arrest these scumbags that caused this?"

Maria Flores wanted to cover her ass with her supervisors, so she said, "You had direct orders, Detective Clarke. Did I or didn't I tell you not to do anything come hell or high water? You have demonstrated a level of recalcitrant behavior from the onset of the assignment. You're lucky you're not being reassigned and suspended. I have the mayor, the City Council, Harlem developers, and ex-mayor David Dinkins calling me in regards to the negative image Harlem is having over your shootout."

Clarke put his feet up on a chair. "This is bullshit. I didn't want the case from the start. Now you're telling me I can't get off it or pursue these scumbags? Whose side are you guys on anyway?"

John Baylor added, "This is New York, the greatest city in the world. Let me remind you that a lot of strings are attached to this Big Apple. Your orders are to assist my unit and observe. Observe Detective Clarke, nothing more. I don't care if it's an all-out assault on Pope John Paul, II. All you do is observe, unless you get clearance to do otherwise."

Bridget Brennan adjusted her skirt and said, "Are we clear, detective?" Detective Clarke agreed, then she said, "Good. Now, we have a press conference to explain this mess. We have to let this thing cool down. What's the data on Rico and Manny Black? Why aren't these men in custody?"

Maria jumped in. "I have information that they were in Panama and will be returning to Kennedy Airport any day now. I was hoping the captain would dispatch an undercover unit to intercept them."

"I didn't get that information. Where are you getting your leads, and why wasn't my unit informed? This is bullshit!" Detective Clarke protested.

Maria's eyes shifted from her bosses to the detective, when she said, "Um...um...I ah...just received this information from my source."

The captain said, "Good. I will take care of it and put these men in custody. Ms. Flores, good luck on your press conference. As of now, my unit is in charge, and we will bring this organization down very quietly." He looked at Clarke, then said, "The right way."

SIXTEEN

The task force agents sat at Kennedy Airport with the intentions of watching every flight that came in from Panama. None of them had the sense to check the departing flights to see if the Black family took another plane out of Panama. That's what their supervisors were paid the big bucks for.

When Manny and Xia flew into Newark, they jumped into a cab and paid the driver in advance. They took the cab to 125th Street and then took another cab up to their residence in Cortland Manor.

Rico landed in Philadelphia and jumped into his girl's Nissan Maxima. The Puerto Rican young girl, whose Section 8 rent he paid and who he bought the car for, was faithfully there with her girlfriend. Rico was pleased that she could follow orders. If it were possible, she would have driven to Panama to get him.

By noon that day, the Black brothers were in Manny's Escalade heading to the M3 Lounge. Manny was thinking about the way he called Rashid and Edeeks to the lounge and if it was safe. He wondered how much the police knew.

His thoughts were interrupted when Rico sarcastically asked, "Yo, how we gonna handle this shit? I know we ain't goin' down here on no fuckin' talkin' shit."

Manny slowly turned to his brother. In a calm voice, he responded, "Hermano, we just got back. We have too much invested out there to leave bodies everywhere. We're coming down here to see what's going on."

For a split second, Rico's forehead wrinkled, and he spat back, "This is what I be tryin' to tell you. You too laid back for this fuckin' business! This a dog-eat-dog situation. This ain't chess. You don't lose and start a new game. In this shit, if you lose, you die! Rah made a bad move. I can feel it. That nigga got to go if this is all his fault!"

Leaning in closer to Rico, Manny asked, "What's more important to you? The money or the killing?"

"It's always 'bout the paper! But, killing a muthafucka is always right behind it."

"Let me handle this. We have to see what's going on? Trust me, 'mano, if someone need to be killed, then it will be done. But, let's talk to Rashid first. We need our team to be solid, not separated."

Manny drove past the empty parking spaces in front of the lounge. The shutters were up and Edeeks' car was parked outside, but Manny drove around the block looking for parked police cars. When he felt the area was safe, he parked around the corner. He and Rico had on all-black Yankee caps pulled way down to their eyes.

When they walked into the lounge, Edeeks was playing pool by himself, and Rashid was playing with the Sony PlayStation on the big screen.

"What the fuck you done did?" Rico barked at Rashid as soon as he walked through the door.

Rashid stood, looked down at Rico, then said, "Man, if you don't get the fuck out of my face wit' that bullshit..."

"That's it!" Manny yelled. Everyone's head turned in his direction. The pressure he was under made him lose control. He looked at Rico, then said, "Remember what I told you. I don't want any shit from nobody. I built this shit, and I will tear it apart, nobody else!"

"That's what I'm sayin', Daddy-O!" Rashid said, happy that his boss set the tone.

Manny turned to Rashid. "You. We left you in charge. What happened?"

Rashid walked closer to Manny, then exhaled. He said, "Daddy-O, you know I would never violate you or M3. The deal is this. This cat Rico, *who used to be* my man, started a war when he bodied that Cuban cat for nothing. When you bust your gun, it gotta be about getting rich. Guns and getting paper don't mix. So, when he hit that cat, they musta known y'all was out 'cause they hit back. Hard! First Stan, then Rich Dice, then Fee-foe, and then Bone from my clique on the Westside. "

"I knew this was going to happen. Who's next?" Edeeks asked.

"And Kev down in Atlanta," Manny said.

"Say word? Damn, Daddy-O, they think this thing is a game," Rashid said.

"So what did you do up here?" Manny asked.

Rashid sighed. "Truth be told, Manny? I don't even need to fuck wit' y'all to get paid, you heard? I'm the one that moved the work, got it cut, and built an army of fifty for M3. *I'm* the one that had M3 buzzing through the town, and *I'm* the one sending all them hundreds of gees to you two cats, and *nobody* ever asked me if I was a'ight. So the way I see it? I been making decisions on my own, but my loyalty to you, Manny, is why I'm still here repping M3. I'm still on the front line and ain't no vacations on *my* watch, you heard? So what I do? I hit them faggots back wit' everything I got. Ain't nothing in The Lower moving without us approving it. We know them Marielitos, or whatever they fucking names is, is supplying them other blocks, so we hit them hard. New York is hot, and I ain't leaving until we decide to leave together." He looked at Rico, then said to Manny, "I know somethin' 'bout loyalty. Our spot Uptown and down is only open from six to twelve. Shit too hot in the daytime, and I ain't got enough work to hold me. I got two hundred and sixty-five gees for you. I'm short and took a lot a losses, but *somebody* forgot to leave me work."

"So who running my spot if Rich Dice, Drama, and Murder is gone?" Rico asked.

Rashid exhaled again. "This nigga only worried 'bout his self. I got Packy up there holding down 17th and 16th Streets. Plus, Tank holding down Bone Fort on the Westside."

"Packy and Tank? I don't even know them niggaz!" Rico complained.

"What the fuck you want me to do? I know them, and I wasn't about to fuck this paper up to check wit' you to see who you liked. If you wasn't trying to control shit all the time, one of your soldiers would a stepped up and held Rich Dice down. When he went to the hospital and the poe-poe locked him to the bed, a few of your cowards broke out. I put the one nigga there who wasn't afraid of holdin' it down, even though the police that was looking for you got murdered up there. Packy got your spot. You work it out wit' him."

Manny looked at Rashid. "You did good. You all right? Did you take care of yourself with the money?"

Rashid looked at Manny, then said, "See? That's why you my man. No doubt I'm alright, but what you want me to do with all this heat and these soldiers?"

Edeeks thought of his dead brother, then stepped in. "What you're going to do is take the cash and make sure the mothers of everyone that died gets seventy-five thousand dollars each. Get Rich Dice, or whatever his name is, a lawyer and make sure his family gets twenty-five thousand for themselves. As a matter of fact, give me the names and tell me where they live. I have to send for Kev's body. None of you M3 guys are to go to the funeral as a group. Have a meeting upstate or in New Jersey and tell them all to sell their cars so the police won't link the team to the officer's death."

"What we suppose to do, run now that a little heat is on? Y'all on some scared bullshit," Rico blasted Edeeks.

Edeeks said, "Run today to fight another day. Stay today and get carried out the wrong way. You can't make a dime in jail or in the grave. Start thinking long term."

"What the fuck you know? Manny, what you wanna do?" Rico asked.

Manny rested his hands on the pool table. *I want to get out and go to Panama,* he thought. "We have to make money, get some lawyers, and finish off the Cubans. We have to find a way to fish them out. Right now, me and Rico have to see the connect. I'm back until this is all over. When this is over, I'm finished." Manny turned to Edeeks. "E, empty the safe and take care of the familia. Then turn this place into a candy store for the children. We are finished with this."

"No man. Hermano, this is M3, man. Money, Murder, and Mayhem. We can get through the mayhem, Manny," Rico pleaded.

"Let's get the fuck outta here, Rico. This ride is over. I'm already doing too much now, but I'm in only because of you, hermano, so don't question me," Manny said, then turned to Rashid. "Get everyone on the same page. Watch out for the police."

"I have your lawyer Robert Boyle downtown. He can take care of all the arrest. I have it covered," Edeeks said, while looking at Manny. "By the way, the gang of four is having a problem with all this heat in Harlem. I told them what they wanted to hear, but if we need political support, then we have to be nice."

Manny nodded. "Okay. Take whatever you need from here. Me and Rico are leaving now."

* * * * *

Manny was driving uptown with the intentions of covering his tracks. He wanted that videotape that Pantera had, and to know why Pedro sent him and his wife on the same hit. If all went well, he wanted to establish a new system with the drugs so that a lower level soldier could meet with the connect. He wanted to remove Rico, Rashid, and himself from out of the loop. Manny wanted out of the game and was going to manipulate things so Rico would leave, too.

While they were driving, Rico didn't say a word, so Manny asked, "You have any suggestions with these people?"

"You can't be serious. This on you!" Rico boldly retorted with a lack of concern written on his face. He leaned back into his seat with his eyes shut.

Havana's Paradise was deserted when Manny and Rico walked through the door. The Cuban with the ponytail was the only one who was sitting out front. Rico cordially greeted the Cuban, "Qué hay?" and Manny nodded.

The Cuban returned the nod, and with one swift move, he went through the procedure of pressing the buzzer behind the counter to indicate to those in the back that they had visitors.

The short brute appeared from the back instead of Pedro. When he saw Manny and Rico he ordered, "Follow me."

Manny and Rico quickly followed the brute towards the back and into the small office. Pantera and Pedro were sitting inside the room looking over paperwork.

"Cómo estan ustedes?" asked Rico.

Pedro stopped what he was doing and looked up at the brothers. "We're good. How was your trip?"

"It was good," Rico replied.

"So tell me, Manny. How is the married life treating you?" Pedro asked.

Displaying a weak smile, Manny responded, "I can't complain."

Pointing to the shopping bag in Manny's hand, Pedro said, "It's been awhile since you come. You usually send Rico. Everything okay?"

"Actually, I came to see you about what took place before I left for Panama."

"Qué bola? Talk to me," said Pedro, while the black beast sat quietly screwing both Manny and Rico with venom in his eyes.

"I want to know why the hell you sent me on a job you sent someone else on. What kind of games you playing, Pedro?"

Rico looked at his brother with a puzzled expression on his face as he stood there wondering what he was talking about.

Pedro glanced over at Pantera, then back at Manny. He lifted his hands andn said, "Take it easy, Manny."

Before anyone could say another word, the black beast slammed his hands down on top of his desk and stood up. "You maricón! You forget when you come to me, you were a nickel-and-dime crook? You don't come in here asking questions. You do what Pedro tell you. My plans are bigger than this operation. Maricón, when Castro dies, who you think Cuba gonna go to? You just like the rest of them Marielitos. You only concern about yourself."

"What?" Rico asked. "You said Marielitos? You know them cats?"

Pantera pointed to Manny, then said, "You be a husband to Xia. You don't worry about nothing else."

Rico put his hand at his waist, then looked at the black beast that he couldn't stand in the first place. "Yo, son, you said Marielito. I need to know about them cats."

Manny held up his hands in an attempt to calm down the tension in the room. "Espérate. Hold up." Manny remembered what they initially came there for. "Pantera, perdóname. I meant no harm. I just wanted to know what was going on." Reaching inside the shopping bag beside his feet, Manny grabbed a stack of money, then asked, "Can we still handle business?"

The black beast glared at Manny and Rico. He mumbled under his breath, then fiercely said, "Salpica!" telling them to leave.

"Pantera, I need to do some business and talk to you," Manny pleaded.

"Salpica!" Pantera said again.

Realizing that he made a blunder, Manny glanced down at the floor with feelings of frustration. He told his brother, "Come on, let's go," then turned and walked back through the office door with Rico trailing.

Before they jumped into Manny's truck, Rico pointed back at Havana's Paradise and asked, "Bro, what the fuck was that about?"

Manny thought about telling Rico the story of how he had killed several people for the black beast, but Manny had too much on his mind. "I'll tell you later when this is all over."

During the ride down the Cross-Bronx Expressway, Rico broke the silence. "Yo bro, fuck them clowns, but we gotta go back. They mentioned them Marielitos. They know something! For the work? They ain't the only candy shop in town. I might be able to get this African kid named Big Ed from a hunned and 24th. Damn, I wish Fee-foe was alive. Them Nigerians got some shit, but it ain't as strong as what we had. Pull over on Jerome Ave so I can cop a hooptie."

"Okay, so what about Self in Atlanta? Who has the coca?"

"Bro, don't sweat that. Dominican Charlie up off of Broadway got yayo by the boatloads. He got bricks at eighteen for five and better. That's who I was seeing before M3. When I pick up my man Baby Born and his brother Sha Bee to hold me down, we gonna take care of everything. If I can't find the powder we need, then I'm going to *take* it from them other spots. If we don't get no paper, nobody getting no paper."

"Okay. Take care of that while I go see Carmen. Find a place to hold everything because we can't go to the club, and hermano..." Rico looked at his brother. "Stop talking to Rashid like that. He is your partner. Don't let the money go to your head."

Manny pulled over at the Jerome Avenue exit in the Bronx. Rico put the bag of cash over his shoulder, then said, "Whatever, man. I gotta make this shit happen for us," and he slammed the door.

Manny got back on the Cross Bronx Expressway and drove the straight line until he was over the George Washington Bridge. He picked up his cell phone and Carmen answered on the first ring. She was paranoid out of her mind and asked him to hurry. Manny stepped on the gas a little harder.

By the time Manny's keys were turning the lock to Carmen's door, she was on the other side of the door with a gun in her hands.

"Puta, qué tú hace? What the fuck are you doing with a gun?" Manny asked.

Carmen exhaled in relief, then lowered the weapon. "Matthew gave it to me. I had to make sure it was you, Negrito." Manny was about to be dumb and ask her how she got the gun on the plane, but then he remembered her connections, the same connections they used to get rich from. Carmen locked the door, then started kissing on Manny. "Oh, papi, I miss you. Dame' pinga."

She reached for his belt buckle, and Manny said, "Puta! They tried to kill you and all you can think about is fucking?"

Carmen was embarrassed. Her eyes shot to the floor and she pouted. "I just miss you. When I saw Kev die, I was thinking of you and how much I love you. I don't care about your wife, Negrito, I need you. Our baby needs you."

"Baby? Oh yeah, how you know you pregnant? That was just a couple of weeks ago."

Carmen sat on her leather couch. "I know, okay? My period was supposed to come and it didn't. My body feels different like the last time." She was talking about her last abortion. "You promised the last time that I could keep it. This is three times, Manny, I'm having *this* baby."

Manny had a seat, rubbed his forehead, then said, "Okay, cuanto dinero from Atlanta?"

Carmen was offended. "Oh, you Mr. Businessman when I tell you I'm having your baby?" She stalled, trying to calculate how much money her and Kev put away on top of the four keys Self had. To cover her tracks, she said, "Nada. Self has the coca, four keys."

Manny said, "Okay, good. You don't go back to Atlanta without talking to me first. You stay here. Your mama and papa are safe in Brooklyn. How much money do you have saved?"

Carmen thought about how much she stashed away on top of what Kev gave her, and she cut it in half when she said, "Three hundred thousand."

Manny knew women too well. When he stood, he said, "That means you have at least five hundred. Good. I made you rich. You keep your job and lay low. I have business to take care of."

Carmen removed her sweat pants as if she was getting in the shower. "You not going to fuck me, Negrito?"

Manny headed for the door and answered, "No."

* * * * *

"Baby, don't go. Master, please don't do this to me," Peaches begged, while Self was packing his things in a duffel bag.

Self cut his eyes at his woman. "Master gotta go. If I stay up in here and somethin' happen to you, then what?"

Peaches was crying. "I can feel it. Something bad going to happen. We can go. We can run away, go back to New York. I can work in a club up there while you stay in. We can leave this place and never come back."

Self strapped on his bulletproof vest, then said, "We suppose to leave Ma too?"

"Baby, please...please don't leave me," Peaches begged on her knees.

BANG! Self's hand flew across her face, leaving a palm print in her cheek. "Get on the bed," he barked. Peaches ran from the floor to the bed, then curled up like a child crying. Self held her face tight. "Bitch, you belong to Self. Ain't no begging! You a trooper." He reached under the bed and pulled out the AR-15, then dropped it next to her with two extra clips. "Self ain't leaving you. Self ain't *never* leaving you! They'll find you in a ditch first, but you can't be weak and say you represent Self. Self going to stay at April's so Self can find them cats that did Self's family dirty and protect you at the same time. If they would've known where Self was at, they would've came already. They around. Self know they around, 'cause Self would've stayed around until the job was done, too. It's only a matter of time before April tell them where they can find you."

"She wouldn't do that," Peaches cried out.

"You don't know what she will do when they splitting her in half and making her feel pain she ain't never felt before. Nuthin' matters but you and Self. You a trooper! Self's queen! They come through that door, you pick that up and use it like Self taught you. Don't go to the club. Stay in a couple of days. You got the paper in case of a emergency. Somethin' happens to Self, you don't do nothin' till Self tell you to. You got fifty thousand under the bed." Self handed her a small bag with some of his jewels in it. The expensive trinkets meant nothing to him. "You hold those. If them Cubans get the drop on Self, sell them and open a business. Stop stripping 'cause Self won't be there to protect you. Tell Ma to keep her mouth shut and come keep you company. Self won't be far, but Self ain't coming back till this is over. If Self die tonight, know you the only one that was Self's wife."

Self did the unthinkable by leaning over and kissing Peaches deep and hard. She couldn't believe that her man's tongue was in her mouth for the first time. She tried to keep it there and felt like she was about to cum just from his kiss. Tears rolled down her cheeks as she watched him strap two 10mm handguns with two 21-round clips on each side of his hip. He then put his jewelry on over his shirt. He grabbed a long bag, kissed her again, and Self was out the door, never to return.

Self took the elevator to the parking garage. He popped the trunk, removed what was inside the duffel bag, and then laid it in the trunk. He then sat in the M3, pushed in his *Hustle Hard* CD from the hot rapper Main-O, and then adjusted his Fortune Hunters sweat suit. Self was going to floss as bait for the Cubans, and before the day was out, he wanted to catch some big fish.

When he walked into April's house, she was sitting on the living room couch staring at the floor. Self looked at her and then she looked up with surprise. "Oh...Master? What's up? What you doing here?"

Self headed for Peaches' old bedroom and said, "Moving in!"

April's whole facial expression changed. She hopped to her feet. "What about Peaches? When she coming?"

Self dropped his bag on the bed. "She ain't. Master here to take care of some business."

April leaned her shapely body against the door frame. "How long you staying? Y'all had a fight or somethin'?"

Self pulled the covers down off the bed and said, "Nah. Master staying for a little while. Make sure everything in order."

April looked at him from head to toe. "You hungry?"

Self shot her a look that suggested she must have been crazy to believe that she could cook his food.

April shrugged her shoulders, then said, "Okay then, I'm 'bout to take a shower. Just call me if you need anything."

Self stashed a stack of cash away in Peaches' old dresser, then hung up the two outfits that he brought with him. He fixed the room to make sure he would know if one single thing was out of place. When he was done, he sat on the bed with his two guns by his side watching television.

Five minutes later, April came to the doorway with a pink towel wrapped around her midsection and baby oil dripping from her dark chocolate skin. She stepped into the bedroom then asked, "Master, I miss Kev, but I accepted that he gone. I'm glad you came over. If there's anything you need me to do just let me know?"

Self looked down at the pink toe nails of her pedicured feet, then at her chocolate calfs, the tightness of the towel that was holding her floppy breast and ass, then at her cute face. He patted the bed, and like a faithful pet, she slithered onto the bed and let the towel drop. She slid her face by Self's neck rubbing on his chest. Self looked her in her face, dug in his pocket, and removed a knot of cash. He placed five hundred dollars in her hand, then said, "Listen here, Slick. First thing you got to know is that there ain't nothing you can do for me that Peaches can't do better. What Master want you to do is take this money and go buy a bunch of fruit, vegetables, juice, and food. Every one of these country-ass ballas that you see on the way and in the club tonight, you let them know Kev's uncle in town and he got what they need. Tell them that Master drives a black M3 and that Master got a lot a coke for whoever wants it. Let them know I'm staying close by here. When them bitches in the club talk about Kev, tell them ain't nothing change and that I left Peaches and came home where I knew it was good at." Self held her face, looked in her eyes, then said, "And every time you

Crime Pays

walk through that door, take off all your clothes as soon as you walk in. You got that, Slick?"

April squeezed the bills tight and nodded rapidly, indicating she understood. Self was glad his plan was coming together. With her clothes always off, she wouldn't be able to hide a weapon and catch him slipping.

Later that night, Self headed over by the Bluff and then to Cascade Pines. He made sure everyone in the area could see the jewelry in his mouth and the remainder of his jewels on his body. When he was leaving the area, he saw a '64 Impala flashing its lights in his direction. He stopped his car, held his weapon in his hand, and rolled the window down. Peanut eased up across from him.

"Aye, man. What's popping, partna?" Peanut asked. "That's fucked up wit' what happened wit' your fam, partna. Since he been gone, things bone dry round here."

Self nodded. "Yeah? You still in business?"

"Hell nah! I'm still spending paper that yo nephew made me. If I had a partna like you to back me, man, I'll have things lined up by morning. Only thing is these bitches over on Commercial Ave got some good yayo all of a sudden, and all they weight is moving. My best people over there scared of them fools."

Self asked, "Yeah? So you ready to take that over if I make the way?"

"Shit yeah! Partna, I'm ready to stay paid."

Self nodded, then said, "Jump in."

Peanut wasn't expecting that response. "Aye...oh...aye, man...right now?"

"If you trying to stay paid, you got to seize the opportunity."

Peanut was thinking hard. "How 'bout you follow me over there and we do it like that?"

Self smirked. "Lead the way."

Peanut made a U-turn, then sped through the streets of Atlanta until he hit the slums of Commercial Avenue. Two girls, five young boys wearing different colored baseball caps, and customers buying drugs from the boys were all Self saw. Peanut slowed his car down, and Self pulled up beside him.

"Aye, man," Peanut began. "That young'n right there, he the one gotta go. The rest of them bitches a move wit' whoever got it."

Self looked over at a young boy that was built like a lineman in football giving orders to the rest of the kids. He checked his rearview mirror and sped off in the direction of the crowd. When the kids saw the black M3 speeding their way, two of them ran, and the lineman stood his ground. Self came to a screeching halt and stepped out of the car.

235

"You want to cop somethin'?" the lineman asked in an effort of bravery.

When Self pulled out the 10mm that sat on his left hip, the two girls and another one of the kids ran. He pointed the gun in the lineman's face, then barked, "Get the fuck on your knees."

"Aye, man, take what you want, man." the lineman screamed out in fear, while his hands were to the sky and he dropped to his knees.

Self shoved the black steel into the lineman's mouth. While the youngster was looking into Self's eyes, Self removed the other gun off his right hip and held it to his side. He said, "This street belong to Master now. Peanut run shit 'round here. If anything happens to him or my money come up short, I'll be back."

The kid nodded and tried to talk with the steel in his mouth. Self then took his right hand and began to whale on the lineman's face with his steel. He then pulled the nozzle out of the linesman's mouth and bloodied his face with massive blows of both gun butts. When the lineman was laying back gasping for air, Self knelt down, put the tip of both guns on each side of the lineman's nose then asked, "How much work you got left?"

"Man...oh, man...I'm sorry, man. Please don't kill me, man...a half a key."

"A'ight. Give that paper to Peanut. When your old boss asks for his paper, tell him you got a new boss, and Master in the black M3 got his paper."

"Yeah, man...I...I got you," was all Self heard when he headed back to his car. Peanut stood there stunned, when Self said to him, "Get money, partna," and he drove away.

Self hit all the nightclubs, the areas where Latinos in Atlanta hung out, and then ended his night at Magic City flirting with April in an attempt to get the streets talking. He was determined to reach out to every major hustler that had heavy amounts of cocaine, hoping to meet up with the men that murdered Kev.

* * * * *

With the new Nigerian and Dominican connects meeting Rico's demand, things in the M3 organization started coming back together. Things were slow uptown due to the police presence, but in The Lower, the heroin was moving because the dope fiends had no place else to go. Rashid held the fort down in The Lower and kept the money coming in for the M3 Boyz.

Rico was determined to gain control of the M3 Boyz all over again. He made sure his presence was felt Uptown and kicked dirt on Rashid every chance he got. He was jealous of Rashid's ability to floss even when he wasn't trying. He also didn't like the way Manny took care of Rashid, so he wanted to prove himself with every chance he got. He and Manny set up a system where they call each other every day so the other could know that they were still alive and out on the streets. Everything went well, until the day Rico didn't call.

A week after they were back from Panama, Manny left his pregnant wife at home. He headed down to 117th Street in an effort to see his brother. He was dressed in his regular casual attire of slacks, a sweater, and a pair of shoes. Tucked in his waistband was his most trusted friend, a Glock-19. As his Escalade burned up the New York State Thruway, Manny thought about the black beast, and the line he and Pantera had with business and being family. Despite Pantera's disrespect, Manny hoped to one day regain the man's trust.

When the black Escalade pulled up on 117th Street at Manhattan Avenue, a young soldier was standing on the far corner away from the spot, talking to two young ladies that were barely dressed. For some strange reason, the block was semi-empty. Usually at that time of the morning, the block would be crowded with customers coming through waiting to purchase their morning fix. Manny looked around for anyone that was familiar in the M3 organization. When he didn't see anyone, he drove around the corner to Morningside Park. He pulled the black fitted cap on his head and then took his time walking up 117th Street.

Manny hit the corner where the young soldier was still talking to the ladies. The young man looked slightly familiar to Manny so he asked, *"Yo, you seen Rico?"*

The young man turned to Manny with arrogance, trying to show off for the girls. When he recognized Manny's face he quickly humbled himself and ignored the girls. "Oh my bad boss." He stuck his hand out. "I'm Packy, I was at your wedding, way in the back. You probably don't 'member."

Manny thought about his army of soldiers and how it was impossible to remember all their names and faces. "Oh yeah, I remember you. You seen Rico?"

Packy put a puzzled look on his face. "Aye yo, you ain't hear 'bout last night?"

"What you talking about?" Manny asked with interest.

"Yo, some Spanish kid ran up on Rico last night and tried to air him out. Dude hit the general twice in the..."

"What?" Manny asked, fearing the worst. "He dead?"

The young soldier held up his hands. "Nah, Rico's a'ight. You know we keep our vest on once you said we had to." Manny wondered what else they were told that he didn't say. Packy said, "Rico play'd dude like he was really hurt, and when dude got up on him, Rico destroyed the kid fo'real. That's why I got the spot closed. Squally been all over here snooping around, asking questions, and looking for Rico, but don't sweat nothing. I got this. I know this whole team from top to bottom. I know everything 'bout M3. Like I know if anybody violate you or Rico, they whole family gonna get murdered. I feel sorry for that kid Scoob family, boss, but this M3, and I'ma hold it down like you told Rah to tell me."

Manny sighed from annoyance. "Bro, where's Rico now? What hospital?"

Packy chuckled. "Nah. He somewhere up at that secret bat cave y'all live in. You ain't see him? That mansion y'all got must be mad big if you ain't see him. I'm feeling how y'all don't let nobody know where y'all rest y'all head at."

"Yeah, that's probably where Rico's at," Manny said, thinking how the young soldiers would let him run them in a brick wall if he asked.

"I'ma hold it down. Right now, I got cats all over me, and you can't even see them, right, boss?" Manny looked up and spotted two kids with guns on fire escapes and nodded his head anyway, telling Packy that he was right. "We got to be real easy. You never know when this shit is coming from them cats we had that drama with. But, I'm here now. I don't think them clowns really want it wit' us. They know I ain't havin' it."

Manny sighed. "Mi pana, we never underestimate no one. Even the strong appears to be weak at times while they actually laying in the cut to kill you."

"Fo'sure. You know I know how cats be tryin' to rock dudes to sleep. That's deep what you just said, boss."

Manny glanced around. "Yo, be safe out here."

"No doubt, boss," Packy said after giving Manny a big hug.

Manny reached for his cell phone, hit a button that automatically dialed a number, then headed towards the Escalade.

"Talk about it," Rico answered when Manny returned to the Escalade.

"Maricón, I been worried sick over you and you at home?" Manny barked.

Rico started laughing. "I was fucking my girl. That shit is mad hard when your whole body is black and blue. Kid tried to do me last night."

"Si, I heard already. I'm on 117th now."

"Bro, get up outta there. It's mad hot. I got my girl over here, so yo, just come over and talk to me here. Make sure nobody follow you."

"Chucha, I don't even know where you live now, estúpido."

Rico laughed again, then said, "Right down the block from that other spot you had."

Manny started the engine and drove towards Riverdale, New York, where he had his condo. Rico gave him the address to his place in Yonkers. Manny flew up the Westside Highway to the Henry Hudson Parkway. He paid the toll and then took the highway until he reached the Riverdale Avenue exit. He then drove through the quiet suburban streets of the upper Bronx until he crossed the Yonkers county line. He followed Rico's directions by staying on Riverdale Avenue until he reached the steepest hill he ever saw in his life. He made the left, and at the bottom of the hill was the parking garage to the beautiful Glenwood Terrace.

Manny stepped into the gorgeous building and took the elevator to the 23rd floor. When he stepped into the carpeted hallway, silence met him, and he wondered why Edeeks didn't move him into a place like that.

Rico's Latin lady opened the door wearing a negligee. Knowing Rico, he probably told the girl to put that on to annoy him, Manny reasoned. When Manny walked through the house, Rico was in bed counting money in front of the television that was originally in the social club. His midsection was bruised, but his hands were working fine.

"Hermano, what's up, kid? Come on in and sit on the bed."

Manny stood in the room while Rico's girl went through the motions to impress him that she really loved Rico. He said, "Qué pasa?"

Rico said, "Bro, this kid came outta nowhere on me when I was getting in a cab. He was about his business and had the drop on me, too. Kid named Scoob that used to come around Rah and me back in the days. I don't know if he was trying to rob me or what, but he blasted my ass when he saw me reach. Yo bro, I was scared to death, but then I had to do what I had to do. I heard he caught a bad one."

Manny didn't like the way Rico was running his mouth in front of the young girl. He asked, "Was it Marielitos?"

"They mighta sent the cat. I don't know. But, I think that was some other shit. Homie was probably hating on me or somethin'."

Manny said, "Okay, lay low. Call me mañana."

While Manny was walking out the door, Rico yelled, "Hey, come back and help me count all this shit up."

Manny reached for the doorknob. He had other plans, like being at home with his pregnant wife.

SEVENTEEN

Commanding officer Captain John Baylor sat in a boardroom repeatedly reviewing the video recording made the night before by his undercover officers. Their job was to secretly record the daily activities of the M3 Boyz in Harlem and on Manhattan's Lower Eastside. On the wall in the boardroom was a large pyramid with all the pictures of as many members of the M3 crew they could find with their names and addresses on it. At the top of the pyramid was Manny and Rico Black.

The city's special narcotics prosecutor, Bridget Brennan, and her protégé, Maria Flores, gave specific instructions regarding the direction of the investigation. The mayor's officer ordered him to take over from where Detective Clarke messed up and conduct a thorough probe of the operation and its primary leaders, Manny and Rico Black. From that day on, his unit made undercover purchases, filed daily reports to Maria Flores, and agreed that under no circumstances would they apprehend any of the M3 Boyz without prior approval from their boss or the prosecutor.

Baylor was becoming extremely frustrated that the probe had yet to turn up anything concrete on Manny and Rico Black. Sure he had charges on each member of the crew that he could file, and he could always bring them in on conspiracy charges, but beyond that they had nothing.

During his progress meeting with the city's special prosecutor and her protégé, he said, "Earlier on I had my men run the names and license plate numbers of all the M3's we saw in the high drug areas, and these guys vehicles were all registered to P.O. Boxes. We know for sure that the man called Manny lives somewhere in the upstate region, but we keep getting a cold trail."

"Well, at least we know who these guys are and what they look like," the special prosecutor said.

"Yes, but what about the videotape?" Maria Flores asked Baylor.

"This is what I have," he said, before pressing the PLAY button.

For the tenth time that morning, Baylor viewed the videotape, trying to identify the man caught on the tape in a shootout with another man who eventually was killed. Due to the poor quality of the tape caused by the pouring rain, he was unable to make out the killer's face.

However, there was no mistake about it, the killer was definitely wounded. The video showed a black male, dressed in black army fatigues with his cap pulled down covering his face. When he was entering a cab, a light-skinned male approached him and shot him several times, causing the victim to drop to the ground. As the gunman walked up to finish the victim off, the victim pulled out a weapon. He fired, hitting the gunman three times in the face and killing him instantly. Before the observing officers who were stationed a block away had an opportunity to act, the wounded male quickly hopped up holding his chest and disappeared into the night.

Baylor's eyes instinctively shifted from the images on the TV's screen to the doorway as one of his officers walked inside the small office. He looked at the two important looking women in the room, then said, "Excuse me, Captain. We checked all the hospitals in Manhattan and the Bronx for anyone who had sustained gunshot wounds to the chest. We even checked the morgue, but we came up empty."

Baylor's hard face turned beet red. "The guy got hit. He had to go somewhere for medical attention. Check the hospitals in the remaining three boroughs and others in Jersey. See what we can come up with."

"I'm on it, Captain," the officer answered, while exiting the room.

When his office door closed, Baylor looked over to the women.

Mrs. Flores said, "We can't see the perp's face good enough to I.D. him because of the poor quality of the videotape. But, we are able to make out that the perp was wearing fatigues, which are the M3 Boyz standard dress code."

Bridget Brennan asked, "So how does that benefit this investigation if we can't identify the perpetrator? It doesn't bring us any closer to indicting the leaders. We need some corroborating evidence to put them away for good. Based on that videotape, the perp or victim, depends on how you look at it, can get a good lawyer and have a possible justification defense."

Baylor thought a moment about their predicament and a similar case he had worked on a few months earlier. He said, "I understand where you two are coming from, but I think I might have a solution to our problem. Based on the numerous videotapes we have of them making sales, we have enough evidence to charge the M3 Boyz under the state's racketeering law for conspiracy to operate a criminal enterprise. Let's not forget criminal sale of a controlled substance in the first degree. We can throw in the murder charge just as a means to apply a little pressure on the soldiers to get them pointing fingers. Once that starts, I'll bet my career on it, we'll have more than enough evidence and witnesses to be able to put the Black brothers away for life." He looked over at the pyramid on the wall. Baylor momentary studied the photos of Manny getting into his Escalade on the day after the shooting, and Rico hanging on 117th and Manhattan Avenue. He sucked his teeth, then said "Ms. Flores, I want to take them all down at the same time, but it's your call."

There was brief moment of silence. Maria's mind raced as she thought about what Baylor was proposing, and how she could hurry up and bring the M3 Boyz case to an end. She wanted to move on so she could focus more on the important cases. Then she thought of her uncle and the bloodbath that was happening in Manhattan. "Okay, Baylor. Do whatever you have to do. Just keep us notified as soon as you bring them in. Are we understood?"

A smile spread across Baylor's face. "That's affirmative. I'll inform you ASAP." Baylor picked up the phone, said a few words, then hurried out his office.

* * * * *

A week later, Rashid stood outside in the heart of Alphabet City on 4th Street and Avenue B. He was watching his twelve-man crew handle their business. From ten o'clock in the morning, the block was packed with customers coming through to buy heroin. Since he had the dope spot open, the M3 Boyz were getting the majority of cash in The Lower.

The vibration from his cell phone caused Rashid to reach for his waistband. Swiftly, he checked the caller I.D. before answering the call. He flipped open the small gadget, put it to his ear. "What's poppin', Daddy-O?" he said, while walking away from his soldiers.

"Meet me around the corner," the voice on the other line said.

Instantly, Rashid walked past a redbrick tenement building and then cut the corner.

A silver Plymouth Prowler with tinted windows was parked at the corner. Rashid walked over to the passenger side and jumped in. "What you doing down here, Daddy-O?" Rashid asked.

Manny looked at all his mirrors and then said, "Nothing. I'm just checking up on the best man for the job. I wanted to make sure you all right"

Rashid followed Manny's eyes to the rearview mirrors. "That's why you my man, Manny! You need to talk to your brother."

"You hear what happened to Rico?"

Rashid faked concern. "Yeah, man, he can't be slipping. I heard it was that cat Scoob. What was that nigga thinking?"

Manny sighed. "I don't want you to take anything for granted, okay? Stay on point. I need things to get back on track so I can get out. Then you can take my place."

Rashid smiled. "Good lookin', but this ain't Uptown. We stay on point. If them faggots try they luck twice, we ready." Rashid checked the side mirror of the car. Four old timers were sitting off to the side, away from all the action, playing dominos. Concealed under their coats and shirts were guns ready for whatever. Rashid smiled knowing he had everything under control. Then he said, "A few of Fee-foe people that just came home is on the payroll ready to hold it down. Them old timers is some funny-ass dangerous dudes."

Manny nodded to the truth. "Okay, hermano, you still doing good. Just be careful."

"Don't worry, Daddy-O. We're good down here." The two men shook hands, then hugged before Rashid left the car.

Manny pulled off and made a U-turn. Rashid cut the corner without noticing the team of undercover officers less than a block away. For twenty minutes, Captain Baylor, Detective Clarke, and a team of Baylor's men watched as the M3 Boyz exchanged dope for cash. Baylor reached on the dashboard of the dark, Chevrolet cargo van and picked up a handheld radio.

"This is Captain Baylor downtown. Units one to twelve do you have a visual on said targets?" he asked, while looking at the group of young hustlers through a pair of high-powered binoculars.

"This is unit one… affirmative!"

"This is unit two... affirmative!"

"This is unit three… affirmative!"

Baylor asked, "Units four to six, are you ready uptown? I need everything to work in unison.

"This is unit four... affirmative!"

"This is unit five… affirmative!"

"This is unit six… affirmative!"

"Units seven to twelve, engage! Bring the whole team down on all locations!"

The remaining units each confirmed that they had a visual on the M3 Boyz at the other spots in the city, and they were moving in.

Again, Baylor talked into his handheld radio. "Listen up! Units one to three, I want everybody in position. On my command, I want to converge on all the subjects. Subjects may be armed." His eyes were glued on Rashid, who was walking back in the direction of his soldiers. He barked into his radio. "Unit one, move now from the roof. All of *my* units…*my units,* the pigeons are in the coop! Shut'em down! Shut'em down!"

Rashid was on the block with his crew when he heard the sound of tires screeching. By the time he looked up, the Major Crime Squad and the Narcotic Task Force were rushing the block from all four directions. Dozens of undercover vehicles, SUV's, Mercedes Benz's, minivans, and a city bus appeared out of nowhere and blocked off the avenue. The M3 crowd made an attempt to flee, but were caught in the web. What seemed like hundreds of officers dressed in street clothes swarmed down on Rashid and his peoples and started locking them all up.

At each M3 spot in the city, each member of the M3 crew were being handcuffed with unbreakable plastic strips and placed into a New York City bus. The four raids was one of the biggest round ups in ex-prosecutor Mayor Giuliani's administration and one of the biggest busts in the history of the city. The police swarmed on all the spots, snatched up workers, customers, and even a few innocent bystanders. By the time all the members of the organization were sent to 100 Centre Street at Central Booking to be fingerprinted, the police had rounded up eighty-three people.

The innocent and guilty both received the humiliating treatment of being fingerprinted and charged with a crime. They sat in holding pens waiting to see the judge the following day, but during their wait, each man was pulled into interrogation rooms so Captain Baylor and his men could offer them deals. Five hours later, two officers came for Rashid. He was sent to Queens where they wanted him separated from all other members of the M3 organization.

Twenty-four hours later, Rashid and the majority of the M3 Boyz saw a judge, and all were denied bails. Rashid was brought back to Manhattan and was sitting inside a cell in the high-security Central Monitoring Case unit on the 11th floor of the Manhattan House of Detention, better known as "The Tombs." When Rashid was finally allowed his phone call, he rushed to call his baby's mother, making sure she was doing what they rehearsed so many times before. Rashid had planned for this day, and his woman was seasoned to handle the pressure for it. He figured that the line was tapped, but he had to do what he hoped someone else would do for him. He asked his girl to call Rico's cell phone.

After five rings, a groggy-voiced Rico answered the phone. "Yo, talk to me."

Without missing a beat, Rashid thought about the last time Rico stood where he was, and he said in haste, "Aye yo, Sundance, this Butch Cassidy. Listen, I don't know how much time I got on this phone, but we in the wrong place. All of us."

There was a short pause. Rico leaned up in his bed, wiped the sleep out of his eyes, then asked, "When? Who?"

"Daddy-O, it's all over the wire. They grabbed the whole team. But, check it, that's only the half of it. Last night, when I was brought in, I ran into Rich Dice. He told me the poe-poe rushed everybody everywhere. Anyway, they got me and Dice. He just came from the hospital, and we up in The Tombs under some shit called CMC status," Rashid said, while looking around at the other detainees playing cards and socializing in the small recreation area within the housing block. "They chargin' us under the state's RICO Law with conspiracy to murder, conspiracy of narcotic distribution, criminal sale of controlled substance."

"Yo, what the fuck happened? What the fuck you done did now?" Rico asked, fully alert as he hopped up out his bed and started pacing the floor.

Rashid sighed. "This nigga. Man, I don't know, but shit seem suspect, and check wit' your brother. He was right there and he skated. Soon as he bounced, we got rushed. And why the fuck y'all ain't here wit' the rest of us?"

Rico lost it. "Bitch nigga, what you sayin', my fam is a snitch? That's it! I'm laying your ass down. In there or out here."

Rashid didn't want to point the finger at anyone without having evidence, so he played it safe by not saying anything. After taking a deep breath and exhaling, he answered, "Daddy-O, I really don't know. I'm just sayin' that it's a hell of a coincidence, and you can eat a dick, faggot. You can get touched right where you at, but I ain't no cell gangster. Plus, the streets is watching. See you when I see you."

"Yeah, see you when I see you. Rot, muthafucka!"

* * * * *

Miguel had just come home, when his phone started ringing nonstop. When he answered it, his niece was on the other end of the line.

"Hello, Tío. I'm so glad I caught you. I have some good news for you," she said excitingly.

"Okay, get to it."

Maria's excitement disappeared. "We are building a strong case against the M3 Boyz as we speak. We apprehended eighty-three members of the organization. The M3 Boyz are no more. All areas where they were selling their product have been cleared of their presence. I am on my way to do a press conference, and I've made sure none of them can receive bail for now. We should have Manny or Rico Black in custody very shortly."

Miguel yelled, "You don't have Rico and Manny Black? Puta, I told you I needed the two brothers to go. The rest are meaningless. Coño! Now I will handle them myself"

"But... but..." The dial tone was the last thing Maria Flores heard on the other end of the line. She held the phone away from her ear, then said to no one in the room, "Fuck you, Uncle Miguel. I got what I want with your help."

Miguel dialed Felix's number. "Oyeme, la policía has created a new market in the enterprises of the Lower Eastside. I suggest your men reorganize and make sure the loss of control never happens again. Ever!" Miguel ordered.

"Si. Bien. My cleansing of the East Coast can now begin. Our children on vacation in Atlanta tells me they will be all done very, very soon."

Miguel chuckled. "Good. Tell the animal I need the other two problems solved now. Immediately. That will guarantee him coming on the council. He can start his celebration as soon as that task is done."

Felix laughed, then said, "Bien. He has the solution already in his grasp. Smoke a celebration cigar for me. I will see you when it is all over. Viva Marielito!"

* * * * *

Manny was at home in bed with Xia playing with the remote control. On one of the channels, he saw two short women surrounded by a group of city officials standing in front of a thousand flashing bulbs. *BREAKING NEWS* flashed across the screen, so he turned up the volume to see what the fuss was about.

When the short Latina on the screen stepped to a podium in front of the mayor, she cleared her throat and said, "Today we have made history in the fight against crime in New York City. We have put an end to the notorious gang called The M3 Boyz."

"Coño!" Manny sat up with Xia, and they both looked at the screen in shock.

"We have made over eighty arrests, and there are more to come. We predict that we will have the leaders, Ricardo and Manuel Black, in custody before the night is over. Some of the men have made statements, so we know for sure that our charges will stick."

"Damn, baby, what are we going to do?" Xia asked.

Instantly, Manny's cell phone rang. He saw that it was Rico's number, and he was scared to answer it. He cut off the television and answered the phone. "What?" he asked in case it wasn't his brother.

Rico was panicking. "Aye yo, the poe-poe swarmed the block and bagged the whole crew. They took everybody."

A pain shot through Manny's head as Rico confirmed that what he saw on television was not a dream. He said, "I know. You on the news."

"I'm on the news? The whole world telling me that *you* on the news!" Rico yelled.

"What the fuck is going on?" Manny questioned. "I was just there with Rah. This is crazy, man."

"Yeah, that faggot called me and tried to say you on some snitch shit 'cause you was there and they ain't got us. I'm laying his ass down."

"Hermano, be easy. We have to figure out what we are going to do? I told you we should've stayed in Panama. Whatever Rashid thinks, we still have to do our part to get him out. That's what a general does for his soldiers."

Rico said, "Yeah, whatever. Right now, I know exactly what I'ma do. We got them Cubans to deal wit' and the poe-poe. I'ma stay my ass right here until your ass come and get me! Don't nobody know where I'm at but you and my girl, and her nervous ass got me bugging. So, I sent her home."

"Okay, hermano, keep your eyes open and lay low until I find out what's what."

"Okay, later! See you when I see you." Rico ended the call.

"Is Rico all right? Is he safe where he is?" Xia asked.

Manny threw the phone on the bed. "Yeah, he's up in Glenwood Terrace in Yonkers. Nobody knows where he's at, so he says."

"What do you need me to do?" Xia asked.

The phone conversation Manny had with his brother disturbed him a great deal. The walls were closing in. Based on everything that took place with the M3 Boyz, his gut feeling told him that he was next. He didn't want to stand still like a sitting duck and allow the unexpected to catch him slipping in a vulnerable position. Assuming that the police were already onto to him, Manny said, "Your car is not registered to here, right?"

Xia said, "No. It's registered to the restaurant downtown. Only the Prowler and the Escalade are in my name to this address."

Manny jumped out of the bed. "Bien, give me your car keys."

He heard the stories about prison before and the way people try to take what's yours, so Manny put on a pair of camouflage fatigues, a black long sleeve shirt, and pair a brown and green low-cut nubuck suede boots. He grabbed a large suitcase, took Xia's car keys, and then headed out the door.

When Manny reached the garage, Xia was knocking on the window. She stuck her head in the door, kissed him, and said, "Be careful. I'll be by your side till death do us part, baby."

Manny gunned the Benz wagon out of the garage and headed towards his apartment in Riverdale.

When he reached the desolate neighborhood, he felt safe. He had never brought anyone there except his family. He assumed that the police would be at his old place in Brooklyn, somewhere near the spots, or trying to track down Carmen. Since her family was at his old apartment, he figured the police would contact her.

Once inside the sparsely decorated condo, Manny wasted no time going to his money. It took him twenty minutes to empty each safe in the hallway and bedroom closet. In haste, Manny double checked the condo looking for anything of importance that he might have overlooked. He didn't even bother taking any of his clothes because they were replaceable.

Manny lugged the heavy suitcase to the rear door of the Benz wagon. After dropping the bag in the car, he rushed to get in the driver's seat. Suddenly, a set of lights beamed down on him as a vehicle was headed his way. Manny thought he was busted, but the lights belonged to an old Jaguar that turned at the parking space next to his. After his breathing slowed down, Manny started the car and headed to Connecticut.

While he drove, Manny started dialing a number from the car phone that was in the steering wheel. When the other party picked up, Manny said, "E, where's your wife and daughter?"

"What? Oh, it's you. Did you see the news? I told you s..."

"I don't need that now, hermano. Where is the family?" Manny was losing patience.

Edeeks yawned. "I see you're safe. They're in Cape Cod visiting her family for the weekend."

"Okay, that's good."

"Bro, what the hell is going on? Where's Rico?"

Manny didn't want to stay on the phone. "I really don't know. I'll see you soon," and he ended the call while stomping the gas.

When Manny pulled up to Edeeks' home in Stanford, Edeeks met Manny at the door. Edeeks watched as Manny quickly hopped out the car, and then after suspiciously scanning the wooded area that surrounded Edeeks' house, he retrieved a suitcase from the trunk. Once they were both safely inside, Manny's eyes nervously scanned the ground floor of the small house looking to see if they were alone.

"What?" Edeeks questioned.

Manny put the suitcase down beside a couch and took a seat. "Man, I have to take precaution. If anything goes down before I get to Panama, I want everything here to be safe."

"You're still not telling me anything," Edeeks said, while waiting for an explanation.

Manny's face turned into a frown. "You want to hear it? Okay, crime doesn't pay. You was right, hermano. The policia came and took everybody. I mean everybody, so that's why I'm here. You have to call all of your lawyer friends, and put that suitcase somewhere safe for me until I get back to Panama. Use what you need for the lawyers, but that is mine! No one else. That is what I saved and planned for this day, thanks to you."

Edeeks glanced down at the suitcase. "How much is in there?"

Manny sighed. "Let me see. A little over one mill."

Edeeks eyes popped open. "Whoa! That's a lot of cash. How did you manage to do that? I thought I had a good grip on things."

Manny said, "E, you think I'm stupid? The day you told me about the law, I knew I had to save. When I was buying the Manteca, I flipped a little here and there, and I didn't tell Rico because he's crazy. The whole world will know. Now you the only one that knows. Not even Xia knows." Manny looked at Edeeks, then said, "Hermano, I trust you with my money like I do with my life. Don't disappoint me."

Meeting Manny's gaze, Edeeks said, "Maybe crime does pay." He then shook his head like he was crazy and said, "You have always entrusted me with a great deal, and I have never once disappointed you. Honor, integrity, loyalty, and love mean everything to me. The HILL; that's what you and my brother taught me when I was a boy. I will never intentionally disappoint you. It would be like betraying myself. On our brother Louie's soul that will never happen."

Manny sighed with relief. "I need you, E. I'm scared, hermano. The whole city is looking for me."

Edeeks looked at the suitcase. "Why don't you just go? With that kind of money, you can just pick a state, jump on your boat, and then lay low for a year or two. We can open another business and keep moving legitimately."

Manny laughed. "It was good, though, huh? We had a lot of fun. The wedding? That was loco, hermano. Crazy-ass Rico. I move and they find me because he will go somewhere else and start a new gang." Manny thought of the Marielitos. "I have some unfinished business, then I'm going to Panama. I'll call you then. If anything goes wrong, take care of Mama and the baby. Carmen, too. Xia can take care of herself better than I can." Manny embraced Edeeks, then whispered in his ear, "I love you, brother."

* * * * *

Early the next morning, Self hit the town to make his rounds for the day. Within the short time that he took over all of Peanut's spots along with Commercial Avenue, word hit the streets of Atlanta about the killer named Master who was from New York. With April's assistance, Peanut had more customers than he could handle, and Matthew and his girl were making more money than when Kev was alive.

Self knew it was only a matter of time before the Marielitos caught up to him, so with the two cannons on his hip and his bulletproof vest, he planned on bringing the fight to them whenever they were ready. All the cash he spread around didn't get him the address of the new connects from Miami, but Self knew for sure that they would be coming. With the rest of the cash he made, he met Peaches in deserted parking garages and handed her the cash. She was begging for his affection, so on one occasion they both expressed their love and relieved their sexual tension out in the empty garage. When Peaches was done sucking and loving her man on the hood of the car, she went home with a couple of hundred thousand that she was keeping safe.

Self's black M3 exited Interstate 75 onto Roswell Road heading in the direction of Marietta. He was on his way to pick up cash from Peanut. As he navigated the M3 across Roswell Road and through the hectic traffic, Self stopped at a red light. While waiting on the light to change at the intersection of the large boulevard, he was captivated by the sight of a new S600 Mercedes Benz pulling into the parking lot, adjacent to the mini mall across from him. Suddenly, a burgundy Dodge Caravan backed into his bumper. The force of the impact caused his vehicle to jerk back along with his neck.

"What the fuck?" Self barked out in his state of vexation.

He beeped his horn, then leaned closer to the windshield to see if the driver ahead realized what he was doing. When the driver didn't acknowledge Self beeping his horn and started backing up again, Self flew the door open and stepped out, hoping to save the front end of his car.

With no delay, the driver, who was an older man with a bandana of the Cuban flag wrapped around his sweaty head, jumped out with a .357 magnum in his hands. By the time Self looked down at the front end of his car, the gunman was raising his hand in an attempt to fire. Like a defensive end getting ready to sack a quarterback, Self took off and didn't stop moving until his left shoulder caught the Cuban in the jaw. The impact of him making contact shook the Caravan, and car horns blared to the display of Georgia road rage.

Self was back on his feet as quick as he went down with the tackle. He looked all around. Traffic and his car was blocked. When he didn't see any police responding to the chorus of car horns begging him to move, Self removed the two hammers off his hips and was ready to end the Cuban.

BING-BING-BING! Three shots hit the thick plate in the center of Self's chest. While he was on the way down to the sticky pavement, he saw another Cuban with a silenced M-92 handgun shooting in his direction. Self didn't even know how he hit the ground so fast, but instead of lying there, he crawled under his open door, reached in his car, and then hit the lever to his trunk.

BING-BING-BING! The silenced M-92 put three more slugs in the open door, right above Self's head, while he half crawled his way to the open trunk.

Another Latino jumped out of the truck wearing all black and toting an automatic machine gun. As the three converged on all angles of the M3, Self appeared on the driver's side of the car wearing black gloves. In his hands was a custom Browning A-bolt rifle, loaded with six 7mm Remington shells inside. The hunter's special had the ability to put any AK 47 to shame and explode cinderbricks upon impact.

Self ducked low, then aimed the rifle in the direction of the shooter with the silencer. Rapidly, he shot and pulled the bolt until three rounds were gone. One of the shots put a massive hole through his open door, and through that hole he saw the remains of the shooter's head splattered across the black asphalt. He heard footsteps on the other side of the car, so instead of raising his head, Self moved the bolt-action and fired off the remainder of the bullets through the door and windows. The massive bullets went through the fiberglass like a hot knife on butter.

Self quickly dropped the rifle and reached under his shirt for his 10mm's while dashing in the direction of the nearest sidewalk. A barrage of shots spit out from the machine gun behind him. Self came to the quick conclusion that he needed to take cover behind the parked cars in the mini-mall. During his run to safety, two hot slugs tore into the back of his vest, and the other tore through the back of his arm. While stumbling forward from the impact of the blows, Self reached under his arm and returned fire at the gunmen behind him.

While crouching down behind a green Buick, Self quickly examined his wounds. He realized he was bleeding badly out of the small hole in his arm. If he didn't make a move soon, he would most likely bleed out on the sidewalk. He peeked through the side window of the Buick and watched as a fourth Latino appeared with an AK-47 and then joined the set of twins as they cautiously advanced. Self crouched his body slightly underneath the car, and then took aim at the moving feet of one of the gunmen. He held his guns low, then squeezed off three rounds from each gun. None of the slugs found the gunmen, but the bullets of the man with the machine gun tore the Buick to shreds. In a panic, Self stood recklessly and squeezed the triggers of both guns, causing constant clapping from his automatic cannon.

Stray shots flew in the direction of the Cubans until one of the slugs found the right heel of the man with the machinegun, severing his Achilles tendon, and instantly dropping him to the ground. His two partners quickly ducked behind a Pepsi truck. While the Cuban that was in plain view hollered in excruciating pain, Self squeezed off more shots. The hot copper hit the man dead center mass in the chest and face, putting him out of his misery.

After the blaze of gunfire cleared, Self was holding two, empty, smoking guns. The ringing in his ears deafened the sounds of the sirens blaring, the footsteps that were quickly approaching, and the sound of the silenced shots that tore into his leg and stomach. The vest he had on was built to stop bullets, not the massive impact of the slugs. The force of the slugs sent Self through a large plate glass window of a store that was behind him.

Self's whole body was hurting, his ears were still humming, and his eyes were closed when he felt a sharp pain at the back of his head. Instantly, he opened his eyes. Hanging from the ceiling above him was a huge assortment of camouflage hunting jumpsuits, a surveillance camera, goggles, and clothes in neon orange. When he painfully turned his head to the side, he saw a camouflaged mask, more goggles, and deer scented spray that was in a rack. He then turned his head to the right and saw a shelf with gun cleaning kits and bullets of all kinds.

With a lot of effort, Self pulled his back off the ground and sat up. He looked for his guns and his extra clips, but they were gone. When he looked behind him, he saw a small crowd of people with red faces staring at him. A fat man that was chewing tobacco and wearing a tee shirt held an empty SPAS 12 automatic shotgun in his hand. Right there, it dawned on Self that he was on the floor of a gun shop. When Self looked through the broken glass in front of him, the two Latinos were tiptoeing his way.

Don't these muthafuckas ever give up? Self asked himself as he reached for a mask from the shelf and slipped it on his face. He then struggled to get up, and with the sight of the black man with a mask, people ran for cover, while others ran out the store.

"Stay down!" a redhead in blue jeans, a white shirt, and who had a sheriff's badge dangling from her neck yelled at Self while she held a Taurus 9mm.

Self looked behind him and saw the Cuban with the AK-47 in his hand coming into the store. Before the Cuban said a word, he let his loud gun announce his presence when he sent a few shots in Self's direction, slamming the lady cop to the floor.

While slowly limping away, Self wasted no time in picking up the woman's weapon and sending a gang of slugs in the direction of the Cubans. The redneck with the empty SPAS 12 tried to stop Self, so he popped the good Samaritan in the shoulder and chest. The man laid slumped over the counter unconscious, bleeding profusely. He had already made up his mind that he was going all the way out, but not without first handling his business. The gun in his hand was emptied after the last two shots he popped into the redneck. Self grabbed the automatic shotgun out of the redneck's grip, then pushed the old man's body to the floor. He then busted opened the glass counter where shotgun shells were held. He grabbed a box of 12 gauge slugs and hurried to load the weapon.

When the two Latinos stepped up into the entrance, Self was already hidden behind the counter. They were determined to carry out their mission at all cost. Without any hesitation, the gunmen started firing all over the gun store. Self cranked the automatic shotgun. When the Cuban with the silencer on his weapon tried to reload his gun, Self fired off two shots, hitting him in the neck and deforming his face. The Cuban's lifeless body flew into a solid rack and lied still with the cold thermoses on the shelf. Quickly, his partner let off another round of slugs from his machine gun, catching Self below his vest and in the other leg. The force of the shots sat Self on his ass. He was bleeding badly from all four of his wounds. He felt dizzy while grasping for air. When he heard the Cuban's footsteps slowly approaching, he knew that time was of essence.

Self was bleeding heavy. He felt himself slowly losing consciousness. He tried to catch his breath so he could get back up, but his strength was disappearing by the second. Sweat poured into his eyes, and through his blurry hunter's mask, he spotted the shadow of a figure coming his way. The man stood directly over him. The figure had the AK-47 in his hand pointing down on Self.

The man chuckled, then said, "Viva Marielito!"

With all the energy he could muster, Self quickly moved the shotgun towards the ruthless gunman and pulled the trigger. He also heard the popping sound of a gun that wasn't his, but never felt a thing as he lost consciousness and slipped into darkness.

LAST

Manny was sitting inside his bedroom depressed and paranoid. For the last hour, Carmen had been calling him, but he ignored her. He didn't answer his phone unless it was Rico, and as far as he was concerned, he wasn't going anywhere. When his phone rang again, he jumped and looked down at his caller ID and saw a number from Atlanta that he didn't know. Manny figured it was Self, so he answered it.

"Yo?"

"Hello? Dude, it's me, Matthew."

Manny never met Matthew and didn't want to, so he said, "Qué paso? Where you get this number?"

Matthew's voice trembled when he said, "Manny, it's about Self!"

"Self?" Manny asked with sudden interest.

"Dude, it's all over the news."

"What's all over the news?" Manny asked, wondering if the police did a raid down in Atlanta. He reached for his remote control and went on all the local news station and didn't find anything. He asked, "What's on the news?"

"Dude, the massacre down here with Self. He's been gunned down, dude!"

"Gunned down? By who? What the fuck you mean he's been gunned down?" Manny started yelling, not realizing his worst fear until he heard it.

"Dude... things are crazy down here. A lot people are dead."

"Gunned down, man? Tell me what happened."

Matthew sighed. "Dude, Self got into a big shootout with some guys on the streets. Dude, he's nuts! A lot of people got killed. Innocent people got shot. They say after he left a trail of dead bodies out on the sidewalk, he ran into a gun store, killed the owner, and continued the shootout with the gunmen until the police arrived. They say six people died altogether, dude, including a sheriff."

"Okay...calm down. Who was the men with the guns?"

"Yeah, dude, the news is saying four Cubans with Miami plates on a Dodge Caravan."

Manny's whole world started spinning. "Damn! What the fuck?" Manny said, while pacing his bedroom floor.

"Dude, I'm shut down. The party over, dude."

"What? You said Miami plates on a Caravan?"

"Yeah, dude, sounds like the ones that killed Kev. With him gone and Self gone, I'm shutting down. I'm all by myself. It was great doing business, but I'll be in the Florida Keys, dude. Come find me and we can talk, but I'm scared shitless right now."

Manny didn't give a damn what happened to Matthew or the money. His only concern was Self. Again, someone died doing his dirt, and for a war his brother started. That was it. Manny had enough. He said, "Hey, gringo, thank you. Enjoy your life," as he hung up the phone.

He dialed another number, then said, "E, they just killed Self, man."

"It's just getting worse, Manny. It's just getting worse. It's time to pull out," Edeeks pleaded.

"Okay, but see if you can get his body back to New York. Somebody have to find out if he had a family. If not, we his family. Please, see what you can do."

Edeeks sighed. "Manny, I took care of things, but someone named Packy is running his mouth. I suggest you pull out, man. Head to Panama. Just let me know where you are."

"Okay, adiós," Manny said as he hung up the phone.

Manny was feeling overwhelmed by a mixture of anger and sadness. The reality of Packy snitching and Self being gunned down had finally sunk in. Time stopped and he suddenly felt sick to his stomach. So many unanswered questions raced through Manny's head. While sitting on the edge of his bed, he visualized Self's bloody body lying somewhere down in Atlanta. "Damn, Slick," he said, mimicking Self's term of endearment. "Why you?" Manny whined out with disappointment.

Not only had he lost a good soldier on his team, he had lost one of his closest friends. It would be difficult replacing their comradeship. He walked into the bathroom and splashed cold water on his face in an attempt to regain his composure. When he picked his head up and looked into the mirror, he didn't like what he saw. *Fucking M3. Everybody died for what? Money? Money can't bring them back. Life is worth more than this shit. Maricónes think this is a joke. Think Manny Black is a joke? Yo soy el mejo, Marielitos! Time for everybody to pay with crime,* Manny thought before walking away from the mirror.

Manny came to the conclusion it was time to bring things to a head. He needed answers and knew exactly the place where to start looking for them. He quickly dressed, then pick up the phone and dialed Rico's cell phone.

"Talk about it," Rico answered.

"Hermano, strap up. I'm on my way!"

Before Rico could say another word, his brother cut the line. Manny walked into his closet and hit Xia's switch. The hidden door slid open, and he pulled the dangling string to spread light through the room. Off the three walls of guns, he pulled down two Colt .45 automatics. He then closed the door. He pulled a pair of black gloves and two wire hangers from his closet. He twisted and bent the hangers until one hook was in the nozzle of the gun, and the other was hooked onto the side of his waist.

When he went into his garage, he didn't want to put any heat on Xia's Benz. He reasoned that his M3 was out of the question, and too many of his soldiers saw him in the Escalade, so he walked outside to the Prowler.

Manny's Prowler burned up the interstate until he reached Glenwood Terrace. The closer he got to Rico's house, the angrier he grew. The only thing on his mind was making those responsible for ordering Self's death pay. His time to grieve would come later. He circled the block to make sure he wasn't being followed, or the police wasn't laying for him and his brother.

When his car pulled up into the garage, Rico peeked from under his black Navigator, then asked, "Hermano, qué está pasando?" asking Manny what was going on.

Manny opened the passenger door. When Rico sat inside and closed the door, his gloved hand placed a mini-Glock on his lap. Manny said, "Hermano, Self got hit up in Atlanta."

Rico eyes opened wide when he heard that the impossible was possible. "Wooord? You serious? Ah man, holmes is dead?" Rico asked, staring blankly at the windshield. "What the fuck happened?"

Manny choked back tears. "El gringo called me scared to death. He said it was all over the news down there about Self in a big shootout. He said when the smoke cleared, six people were dead. The four Cubans from Miami had guns. Then I called E and he said Packy snitching."

Manny pulled out of the garage, made a left, and was heading to the Bronx, when Rico said, "Fuck Packy, Rah, and all the rest of them rat bastards. Rah threatened to get me killed, but he can eat a dick. I ain't going to live in no cage. Poe-poe gonna have to kill me first. What's up with Self?" Rico put his head in his hands. "Self laid them down? That's how son is. Cubans, huh? You think it came from those Marielitos cats we had that drama wit'?"

"Si, the same ones that did Kev," Manny said with exhaustion in his voice.

"A'ight, whatever, whatever. What we gonna do to find these cats?"

Manny stepped on the gas, then growled, "If we want to find Cubans, then we have to go see some Cubans."

* * * * *

Manny and Rico jetted to the Henry Hudson where they took the Westside Highway down to the Lincoln Tunnel. From there, they maneuvered the vehicle through the heavy evening traffic that was headed to New Jersey. Once they were on the Jersey side, they quickly drove on the New Jersey Turnpike until they were heading in the direction of the George Washington Bridge. After paying their toll, they headed to the Bronx, knowing for sure that no vehicle was going to follow them for what they were about to do.

When the Prowler pulled up in front of the Havana's Paradise, the block was quiet. Manny's eyes swept the block and noticed that most of the stores along the street were closed and traffic was minimal. He hopped out of his car and marched into the social club with Rico in tow.

The short brute met the brothers inside at the door. After looking them up and down like they were suspicious, he asked, "Cabrón what you want? Nobody say you was coming."

"We need to see Pantera or Pedro," Manny replied, while looking over the brute's shoulder.

"It's important," Rico added, maintaining eye contact with the brute.

The brute listened, then said, "Wait here!"

Less than a minute later, the brute reappeared and said, "Okay, go in the back."

Manny was expecting to see both Pantera and Pedro when he walked into the office. Instead he only saw Pedro leaning on the front of the desk with his legs crossed.

When Pedro saw the brothers come through the door, a faint smile appeared on his face as he asked, "Tell me what brings you two up here?"

"I came because I need some answers," Manny said, walking closer to the desk. "The last time we was here Pantera mentioned los Marielitos. I need some answers."

Rico eased his way back to the entrance of the office.

Pedro watched the two brothers, then asked, "Answers? Answers to what questions? What are you talking about? Marielitos is a myth."

Manny remained calm. "Cubano, a lot of strange shit has been happening. First, you send me on a mission that you sent somebody else on. Then I get there and the guy is already dead, and he is also one of the Marielitos that my family had a problem with. Next, I come and talk to you like a man, you cut off my supply. How could I be wrong for wanting to know what the hell is going on? Now the Marielitos murdered one of my closest friends in Atlanta, and you tell me in my face that it's a myth? Too many coincidences, and I don't believe in coincidences, Cubano." Manny lost his temper when he said, "Pinga, I want some answers!"

Pedro lit a cigarette with the same gold lighter that started all of Manny's troubles. On the exhale, he said, "Esperate. We already dealt with your questions. We're not dealing with this again. Comprende?"

When the short brute heard Pedro's voice go up a notch, he marched through the office door with his right hand glued to the butt of the gun that was in his waistband. He looked at Pedro, then asked, "Is everything okay?" He then started staring intensely at Manny and Rico.

Manny was tired of playing games. He wasn't leaving there without getting the answers he came for. When he saw Pedro leaning up against the edge of the desk smirking and trying to dismiss him, Manny's mind snapped. Before anyone understood what was happening Manny pulled out his two .45's. With his right hand, he gun-butted Pedro on left side of his head. A three-inch gash quickly opened up and blood poured down the side of his face. Pedro's thin frame partially slumped over the desk.

When the brute saw what Manny did, he made an attempt to pull his gun, but Rico quickly stuck the mini-Glock under his chin and disarmed him. "Bro, you want me to air him out?" Rico asked, while looking the brute in his eyes.

"No," Manny said, while holding Pedro tightly by the collar of his linen button-up shirt. Pedro's hardened face didn't reveal any emotions. "I'm not gonna ask you again. Answer me," Manny barked, raising his gun in the air to gun-butt Pedro again.

Pedro looked at Manny and said, "I don't know what you're talking about. You already went too far, so do what you have to do."

"Cabrón! When this is over, I'm going to kill you," the brute said through clinched teeth.

Manny was disgusted. He looked over to Rico, then said, "Give him his gun and let him go."

Rico held the gun under the brute's chin, then asked, "What?"

" You heard what he said?" The brute spat out.

Manny barked, "Ahora!" Instantly, Rico did what he was told. When the brute grabbed his gun, Manny said, "Vete pa'l carajo," telling the man to go to hell and aimed his gun, firing two hot slugs from the .45 into the brute's face.

Pedro hands quickly shot up in surrender. He screamed, "Wait! I'll tell you what you want to know."

Manny looked at the bloody mess the brute turned into and said, "I never liked that puta from the first day he called me a cabrón. Now somebody else can fuck his wife tonight."

"Whoa, whoa, whoa!" Pedro tried to sink through the carpet under him when he saw the rage in Manny's eyes. "It's all Pantera," Pedro cried out. "You were sent to that place on your wedding night because Pantera wanted to get rid of two birds with one stone. He knew armed soldiers would be inside the garage after their boss was gunned down. That's the way it goes. He planned for you to walk into an ambush. You were never supposed to walk out of that garage that night alive."

"But why he want me dead?" Manny questioned, towering over Pedro.

"Because you got too close to something that he loved dearly...Xia."   Manny shook the cobwebs from his head. "Xia? But he gave us his blessing."

Pedro took his time wiping a fresh napkin against his head. "Do you really believe that Pantera approved of you two being together? Why do you think he stopped supplying you with product?" Manny looked at Pedro blankly. "You two were never supposed to be together. You were only here to serve a purpose...that's it! Pantera felt you manipulated Xia, and that's nearly impossible. He only needed you to help his plans materialize."

Manny waved his gun. "Yeah, and what was that?"

"To help Pantera wipe out his competition so he could get on the council."

"What council? What are you talking about?" Manny asked in a state of confusion.

Pedro sighed at his ignorance. "The Marielitos? In Pantera's eyes, you were nothing more than a pawn. The day you walked into the back of the restaurant and attempted to rob me, Pantera knew then that you would run through fire to get to the pot of gold. He saw the hunger in your eyes. He exploited you until he felt you overstepped your boundaries."

"Why is Pantera trying to get rid of the Marielitos?" Rico asked. He was confused and impatiently tapping his gun against his thigh.

Pedro looked over Manny's shoulder, then said, "Roberto and I are Marielito."

Manny heard the new name, then asked in confusion, "Who the fuck is Roberto, maricón?"

Pedro's eyes ballooned when he saw the hole from Manny's gun. He trembled as he answered, "Roberto Sazón. That's Pantera. He was once a soldier for La Familia Mariel, but from the start, he didn't agree with their politics. His outfit did all the dirty work to help the family rise to power. In the end, Pantera was only rewarded with peanuts in comparison to what the heads of the family took for themselves. Some of the top men started working with the U.S. government, and Pantera soon grew tired of being used. He started defying the Marielitos rules. He started making moves on his own in order to survive, and take care of our family. Because of La Familia Mariel, Pantera lost his wife and only daughter. From that day forward, he swore to become the head of the family. With your help, that day might come soon. You were just one of his many pawns."

"So the first hit I did? He was a Marielito?" Manny asked, growing angrier. Pedro nodded. "So that's why he held on to the tape?"

Pedro motioned for permission to light another cigarette. When Manny nodded, he lit it, inhaled with all of his breath, and on the exhale he said, "The tape was his insurance policy just in case you didn't play ball or ever went sour. It was something he could always dangle over you to do what he wanted. He does that with all of us. Like you are the thing he now dangles to Xia."

Manny eyes turned bloodshot red. He couldn't believe what he was hearing. "Who ordered the killing of my man down in Atlanta?" he asked.

Pedro put his hands together like he was praying. "It wasn't us. We had nothing to do with that. You made us a lot of money with that operation."

"If not you, then who?" Manny questioned, stepping forward and gripping the .45 a bit tighter.

Pedro shrugged his shoulders. "You should ask yourself that. Who else has the power to make such things happen with the Marielitos?"

Manny raised his gun. "Where can I find Pantera and the Marielitos? Where does he live?"

Pedro stared into space, then said, "I don't know where Pantera lives, and I'm the closest one to him. The top men of the Marielitos are well organized. These men live in secrecy. We do what we are told the way you did. You don't find them; they find you."

"Where does he live?" Manny asked, while snatching Pedro by his collar again. "How can I find him?"

Pedro looked up at Manny. "Look, nobody knows where Pantera lives. He only tells us what he wants us to know and nothing more."

"Well, call his cell phone!" Manny ordered, releasing Pedro from his hold and grabbing the phone off of the desk. "Here, call him!" Manny ordered again, while handing the phone to Pedro.

Pedro shook his head. "You don't understand. Pantera doesn't believe in such devices. He feels they could be used by the government to monitor his whereabouts. So, he calls us. No one ever calls him. Ask Xia."

"What about that restaurant? Is he down there? Dígame!" Rico asked.

Pedro shook his head. "I told you guys, he just comes and goes unannounced."

Manny frowned. "Okay, I'll deal with him later." He stepped away from Pedro, then turned to his brother and said, "Come on, we leaving."

Rico shot Manny a puzzled looked, then asked, "Bro, what about him?" while he nodded towards Pedro.

Manny looked at the pathetic man and thought of the riches the man made him. "Leave him. We have other things to do."

"What?" Rico retorted, glaring back at his brother.

"Just come on," Manny ordered and started walking towards the office door while putting his gun in his waistband.

"Hey, where are you going?" Pedro shouted out. He got down on his knees, then clasped his hands together. He said a quick prayer, then opened his eyes. "After all that I revealed to you, I'm already a dead man. I'd rather die by the hands of you then to die a thousand deaths by the hands of Pantera."

Manny was bugging off the old man. He frowned, then asked, "How the hell will he know what you told me?" Manny pointed to the dead brute, then said, "The only witness is him."

Again, Pedro sighed at Manny's ignorance. Since he knew things that Manny would never know, he said, "He already knows. Please have some honor and punish me for my disloyalty." Manny didn't give it a second thought. He quickly stepped forward and violently drew his .45. He placed it to Pedro's head. "Viva Marielito," Pedro said, and Manny squeezed off two shots, ending another Cuban's life.

Rico smiled when he watched his brother killing Pedro. For good incentive, he opened fire on the brute and Pedro, blowing their faces to pieces and making sure they were dead.

Together, Manny and Rico marched out of the social club unnoticed. They hopped into the Prowler and raced for the highway.

* * * * *

Back at One Police Plaza, Captain Baylor and Maria Flores were in the darkness of the boardroom reviewing the bust that was getting them promotions. They still needed to capture the Black brothers to make history.

After watching the tapes from each unit, the captain reviewed the tapes from his own unit, then said, "See, there he goes again."

Maria looked blankly at the screen. "Okay Rashid goes around the corner and he comes back. That's when you stormed the building. What's the problem?"

Baylor rewound the tape. He played it, then stopped it when a silver Plymouth Prowler did a slow creep by the block. He pointed. "See?" He played it again, then stopped it where Rashid was talking into his cell phone. He froze the frame again, then asked, "See?" He then played it and quickly watched as Rashid cut the corner. More action from the M3 Boyz took place, then Rashid cut the corner again. Behind him, a silver Plymouth Prowler passed by the corner again. Captain Baylor pressed pause, turned to Maria, then said, "I know you know what I'm talking about now."

She stared at the image of Rashid walking back to his spot. "Sir, I guess that's what they pay you the big bucks for. Pardon my French, though, but I don't know what the fuck you're talking about."

"The silver Plymouth Prowler!" Captain Baylor announced, as if that was suppose to bring some clarity to the tape.

"Okay?" Maria Flores said sarcastically.

Captain Baylor rewinded the tape then pressed play before he said, "It's simple." While the tape played the events, the captain narrated and said, "Rashid is hanging around and then the car goes by. Suddenly, he gets a call. He walks around the corner and stays for awhile. Then when he cuts the corner again, if you look over his shoulder, the same car goes by."

"And?"

The captain paused for effect. "And it's possible that Rashid went to the car. It's possible that such a car belongs to Ricardo or Manuel Black. It's also possible that if we go get his cell phone out of storage and check the incoming calls, that it may have the numbers to the phones, and we can find the address or track it with a GPS. There can't be too many of those brand-new cars registered to New York State, so? We run a scan on every silver Plymouth Prowler in New York and see if the Black name comes up."

Maria said, "But the other cars came up to P.O. boxes. These guys can't be that dumb."

"That's what they pay me the big bucks for, finding where they are dumb so I can use it against them."

Maria hopped out of her chair. "I'll get on it right away."

The captain said, "Already did that. Every officer on the road is looking for that car." He laughed at Maria and then said, "Just earning my pay, Miss Prosecutor, just earning my pay."

* * * * *

Five o'clock the following morning, Xia was laying across the bed dressed in a short night grown, watching television. Her stomach was already getting hard and her emotions were like a roller coaster.

When Manny's eyes opened from her constant shifting, he affectionately said, "Hey, Bonita."

"Hi, baby," Xia responded. She leaned up and kissed Manny's morning breath. She then grabbed the TV remote and turned up the volume before asking, "Are you hungry? I can make some breakfast or heat up that chicken, rice, and beans."

Manny sat up beside Xia and started rubbing her little stomach. "No, I'm good. I'm not hungry."

He closed his eyes, and the events from the social club shot through his head. Manny didn't plan for things to turn out that way, but it already happened, and it was definitely too late to cry about it. He knew it wouldn't be any turning back after what took place the day before. For a moment, he wondered if Xia knew all along about the plot to get rid of him. He knew that she was like a daughter to Pantera, and he was sure that Pantera shared many secrets with her. He already decided not to tell Xia about what took place down at the social club. If she found out, he would act just as surprised as she about Pedro and the brute being murdered.

Xia sat there observing her husband lying beside her with his eyes closed. From the hardness of his face, she could tell that something was troubling him and that he was in deep thought. She leaned over and ran her fingers through his curly hair, when she asked, "Baby, what's wrong?" Manny's eyes opened, then stared into space. "Nada. I'm just a little tired."

"My baby tired?" Xia playfully asked, while reaching her hand further down and slipping it inside of his opened boxers. She started stoking his dick slowly. After a few minutes of playing with it, she started getting wet.

Manny pretended for a moment like he was enjoying what Xia was doing, but the truth of the matter was that his mind was on trying to figure out how he was going to find Pantera and the heads of the La Familia Mariel. Being intimate was the last thing on his mind.

He leaned up slowly, then said, "Bonita suave," without sounding harsh.

Xia's hormones kicked in and her emotional roller coaster went out on a ride. "What the fuck is wrong with you? You don't want to eat the food I made for you. You don't want to fuck me. You just lying here all quiet and shit not saying anything. I'm your wife! The least you can do is talk to me! If you don't want to talk, then fuck me!"

A faint smile appeared on Manny's face. He tried to ease her irritation. "Bonita, you a sexy puta when you get mad."

Manny reached for her crotch, and she said, "I'm fat. Stop playing with me."

He reached again, then said, "I'm serious, Bonita. You sexy. Don't make something out of nothing."

She opened her legs, eased closer to her husband, and while her roller coaster was on the way down, she whispered, "Okay. So what's wrong?"

Manny put his finger on her clit, then looked at Xia and asked, "Tell me something, can you get in touch with Pantera?"

Xia kissed him, then asked, "Why?"

Manny sucked on her breast. "If I need you to get in touch with him right now, can you?" He was trying to test the validity of what Pedro had disclosed to him.

While Manny rubbed her clit and sucked on her breast, she moaned, "Baby, it's not like that. Oooh, that feels good. I never call him. Yes, baby, right there. I see him when he calls for me. That's how he operates."

Manny hoped she would disclose more about the black beast when he was sliding his tongue down her stomach and towards her clit, when he asked, "You're his daughter. I know you can reach him."

Xia turned cold and the roller coaster shot up again. "Listen! That's the rules! You want to talk or fuck your wife?" Manny didn't know who she was at times. As soon as he was trying to work his dick into her, her phone rang.

Xia stopped, looked at the clock, and then jumped up quickly to answer her phone. Manny overheard her saying, "What? Who? Uncle Pedro? You need me to do what? No, okay, I'll be right there to talk about it." Xia cut off her phone, dropped it on the bed, and headed for the shower.

"Qué pasa?" Manny asked.

Xia peeked her head out of the bathroom, then said, "Just business. Don't ask. You promised."

Manny already knew what the phone call was about. He hoped when his wife received the news that she would come home to his arms and cry on his shoulder. Manny still didn't realize that Xia wasn't that type of woman.

When she exited the shower, she dried herself off and asked, "Two of my .45's are missing. You took them, right?"

Oh shit, Manny thought. He said, "Yeah, I had to give them to one of my soldiers."

While she was rubbing on lotion, she said, "Please replace them. If you need someone to get them from you, let me know." Xia got dressed, then asked, "Are you going anywhere?"

Manny was pleased that she accepted the answer he gave about the guns. He pulled the covers over his head and said, "No, I'm going back to sleep."

"Good. Don't leave the house. I'll be right back to finish what you started. I love you."

Manny didn't answer his wife. He fought the hundreds of thoughts that were rushing through his head and then closed his eyes. He wanted to sleep for two more hours, then call Rico so they could go Marielito hunting.

Two and a half hours later, Xia still wasn't home. Manny was busy trying to get in touch with Rico. He didn't know whether his brother was still alive or dead. He tried three more times to call, but his calls went unanswered. After leaving his brother several messages on his voice mail and not having his calls returned, Manny began to worry. He wondered if Pantera had found out that they were responsible for what had happened at the social club, but he quickly dismissed the thought. Dead men tell no tales, he reasoned.

This fucker is doing it to me again. He's probably at home getting his bicho sucked, Manny thought when he raced into his closet. He got dressed, then lifted a short barrel .40 caliber automatic from Xia's stash. He raced down the stairs and stopped at the garage. When he got there, the Prowler was gone. He didn't know which one of the cars he should take. He felt like an animal trapped in the corner. Just then, he figured that if he was going to be cornered in, he might as well have the fastest ride to get him out.

Manny's M3 raced down the New York State thruway until he reached the Yonkers county line on Riverdale drive. While on the road, he made another attempt to contact Rico on his cell phone, but he got his voice mail again. That was definitely unlike his brother to not answer his phone. In an effort to make sure he wasn't being tailed, he made a right on Riverdale until he reached Post Road. He drove down the residential block, then turned to go back the way he came. He hit Broadway then made a left until he reached Getty Square. He maneuvered his way through downtown, hit Locust Hill, and made his way down the hill until he reached the terrace condos on Glenwood Avenue.

After circling the block, Manny drove into Rico's parking garage. When he got inside the dark enclosure he quickly scanned the parking lot, searching for his brother's black M3 and his black Navigator. Both vehicles were parked in their regular spots.

In haste, Manny jumped out of his car, and entered the building heading for the elevator. When the elevator stopped his heart pumped harder as he got closer to the apartment door. A familiar scent hit his nose, but he was more concerned with why his brother's front door was ajar.

He pulled the .40 caliber out and slowly crept inside. The empty space was consumed with a haunting stillness. Manny moved slowly down the hallway. When he walked through the open bedroom door, his world started crashing and his mother's words started to haunt him. While Manny stood over his dead brother's naked body, he stared at the hole in Rico's head and heard, *Ricardo has been wild since he was inside of me. Please son, be careful and don't send any coffins home to me.*

Manny was momentarily stuck in shock. He couldn't stop staring at Rico's dead body. His mind raced. He was trying to comprehend how Rico could have slipped up and let somebody kill him. He looked at Rico's limp dick and figured it was his girl that did it. *The Marielitos got the Puerto Rican chick to put in the work, Manny thought.*

He sat next to his dead brother and then hugged him as the tears rolled down his eyes. An excruciating pain shot through his head. It felt like someone had dropped a boulder on it. For the second time reality started setting in and everything hit Manny all at once. He lost everything; his operation was over, Rashid was locked up, Self was dead in Atlanta, and now his brother was dead. Manny felt like life was cheating him. Suddenly, all the money, cars, and material items didn't mean a thing to him. What was life worth without those he loved by his side. Manny wondered how he would tell his mother about Rico's death. He knew his father would place the blame on him, and how was he supposed to bury his brother in America. With the police after him, he wouldn't even be able to identify the body, give him a proper funeral, or see Rico go to a decent grave.

Manny stood and headed to the kitchen. He searched through the cupboards until he found matches and a tall bottle of Bacardi Lemon. He rushed back into to the bedroom and thought like Rico. He looked under the bed, and under a MP5 machine gun was a huge suitcase. Manny opened the suitcase and poured the stacks of money unto Rico's bed. He then took all the bed sheets and curtains he could find and placed them over his brother's body. Like a lush, Manny tilted the bottle and took it to his head. With the remainder of the liquor, he poured it all over his brother's body and lit the bed on fire.

I'm going home to get Xia, and we're driving our boat to Panama, Manny was thinking when he hit the steps, heading for the parking garage.

* * * * *

Back at One Police Plaza, Captain Baylor had just received some of the best news in his career that he wanted to share. He picked up his phone and called Maria Flores.

"Maria Flores' office," the sexy voice said on the other line.

"The wonderful Mrs. Flores, I was wondering if you were interested in accompanying me to Westchester County."

"Who is this?" Maria asked with her Latina attitude.

"This is Captain Baylor."

"Well, Captain, in case you didn't know, I'm married."

The captain cleared his throat, then changed his tone of voice before he said, "Oh...no. This is a professional matter. My men found the residence of one Xia Black."

"Is that the mother of the perps?" Maria asked while excited.

Captain Baylor was happy she knew who the smarter one was. He said, "No, his wife. The same wife that took a trip with him to Panama after their honeymoon. The one who is aiding and abetting a wanted man, and that flew into Newark International when my men were at Kennedy. She's the woman the 2000 Plymouth Prowler belongs to."

"They may have fled by now."

The captain said, "Nope. We sent an unmarked Westchester County sheriff's department car out to the address. The deputy saw the Prowler pull up a half-hour ago. Ten minutes later, a black M3 rolled into the garage. And get this. They even have a sign that reads *The Blacks* on the mailbox. I'm taking one of my units up there with the sirens blaring, and I wanted to know if you were interested."

Maria shuffled her papers, then said, "I'll be downstairs waiting for you."

* * * * *

Manny wasted no time rushing home to Xia. When he walked through the door with his gun in hand, he had agony etched on his face. He walked into his bedroom and saw Xia's clothes on the floor. He sat on the edge of the bed, then laid back and closed his eyes.

Xia's water stopped running, and when the bathroom door opened, he heard her walking towards the closet. Manny's eyes suddenly popped opened when he caught whiff of the familiar scent that was lingering inside Rico's condo. He quickly sat up. Xia walked into the room wearing a black, wraparound dress that covered her whole body. In her hand, she held a silenced .380 Beretta.

Manny looked at his wife and asked, "Qué pasa, Bonita?" He glanced down at the gun in her hand. "What you doing?"

Xia had undergone a metamorphous. Her face belonged to the killer from the night in the storage room of the restaurant. She stared at Manny with eyes that were cold as the dead. "You just had to go and cross the lines. Why couldn't you just leave well enough alone, Manny?"

Manny's gripped his gun tighter. "Bonita, what are you talking about?"

Xia let out a cold laugh. "Don't call me that. I am not beautiful. I'm fat! You knew that from the start and used me to get closer to Pantera. I'll give it to you; I thought you were smart, but how could you have been so stupid? You should have known Pantera would find out about you and Rico killing Pedro and his bodyguard last night."

Manny pretended like he didn't know what she was talking about. "Que? I don't even know what you talking about."

Xia inched a step closer. "Oh, you don't know what I'm talking about? Manny, I saw the tape!"

"What tape?" Manny yelled back.

"The one you left behind at the social club. After you used my guns."

Manny had a dumb look on his face. *Coño! Of course he would have security cameras. He always has cameras!* he thought, while looking at Xia inching her way closer to him. "Xia, put the gun down."

Tears dripped from her cheeks when she said, "I had to fuck your brother to get close enough to kill him."

"No," Manny groaned.

"Yes, I did. He fucked me and told me how he wanted me the first time he saw me. While his dick was cumming onto your baby's head, he told me how he was the brains of M3. Not even your brother had loyalty to you. I was the only one! Then, when he was tired, I put a bullet in his head. You should thank me."

Manny stood on the other side of the bed with his back to his window and his gun pointed to the floor. His emotions were getting the best of him as the images of Rico fucking his wife danced around in his head.

"Cállate Puta!" Manny screamed for her to be quiet.

She inched closer. "I had no choice. You put me in a position to choose between Pantera and you. I asked you before to never do that. So, now you have to die, too."

Manny shook his head. "Xia, no! It doesn't have to be this way. What about the baby?" Manny was trying to buy himself some time in hopes of getting close enough to take her gun away.

Again, Xia let out a cold laugh and shot him a piercing stare. "Don't worry; Pantera will be the father of my son." Xia raised the Beretta. "I see your gun, Manny. You know I'm the better shot."

Manny quickly lifted his .40 caliber, but Xia was quick on the trigger. In a flash, she squeezed off two slugs that violently tore into the right side of Manny's chest and stomach, causing his body to erupt in excruciating pain.

He swiftly swung his arm forward, then fired three shots into his wife's midsection. By the time the second slug tore into her uterus, Xia fell back, but emptied her gun into her husband. The brutal force of the small, but deadly slugs pushed Manny back through his bedroom window.

The soft grass broke his fall, but while he lay in the shards of glass, he heard a group of cars screeching, and someone in the distance yelling, "Freeze!" as if he was going somewhere. Manny looked up at the cloudy skies above him, and while his life flashed before his eyes, he thought, *Damn! Everything I have has turned to poison. I guess that shit called karma is catching up to me.*

Manny's thoughts were interrupted when, above him, the face of Captain Baylor and Maria Flores blocked out the clouds.

"Manuel Black, you are under arrest."

EPILOGUE

"Damn, Manny, that was some bugged out shit!" Baby J said, while pacing the floor in the middle of the night.

"I hope you see, mi pana, that crime don't pay," Manny said.

Baby J asked, "How much time you got for all that?"

"Ten flat," Manny said, not sounding proud.

"Ten flit-at? Damn, who you folded on? All that shit and all you got is ten years? Yo, just let me know."

Manny sighed at the youngster's ignorance. "Mi pana, I copped out to all known and unknown cases. I got manslaughter for my wife and unborn child, and could have beaten it because she shot me before I shot her. Packy didn't snitch on me. He shifted all the weight on my brother since he died. I was never in Atlanta, and I ain't had nobody else telling. That whole M3 shit you read about in the papers came from somebody giving a tip. Plus, I had the political connections in Harlem with my man E, and Robert Boyle is the best lawyer in New York."

"Damn, that's fucked up wit' what happen to Self thou, the way he got bodied."

Manny sat up, then said, "Got bodied? I never told you that Self died."

Baby J looked up and asked, "What happened to him? You said…"

"He went to the hospital. They took like a few feet of his intestines out. Then his girl Peaches helped him escape. He later got locked up for the shootout, but he proved self-defense and copped out to ten years for everything else. With the law in Georgia, he'll be home this year. Peaches still by his side."

"Now that's what's good. What about Carmen?"

Manny smiled, then pulled a picture that he had glued with toothpaste off the wall. He handed him the picture of a woman and little boy, and said, "That's her and my little man Rico. That's who always come visit me. We're going to get married when I get out of here."

Baby J studied the picture real well, then blurted out, "Man, this baby don't look like you."

Manny laughed. "Yeah, he looks like his mother."

Baby J was thinking that Manny must have been crazy, but in prison, a man needs all the hope he can get.

He handed the picture back and said, "You the man, Manny. What up wit' Edeeks, Pantera, and Rashid?"

Manny said, "E is all right. He come up every now and then. Rashid and Rich Dice got fifty years apiece, but we got connections that's trying to get them out." His whole expression changed when he said, "Pantera is why I stay in the hole. He keeps sending hits on me inside, so I get them before they get me. I'll cross the bridge with Pantera and the Marielitos when I get to it."

"Man, I still think you came out better. You gotta still be paid. Plus, your people in Panama is straight."

"I will give it all away to have my wife, my child, and my brother back. I know now that I can use my mind to make millions."

Baby J closed his eyes. "We'll see if you still talking that positive shit when you get out."

Manny said, "Si, we will see. We will see, Baby J."

"BLACK-BLACK!" a voice said in the distance. "Inmate Black!" Manny heard before jumping awake.

"Damn" Manny uttered when he awoke from his reoccurring nightmare.

"Inmate Black," yelled the Correction Officer who stood in front of Manny's cell.

"What?" he asked when he finally cleared the cobwebs from his head.

"Get up and get dressed. They want you down at the chaplain's office," an officer he knew as Nugent barked.

Manny quickly sat up to face the officer. The red-faced man stood six feet three inches. His huge shoulders and head looked joined, and he looked like he drank steroid cocktails. His massive arms were bursting from his light blue shirt and his dark blue pants were high-waters that stopped above massive combat boots. In his hand was a long wooded club with an attached rope that was wrapped so tight around his fat hands that Manny could see the whites of his knuckles.

"What do they want me for?" Manny asked as he was washing his face in the stainless steel sink that was directly over a matching seatless toilet.

"Get yourself together," Nugent said with a Southern drawl. "They want you down at the chaplain's office. Let's get a move on it. I'm your escort and I don't have all day."

Manny's heart suddenly did a sprint. Thick beads of sweat burst onto his forehead. For a prisoner, a trip to the chaplain's office meant someone in their family was either gravely ill or had passed away. The thought of losing another loved one sent chills through Manny's body. Prior to his incarceration, besides losing Rico, he'd lost too many soldiers from his M3 gang. Death was always chasing Manny. Either he was doing the killing, or someone close to him was dying. Now he was being called to face another tragedy.

Instantly, images of his girlfriend Carmen and their eight-year-old son Rico flashed in his head. He quickly dressed in his prison issued green uniform. He took a moment to examine the reflection of himself in the small plastic mirror that was mounted directly above the sink. Manny touched the skin on his smooth chocolate face and then ran his hands through his thick head of dark black curls. He was still pleasantly handsome for thirty-eight years old. He silently prayed for the wellbeing of the only family he had left. Then he took a deep breath and walked out of the cell.

"Put your hands inside your pockets and keep them there. If you take your hands out of your pockets for anything, I'm dropping you where you stand. We understand?" the redneck barked.

Manny stopped short, stared at the officer, slipped his hands into his pockets, and headed down the row of cells that were separated by huge steel doors.

For Manny, the walk out of the cellblock was a chance to see different scenery. Most of his time in prison was spent in solitary confinement, special housing units, or involuntary protective custody. Now that he was at the end of his stretch, he was "Keep-Locked"— spending twenty-three hours a day in his cell—just him and his personal property.

The long corridor that led to the chaplain's office was dim due to dusty florescent lights that lined the ceiling. Stained paint chips dangled from the moist, cold walls that exaggerated the temperature outside by twenty degrees. A repugnant odor of old garbage and dirty mops consumed the air. Manny was disgusted during his walk. No matter how much time he did, he never got used to being trapped and at someone else's whim.

With each step Manny took, Nugent tapped the chips on the wall with his nightstick. The annoying bang echoed down the cramped corridor, getting the attention of two inmate porters twenty feet in front of him.

Manny looked up ahead, checking if he recognized any of the males who swept the dull concrete floor. He had had too much drama with the Marielitos in the prison system and the huge contract on his head was enough to feed an American family for a year.

As Manny tried to make out the porter's faces, the men stopped to stare at who was coming. As Manny closed the distance between them, he looked at one man who had a middleweight boxer's physique and a blue-black complexion. His Latino partner favored an Inca Indian, with long twin braids hanging down the middle of his back.

Blue-Black, and Braids, Manny thought while playing a game of naming the men.

As Manny was quickly approaching the men, the Latino with the twin braids made eye contact. "Oh shit," Braids said when he looked at Manny. "Yo, whut up, Papi? Chu Manny Black, no?" he asked like a fan seeing his favorite movie star.

Manny gave a slight nod, acknowledging the man while the other one continued sweeping.

"Oye, that's that kid Manny that ran tha M3 Boyz." Blue-Black muttered to his partner like Manny wasn't right there passing by.

Braids nodded in awe, and then whispered, "They was getting crazy money and laying mad nigga's down."

That type of thing was nothing new to Manny. It was his gift and his curse. Over the years he often received praise for the reign of terror that he, Rico and the M3 Boyz unleashed on the streets of New York.

"*Coño, man,*" Manny heard behind him. "Dem boyz was millionaires, Bee," one of the men said as Manny was cutting the corner to the chaplain's office.

* * * * *

Officer Nugent knocked twice.

"Enter," a deep voice commanded from inside the chaplain's office.

The officer pushed the frail wooden door open and pushed Manny into the brightly lit room.

"I'll be waiting outside," the officer said to the chaplain while his eyes were glued to Manny. The door slammed behind him.

Manny walked inside and causally scanned the small room that was cluttered with bookshelves. Under a gated covered window and sitting at a huge desk that was out of place in the small room, sat the prison chaplain. The fat, clean-shaven, rosy-cheeked Catholic priest met Manny with a sinister grin.

"Manuel Black?" the priest meekly inquired. He extended his short, obese arm to the empty folding chair that sat directly in front of his desk. "Please, have a seat," he suggested.

Manny shook his head. "No thank you. Whatever you got to say, tell me now." He stepped his six-foot, athletic frame forward until he towered over the priest.

The priest fidgeted uncomfortably with a manila folder before reading from it.

"Um... Mr. Black. When was the last time you spoke with your family?" he asked sheepishly.

"Did something happen to my son or his mother?" Manny questioned impatiently, fearing the worst.

The priest flatly responded, "No. I was referring to your family in Panama."

It had been a year since Manny wrote his mother, father and little brother Puncho. The unanswered letters that filled a shoebox underneath his bunk crossed his mind. Guilt kept him from reaching out and now he was paying for it.

"I... I don't know," he stammered, feeling ashamed for neglecting his family.

The priest gently smiled without showing teeth before saying, "Ah, Mr. Black... I hate to be the bearer of bad news. I received a call this morning from your brother. I'm sorry to inform you that your mother has passed away."

"What?" Manny asked, stunned.

"Mr. Black, I promised your brother that I would call so you could speak with them." The chaplain reached for the telephone on his desk. He picked up the receiver and started dialing numbers.

Mamá died? Manny asked himself. *How?*

His mother's death was the last words he expected to hear from the priest. Life was passing by in a blur. Agony numbed his senses. Manny was paralyzed with regret.

"Mr. Black," Manny heard before snapping out of his daze. The priest handed him the phone.

"Manny? You there?" his younger brother Puncho asked on the other end.

"Si, I'm here," Manny mumbled. *"Qué sopa mi hermarito?"* he painfully inquired about the situation.

"Mama's gone, Manny!" Puncho sadly responded. Although he was twenty-five years old, he sounded like he was fifteen. "She had a massive heart attack last night. She died before we could get her to the hospital."

Manny instantly remembered when he and Rico had visited Panama in 2000. Right there in the chaplain's office he could hear the last thing his mother said to him in private.

Please son, be careful and don't send any coffins home to me. Promise me.

Manny winched, fighting back tears. "Where's papá?" he asked, slowly turning his back to the priest.

"He's out making funeral arrangements. I stayed for your call. Why haven't you been writing or calling? You had everybody worried."

"I know," he said while swallowing a dry gulp. "I fucked up. *Perdoneme,*" Manny apologized.

Puncho sighed. "And what's up wit' Rico? Nobody hear from him. Since you went in we can't find him. What's up with that, hermano?"

Manny flashed back eight years earlier to the time when he, Rico and their infamous M3 Boyz were under the microscope of the New York City Major Crime Squad. The investigation that was prompted by one of their Cuban enemies from a gang called the Marielitos, who they were in the middle of a nasty war with. Manny winced again, this time for keeping Rico's death a secret from his family while the image of his naked bullet riddled body returned.

"It's a long story. I'll tell you 'bout it later," Manny said firmly. "Tell me, how's the old man holding up?"

Puncho's voice dropped a notch. "It's hard on him too, but we keeping each other strong."

"What about everything else?"

"We good. The Real Estate and food markets you and Rico set up for the family is doing good. We good," Puncho said with pride.

"Okay, that's good," Manny, whispered, "I'll be home in six months. Just be easy."

"Good. Hermano, I know you ain't tell nobody in there about your case or when you're coming home, right?" Puncho foolishly questioned.

The only person Manny ever revealed the facts of his life to was his ex-cellmate, Baby J. Manny told the youngster a story mixed with deception in an effort to deter the youngster from crime. Since he didn't know whom to trust, the most important part of his story was always left out.

"Hell no," he whispered to Puncho. "I don't know who's who in here. Any stories I told were lies," Manny exclaimed while staring at a painting of Jesus Christ on the wood paneled wall.

"*Bien*, I'll be waiting for you to come home, hermano. You'll be proud of me and my team."

"Just take care of Papá for me. Six months. That's all I have left. I'll call you then."

"I will represent you, Manny. Mamá will go off in style. Love you," Puncho said with a sniffle.

Manny held back his own tears. "Love you. Six months," he said before ending the call. Manny slowly turned to face the priest. When the man of God looked into Manny's piercing stare, Manny said, "Sir, I appreciate your efforts. If it isn't too much, I would appreciate if you allow me to contact my family here in New York. It would mean a great deal to me."

The priest looked away from Manny before saying, "I understand Mr. Black. It's not a problem. It's a direct line—dial away. Please try to be quick," he said while cautiously looking at the door, fearing the officer would walk in and call him an inmate lover.

"MB Enterprises, how may I help you?" a woman asked on the other end of the line.

"This is Manny Black, where's Edeeks?"

"Oh… oh… good day, Sir, it's a pleasure to hear from you. This is Lacey McCloud. Edeeks stepped out, would you like me to connect you to his office so you can leave a message?"

"Sure," Manny said with professionalism.

"Hold one minute. It was a pleasure hearing from you," Lacey said before she clicked over and Edeeks' phone started ringing.

"Hello?" another woman answered.

"Who's this?"

"I beg your pardon?" the woman snapped like his question was all wrong.

Manny lost his patience. "This is Manny Black. Who is this and where is Edeeks?" he whispered, not wanting the priest in on any more of his private affairs.

"My apologies, Sir. This is Racheal."

"Racheal?" he asked, not certain of his own employee's names. "Racheal what are you doing in Edeeks' office?" Manny asked authoritatively.

There was a pregnant pause before she said, "Ummm, well... I was...I was just searching for an account and, oh! Here comes Edeeks now."

Seconds later Edeeks said, "Hello?"

"Yo, it's me," Manny said, instantly feeling more comfortable when the man who controlled his life on the outside answered. "Yo, E, Mamá died."

"*Coño*, no," Edeeks exclaimed. "When? What happened?" he asked painfully. "Manny, I'm so sorry. I'll get in touch with Puncho and Papá right now."

"I appreciate that." Manny paused for what seemed like forever before switching to more pressing issues. "Do what you gotta do for the fam," he whispered. "But yo, what did your people find out about her?" Manny questioned.

Edeeks dropped his voice to a whisper too. "According to the investigator's report, Xia was rushed to Westchester Medical Center, they performed emergency surgery on her. The next day, she vanished from the hospital. We don't know if she is dead or alive."

"What about the baby?"

"Like I told you before, the only mention of a baby in the report was the fact that she was pregnant. So I don't know if the baby made it or not."

Manny fell silent again. Thoughts of his deadly wife being out there had been taking up most of the space in his mind during the hours he was awake. He didn't want to go home and be caught on the wrong side of the law again.

"Okay, Yo. I'm a give the phone a break for a minute. I gotta get my mind right. I'll see you at the office when I touch down."

"You sure?" he asked, but Manny didn't answer. "Okay, but hold your head in there. Remember, you got an empire waiting on you out here so don't do anything stupid."

"I got you. Hold things down for me and take care of Mamá. I love you, bro," Manny said before ending the call.

Pain surged through Manny's veins. Now that his mother was dead and gone, nothing else really mattered. He turned his back to the priest and didn't wait for him to call the officer. Manny would meet the redneck in the hallway.

* * * * *

"You took long enough," Officer Nugent said when Manny stepped out of the chaplain's office. "Hands in your pocket and let's go."

Manny held back tears during his walk down the hall. He went from being on top of the world to being reduced to taking orders from a man he knew was not as dangerous as him. On the other side of the wall the correctional officer would be scared to walk through the neighborhoods that Manny once ruled.

Thoughts of his condition, how living in prison was almost over flooded his mind. Time wasn't moving fast enough.

"Yo! Yo!" Manny heard up ahead and snapped out of his daze.

The two porters he passed earlier were debating in Spanish while their eyes bounced from Manny and then down to the filthy floor they mopped. Manny wasn't looking forward to hearing their praises or small talk. He wanted to get back to his cell, work out, and plan out his future.

Suddenly, one of the yellow Wet Floor signs dropped, echoing in the hallway.

Manny jumped and then quickly stopped.

Less than ten feet away, the dark Latino porter and his partner with the braids locked eyes with him. They quickly leaned the mop handles against the grimy walls. Like synchronized dancers, they bent over at the waist, dipped their hands into each of their filthy mop buckets and pulled out long, flat pieces of steel with a sharp tip at the end of it.

Manny quickly pulled his hands out of his pockets.

"What the fuck are you doing?" Nugent barked until he saw Manny quickly place his back against the wall.

"Viva Marielitos!" Braids yelled out the name of the Cuban crime family that Manny had warred with before and during his time in prison.

"Aww fuck!" Nugent screeched in fear as he backed away from Manny while fumbling with the emergency pin on his walkie-talkie.

Manny stared at the homemade weapons. He started backing away. The two men moved closer, cutting off his space.

"Los Marielitos sends our deepest and sharpest regards," Braids said to Manny with a smile.

The sound of the officer's stick dropping startled Manny. He quickly looked behind him to find the stick ten feet away, and the muscular officer running fast down the hall.

"HELP! HELP! These spics are about to kill each other," Nugent yelled.

"Just you and us, *puta*," Blue-black yelled as he jogged to Manny.

Manny took off. The killers followed. Manny ran as fast as he could until he slid, picked up the officer's stick and then faced his soon to be attackers.

"Drop my stick! Drop it!" Nugent, the foolish officer yelled from a hundred feet away.

"Bring it!" Manny yelled before rushing to Braids, the one he thought was the leader.

Kill the head and the body falls was Manny's strategy.

"Viva Marielitos!" Braids yelled out in the hall, causing his echo to send chills through it.

Blue-black lunged at Manny's left side, stabbing for his neck.

Manny swung the stick, missing and only catching air. Like a seasoned boxer, he swiftly pivoted towards his right and managed to slip underneath Blue-black's sharp blade.

"Come on, mother fucker," Braids said in frustration while swinging his blade.

Most victims froze in fright, taking what came to them. Not Manny. Since going to prison, he had been in too many knife fights to back down now.

"Ah!" Manny yelped when Blue-blacks sharp blade pierced his left shoulder.

Manny swung the stick and learned a valuable lesson: Wrap the cord around your wrist, because the force of the stick struck his attacker and flew from his hand.

"Ah," he growled when his forearms took the blunt of the blade jigging at him.

Manny bobbed and weaved. His attacker moved in while his leader Braids was smiling behind him. That frustrated Manny more.

"Back up," Blue-black yelled to his partner. He wanted Manny to himself. In the distance was the sound of feet pounding and keys jingling.

Manny rushed Blue-black. He threw a left-right combination that shook the man. Manny quickly followed up with a solid overhand left that landed on the right side of the Latino's his temple. Blue-black stumbled, slipped on the floor he mopped, and fell back, landing on his ass.

Before Manny could fully turn towards Braids, he plunged the tip of the seven-inch blade into Manny's back. Manny flinched backwards. Then he stepped forward as the blade came his way again.

His adrenaline was pumping too hard to feel the second blow, but before his blood could drip to the concrete, Manny grabbed at the blade, clutched the pieces of ripped bed sheet at the handle of the blade and held on for dear life.

"Ahhhh," Braids yelled while trying to get away from Manny's clutch. He twisted the sharp blade, slicing Manny's hand, as they tussled for control.

"*Puta, maricón*," Blue-black yelled before quickly getting to his feet. He jabbed his deadly blade under Manny's armpit, piercing his left lung.

Manny swung Braids like a shield, letting him catch the direct hit of Blue-black's blade.

"Awwh," Braids cried while tussling with Manny.

"Not me. Not me!" Manny cried in fear before sinking his jaws into Braids neck until he drew blood and the man let the knife go.

Manny took another heavy blow in his back that felt like someone hit him with a hard jab.

Instantly, he snatched Braids by his hair, yanked his head forward and plunged the sharpen blade down into his collarbone. When his hand recoiled, a mist of scarlet blood sprayed Manny's face. He quickly let Braids flop to the concrete.

Manny didn't hesitate. Blue-black was determined, so Manny rushed his attacker and threw a left jab. As Blue-black instinctively swung the blade upward towards Manny's jab, like Manny was hoping for. Manny crouched down, thrust his blade forward, and stuck the prison steel into the overweight pouch that the Latino called a belly.

Footsteps were running in from the distance.

Manny's mind was gone, he was in survival mode. Although his stomach was bleeding, the Latino didn't stop. Blue-black bounced his thick, flat-headed blade from one hand to the other with a smile on his face. "Viva Marielitos, motherfucker," he uttered before making three quick jabs at Manny's torso.

Manny jumped back, but it took a lot of effort. He saw the way the man swung the blade and knew he was a pro. For some reason he couldn't breathe and his energy was gone.

Manny fell against the wall. Black-blue moved in, snatching Manny's dark curls. As Manny tried to block the blade with his elbow, Blue-black plunged his blade into Manny chest.

"Hey! Hey! Stop! Stop!" a Correctional Officer shouted, but it was too late.

Blue-black was plunging his blade in and out of Manny. The whole incident took a matter of seconds.

As the corridor was being filled with officers, Manny's bloody frame was slowly sliding down to the grimy concrete. His determined enemy Pantera had won again.

"Someone call a medic!" were the last words Manny Black heard.

☐ ☐ ☐

☐ ☐ ☐ MON-D

☐ ☐ ☐

SPECIAL OFFER: **$13.00 Each**   **S/H $4.00 PER BK**

FORMS OF PAYMENT:
Cashier's Checks, Institutional Checks, & Money Orders
Prestige Communication Group,PO Box 1129, NY, NY 10027
Credit Cards: PRESTIGECOMMUNICATIONGROUP.COM

Total Title(s) Checked _____   Amount enclosed_____

Name/ID #_____

Address: _____

City/State/Zip: _____

Made in the USA
Middletown, DE
03 November 2014